HOPE

Also by Andrew Ridker

The Altruists

HOPE

A Novel

ANDREW RIDKER

VIKING

VIKING
An imprint of Penguin Random House LLC
penguinrandomhouse.com

LIBRARY OF CONGRESS CATALOGING-IN-PUBLICATION DATA
Names: Ridker, Andrew, author.
Title: Hope : a novel / Andrew Ridker.
Description: New York : Viking, [2023]
Identifiers: LCCN 2022054137 (print) |
LCCN 2022054138 (ebook) | ISBN 9780593493335 (hardcover) |
ISBN 9780593493342 (ebook)
Classification: LCC PS3618.I392246 H66 2023 (print) |
LCC PS3618.I392246 (ebook) | DDC 813/.6—dc23
LC record available at https://lccn.loc.gov/2022054137
LC ebook record available at https://lccn.loc.gov/2022054138

Printed in the United States of America
1st Printing

Designed by Alexis Farabaugh

forever Erin Sellers

HOPE

The Hunger Banquet

•

AUGUST 2013

E veryone will take a card," said Deborah Greenspan, cradling a wicker basket in her arms. "The cards are divided into three tiers of income. Your tier will determine where you sit, with whom, and, most importantly, how much food you'll eat tonight." She was small and stringy, all sinew and knob, standing with her shoulders squared and spine erect before a wall papered with William Morris pomegranates. "I should add that the cards come with names and nationalities. We'll spend the night in character. Almost like a game. It's educational, of course, but let's not forget that it's also supposed to be *fun*."

"Excuse me," Karla Cantor said. "I thought this was a potluck."

Karla sat beside her husband, Sidney, on a silver damask sofa Deb had recently purchased to replace the love seat that for years had occupied its place. In addition to the Cantors that evening, there were three other couples, the Selzers, Sackses, and Steins, clustered like a class of schoolchildren eagerly awaiting instructions from their teacher. Deb's mother-in-law, Marjorie, sat in one of two mahogany bergères—also new—her head bobbing as she slipped in and out of consciousness.

"Not quite, Karla, but I appreciate the babka. No, the purpose of this evening is to replicate, in a controlled environment, the lottery of birth and its consequences."

Karla blinked. "The lottery of birth."

"And its consequences. It's important that you pick your card at random—no peeking—to make sure that we emphasize the element of chance."

"I'm sorry," said Karla. "I'm not sure I understand."

Deb flashed a diplomatic smile. "Then I guess you'll just have to wait and see."

The Greenspans lived in an eccentric Queen Anne at the northern end of Crowninshield Road, where the quaint suburban quiet of Brookline, Massachusetts, gives way to the tremble and clamor of Commonwealth Avenue. It was here that Deb dreamed up her neighborhood initiatives, here that she held house parties for Democratic hopefuls, here that she hosted Passover seders where she served her celebrated brisket—the secret: a dusting of Lipton powdered onion soup—and homemade gefilte fish on plates her grandparents had smuggled out of Poland. With its canary-yellow siding, white window trim, and red pagoda roof above the door, the house, like its inhabitants, stood out among its gray, stucco neighbors.

Unlike the other couples in her social circle, Deb hadn't moved to Brookline "for the schools." She was born in this sylvan streetcar suburb and more than anyone embodied the spirit of civic engagement that made it such a special place to live. When she wasn't raising money for the high school's Innovation Fund, she chaired her synagogue's Resettlement Committee, procuring housing and furniture and steady work for immigrants. She baked flourless cookies for the crossing guard with celiac and invited Holocaust survivors to speak to local students. She remained a reliable chaperone for field trips long after her own kids had left for college, guiding sixth graders through the dead mills of Lowell, passing out condoms and bottles of water at the LGBT youth dance held each year at city hall.

Where Deb found the time to perform these good works while bringing up two apparently well-adjusted children was a mystery. She had raised them on salmon and *Positive Discipline*, T. Berry Brazelton and after-school enrichment, prearranged playdates and *Bill Nye the Science Guy*, birthdays at the Boston Children's Museum and Plaster Fun Time. She had read them Maurice Sendak to fall asleep and played Caribbean folk tales on cassette. She'd bought Legos and K'Nex and Mavis Beacon Teaches Typing, tickets to the MFA and Puppet Showplace Theater. She'd signed them up for swimming lessons at the JCC and classes at the Russian math school in the afternoons. There were some, like Karla Cantor, who believed that Deb had invested *too much* time in her children—that there was something almost *pathological* about her level of involvement—but if Deb's critics disapproved of her methods, they couldn't argue with the results. Her daughter, Maya, worked at an august New York publishing house whose colophon, a fruit tree representing Knowledge, was stamped on the spines of all the best books in the house. Her son, Gideon, was premed at Columbia, preparing to follow in the footsteps of her husband, Scott.

"I love what you've done in here," said Gail Sacks, stroking the arm of the silver sofa. Gail, whose expansiveness was covered by a flowing floral caftan, owned a women's clothing boutique on Harvard Street and knew something about fabric and color.

"After dinner," Deb said, "I'll give you the grand tour."

Her financial planner, Marty Selzer, feigned offense. "Redecorating can be costly," he said. "I can't believe you didn't consult with me first."

"She hardly consulted with *me*," Scott said. He sat in the second bergère and seemed to be resisting the urge to rest his feet on the beveled surface of the coffee table, at the center of which sat a hardcover copy of *Frederick Law Olmsted: Designing the American Landscape.* "I feel like a stranger in my own living room."

Scott ran a private cardiology practice in the heart of the Longwood Medical Area, a concentration of hospitals and medical schools that accounted for roughly a billion dollars of NIH funding each year. Despite his professional success, he made himself available to friends and family, dispensing free medical advice to anyone who asked. Standing five foot ten in his New Balance sneakers, Scott was, by far, the tallest of the Greenspans, with a forehead so vast it seemed to refer to the size of the brain tucked behind it. Owing to an infection he'd contracted as a child, his left eye was locked in a squint, fixing his face with a look of permanent irony. He always seemed to be staring at his life from afar and finding it almost too good to be believed.

"I didn't know I needed permission," Deb said, watching the basket make its way around the room. "I didn't know I had to clear it with the *man* of the house."

"Hey now," Scott said. "Perlman is the man of the house, not me."

"Where *is* he, anyway?"

"I've got him," said Buddy Stein, stroking the striped tabby on his lap. Buddy, who had served as the city's transportation commissioner before retiring to consult on the Seaport development, occupied the wide cushion next to Karla Cantor. His petite wife, Judy, perched on the armrest. "Grab a card for me, will you, honey? Little guy's purring like an engine over here."

"Get this," Scott said, his thin lips canted in a crabwise smile. "My lovely wife gave our cat an IQ test."

"You're kidding."

Deb beamed. "Perlman is a genius."

"Allegedly," Scott said. "But I've got scars that suggest otherwise."

Sidney Cantor, scrolling through the news on his phone, dipped his free hand into the basket. "Nelson Mandela was just discharged from the hospital."

"Put that away," Karla whispered.

The word *hospital* roused Scott's mother from her sleep. "Oh!" she said suddenly. "My shoulder!"

"Is everything all right, Marjorie?" asked Judy Stein.

"It's my shoulder! It *hurts*! I can't drive back tomorrow, not like this." Though she lived most of the year in Washington, DC, Marjorie spent her summers on Cape Cod and dropped in on her son whenever possible. A stately woman with a hive of cotton-candy hair, she was a regular presence at Greenspan family functions and could be counted on to liven up a party with incredible—Scott would say fictitious—stories.

He sighed. "*I'm* driving you, Mom. All you have to do is sit still. You can sleep, for all I care. Matter of fact, that might make the trip easier."

"I won't get behind the wheel of a car, not like this," she said, clutching her right shoulder. "I'm a danger to myself and others! I guess I'll have to stay a few more nights here with you."

"For the last time, you aren't driving. *I* am. And you had surgery on your *left* shoulder. Not your right."

"Well!" she said, blushing and lowering her hand. "Thank God for that."

"Come here, Mom. I want to look at your Pinocchial lobe."

She smiled at the thought that something might be wrong with her after all. "Pinocchial lobe?" she asked. "What's that?"

"Tell her, Deb."

His wife waved her hand. "Don't drag me into this."

"What is it?" Marjorie asked. "I want to know!"

Scott smirked. "It's the part of the brain that makes shit up."

"Oh!" Marjorie cried. "Do you see how he treats me?"

"Madiba is a hero of mine," Sidney murmured.

Gail's husband, the Honorable Larry Sacks, stroked the beard he'd been growing all summer in solidarity with the Red Sox. "*Graceland* is perhaps the single greatest album of the twentieth century."

Once the wicker basket made its way around the room, the group divided up into their designated places. Scott had carried card tables in from the garage for guests who had drawn high- and middle-income cards. Low-income cardholders sat on the floor.

"After everyone has found their seats," Deb said, "we'll start by introducing ourselves."

Gail, who had drawn a high-income card, went first. "My name is Natasha," she said. "It says here that I'm a wife and mother of six." She whistled. "Six! . . . I live in Moscow, where I run a shop selling hand-painted teakettles. I don't have much in savings, but I can afford to feed my family, and all of us have access to basic social services."

Marty, at the middle-income table, raised his glass. "To basic social services!"

"Why don't you go next, Marty," Deb suggested. "Since you seem so eager to participate."

"Okay, let's see," he said, squinting at his card. "My name is Ja-mala. I live with my husband and children in Yemen. We have a small farm with three cows, which we use to make milk, butter, and ghee." He looked at Deb. "You *do* know I'm lactose intolerant."

"You picked the card, Marty, not me."

"I'm just saying, if anybody wants to trade . . ."

She wagged her finger. "No trading."

"Of course," Marty said. "The lottery of birth."

One by one, they introduced themselves, reading the character biographies on their cards. Karla, who thought the exercise was stupid even as she wished that she'd come up with it herself, was surprised to find her fellow guests enjoying themselves. They seemed to relish the game, if that's what it was, the permission Deb had granted them to inhabit lives much different from their own. Some of them even improvised details that weren't on their cards, while others attempted to speak in accents authentic to their characters' countries of origin. The thrill of pretending to be from somewhere else, of pretending to *be* someone else, and the knowledge that this pretending served a social cause, only enlivened the atmosphere at the Greenspan house.

Karla was even more surprised when Deb, true to her word, began distributing three completely different dinners. To the high-income table, she brought roast chicken with saffron served on a bed of pearl couscous; the skin, still sizzling, smelled of cinnamon. Then she went back to the kitchen and returned with shallow bowls of buttered pasta, which she distributed to the guests at the middle-income table. Though the portions were small and the pasta ungarnished, the steam rising from the bowls made Karla salivate. Deb served the low-income group last, passing around saucers of brown rice. Karla furrowed her brow as she accepted her saucer and saw that no more food was forthcoming. Deb assumed her place before the wall of pomegranates.

"As we enter this next stage of the evening, I'd like each of you to start reflecting on how you feel. High-income guests: Do you feel grateful? Guilty? Low-income guests: Are you upset? Does this system strike you as fair? Let those questions inform your conversations as you eat."

Karla's prevailing feeling at the moment was hunger. "Sidney," she whispered in an attempt to reach her husband, and his pasta, at the middle-income table. He didn't hear her, preoccupied as he was with the cascade of headlines on his phone.

"Amsterdam museum identifies a new Van Gogh," he murmured.

"How can a Van Gogh be 'new'?" Marty asked. "The guy's been dead a hundred years!"

"Honey," said his wife, Miranda. "How much have you had to drink?"

Karla consumed the contents of her saucer, but it was hardly enough to satisfy the ache in her side. During a lull, she caught Deb's eye and waved her over. "I'm having a wonderful time," she said, "wonderful. But do you think it would be possible to switch the cards around? Now that we've all had a taste, pardon the pun, of what this is all about?"

"Well," Deb said, crouching to meet her at eye level, "the idea is that you can't control the world you were born into."

"I understand. But I think by this point, we've all got the picture." She looked to the other low-income guests for support. "We recognize that life can be unfair. So maybe now we can all share in the delicious food you've made."

"I don't mind," Judy said. "I'm having fun!"

"I'm glad to hear that," Deb said. "And I'm sorry, Karla, I can't just change the rules. It would completely undermine the purpose of the evening."

"I'm not trying to be critical. It's only a suggestion."

"I understand, but I think we should stick to the plan. Once everyone finishes their meal, we'll have a discussion about what, if anything, we've learned."

"It's just that I haven't eaten anything all day."

"I don't know what to tell you. I've been planning this for weeks."

"I thought it was a potluck."

"Did you read my email?"

Karla cupped her bowl, a beggar in a Chico's blouse. "I'm just ask-ing for *something*. Something other than rice."

"What does your card say?"

Karla picked her card off the area rug. "It says my name is Esther. I'm a rice farmer from Haiti."

"So what do you suppose she eats most of the time?"

"Rice . . ."

"Exactly."

". . . among other things."

"Esther doesn't have the luxury of roast chicken."

"But I do. I, Karla Cantor, *do* have that luxury. At least give me the babka I brought."

"I can't do that."

"But I made it! It's *mine*! You can't just hold a babka hostage—"

She was interrupted by a bleating landline phone.

"Excuse me," Deb said. She rose and walked off on the balls of her feet, like her heels were too good to grace the floor. Karla looked across the room at Scott, who sat with one leg crossed over the other, his fingers knit behind his head in a tableau of total satisfaction. It seemed wrong that he should be sitting at the middle-income table when some of his guests were on the floor, but if Karla pointed this out, Deb would probably say that the wrongness—the *unfairness*—was the point.

Scott was telling a medical story. "Here you have a sixty-year-old man with diabetes, peripheral vascular disease, and hypertension, and he's admitted to the hospital for a below-the-knee amputation."

"And they say healthcare doesn't cost an arm and a leg!"

"My god, Marty," said Miranda. "Let him finish."

"They're prepping him for surgery when they find the letters *DNR* tattooed across his chest. They check his file, which says he *does* want to be resuscitated in the event of cardiac arrest. Naturally, they ask him why his tattoo appears to contradict his file."

"So?" said Marty. "What'd he say?"

Deb poked her head into the living room. "Scott? It's for you."

"Hold on," he said. "I'm finishing a story."

"I really think you should take it."

"I'm almost done. He says—"

"*You should take it*," she said, more forcefully this time.

"All right," he said, rising from his chair. "All *right*."

Maybe the most galling thing about the Greenspans was that they were rumored to have "opened" their marriage. These rumors, while never confirmed, had long outlasted the shelf life of idle gossip, refreshed by semi-regular sightings of the Greenspans on the town with strange characters. Larry Sacks claimed to have seen Scott at Aquitaine, the French bistro on Tremont Street, in the company of a young woman too blond and too provocatively dressed to be his daughter. Judy Stein and Miranda Selzer both saw Deb in Inman Square holding hands with a shaggy man in a leather jacket, though Miranda maintained that the man was, in fact, a woman. Whether or not the rumors were true—the fact that no one knew for certain suggested that, for all their popularity, the Greenspans were short on genuine friends—they certainly *seemed* plausible. The Greenspans had always been early adopters of customs that sounded strange until they caught on; Deb was composting long before her neighbors. Besides, most of married Brookline *wanted* the rumors to be true. Though few were brave enough to say so, the rumors gave them hope for the possibility, however remote, that they, too, might open their marriages someday.

Their guests hushed as Scott followed Deb out of the room in deference to this rare moment of marital tension.

With both Greenspans gone, Karla saw her chance. "Gail," she whispered, tugging on the hem of her caftan. "Are you finished with that?"

"Who is this 'Gail' you speak of?" Gail asked in her best Russian accent. "My name is Natasha."

"Come on, Gail. I'm starving over here."

"Who are you?"

"For God's sake. It's me, Karla. I just want a bite of chicken."

"I do not know this 'Karla.'" Her accent, like her ancestors, had fled to Brooklyn.

"Come on, Gail. Be serious."

"But I am Natasha!"

Karla shook her head in disbelief and picked the last few grains of rice from her saucer. She stewed in silence while the rest of the group finished eating, the ambient chatter supplanted by the ring of silverware on bare china.

"They've been gone an awfully long time," Judy said.

Marty bounced his heel. "I want to hear the end of that story."

"Is it over?" Sidney asked, looking up from his phone for the first time all night. "The game, I mean. Are we done?"

"I bet the guy was in a gang. A biker gang! That's why he had the tattoo."

"This is no way to treat dinner guests," Marjorie huffed.

"Maybe we should clear our plates?" Miranda said.

Gail nodded. "That's a good idea."

But Gail didn't move. No one did. They just sat there, silent but for the turning of their stomachs, as the sky grew dark and the new floor lamps turned the living room windows into mirrors.

It was a long while before Deb returned. When, at last, she appeared in the living room, she seemed to have lost all trace of the patience that made her such a superlative host. Her face was flushed pink, and a few stray grays frizzed out from her neat brown bob.

"I'm sorry," she said, clearing her throat, "but I think we're going to have to call it a night."

The wind was picking up outside, overturning the big blue recycling bins on the curb. Not a storm, nor a nor'easter—too soon in the season for anything like that—but a mounting sense that something was wrong, the weather out of whack, a glitch in the atmosphere. Sirens sped down Commonwealth Avenue. Tree branches ticked against the windows.

"Is everything all right?" Gail asked.

"Everything's fine."

Marty raised his hand. "Where's Scott?"

Deb's throat pulsed as she swallowed, as though a second, smaller heart were lodged inside it. "I'm afraid Scott is indisposed."

"Lactose intolerance. He has my sympathies."

"I didn't mean it like that." She closed her eyes, taking a moment to compose herself before the diplomatic smile returned to her lips. "He wanted me to apologize on his behalf. Something came up at work."

"Medical emergency?" Karla asked, raising a single, accusatory eyebrow. It wasn't like Deb to end a dinner party so early, and so abruptly, especially when she'd gone to the trouble of preparing multiple entrées. Karla was determined to figure out why. "It must be an emergency to tie him up like this."

Deb met her eyes. "That remains to be seen."

"At least let us help tidy up," Gail said. She got up and started stacking dishes.

"Leave those," Deb said.

"It's no trouble."

"Really. I'll take care of it. I insist."

"And the discussion?" Karla asked. "I thought we were supposed to go around and talk about the meaning of the evening. What we *learned*." She would wring the answer out of Deb if she had to.

"Honestly?" Deb said. "It's pretty self-explanatory."

"The lottery of birth."

"Exactly."

"What about my babka?"

"I'll drop it off tomorrow."

"If you don't mind," Karla said, with a neighborly smile, "I'd rather take it home tonight. For some reason, I'm absolutely *ravenous*."

Deb glared at her a moment before giving in. When she returned from the kitchen, she handed Karla the babka, still sealed in saran, and went to the front door, where she waited for her guests to gather their things. Though her posture was perfect, even balletic, heels together with her toes pointed out in first position, she seemed to be blinking more than usual, as though whatever disturbance the phone call had caused had lodged itself in the corner of her eye. As Karla passed Deb on her way out of the house, she swore she could smell the bitter tang of stress on her host.

Out they went, the couples huddled close together as they descended the six stone steps to the sidewalk. The power lines cut precariously through the trees that formed a canopy over Crowninshield Road, rippling like waves in an EKG. The wind bent the branches overhead.

Sidney pocketed his phone and pulled out his keys, the ring crowded with loyalty cards to Whole Foods and Costco. Though the Cantors lived around the corner, Sidney, who wanted to show off his hybrid car ("A hundred miles to the gallon when the battery is running"), had insisted that they drive. He pressed a button on the key fob. The headlights flared. "That was strange," he said. "Don't you think?"

Karla stared through the window on the passenger side. Deb was standing in the portico beneath the red pagoda roof, clutching a tea towel to her chest like a security blanket.

"Don't you think?"

Karla craned her neck as the car pulled off the curb, Sidney's question hanging in the unpolluted air behind them. Deb was still standing in the doorway, as if to forestall confronting whatever it was that awaited her inside.

My Son, the Doctor, Is Drowning

•

MAY–OCTOBER 2013

Every summer since his mother's shoulder surgery, Scott Greenspan had chauffeured her from Boston's Logan Airport to her little shingled cottage down in Wellfleet. Never mind that she could make the drive herself—at eighty-one, she still traveled to Lisbon, Nice, and Rome—or that the aches and pains that plagued her only ever seemed to flare up in his presence. The surgery, which she had undertaken against Scott's counsel and that of every half-decent physician in Washington, had left her with a persistent yet elusive soreness that seemed to leap from one arm to the other at will and prevented her from driving long distances. Scott fulfilled this obligation with the same practiced indifference that he'd brought to dealings with her as a child. But this year, she met him at the curb in a wheelchair, pushed along by a heavyset kid with half a mustache. She'd dyed her hair white and acquired a cane, which she held in place across her lap. "Dr. Greenspan!" she cried as he approached, her narrow eyes brightening at the sight of him. She was wearing one of her summer outfits, white capri pants and a solid blue top with a sheer kimono jacket draped over her shoulders. Scott wasn't sure what depressed him more, the fact that she didn't really need the wheelchair or how happy she looked riding in it. He ran a hand through his head of thinning curls and steeled himself against the day ahead.

"Mom," he said. "You're looking well."

She surprised him by waiting for the kid to leave before she started to complain. "Twenty minutes I sat at my gate, waiting for that chair. I told that boy to tell United they just lost my business."

Though Scott had inherited his father's lean frame, his face was a faithful reproduction of his mother's. They shared the same sly lips and narrow eyes, the same arrow-straight nose and kinky coils in their hair. Standing now, she seemed at least an inch shorter than last summer.

"I'm sure they're broken up about it," he said, grabbing her bags.

"They won't get another cent out of me. Not one solitary cent!"

She hooked her arm around his in the manner of a woman for whom male attention was even more valuable than money. Scott winced as he recalled his med school graduation, when she had collapsed on the Longwood Quad, struck by an acute case of neglect. "I guess you could say I'm your first patient!" she'd gushed, after he had helped her to her feet.

"How long have you had the cane?" he asked, guiding her toward his car. She seemed to be shuffling at a slower pace than usual. It might have been the osteoarthritis in her knees, but Scott suspected she was simply savoring the walk. They both knew that until they reached the car, Scott would not be able to let go.

"Six or seven weeks. Your sister picked it out. My doctor says I have two S curves in my spine. Compared to the couples in my building, of course, I'm practically the picture of health. I'm taking all my pills. I've been a very good girl." A Silver Line bus sighed as it pulled up to the curb. "My dear friend Dottie, down the hall? She's had a—what's that called, when they cut off your breasts? Her Ted has no one to take care of him while she's laid up in bed recovering. Ted's a charmer, but the man can't boil water. He must be eighty-eight, eighty-nine?

And a charmer. It would be awful if something happened to Dottie and Ted was left all alone. You remember their son Robert killed himself."

She lived to shock, but Scott had heard it all. Suicide, sex, money, disease: no trip with his mother was complete until she'd touched at least once on each of her four favorite subjects. Wresting his arm from her grip, he opened the trunk of his Honda Insight and hoisted her suitcase inside.

"New car?"

"I've had it for a while now."

"Oh oh oh!" she said. "Fancy!"

"It really isn't," he said, slamming the trunk.

"I invited Ted to see my kitchen. I thought I'd teach him a few things. I was showing him around when the doorbell rang—it was Dottie. You should have seen Ted's face! He ran away as fast as he could and jumped right through the window. He was terrified of being caught with me in my apartment. I've never understood it, I really never have, but women tend to see me as a threat." She tapped her cane on the curb. "You'll stay the night, of course."

"Actually, I'm driving back tonight." He stepped around the car so he wouldn't have to face her while the fact of his early departure sank in.

"*Tonight?*" She dropped into the passenger seat and pulled the cane in after her. A wrist strap hung from the handle like a noose. "But there's so much to do! And in my condition, I won't be much help. Dr. Trask forbade me from physical exertion."

"Is that right?" he asked, in a tone that he hoped expressed his professional opinion of her doctor. "Well, of course, if Trask says so."

"Apparently I'm a so-called fall risk. My mind is always on, he said.

I have hypomania—energy, in other words—and my body can't keep up. I'm always racing to the next thing, and the next."

"Well, he's right about that."

"Is Gideon coming to see me this summer?" she asked as he pulled off the curb.

"I'm not sure, Mom. You'll have to ask him."

"First you throw away all that furniture I gave you, and now you won't let Gideon see me?"

"We didn't throw anything away."

"It's hideous what Deb has done with the living room. Who ever knew she was such a glamour-pussy?"

"Glamour-puss, Mom. The word you're looking for is Glamour-*puss*. And believe it or not, Gideon is an autonomous being. He can do what he wants."

"Oh, hush. That boy will do anything you say."

He slowed to a stop at a tollbooth. The operator was a weathered-looking woman with thinning orange hair and no eyebrows. For a moment, Scott imagined switching places with her. He would trade in his house, his income, his eyebrows, if only she drove his mother to the Cape.

"How's the study coming?" Marjorie asked once he'd rolled the window up. She sat up straight and adopted the expression of a helplessly innocent ten-year-old girl.

"We're having a hard time recruiting patients, actually," he said, passing through the concrete womb of the Ted Williams Tunnel.

"You've never had trouble finding patients before. Who's running this thing?"

"Braverman. In Dallas."

She rapped the dashboard with the butt of her cane. "You're the one who should be in charge. *He* should be recruiting patients for *you*."

"It was Braverman who thought to study inflammation."

"You were one of *Boston* magazine's Top Docs of 1999."

"That was *fourteen years ago*."

"Why you haven't been a Top Doc since, I can't say, but I have many close friends in the publishing business who tell me the new editors are terrible, terrible."

"Mom."

"You were top of your class at Harvard."

"Mom!"

"What's this Braverman hoping to find, anyway?"

The Human Outpatient Pericarditis Evaluation study, so named to force a snappy acronym, sought to investigate the effects of interleukin inhibitors on pericarditis. "In layman's terms?" he said. "It's for people whose white blood cells aren't communicating."

"There's an opening ahead," she said.

"They attack the pericardium like it's a foreign body."

"You're missing your chance."

"By and large, ibuprofen does the trick. The problem for Big Pharma is, ibuprofen's cheap."

"Switch lanes!"

"For God's sake, Mom, I can't!" The highway was choked with traffic. "You should see the money they throw at him."

"Who?"

"Braverman."

As an undergraduate, and well into medical school, Scott had believed that science was synonymous with progress, and so moved in a single direction, separate and apart from fads and trends. But the moral of Scott's career, and Braverman's, was that the institutions that made research possible were as fickle as fashion.

"What's that blinking light?" his mother asked.

He followed her eyes to the orange exclamation mark lit up on the dash.

"I don't know," he said. "I've never seen it before."

"Pull over and check the engine."

"Check the engine for what?"

"I refuse to ride in an unsafe vehicle!"

"It's safe, for God's sake. I just bought the thing."

"So it *is* a new car."

"Last year, Mom. I bought it last year, okay?"

She folded her hands over her lap and pouted out the passenger-side window. The highway ran above a run-down neighborhood of clapboard homes and slanted telephone poles. A billboard for a bank sat atop a charter school. LOOKING FOR A SIGN OF RESPECT? it read. THIS ONE IS 40 FEET LONG.

"It's bad enough you threw my furniture away," she said.

"We didn't throw anything away. Deb redecorated."

"I gave you some very valuable pieces."

"Most of the old stuff is with Maya now."

The light in her eyes had changed. The innocent ten-year-old girl was gone. A wicked, ill-tempered witch sat in her place. "This is what Deb wants. She's trying to poison you against me."

"Will you leave my wife out of it, please?"

"Maybe she's depressed again. Is that it? She's depressed?"

"She's not depressed and never was."

"Well, *something's* going on. Something you're not telling me. I went

to see a shrink, you know. Not for me—for you. I told her how Deb
threw away my furniture and she said, Marjorie, this isn't your problem. There's something going on in that marriage they're not telling you."

Scott felt her eyes raking over his face as she searched for some
small, unconscious movement—a half-hidden scowl, a fluttering
lash—to indicate that she was homing in on something. "I promise
you, there's nothing going on."

"You probably aren't used to an empty nest. Children are a wonderful diversion in a marriage. Your father first stepped out on me
when you went off to college." She then proceeded to enumerate her
late husband's affairs. Scott could hardly blame his father for any
indiscretions—the man had, after all, put up with her for years—but
the number of women increased with every telling, and it had become impossible to distinguish fact from fiction. "I used to blame
myself, you know. I thought I'd failed in my duties as a wife. Despite
my formidable appetite for sex, I felt I couldn't satisfy him. Now, of
course, I know better. The problem wasn't me. The problem was men!
Sometimes I think I should have been a lesbian. I have many, many
lesbian friends, and they're the happiest people I know."

Since Scott had been a preteen, he'd possessed the rare ability—
superpower, crutch—to detach himself from any circumstance that
threatened his composure. His father had worked in the State Department, and his itinerant career had taken the family from Chicago to New Delhi and then to Washington, DC. Scott was never at
the same school longer than two years, learning early that to form
friendships with other students was to cultivate and harvest his own
heartbreak. The moves also meant that his mother never met a more
age-appropriate confidante. Most nights, Marjorie sneaked into Scott's

room and sat at the foot of his bed, where she described to him, in chilling detail, the consistency of her bowel movements or the erotic charge she got while riding a bicycle over gravel. Lying in the dark beneath a heavy comforter, Scott slipped through the trap door in his mind.

In college, he'd learned that particles can exist in two places at once, a phenomenon known as quantum superposition, and it was there, at Johns Hopkins, where he put the theory into practice. He wasn't talking to his mother, a cramp in his leg as a line formed behind the phone on the dormitory wall; he was in a comfortable, cavernous, well-appointed room with walls so thick her voice could hardly reach him. Scott would not have survived his college years—thrived, really, graduating with honors while dating the great-granddaughter of a philosopher-poet whose books are still in print—were it not for this ability to project himself into another realm. And if occasionally Beth complained that he did not live *in the moment*, that he was never *fully present*, that his prized composure was a bulwark that prevented her soul from merging with his—when she was feeling threatened, she fell into the mystic babble of her great-grandfather's poetry—one call to his mother would remind him why he'd secluded himself in the first place.

Marjorie, for her part, was less interested in withdrawing from reality than in stretching it to suit her whims. She had studied art and architecture as an undergraduate; from these raw materials, she had fashioned a story about a torrid love affair with I. M. Pei. But as her calls grew increasingly frantic, contradictory, and repetitive—"Your father is incapable of love. He doesn't know how to love. You can't trust a word he says, even if he says he loves you, because he said he loves me, and look how that turned out. I'm telling you this for your own good. Protect yourself. Me, I have no protection. I'm a woman in the world! The world will eat a woman up and spit her out unless she's independent. I've always had an independent streak. That's what your father loves about me. That's what every man I've loved has loved about me. Did you know that I. M. Pei refused to pay for my abortion?"—he began to withdraw into himself more frequently and with greater intensity until nothing she or anyone else said could touch him.

They passed the drive this way, Marjorie tallying her grievances while Scott took cover in his well-appointed room, which lately resembled an upscale ski lodge, with exposed wood beams and a large stone fireplace and—why not—a deer antler chandelier. It was not until they could see the Sagamore Bridge that she said something that caused the chandelier to crash through the floor of his vision.

"Hold on," he said. "Why on earth would *you* need money?"

She feigned surprise. "Why, for Green Pastures, of course!"

For years she'd been reluctant to leave her grand apartment with its impressive collection of Indian sculpture and her vast library of books. But living alone was no easy feat for a woman of her age, and Scott and his sister had worked tirelessly to find a retirement home to suit the lifestyle she was stubbornly unwilling to relinquish. They'd toured a number of facilities before finding Green Pastures, a high-end community of professors emeriti, career bureaucrats, and former ambassadors. There were chamber music concerts and a well-attended lecture series, art lessons, and views of Rock Creek Park. After much convincing, Marjorie had sold her Kalorama co-op and used the proceeds to put down a deposit at Green Pastures. She was slated to move in at the end of the summer, but not until she paid what remained of her balance.

"You have plenty of money, Mom," he said.

"Whatever gave you that idea?"

She had never divorced his father, who died at sixty-five, and whose savings and social security checks had allowed her to live in her building for the better part of the past twenty years. As far as Scott could tell, and despite her liberal leanings, she had slipped through tax loopholes all her life. "You're right," he sighed, "I don't know why I thought you did."

"If you *listened* to me, instead of tuning out—don't think I can't see you staring blankly through the windshield—you'd know that all my money is tied up overseas."

He peeled his hands off the steering wheel and wiped them on his jeans. "Tied up overseas where?"

"Most of it is with my boyfriend right now." The ten-year-old girl was back, an ingenue batting her eyelashes and trying to make sense of the world.

Scott could never keep up with her boyfriends. Since his father's death, he'd met a slew of Davids, Bobs, and Henrys, Harolds and Dicks and Eugenes and Toms, each man a float in a dull parade of corduroy and cardigans. They were engineers and economists, historians and experts on foreign policy. If she were to be believed, and this was no small *if*, his mother had slept with half the Brookings Institution.

"And which boyfriend is this?" he asked.

"As a matter of fact, he's new."

"And your money is tied up with him why?"

"He needs it," she said. "For his education. You know me, I don't like fancy things"—the moving boxes full of antique Asian statuary that cluttered her apartment argued otherwise—"but you can't put a price on education."

"I'm sorry, Mom. I don't understand."

"Who paid *your* college tuition? Who paid for med school? You owe me."

"I'm pretty sure Dad took care of college. For med school, you'll recall, I took out loans."

"And who paid for your kids to go to school?"

"I did, Mom. Deb and I, together."

"I sent you a check!"

"For five thousand dollars. And while we're on the subject, I have nothing to loan you."

"I don't believe that for a minute."

Her insistence that he was not merely comfortable but *wealthy* tore the tough muscle of his heart. Yes, he had a private practice, but his mother didn't know the first thing about what it cost to run a family in the twenty-first century. On top of taxes and mortgage payments, his daughter had just graduated from one of the most expensive universities in the country, and his son had two years left at Columbia. Still, there was some hope of turning things around. Recently, on the advice of his financial planner, Marty Selzer, Scott had pulled $97,000 from the market, a not insignificant share of the family savings, and invested in SOAR, a green-energy startup run by Marty's cousin Mike that was presently worth nothing but whose value was expected to skyrocket—that was Marty's word, "skyrocket"—as soon as Mike received the necessary permits.

Activists and entrepreneurs had been trying to build wind farms off the coast of Cape Cod for more than a decade. The most recent effort to harness the powerful currents that sweep through Nantucket Sound had been met with pushback from an unlikely federation of blue-collar Cape Codders and fossil fuel barons, Kochs and Kennedys, who had come together to "preserve" the "sanctity" of the sound and, with it, their property values. They tanked the project by arguing that wind farms were bad for not only property values but birds. One memorable editorial called the proposed field of offshore wind turbines "pole-mounted Cuisinarts" for migrating species.

Mike Selzer had a different approach. An engineer in the energy field, he'd paid close attention as previous projects collapsed and come up with a solution that he believed would satisfy summer people, year-round residents, and activists alike. He'd patented a device he called an eGull™, a sort of parafoil parachute that resembled, at a distance, a bird with outstretched wings. The eGull™ was tethered to a launch-and-recovery system that sat on a floating platform, which in turn was connected to an underwater generator. They flew between six hundred and two thousand feet in the air, pulling on a tether, generating two hundred kilowatts of energy each, without obstructing valuable views; from the shore, they really did look like a colony of gulls. What's more, they were a fraction of the cost of the wind turbines and posed no threat to actual birds.

It wasn't like Scott to make such a dramatic investment, but a tour of Mike's warehouse in New Bedford changed his mind. Mike, like Marty, was a small, spring-loaded man of middle age, a compressed coil of manic energy. "The beauty of this concept is its simplicity," he said with the self-effacing candor of a seasoned pitchman. "My eGulls™ are basically kites. That's it. That's the whole idea. The ancient Maori people flew kites, you know. Only priests were allowed to make them. Kites were thought to be the direct descendants of the god of birds."

Scott was less taken with the mythology than he was the science. He geeked out over the simulations, studying the birds' figure eight patterns, checking Mike's math as he calculated the energy generated by the spooling and unspooling of the tether. He hadn't felt this excited since medical school, when he'd been young and curious and eager to learn the structures underpinning life on earth. After the warehouse visit, he gave himself a crash course in the physics of flight, drag, and traction. Mike's math was accurate, and, according to Marty, he was just a few pesky permits away from getting permission to build a fleet of eGulls™ that would fly above Cape Cod Bay, as opposed to the sound, so as not to provoke the ire of the one percenters on Martha's Vineyard and Nantucket. Once the permits came through, Mike expected to be swarmed with investors. Handing over some seed funding now would secure Scott a spot on the ground floor. It was risky, investing before the permits were in place, but by doing so he bought himself a 10 percent share in the company—a level of control he couldn't wield if the VCs invested first. Scott envisioned himself changing course, maybe leaving medicine altogether to become, in the second half of his life, a pioneer in the field of clean energy.

"One hundred fifty thousand dollars," Marjorie said. "That's all I need to complete the down payment. I can cover the monthly rent myself."

"One hundred fifty—Jesus, Mom. You think I have that kind of cash lying around?"

"They're threatening to release the hold on my apartment!"

"Write your boyfriend. Get the money back from him."

"I *told* you," she said, "he needs it for school! Who am I to deny a man his education?"

An Audi tore past Scott in the passing lane. It was hard not to take its reckless speed and the purr of its Bavarian engine as a rebuke to Scott's judiciousness in driving and in life, his stable career and respect for the speed limit, the abuse he freely accepted from his mother. "Why," he asked, "are you paying for an eighty-year-old man's education?"

"Because he isn't eighty. He's eighteen."

"Now I know you're losing it."

"Dr. Trask says I have more brain in my body than the rest of his patients combined. Now listen!"

Scott's grip tightened on the wheel of the Insight as his mother explained that she had struck up a relationship with a Turkish teenager based in Berlin. He wanted a higher education more than anything—his grandparents had been Gastarbeiter, "guest workers," and his parents cleaned houses for a living—so she had transferred most of her savings to him for tuition.

"You did *what?*" Suppressed rage shot up through Scott's body like a geyser. But before the force of his anger knocked his head off, he remembered her fondness for grotesque exaggeration and comforted himself with the reassuring thought that nothing she had said could possibly be true.

"I'll explain one more time because for some reason you don't seem to want to hear what it is I'm telling you. I sent my boyfriend money so that he could go to college."

There would be no greater pleasure than in proving her wrong, in dismantling her falsehood piece by piece. "College is free in Germany, Mom. Or as close to free as possible."

"He wants to study in America. He's very bright. And for his age, very ma-*toor.*"

"And how did you meet?"

"On OkCupid."

"Who taught you how to get on OkCupid?"

"Gideon."

"And how do you communicate with this boyfriend of yours?"

"Email. Sometimes we Gchat."

"Who showed you Gchat?"

"Gideon! Now, I know how much you want him to be a doctor, and God knows he looks up to you, but I wouldn't rule out a future in technology."

She seemed to have an answer to all of his questions. She had been chatting with the boy, Ahmet, for almost a year; he lived with his parents in a flat in Neukölln; she'd drained her Roth IRA—she pronounced it "Roth, Ira," as if taking attendance at a Hebrew school—and called in a bank transfer. "If you can't cover my Green Pastures payment, I guess I'll have to move in with you."

Scott laughed. "That is *not* going to happen."

"I knew it! You don't want me around!"

"Mom."

"Maybe it's something in your marriage. Something you're trying to keep hidden from me."

"Why don't you move in with Sarah?"

"Your sister lives in the woods! And hates Western medicine. If I fell, she'd try to revive me with crystals."

"Well, you're not coming to live with us."

"Every man I've ever loved leaves." There was a tremor in her voice and tears in her eyes. "My husband abandoned me, my boyfriends abandon me, and now my only son won't take me in."

"Have you ever wondered why that is?"

"Oh! Oh! The way he speaks to me!"

Scott shut his eyes for as long as he could without veering off the road. No one deserved to be as lonely as his mother was, even if her loneliness was of her own making.

"I'm sorry, Mom, okay? I didn't mean it."

"Pull over. I'm getting out."

Scott sighed. "I can't stop, Mom. I'm on the highway."

"I'll let myself out. They'll find me in the morning, strewn about Route 6."

"I said I was sorry."

"Try living all alone. See how *you* like it."

He dropped the subject, and they drove in silence until they reached the house.

Marjorie's cottage sat at the dead end of a street lined with scrubby trees and tall, tick-infested grass. She and Scott's father had bought the place in a last-ditch attempt to save their marriage six months before his fatal heart attack. She liked to say it was the place where she was happiest on earth.

"They're going to build a monstrosity here," she said, pointing at a clearing in the trees. Four roofless walls wrapped in Tyvek paper stood on a raised wooden platform. "A hideous thing. I've been fighting it for months."

Scott pulled into the driveway, soothed by the familiar crunch of seashells under the tires and the brackish funk in the air. He carried her bags inside the cottage, nearly knocking over a ceramic vase containing blooms of dried hydrangeas. The recessed shelves were crammed with books: *More Die of Heartbreak*, Kissinger's *On China*, *Edward Hopper: Portraits of America*, *The Doctors' Guide to Better Tennis and Health*, *Darwin's Influence on Freud*. Four tribal masks hung above the fireplace. "My exes," Marjorie said when she came in, a joke Scott had heard a thousand times.

The small living room, with its sagging ceiling, was stifling, and Scott stepped out onto the deck for air. He stared through the gap in the scrubby pitch pines at the porthole view of the bay below. He could almost see, set against the whiteness of the sky, a fleet of eGulls™ sweeping through the clouds.

"Dr. Greenspan?" his mother called. "I need your help in here."

Wordlessly, he set to opening the house. She appeared to have forgotten her earlier outburst and assumed the traditional maternal role of telling him what he was doing wrong. She stood beside him as he flushed out the pipes and turned on the water heating system. She watched him as he swept up the bodies of dead mice and pointed out droppings he'd missed. She told him he had dusted off the wrong set of deck chairs and chastised him for throwing out a frostbitten pint of Breyers chocolate ice cream from the freezer. "I'd give you a hand," Marjorie said as she clawed at the last tattered scraps of his composure, "but I have two S curves in my spine."

By sunset, Scott was dizzy with hunger, his lower back tense from the drive. Marjorie chopped carrots while he waited like a child at the dining room table for his dinner.

"The catbirds are back!" she called from the kitchen. "You can tell they're catbirds by the yarmulkes on their heads."

Scott scrolled through the emails on his phone. His inbox was clogged with ads for Viagra and come-ons from Sexy Eastern European Singles. Braverman's team had sent out an updated consent form for patients; his neighbor Karla Cantor was asking for medical advice on behalf of her sister. Farther down, he saw a message from the editors of *The New England Journal of Medicine*. He had sent them a paper just yesterday and hadn't expected to hear back for weeks. His heart jumped.

"Dear Dr. Greenspan," it read, "After a preliminary review, the editorial board does not feel your manuscript merits external evaluation. We are uncertain that the design of your study, the methodology used, the statistics employed, or the control group evaluated are adequate to shed light on the question you have raised, itself of uncertain interest to our readers. We hope the speed by which we reached our decision allows you to re-submit to another journal without further delay."

"Last summer," Marjorie said, "the mama bird sat on her eggs all day with no help whatsoever from her husband. I only saw him once, and you could tell he wanted nothing to do with her or the children. He was itching, just itching, to fly away. I wonder if they got divorced."

Scott set his phone facedown on the table. "You're projecting again, Mom. Birds don't get divorced."

"That birdhouse you built me is falling apart. I told you not to use pine, but did you listen? Now it's rotting through. What is it, C grade? D? Maybe that's why the papa bird never came back."

He clenched his jaw. "That's quality wood."

"Someone's cranky! We'll see how you feel after you eat. Maybe you'll be so tired that you have to stay the night."

"Yeah," he said. "We'll see."

"Unless you're still worried about recruiting patients and need to get back home for work." She was like a blind nurse searching for a vein, sticking his arm until she found it.

"I'll drive back after dinner," Scott said, "but not because of work."

"Or maybe something's going on with Gideon."

He winced at the prick of another needle. "Nothing is going on with Gideon."

"Maya? I know how hard it is for young people to find a job these days."

"Maya's fine."

"I just keep thinking about what my friend told me." She was bent before the oven, her back turned to the table, her rear end stretching the seat of her capris.

"What friend?"

"The shrink. She thinks Deb is cheating on you."

She had found the vein at last. Scott leaped to his feet, knocking his glass of water off the table. "Give it a fucking rest! I don't know how you spend your money, and I honestly don't care. But I will *not* sit back while you *shit* on my family and *then* ask me for help! You are not my problem, understand? *You are not my fucking problem!*"

His shoulders heaved. He wiped spittle from his lips. She raised her shoulders defensively and shot the linoleum floor a bashful look.

"Okay," she said, "okay!" She looked chastened, but he thought he saw a smile breaking like a wave across her cheeks. The smile said he'd given her the response she wanted; he had shown that it was still in her power to provoke him. "I don't know how I whip these meals up out of nothing," she said, opening the oven door. "Out of nothing! I guess I've just always been gifted that way."

He dispatched his dinner as quickly as possible and left without waiting for dessert. Instead of heading home, he drove north, toward the fist at the tip of the state's curled bicep, making and unmaking his own fist the whole way. Colleen Quinn's cottage wasn't easy to find, tucked away as it was on a dark, country road, but Scott had made the trip enough times that he could get himself there on muscle memory alone.

"I just put the kids down," Colleen said when he arrived. "Try not to make any loud noises."

Colleen's cottage was not much larger than Marjorie's, though she lived there year-round with her three young children. The screen around the porch was riddled with holes, and the paint on the window box was chipped. The door whined as it shut behind him. He followed her to the kitchen and put his hands on her wide, sloping waist. "I'm not the one prone to making loud noises."

"I'm not kidding. If they wake up, it's your ass. Coffee?"

"Sure."

Scott leaned against the laminate countertop while Colleen put the moka pot he'd bought her on the stove. "I still don't know how this fucking thing works," she said. She wore an oversize T-shirt that read I DIG CLAMS and a pair of Red Sox boxer shorts.

"One call," he said, watching a troop of ants march up the wall, "and I could get you and the kids out of here."

The electric coil on the stovetop blushed. "I told you," she said, "I like where I live."

"Pick any hospital you want. Mass General is WASPy. But Beth Israel? The pay would be better, the schools would be *much* better, and you could put some space between yourself and what's his name."

"Maybe my life is fine the way it is."

"Maybe I just want to be closer to you." As soon as he said it, he knew it wasn't true. He couldn't fold Colleen into his world when he depended on her to help him escape it.

"But who would be left to look after Marjorie when she comes down with some medieval disease?"

Scott and Colleen met the previous summer when his mother decided that her upset stomach was a case of full-blown dysentery. She begged him to drive her to the Outer Cape Clinic, and when Scott finally caved, he was thrilled that the raven-haired nurse with the ice-blue eyes was neither convinced by nor impressed with her performance. Colleen wasted no time informing Marjorie that she had not, in fact, contracted dysentery, and no, she would not need to provide a stool sample, and that the best thing for her was to go home and lie down. Anything more would be a waste of time and money. Scott was smitten.

"I'm sorry," he said. "I don't mean to push."

She switched off the stovetop. "You don't?"

Colleen pressed him up against the counter, and they kissed. She pulled him close, her fingers hooked into his pockets, and he slipped his hands up the back of her shirt. She was a boxy woman with large breasts, and her bra had six or seven clasps. As he struggled to unhook them, he thought about his mother. It was almost as if, by mentioning her name, Colleen had summoned her into the room. Had she really sent her retirement savings to some kid in Germany? Did she mean it when she threatened to move in? Colleen stroked the front of his jeans, the denim wilting under her fingers.

"Something wrong?" she asked.

"Just give me a minute."

"You sure you're okay?"

"I don't know."

"Come with me," she said and pulled him toward her bedroom. He spotted a spatter of black mold above the mirror in the corner where the drywall met the ceiling.

"You should really get that looked at," he said.

She didn't turn around. "Get what looked at?"

"That mold. At least let me pay someone to come by." He wondered, with delight, what his mother would say if she discovered he was doing someone else financial favors.

Colleen shut the bedroom door behind her and pushed him down onto her unmade bed. She climbed on top of him and straddled his hips. "I don't need anything from you," she said, pulling her T-shirt over her head.

"Say that again."

She reached behind her and unhooked the clasps. The light on the ceiling smoke alarm winked.

"I don't need anything from you," she repeated, tossing the bra across the room. Lying on his back, staring up at Colleen, Scott was pleased to discover that lust had not yet abandoned him for good.

Most of the houses on Crowninshield Road were dark by the time Scott got home. The old neighbors had downsized or moved out of state, making way for a new class of eager young parents, biologists jogging with their strollers in the small hours, pushing babies with antique names like Cecil and Maude. But the light was still on in the Greenspan kitchen, and from the sidewalk, Scott could see Deb at the sink, washing her hands. There were a few threads of gray in her bobbed brown hair; a pair of scarab beetle pendants dangled from her ears. She looked in Scott's direction with no sign of recognition,

her reflection in the lighted window blocking him out. He wanted
her to notice him, to register his presence, and considered calling out
to her or jumping up and down. He even thought to do a cartwheel
right there in the street, like a schoolboy desperate for a pretty girl's
attention, but his back was sore from the drive, and he settled for
the front door instead. "Deb?" he said, kneeling to pet Perlman. "I'm
home."

"Oh! Hi! I was just heading out." She flew through the foyer.
"How's your mom?"

"Manipulative, anxious, overbearing, and critical. Where are you
going?"

"Good to know she hasn't changed." Deb dug through the open
bag she'd left on the counter. "I'm running late. I told Joan I'm coming over."

"You're seeing Joan? Tonight?"

"I figured you were staying with your mom. Or Nurse Betty."

"That's not fair."

"I'm sorry. Did you eat?"

"I've never spent the night at Colleen's."

She looked up from her bag and kissed his cheek. "I'm *sorry*."

He could feel, already, the sense of loss that would strike him as
soon as Deb left the house. "I ate."

"I got a funny call from Maya's boyfriend today. He said he left a
message with you."

"I haven't checked my voicemail in ages."

"Well, I think he wants to ask you something." Deb raised an eyebrow. "I think he wants your *blessing* for something."

"My blessing? What century is this?"

"I think it's kind of sweet."

"She doesn't come with a dowry, if that's what he's after."

"Just do me a favor and call him, okay?"

"I can't spare any goats."

Deb slid into her flats. "Leftovers are in the fridge if you get hungry."

"I had to leave my car in the shop. All the way down the Cape, I was getting this weird blinking light on the dash."

"Weird," she said, opening the door.

"I was almost home when it started making this buzzing sound, like there was a hornet's nest in the engine. I had to pull off I-93. I thought the car was going to explode." He could hear himself stretching the story, exaggerating details, to hold her attention. He was no better than his mother, but he couldn't stop himself. "I rolled to a stop right on Methadone Mile," he said. "Some of the homeless were wrapped in soiled bedsheets, haunting Mass Ave like actual ghosts. I saw one girl, about Maya's age, pushing a shopping cart around. A prosthetic leg was sticking out of it."

Deb, never one to take the suffering of others lightly, lingered in the doorway. "That's terrible."

"It's like a third-world country over there. One guy shot up in the middle of the sidewalk while I was calling AAA."

"Terrible."

"It was right around where Gideon volunteered that summer. Hope House, or whatever it's called. I've got to give the kid credit for even going down there. You know what the AAA guy told me when he showed up?"

"I'm eager to hear all about it tomorrow."

"There was one other thing," he said suddenly. Anything to keep her there a minute longer. "My mom says she's dating some Turk in Germany."

"He's Turkish or he's German?"

"Both, I guess."

"So far, this sounds just like her."

"She says she sent him her savings so that he could go to college."

"And you believe her?"

"She wants me to pay for Green Pastures."

"Ah," she said. "There it is."

"And if I don't, she'll move in with us."

"Well, *that's* not happening," she said with a laugh, starting down the stone steps. "Don't wait up. I'll see you in the morning."

"Wait!" he said, lunging after her. He stood at the edge of the portico, the door open behind him, staring down at Deb on the pavement below. "Tell me she's crazy and I'm nothing like her."

Deb climbed up the stairs to meet him. She held his head against the hard, flat surface of her chest. "She's crazy, Scott, and you're nothing like her."

He watched as she made her way back down the steps and waved as she pulled off the curb. The loss struck on cue and he hurried inside, as if to stop the feeling from following him in. The eerie quiet of the house depressed him, and he switched on the radio. A woman's voice came through the kitchen speakers and said that three more individuals had been arrested in connection with the Boston Marathon bombing on charges of obstructing justice. Scott envisioned the journalist's lips, the warmth of her breath on his ear.

When he looked up, he noticed a basket on the counter, drawing the attention of the track lights overhead. Through the clear plastic wrapping, he saw apples and pears, a block of cheddar cheese, and a sleeve of crackers, all assembled on a bed of crinkle-cut paper. Scott tore off the plastic wrap and picked up the card leaning against the block of cheese. "Thank you for all that you do," it read, "to help us meet our goals!" Below the typed text was a dashed-off signature that Scott knew to be Rich Braverman's. The corporate condescension of the note turned Scott's stomach. The HOPE study was a sham, and Braverman should have counted himself lucky to have someone of Scott's caliber working for him. The least he could do was write something personal. He shoved the basket to the back of the counter, where it fell into shadow underneath the kitchen cabinets. Then he went to the fridge to mix a drink.

The previous summer, high off of having met Colleen, Scott had driven to Manhattan to pay a surprise visit to his children. They took him to the Rusty Knot, a naval-themed bar near the bank of the Hudson River, where Maya was confident that Gideon, then only twenty, wouldn't be carded. It was there, bathed in the aqueous green light of a fish tank, that Scott had tried his first Painkiller. For Scott, who drank alcohol only on occasion and rarely, if ever, consumed sugar, the first sip was a revelation. His taste buds, deprived of sweetness for years, all seemed to stand at attention. He'd been experimenting with tiki drinks ever since—Scorpions and Zombies, slings and sours—stocking up on lemons, limes, and pineapple wedges. Ginger syrup. Pandan leaves. Rum from Martinique. There was something subversive about sipping a fruity cocktail in the dead of winter, but now that it was summer and fresh fruit was in season, Scott looked forward to evenings on the patio, a drink on the arm of his Adirondack chair. Preferably a Painkiller: high-proof navy rum, pineapple juice, orange juice, and cream of coconut, served over ice in a thick, stout glass and garnished with freshly grated nutmeg.

He took a sip—still refreshing, still cheerful, still delicious—and carried the drink upstairs with him. When she redecorated, Deb had hung a series of family portraits, arranged chronologically, on the wall beside the stairs. Scott watched his hair thin as he ascended.

He paused on the landing. There were strange sounds coming from Gideon's room, muffled voices and grinding shrieks. He pushed open the door and found his son, home from college for the summer, sitting up in bed beside his girlfriend. Between them sat the laptop Scott had bought Gideon when he graduated from high school. A scream came through the speakers, followed by a gargle of blood.

"Japanese body horror," Gideon said. Those three words in sequence meant no more to Scott than any three picked at random from the dictionary. "Do you want to watch with us? We can put it on the projector downstairs." The room was dark, and the blue light of the laptop strobed across their faces.

The girlfriend, Astra, said, "You'd like it, Dr. Greenspan. It's about a guy who slowly turns into a machine. Kind of like, beware the hubris of science. As in, just because we can, does that mean we should?" She wore winged eyeliner, and her hair, dyed turquoise, was beginning to show its darkness at the roots.

"That's all right." The light strobed again, and a woman screamed. "Astra, what are your plans for the summer?"

"I'm going with my family to the Bahamas."

"Lucky you."

She shrugged. "It's kind of effed up, actually? Lying on the beach with a cocktail when so many people on the island don't have running water."

Scott tucked the Painkiller behind his back. "That reminds me, Gideon. I left a message with Cal Christopoulos at the NIEHS in North Carolina. I asked if they needed summer interns. Any interest?"

"I don't know," Gideon said. "What do you think?"

Scott shrugged. "I'm not sure how much fun you'll have in Durham."

"Then I won't."

"But Cal is a brilliant scientist, and I'm sure it'll look good on your CV."

"Good point. Tell him I'll take it."

There were times when Scott wondered whether his son was not too dependent on his counsel. Gideon always made the right decisions, but only after asking Scott's advice. He wished his son would think for himself, and *then* reach Scott's conclusion on his own.

"Well, you think on it."

Gideon nodded thoughtfully. "All right, then. I'll think on it."

"Some interesting news from Grandma today. Apparently, she's dating a teenager. Did you set her up on OkCupid?"

"Yeah."

"I really wish you hadn't."

"She asked me to!"

"Hey, Dr. Greenspan," Astra said. "Have you ever taken the Enneagram?"

"I'm not sure I know what that is."

"It's a map of the nine personality types. I'm a Loyal Skeptic," she said, tapping at the keyboard. A brighter light was coming off the screen now, casting dark shadows under her eyes. "Gideon is an Enthusiast-Epicure. You can take the quiz online."

"I think I'll sit this one out."

"But Gideon said you used to study this stuff."

While fulfilling his fellowship in the early nineties, Scott apprenticed himself to an esteemed Viennese cardiologist called Krebs, who studied the relationship between personality and coronary heart disease. Patients enrolled in these studies would be asked a series of questions to determine their personality type. Do you struggle to unwind at the end of a long day? Are you a sore loser? How often do you multitask? These questions helped determine whether the patients were type A (competitive, aggressive) or type B (relaxed, easygoing). The pioneering studies, which Krebs had carried out while Scott was still in college, found that men identified as type A individuals were more than twice as likely to develop coronary heart disease as compared with those identified as type B. The underlying premise was so simple it was hard to believe no one had seen it before: emotional distress—a risk factor for mortality after myocardial infarction—was linked to stable personality traits.

Scott's research, which he continued after his fellowship, centered on a simple question: Could a man change? He ran generously funded clinical trials in which half of the competitive, aggressive men enrolled received behavioral counseling. They were taught to practice patience in their daily lives; to express themselves in measured tones; to see their friends, colleagues, and spouses as collaborators and not adversaries. The results were not only medically significant, but offered hope to a population prone to premature exhaustion. It seemed that if a man could change his behavior, he could dramatically extend his life.

Scott had been unstoppable then. He flew first class to meetings of the AHA and ACC, shuffling slides between sips of champagne so his lectures would sound sufficiently new. He developed a following of young physicians who accosted him after every event in the hopes he might attach his name to one of their studies. He received more dinner invitations on those trips than he could possibly accept and took to ordering room service just so he could have some time alone.

Not that Scott could be accused of callousness. When he wasn't on tour, he volunteered at a clinic in Dorchester, lending his time and attention to indigent patients on a pro bono basis. And when he wasn't doing *that*, he was writing a book proposal based upon his research, tentatively titled *In the Hearts of Men*, that an agent in New York thought he could sell for six figures.

"I do," Scott said, "I did, but it's a lot more complex than an online quiz. My mentor, Dr. Krebs, was the first to define the criteria for type A and type B individuals—"

"But that's just two different types of people," Astra said. "The Enneagram has *nine*."

In the early aughts, at the peak of Scott's success, when he had amassed more grant money than he could spend, a series of international studies failed to replicate his findings. Those that did produce relevant results found correlations between heart disease and hostility but no other type A personality traits. One damning study found *lower* mortality rates among its type A participants. It then came to light that much of Krebs's early research had been funded by the tobacco industry, which sought to blame the deaths of its customers on behavioral types rather than their smoking habits, but by that time, Krebs had become one of those rare and lucky scientists who die before the world proves them wrong.

"It's not enough to break people into groups," he said, wincing at the note of defensiveness in his voice. You need physical *and* psychological benchmarks."

"If you had to guess," Astra asked, "what type would he be?"

"Achiever-Performer," Gideon said.

Astra swiped her fingers on the track pad. "Achiever-Performer, Achiever-Performer . . ."

The Painkiller was numbing his hand.

"Your basic desire is to feel valuable," Astra said, squinting over the screen. "Your basic fear is worthlessness. You're always pushing yourself to be the best. Hope and Law are your Holy Ideas. Your virtue is truthfulness and your vice is deceit. Your ego fixation is vanity."

"Well, there it is," he said. "You've got me pegged."

Gideon grinned. "You have to admit, it's kind of on point."

"It's no more legitimate than a horoscope."

"You don't believe in horoscopes?" Astra asked.

Scott stepped back into the hall, closing the bedroom door behind him. He started down the stairs, unwinding time, growing younger and younger with each photo he passed.

He could hardly recognize his own house. Deb had replaced his mother's Persian rugs and floral-print furniture with sleek silver couches and synthetic carpeting. All that remained of the previous decor was the large Chagall print hanging in the foyer, a wedding present from his mother. It depicted a newlywed couple taking flight on the back of an enormous chicken. The groom's arm was wrapped around his wife's waist while the chicken, in profile, stared into the distance, its expression mute and indecipherable.

"The problem," Carol Chin explained, "is that I live in a buffer zone." She and Scott were walking down the hallway of his practice two weeks after Scott took his mother to the Cape. "The twins could wind up at either Lincoln or Pierce. I'm waiting on an email from the enrollment office. They're both good schools, and Pierce is closer, but it's on the other side of Route 9. That's four lanes of highway the kids would have to cross just to get to class every morning! And then again on their way home, of course. What kind of mother would let their kids cross Route 9 for a playdate, much less school? It's a barrier that, socially, most moms won't breach. It might as well be the Berlin Wall."

Scott perked up at the mention of Berlin. He was only half listening, his mind occupied by the call he'd received that morning from the auto body shop. He'd been biking to work since taking in the Honda, and now that it was ready, he'd been told that the mechanic had replaced the transmission. The car was practically new, Scott protested, but the mechanic would not release it to him until he coughed up $2,800. Scott hadn't asked for a new transmission; it was not, he maintained, the mechanic's prerogative to fix what didn't need fixing in the first place.

"Where are we," he asked, "with the Braverman study?"

Carol stopped outside the examination room. The wall behind her was a nauseating shade of teal, and to the left of her head hung a canvas print, a color-saturated field of bluebells. Noticing these details as if for the first time, Scott wondered who had been responsible for choosing them.

Carol sucked her teeth. "More bad news. Mr. Hatch withdrew last night."

Scott shut his eyes and rubbed his temples. Hatch's departure seemed like one more decision in a series of decisions—the color of the wall, the canvas print—that had, for some reason, been made without him. "Why?"

Carol shrugged. "Too big a commitment."

Braverman's study was a commitment to the extent that it was likely to last a few years, but that didn't account for Scott's recent difficulty finding patients to enroll and keeping them. There had been a time when he felt confident in his ability to talk any patient into any course of treatment, but he seemed to have lost his gift for persuasion. It was a kind of impotence, he thought, and it seemed to him that this problem was related to his wife's entanglement with Joan Portafoglio.

"That's the second patient to drop this month," he said, though he was certain Carol already knew that.

Chatty, competent, and chronically upbeat, Carol Chin had served under Scott for so long he could hardly remember a working life without her. He'd introduced her to her wife, an occupational therapist at the Brigham, and counseled her through an especially tough pregnancy; Carol, barely five feet tall, had carried her twins into work until her water broke at her desk. He'd encouraged her to take off as much time as she needed and promised to continue paying her in full, but was relieved when she returned to work just six weeks later. During her absence, the staff brought their grievances to him, and he could not have imagined the extent of the interpersonal dramas that had been brewing in his office all this time. Two of Scott's employees were engaged in a turbulent on-again, off-again relationship. A patient was calling and leaving lewd voicemails for the receptionist. Everyone had strong feelings about the thermostat. They came to Scott hoping he would settle their disputes. It was as though he had been running not a practice but a country whose citizens' needs were not known to him. Carol was the empress of this shadow office, the queen of all that Scott couldn't see.

"Hey," she said, hugging a clipboard to her chest and looking up at him with wide-set, guileless eyes. "At least we still got paid."

"How's that?"

Carol explained that Mr. Hatch had been enrolled just long enough to have passed the randomization deadline. In addition to the thousand dollars Scott was sent for screening him, the office would receive a check for an additional four thousand to cover the costs of the next round of tests, which Mr. Hatch would no longer receive.

"Well," Scott said, "I guess that's something."

She followed his eyes to the field of bluebells behind her. "If, God forbid, something happened to my kids while crossing Route 9," she said, her voice no longer bright but leaden and low, "I don't know how I could live with myself."

Scott saw patients until four o'clock and then biked to the indoor tennis courts at BU. Though the sky would be lit for at least another hour, Scott preferred practicing his serve indoors. There were no sur-prises indoors, nothing left to chance, and he liked the heavy blanket-ing stillness of the air, the smell of glue and rubber gassing off the balls. He hit until he'd sweat through his gray Novartis T-shirt, which he peeled off as soon as he got home.

"Keep your shirt on," Deb said. "Dinner's ready. Gideon!"

He could hardly remember their last family dinner, and the thought of it suddenly lifted his spirits. "Smells terrific."

"Did you call Louis?" Deb asked.

"Who?"

"Your daughter's boyfriend."

Scott summoned a mental image of Louis, a beefy little guy with broad shoulders and kind eyes. Sweet kid. Not entirely deserving of his daughter, but who was?

"Not yet."

"I wonder if he's started looking at rings. They're growing dia-monds in labs now, you know. Conflict-free."

"I have yet to work in a single lab that I'd describe as 'conflict-free.'"

"Is that the kind of shtick we can expect at the wedding?"

Gideon pulled up to the table with Astra.

"Hey, Gideon," Scott said. "Who am I? 'You come to me, on the day of my daughter's wedding . . .'"

"Orzo with shrimp and feta," Deb said, setting the cast-iron dish on a trivet.

"Come on." Scott pinched his fingers. "'I'm going to make him an offer he can't refuse.'"

"You shouldn't do that," Astra said.

"Do what?"

"That thing with your hands. It's offensive."

"Offensive to who?"

"To *whom*," Deb said.

"Italians."

Scott was determined not to let his son's girlfriend spoil his rare buoyant mood. "Hey, Gideon," he said. "I heard back from Cal Christopoulos. He says they don't usually take interns, but if you wanted to shadow him for a few weeks, he'd be happy to set something up for later in the summer."

"Cool!" he said. "But what about Astra?"

"I thought she was going to the Bahamas."

"Scott," Deb said. "She's sitting right here."

"Only for a week," Gideon said.

Deb spooned orzo onto Scott's plate. "I'm sure Astra is pursuing her own internships. Aren't you, honey?"

"Not really, no."

"By the way, Scott, your mom keeps calling the house."

"She just wants someone to talk to."

"She wants money, is what she wants."

"I think it's cool about your grandma," Astra said. "Having a hot young internet boyfriend."

"For all we know, she's lying," Deb said. "It wouldn't be the first time."

Scott sucked a shrimp out of its shell and dropped the brittle tail on his plate. "For once, I'm sorry to say, I think she's telling the truth."

On the drive home from BU that evening, Scott had called his mother's financial planner, Gary Weed, in DC. The two men had developed a close relationship over the past decade as Marjorie descended deeper into the uncharted waters of her mania. Weed was probably violating some kind of professional code by discussing her finances with Scott, but he understood that it was in her best interest to keep her son apprised of her situation. It was the kind of relationship Scott had developed over the years with the men and women who kept his mother afloat: her accountant, her physician, the woman who cleaned her apartment.

On the phone that evening, Scott had asked if there was any truth to her claim that she'd transferred her savings to a boyfriend overseas. Weed, to Scott's surprise, said that yes, she had ordered a significant transfer of funds to an account in Berlin. He'd tried to talk her out of it, to no avail. As far as the boyfriend business was concerned, he could neither confirm nor deny, but she *had* seemed especially giddy—lovestruck, even—when she instructed him to make the transfer.

"Who cares how Grandma spends her money?" Gideon asked.

"Because," Deb said, "then she comes to Dad and begs him to pay for her retirement home."

"What's your grandma's personality type?" Astra asked.

"Good question," Gideon said. "She defies all categories."

"That," Scott said, "is the understatement of the century. Couldn't you go to Durham by yourself?"

"But what about Astra?"

"We're due at the Waxmans' at eight," Deb said. "I need to shower."

"*I* need to shower," Scott said. "You aren't eating?"

"No one escapes the Enneagram," Astra said.

"Have you heard about this?"

"Of course," Deb said, rising from her chair. "I'm a Reformer-Perfectionist."

"What's his name again?" Scott asked as Deb pulled up to the curb.

"We've had them for dinner a hundred times. Doug did Gideon *and* Maya's braces."

Scott looked up at the Waxmans' colonial. Paper lanterns, round and white, were strung above the doorway, curving like a toothy smile.

"Doug," he said. "Doug Waxman. And Dawn."

"She runs that gallery you hate on Newbury Street."

"I don't hate it," Scott protested. "I don't 'hate' anything."

A flushed Doug Waxman greeted them at the door. Deb wished him a happy birthday, and Scott, who had not known the cause for the occasion, wished him a happy birthday, too.

"The Greenspans!" Doug beamed. "I'm honored by your very presence. Do me a favor and kick off your shoes."

The house was full of people, most of whom Scott didn't recognize: bald or balding men in button-downs and khakis, women in caftans or cardigans. A woman approached and pulled Deb into the scrum.

"Tell me something," Doug said, guiding Scott into the living room. "Do you read the Ethicist?"

Scott was embarrassed to be standing in his socks. "The what?"

"The Ethicist. It's a column in the *Times*."

A caterer appeared with a tray of water crackers topped with avocado and crab meat.

"Oh," Scott said, watching with longing as the caterer passed. "The Ethicist. Sure."

"So Dawn and I were on a flight to Tokyo last month. And who else is on board but these Hasidic Jews. Black hats, curly sideburns, the whole deal. What they want in Tokyo is a mystery to me. Do they have Jews in Japan?"

"No idea."

"Anyway, the plane is scheduled to depart Thursday morning, but we keep getting hit with delays. The more we wait, the more the Hasids are starting to get nervous. Because Japan is thirteen hours ahead, the flight is even longer, and of course, they can't fly on Shabbat. Or, wait—if it's thirteen hours—because the sun sets later in the west . . ." His lips moved wordlessly as he made a calculation. "The point is, the Hasids are starting to get nervous."

Scott nodded along, looking over Doug's shoulder. He strained his eyes but couldn't find Deb in the crowd. The only face he recognized belonged to Larry Sacks, who stood by the fireplace gesticulating wildly beneath a painting of Mount Fuji. Scott looked down and realized that he and Doug were standing on a straw tatami mat.

". . . so they canceled the flight!" Doug exclaimed. "I mean, is that not perfect for the Ethicist?"

"Great story," Scott said. He was staring at a bowl of brown billiard-size balls that sat at the center of the Waxmans' coffee table. The balls were glossy and spotted with light. "I mean, you're right. It's great for the Ethicist."

"I see you admiring my hikaru dorodango."

"Pardon?"

Doug reached into the bowl and handed Scott a ball. It was smooth and solid in his hands.

"Hikaru dorodango. It means, literally, 'shiny dumpling.'"

"What are they made of?"

"Mud! That's all it is. Dirt and mud and clay and sand, rolled into a ball and polished to perfection."

Scott held the ball up to his eyes. "You *made* this?"

"It's a simple process, really. I collect mud from the bank of the pond, and I shape it. Then I cover the ball with increasingly fine layers of dirt. I find it very relaxing."

Marty Selzer materialized at Doug's side. "Your wife is looking for you," he said. "Sorry to break up the party."

"Don't move," Doug said, taking the ball from Scott's hands. "When I come back, I'm showing you my studio."

Marty arched an eyebrow. "I won't ask."

"You don't realize the favor you did me just now."

Marty's bald head blazed beneath the eco-friendly glare of the living room's helical bulbs. "Believe me, I do. Look, I need to ask you something."

"Ask away."

"It's private. Here, come with me."

Scott followed Marty through the crush of guests and up the stairs. They reached the landing at the top of the staircase, where a bamboo fan was mounted on the wall.

"What's with all the Japanese stuff?" Scott asked.

"They go every year. It's like a coping mechanism."

"Coping for what?"

"This way." Marty beckoned, and opened the door to what appeared to be a teenage boy's bedroom. The walls and ceiling were painted black. The bed was a mess of rumpled black sheets, and the poster above it read GET RICH OR DIE TRYIN'. When Scott turned around, he found Marty in his underwear, his corduroy pants in a puddle at his feet.

"Marty, for God's sake——"

"Scott. Please." Marty hooked his thumbs inside the waistband of his briefs and pulled it down to reveal a nest of coarse pubic hair.

Scott raised his eyes to the black ceiling. "Marty . . ."

"Is it herpes?" Marty asked. "I have a feeling it's herpes. Just look really quick and tell me if it's herpes."

Scott drew in a long breath and exhaled. He made a quick inspection of the huddle of white sores at the base of Marty's penis. "It's herpes," he said. "Now, for God's sake, get dressed. I'll write you a scrip for Valtrex."

"Thanks, pardner. I knew you'd come through. And I hope I can count on your discretion."

"Of course you can. But I won't pretend not to be curious about where you contracted it."

Marty zipped his fly, fixing Scott with a knowing glance. "I won't trouble you with the sordid details. Let's just say that not all of our marriages are quite so sound as yours."

A skateboard was mounted on the wall behind Marty, a cartoon alien painted on its underside.

"Herpes," Marty said, buckling his belt. "My god. Hey, by the way, how's your mom?"

"I won't ask how you made that mental leap."

"Just being polite."

Scott sighed. "She's the same. It's like the old joke. If I was drowning, she'd shout—"

"My son, the doctor, is drowning."

"Exactly. How's Mike doing with those permits, by the way?"

"Beautifully. He's been cleared by the Cape Cod Commission and the Army Corps of Engineers. He's got a power purchase agreement all lined up with National Grid. The Wampanoag are on board—the Nauset branch. The Mashpee will come around."

"That all sounds like good news."

"Soon as he gets FAA approval, the sky over Massachusetts is going to be full of those big, beautiful birds. And you, my friend, will be a very rich man."

"I'm glad to hear it." Scott sat on the bed. Orange snack dust had been ground into the rug near the toe of his shoe. "I really need this to work, you know. I haven't told Deb about it."

"You *didn't*? Pardon my tone, I'm just surprised. You seem like the kind of couple that talks about everything."

"I guess I didn't think she'd go for it."

This much was true. While Deb might have supported Mike's mission in principle, she would have balked at Scott's investing so much in SOAR. But the money wasn't the main reason he hadn't told her. The truth was, he wanted something of his own, something for himself. Mike's company provided just that opportunity. He looked forward to surprising her when the investment paid off.

"Trouble in paradise?" Marty asked.

"I wouldn't go that far."

"I've been a financial planner for a long time, Scott. I know what it means when one spouse makes an investment without telling the other. I've seen how that story ends."

Scott sighed. "It's just that Deb's been acting a little *strange* lately."

"Strange how?"

"For one thing, she just redecorated. Replaced the furniture, everything. I hardly recognize the place."

"Right . . ."

"And then"—he knew he shouldn't go on, but he couldn't help himself—"there's the whole thing with the open marriage."

"Open marriage? You're kidding." Marty sat beside him on the bed. "My god. You aren't kidding. I knew it. I knew it! How'd you talk her into it?"

It was a relief to share the secret with someone, even Marty. The tension he was holding in his chest deflated like a blood pressure cuff. "Actually?" Scott said. "It was Deb's idea."

"Now I *know* you're kidding."

"I'm not."

"What did you say when she proposed it?" he asked. "Were you paranoid? Concerned? Speaking for myself, I might have been concerned."

In fact, Scott *had* been concerned when Deb sat him down almost five years earlier and asked how he felt about opening their marriage. He didn't know how to answer her. At first, he thought she was testing him somehow. Then he worried she was seeing someone else. But over the course of an hour's conversation, concluding in the best sex they'd had in years, she had persuaded him.

"I did what anyone would do," Scott said. "I went with it."

"I can't believe what I'm hearing," Marty said.

"A one-night stand here or there, I could live with. That was our deal. But she's spending two, three nights a week with this woman. Staying over at her house. I feel like I'm sharing my wife."

"A woman, you said?"

"Joan Portafoglio."

"The charter school advocate?"

"You know her?"

Marty picked up the magazine that lay on the duvet, and began flipping through pictures of models in swimsuits. The magazine cover read ATOMIC SEX: DROP THE BIG ONE ON HER TONIGHT! "No one has done more to weaken the position of public schools in the state than Joan Portafoglio."

"It's not like I haven't had my fun," Scott said.

"Handsome guy like you? And a doctor at that?"

"I see a woman on the Cape every now and then. She works at a clinic out there."

"Hello, nurse!"

"And every now and then, I meet a drug rep at a conference."

"Attaboy."

"But I'm not moving in with any of them. And I never stay the night!"

Marty set the magazine down. "I wouldn't worry about it, Scott. Really, I wouldn't."

"Yeah? Why not?"

Marty rose and put a hand on Scott's shoulder. "Would a woman who just redecorated up and leave?"

Scott chewed the inside of his cheek. "You have a point."

"You're the Greenspans, for God's sake. This kind of thing doesn't happen to people like you."

"You're right. You're right."

"Of course I'm right. Now let's get me a drink. My doctor just told me I have herpes."

Scott followed Marty back downstairs. The living room was more crowded than when Scott had first arrived. He found his wife by the bar cart, talking to a couple that he didn't recognize.

"Did you see that *Rolling Stone* cover?" the husband asked. "They have him looking like some kind of rock star."

"He wanted to be famous," the wife said. "They all do."

"There are easier ways to get famous than blowing up a marathon."

"But look where it got him," Deb said.

The wife nodded. "He *was* a cute kid. Or is it wrong to say so?"

"You're not wrong. You're human."

The husband shook his head. "I don't see what looks have to do with it."

"Honey," said his wife, "looks have *everything* to do with it."

"Can I refresh anyone's drink?" Scott asked.

Deb held her empty glass in front of her. "Make me something?" she asked and flashed a goofy grin. Scott smiled at his wife, whom he rarely saw drunk; she was a woman who prized control above all else.

"One Painkiller, coming up. I'll have to check the fridge for juice." He turned to the couple. "Have you two had a Painkiller? Deb and I are completely addicted."

"That's not entirely true," she said.

"Sure it is!"

"I'm sorry, honey. They're just too sweet for me."

Scott paled. "But I've been making them all year."

"I've upset him. Oh no, look, he's upset."

"It's no problem," he said, forcing a smile. "I'll just make something else."

She was in no condition to drive. When they left the party an hour later, Scott fought her for the keys and claimed the driver's seat. Deb closed her eyes and leaned her head against the window, her breath taking on the slow rhythm of sleep.

A light rain was falling, scattering the brake lights of cars up ahead into beads on the windshield. The squeaking wipers kept irregular time. Waiting for traffic on Beacon Street, Scott could see inside the Green Line car that had stopped to let passengers debark at Summit Avenue. An old woman draped in a black rain poncho sat with her hands folded across her lap. On second glance, the poncho might have been a garbage bag—it was hard to make out through the rain-streaked window—and the train lurched forward before Scott could say for sure.

"I didn't know Doug had a son," Scott said to himself. He was thinking of the black room, the magazine, the skateboard.

Deb yawned and shifted in her seat. "He died," she said. "On a trip to Japan."

He poured her into bed when they got home. Scott, who was too anxious to sleep, installed himself at the desk in his home office. He Googled "internet money love scam," hoping to find documented evidence of young men bilking old ladies online. He found what he was looking for—reports from the Federal Trade Commission, FBI, AARP, a victim testimonial published in *The Guardian*—but he was at once too tired and too jittery to focus. He clicked one link after another, and another, watching the cursor flit between black arrow and white glove, until he found himself watching a livestream of a blue-haired girl called Pussy Katz pleasuring herself with a toy light-saber. She seemed to be broadcasting from inside her bedroom; a dream catcher hung on the wall behind her, and he could read the spine of the microeconomics textbook on her bedside table. Periodically, a sound that signified a cash register opening would ping through the speakers. Other viewers were sending her digital tips. Scott watched while Pussy worked the saber and the speakers went *ka-ching, ka-ching, ka-ching.*

Deb slept through her alarm the next morning. Scott, who had tossed and turned all night, drank his morning coffee from a mug that read KEEP YOUR ROSARIES OFF MY OVARIES. On his way out of the house, he paused before the basket that Braverman had sent him. It was in the same place where he'd left it on the counter, concealed in shadow beneath the kitchen cabinets. The apples were now poxed with mold, caving in on themselves like collapsed lungs. He reached for a pear and it withered on contact, the flesh giving way to the pressure of his fingers. A fruit fly alighted on his thumb. On his way out, he walked the basket to the trash can on the curb and dropped it in.

At work, he shut himself inside his office, folded his arms, and laid his head on his desk. He had just begun to fall asleep when the office phone rang.

"When are you coming to get it?" the voice on the other end asked in a heavy Greek accent.

"Get what?"

"Your Insight." It was the mechanic.

"Oh," Scott said. "I'll come by soon."

"She is taking up much space in the lot."

"You had it for weeks. Much longer than expected. Very long

time." When Scott dealt with people who spoke broken English, his language skills automatically regressed.

"A man without a car," the Greek said, "is like a woman."

The light on the phone was blinking.

"Christ," Scott said. "Can you—hold on a sec."

He switched to the second line. "Hello?"

"Scott? It's Marty."

"Hey, Marty. I've got someone on the other line."

"Listen, I've got some news."

"Now really isn't the best time, but if you—"

"Mike didn't get the permit."

"He *what?*"

"The FAA. They denied Mike the permit. Looks like he won't be building those eGulls after all."

"You can't be serious."

"You know, I feel a little bit responsible, seeing as he's my cousin and all."

Scott could feel his body rejecting the news, a case of graft versus host. "What does the FAA care? Mike's kites don't fly high enough to mess with air traffic."

"I just got off the phone with Mike. I guess some environmental group made a stink. They say the generators make too much underwater noise. They say it'll traumatize the fishes."

Scott pressed his palm to his forehead. "What about you? Didn't you invest in SOAR?"

"Nope."

"Why not?"

"One time, when me and Mike were kids, he was showing me

around his room, and I noticed this little green speck on the wall behind the headboard of his bed. I looked closer and saw that it was,
you know, a booger. And the closer I came, the more of them I saw. I
mean, they were *everywhere*. It was like a museum exhibit. The guy was
picking his nose and wiping his finger on the wall behind his bed."

"So?"

"So I could never really trust him after that."

"Marty."

"By the way, how's that Valtrex scrip coming?"

He'd hardly begun to take in the news when yet another light on
the phone console started blinking. "Can you give me a second?"
Scott switched lines. "Hello?"

"I wait and I wait and I wait," said the Greek.

"Hold on—wrong line—be right back," Scott said. "Yes?"

"I've been calling you all morning!" Marjorie said.

Scott checked his pockets and realized his cell phone was missing.
"Sorry, Mom. I can't find my cell."

"If I don't pay Green Pastures by July, I'll lose my spot. They mean
it this time. They're not messing around."

"I have nothing to give you, Mom. Okay? I have nothing."

"Why? What's wrong?"

"I don't know what you expect me to do. If you're unwilling to talk
to this boyfriend of yours and see about getting your money back, it
might be time to look at some less expensive options as far as retirement homes are concerned."

"This is the place where I'm going to die. I would think you'd want
me to be comfortable."

"I'm not the one who got scammed by a teenager."

"Ahmet and I are in love! How would you feel if *I* started trying to poke holes in *your* marriage?"

"How would I feel if you started to do the thing you've been doing for the past twenty years?"

"All the good homes in DC have a waiting list. Unless you want to stick me in some roach-infested hospice, subjecting me to elder abuse . . ."

Scott set the office phone down on his desk and pulled up a website to track his cell phone. The site showed a digital map of Boston and its suburbs; his cell, a blue pulse, beat on the white line that represented Crowninshield Road. He must have left it in Deb's car the night before.

". . . it's not that I'm *blaming* the nurses for stealing, it's a shame what those people are paid in this country . . ." His mother's voice was small through the earpiece.

The pulse on the screen started to move. It crept up Crowninshield, picking up speed as it turned onto Commonwealth Avenue. Scott inched his chair toward the monitor.

". . . and with my shoulder like it is, and the S curves in my spine . . ."

The pulse raced east, past Boston University and Kenmore Square, until it crossed the green stripe that signified the Comm Ave Mall and then turned right, where it suddenly stopped. The pulse beat in the heart of Back Bay. Scott plucked the little yellow man from the corner of the screen and held him above the pulse. The man dangled there a moment, his legs swinging back and forth before Scott dropped him, and the screen switched to street view. There it was, Joan Portafoglio's brownstone, set back from the brick sidewalk. An old gas lamp burned in the foreground. The view was so vivid—a sodden newspaper sat on the front steps—that he half expected to see his wife on her way in.

His hand groped for the office phone, his eyes fixed on the screen. "I have to go," he said and returned it to its cradle. A moment later, the phone started ringing again.

Scott stared at the pulse for what must have been minutes until the phone stopped and Carol Chin knocked on his door. Sue Lamb was here for her appointment, she said. His brain registered the words after a few seconds' delay. Without thinking—his body seemed to be working on its own, separate and apart from his conscious mind—he instructed Carol to draw from Sue Lamb twice as much blood as she normally would and then to go home for the day.

"Are you sure?" she asked.

"Tell me something, Carol. Have you ever been to the Bahamas?"

Carol cocked her head, confused. "I haven't."

As a first-year cardiology fellow, Scott had flown on a prop plane to a private island in the Bimini chain of the Bahamas. The island was owned by a rheumy Raytheon executive from Tucson with an implantable defibrillator. He wanted a cardiologist on call at all times and rotated young physicians in and out all summer in exchange for room and board on the island. Scott was free to roam around all day, so long as he kept a walkie-talkie on hand in case the executive had a heart attack or one of the Bahamian workers, who called him "Island Doctor," came down with a cold. But the walkie-talkie rarely rang, and soon Scott realized his true purpose on the island was to keep the executive company. In the evenings, over fresh marlin and mahi-mahi, he sat and listened while the Raytheon executive dropped verbal bombs on his estranged son and ex-wife. A life of hard drinking had drilled holes in his memory, and Scott was treated to the same stories night after night. By the end of his three weeks on the island, Scott was desperate to leave.

"You'd love it," he said.

After Carol left the office, he opened a new window on the computer and began to fill out an enrollment form. Under PATIENT NAME, he typed "Doug Waxman." He entered a date of birth, 6/9/45, composed of the retired jersey numbers of Johnny Pesky, Ted Williams, and Pedro Martínez, before filling out the rest of the questionnaire. Is the patient in good health? Yes. Is the patient a smoker? Not anymore. What medications does the patient take? And so on. Then he examined Sue Lamb.

Scott asked a nurse to print the labels for his new patient, a sixty-eight-year-old former smoker named Doug Waxman. He walked the labels to the medical refrigerator, where he found the four tiger-top tubes of Sue Lamb's blood. He wrapped the labels around two of the tubes. Before leaving work, he sent the blood to Braverman. The check arrived in the mail one week later.

One bright afternoon in mid-July, Scott called Carol into his office. There were grooves in the corners of her eyes, he noticed, and her thin black hair lay close her to skull. "You look tired," he said.

She raised a hand to her cheek. "I do?"

"Oh, Christ. I didn't mean it like that. Come, sit."

She pulled out the chair opposite Scott's, a space-age contraption of steel tubing and leather that whoever bought the office furniture must have found appealing. She pressed her thighs together, looking altogether more nervous than Scott had ever seen her.

"Am I fired?"

"What? No! Of course not. I wanted to give you these." He slid an envelope across the desk. "It's time you and Celeste took a well-deserved vacation."

She furrowed her brow as she opened the envelope and found a pair of tickets inside. "Carnival Cruise Line?"

"You set sail for the Bahamas this weekend."

Her expression darkened momentarily. "Scott," she said, "this is beyond generous, but don't you think you need me here?"

"I'll do my best to keep the lights on until you're back."

"But our patients—"

"I'll be *fine.*"

Her cheeks flushed as she allowed herself to believe in the reality of the tickets. Scott could see her picturing the sunset, tasting a tropical cocktail on her tongue. "I need to pack!" she cried. "I need a new bathing suit!"

"You'd better get to it, then."

She held the tickets over her heart. "Thank you, Scott. Thank you so, so much."

Scott spent the first week of Carol's vacation drawing blood from patients who didn't need it drawn and shipping it to Dallas under a variety of fictitious names. His patients didn't object to his drawing blood; no one bothered to ask what it was for. When Braverman requested patient EKGs, Scott simply made copies of Sue Lamb's printouts and relabeled them with different initials and dates. It was hard to feel as though he had transgressed; surely, any rule worth taking seriously would be more difficult to break. Besides, he thought, he was doing it for his mother, and what could be wrong with that?

And yet there *was* something thrilling about the transgression, minor though it seemed to Scott. His whole life, he'd been climbing a ladder to respectable living. One rung was med school, another rung was marriage, and yet another was the yellow house on Crownin-shield Road. He'd proceeded with caution, taking the slow route, se-cure in the knowledge that the world would reward his patience as it had rewarded his hard work and intellect. Now he relished the feel-ing of skipping a step, of altitude gained at minimal expense. It was so *easy*. Why hadn't he tried it before?

He only saw so many patients, however, and they only had so much blood. At the rate he was going, he wouldn't have nearly enough blood to pay for Marjorie's room at Green Pastures, to make up for his losses, to get Braverman off his back—to convince himself, and Deb, that he was capable of keeping up the life they'd built for themselves. He needed more.

Scott's breakthrough occurred to him over the weekend when he nicked himself while shaving. A red bead of blood blossomed on his chin and fell into the bowl of the sink, the white porcelain studded with the grit of his stubble. Scott tore a scrap of toilet paper from the roll and stuck it to his chin to stanch the bleeding. But the blood kept coming, soaking through the paper, like his body was trying to tell him something.

He stuck a Band-Aid to his face and drove to work. There was something vaguely menacing about an empty office, he thought as he passed a bin marked with the horned biohazard icon. It was quiet enough to hear the cool air in the vents; the squeak of his sneakers on the tile resounded through the halls. When he reached the supply cabinets, he set to searching for a tourniquet and butterfly needle. Carol had devised a detailed storage system, but Scott hadn't paid attention when she explained it. He threw open one drawer after another, growing more frustrated and frantic by the minute. After some digging, he found the tourniquets, and had just discovered where Carol kept the butterflies when he heard a voice calling out to him.

A man in a blue uniform stood at the far end of the hall. Scott raised his hands above his head and released the tourniquet. It was over. Maybe if he turned himself in, he thought, they'd shave a few years off his sentence. Then another few for good behavior. Scott started toward the uniformed man, silently signing his confession when he noticed the mop the man was holding and the yellow sign beside him that read SLIPPERY WHEN WET.

"Mister?" the man called again. "You lost?"

"No, thank you," he said and stopped in his tracks. "I'm fine!"

The man shrugged and returned to mopping the floor. Sweating now, Scott bent to pick up the equipment and stole away into one of the examination rooms. He dropped the supplies on the counter and dipped his hand beneath the sanitizer dispenser. It whirred and deposited a mound of foam in his palm, which he rubbed vigorously into his skin. Then he rolled his left sleeve to the elbow and wrapped the tourniquet around his arm. Scott struggled to tie it and took one end in his teeth, jerking his head away from his arm. A vein surfaced like a dead body in a lake, like a crucial piece of evidence someone had suppressed. He swabbed the inner crook of his elbow with alcohol, popped the cap off the butterfly, and stuck the needle in. He hadn't drawn blood, or had his own drawn, in years, and he watched with childlike wonder as the tube attached to the butterfly turned crimson.

No one would ever have to know. The trial was double-blind by design. Not even Braverman had access to patient records. The trial's integrity *depended* on his not having access. And so, each night of the following week, Scott stayed at the office after sending home his staff and made a fresh deposit in his personal blood bank, pulling half a pint of hemoglobin out of his arm. Then he divided the pint into tiger-top tubes, diluting each sample with a discrete amount of saline to differentiate their lab values. He shipped the tubes to Dallas under various names, some real and some invented. The money followed. It wasn't so different, Scott thought, from getting paid for donating plasma. Apart from the occasional spell of light-headedness, he hadn't felt better in months.

On account of all the time she spent with Joan, Deb didn't seem to notice his late nights at the office. That, of course, was an advantage. But a part of him wished she *would* notice. It didn't seem to be the sign of a happy marriage that he was able to get away with so much under her nose. He almost wanted her to catch him in the act. He fantasized about confessing, the secret drawing them closer together.

In the meantime, he devoted himself to his children. He started calling Maya on a regular basis and committed himself to learning the names of her coworkers and her friends, names that sounded entirely new to his ears. He asked Gideon, who would soon be shadowing Cal Christopoulos in Durham, if he would help him build a birdhouse.

"Grandma says the old one is falling apart," he said, walking through the aisles of the Home Depot in Watertown. "She's grown pretty attached to those catbirds."

"The ones with the yarmulkes?" Gideon asked.

Scott laughed. "That's right."

"I haven't been here in forever," Gideon said. He looked around, apparently bewildered by the vast warehouse space—the air ducts hanging from the ceiling, the stacks of flattened cardboard boxes, fissures in the concrete floor.

"I used to bring you all the time. You loved helping with my home improvement projects."

"I did?"

"You bet." Scott walked slowly through the lumber aisle, reading the paper tags zip-tied to the orange shelves. "She doesn't want pine. She was very specific on that point."

"I only remember the time you left me here."

Scott looked up. "I never left you here."

"Yeah, you did! Remember? I was hanging out in the display kitchen while you shopped, and then you left without me. I remember being scared because you'd been gone a while. This old woman came up and asked if I was alone. It hadn't occurred to me until she said anything, but I guess I must have *felt* alone, because I said yes."

Scott winced. "But I came back for you, right? I mean, obviously someone did."

"I remember hearing my name on the PA system. It was so loud." He cupped his hands over his mouth. "'Gideon Greenspan, please report to checkout. Your father is looking for you.'"

"So I *did* come back."

Gideon shrugged as if this were beside the point. "It was cool, in a kind of terrifying way, hearing my name echoing across the store."

"But it's not like you were traumatized or anything." Scott forced a laugh. "I mean, right?"

"No, I wasn't traumatized." Gideon gave a reassuring smile. "But you *were* gone a really long time."

They bought the necessary materials, drove home, and set up on the front steps of the house. Scott ran an extension cord outside, which he used to power the circular saw that sat on his portable workbench. Gideon, goggled, sat on the bottom step and watched as Scott cut the pieces for the base, walls, and roof.

"It's not enough to get good grades anymore," Gideon said. He'd been talking since the car ride home about his application to medical school. "You have to tell the adcoms a compelling story about yourself. That's where I'm stuck. I can't figure out what to say."

Scott was paying as much attention to his son as he could while operating dangerous machinery. "You've led an interesting life," he said. "You've traveled."

"I'm not interesting in the way they want. I haven't really *overcome* anything."

"I'm sure the admissions committee gets tired of hearing sob stories. I'm sure everyone else is going to write about how they lost their grandmother to cancer, which inspired them to find a cure, et cetera." The blade of the circular saw cleaved a board in two. One of the pieces clattered to the ground. "You're lucky, you know. My dad wasn't around to do things like this."

"Is that what you wrote your essay about? Losing your dad?"

"I don't remember if I even *had* to write an essay. But it wasn't so competitive then. Not like it is now."

Scott had been in private practice long enough that he was insulated from, though not unaware of, the changes taking place in American medical schools. He didn't remember stressing this much about his application, but his time at Harvard and his residency afterward had been so grueling as to be unethical, at least according to the new regulations. Scott had spent so many hours at Brigham and Women's during his residency—eating in the cafeteria, running up and down the stairs for exercise—that he routinely considered surrendering his apartment and living full time at the hospital. It was harder than ever to get into med school these days, but it had never been easier to graduate.

The door to the house opened, and Deb stepped out. "Look at my boys," she said, beaming. "Such hard workers."

Scott asked where she was going.

"I have to run some errands. I might be home late." She shot Scott a look that meant she'd be seeing Joan. "I'm pretty sure I won't be back for dinner."

"I'm sure Gideon and I can rustle something up," he said uncertainly.

Deb bent to kiss Gideon's head. "I love having you home."

She got in her car and waved at them through the window. Scott switched off the saw and looked at his son.

"I hope you don't take your mother for granted," he said.

"Why would I do that?"

"You wouldn't. I mean, I hope you don't take your girlfriend for granted. Or your wife, when you're older."

"I didn't think you liked Astra that much."

"I'm not talking about Astra, per se. And—hey!—I like her just fine."

"So what are you talking about?"

"Are you familiar with the concept of an open marriage?"

"Um . . . yes?"

Scott second-guessed himself. Maybe he *shouldn't* tell his son. But if they were going to bond—and what was this birdhouse business about, anyway, if not bonding?—he would have to tell the truth. He set the saw down and removed his gloves. "Can I share something with you? Man to, er, man?"

Gideon seemed to realize the gravity of the moment. He took off his goggles, which had left pale impressions in his skin. "Of course."

"About, oh, I don't know, five years ago, your mother proposed we open our marriage." He felt a twinge of cowardice for pinning the decision on Deb, but it was the truth. "We've been seeing other people, on and off, for some time now. I'm sure this comes as something of a shock, and I can only imagine how you feel. I want to give you the space to ask me any questions you might have."

Gideon blinked. "You and Mom have an open marriage?"

Scott nodded. He was suddenly overcome with dread at the idea of answering Gideon's questions. "Of course, if you don't have any questions, that's fine, too. Or if you need to mull it over for a while. This whole thing, it's not that big a deal. It's just something I wanted to share."

Gideon nodded. The newish neighbors across the street, a young couple with a toddler named Abe, the very picture of contented young marrieds, waved at them on their way to the car. Scott waved back. It was like looking into his past.

"I guess my question is . . . why?"

Scott thought for a minute. As he prepared to explain his open marriage to his son, it occurred to him that he'd never quite managed to explain it to himself.

"It's practical," he said at last. "When you've been married as long as your mother and I have, you come to understand that one person can't fulfill all of your needs. It's kind of crazy, isn't it, the way we ask our spouses to be everything to us, all the time? Your mother is a remarkable woman, don't get me wrong, but even she can't possibly provide everything our society asks of a partner: financial security, emotional dependability, sexual novelty—sorry. You get the picture."

Gideon's eyebrows knit together. "I thought you said it was Mom's idea."

"Right. That's right. Good listening. It was." This was proving more complicated than Scott expected. He elbowed his son in the side, trying to lighten the mood. "But it's not like I haven't had my fun. Huh? Huh?" He elbowed him again. "Huh? You know what I mean?"

"I think so, yeah."

"But the important thing—the reason I'm bringing this up—is that we're going to put a stop to it. The open marriage, I mean. We tried it for a while, but ultimately, I don't think it's brought us any closer. In fact, I think it's had the opposite effect. But that doesn't mean Mom and I aren't still happy together. Think of it like a science experiment. We tested a hypothesis. The hypothesis failed. That's just part of the process."

"Are you getting a divorce?"

"No! Of course not. This is the opposite of that."

"That's good."

"It is. It *is* good."

"So you, like, went on dates and stuff?"

"I bet you didn't think your old man had it in him, huh?"

"No, I guess I didn't."

"Huh? Huh?" Scott elbowed him again. "Pick up that hammer, would you? I can't do this all by myself."

Gideon grabbed the hammer. With his free hand, he positioned a nail at the end of a wood panel. He brought the hammer down, missed, and crushed his thumb.

"Ow! Ow! Shit! Sorry! Fuck!"

"Whoa there," Scott said. "Take it easy. There's no rush."

"It isn't my fault," Gideon said. "I can't hold the boards steady. I don't have enough hands."

"I didn't say it was your fault," Scott said. He'd seen his son worked up like this before. "Let me take a crack at it."

"I can do it."

"I know you *can* do it, but I'm offering to help," Scott said, reaching for the hammer.

Gideon jerked his hand back. "I've *got* it, I've *got* it."

Scott watched him struggle with the hammer for a while. Through the goggles, he could see his son's eyes welling up. "You're doing great, G-Money," he said. "You're doing great."

On the weekend that Carol was due to return, Scott drove down to see his mother on the Cape. He presented her with the birdhouse and spent the rest of Saturday fixing up the cottage, ignoring the hints she dropped like anvils about her bill from Green Pastures. That evening, he took her out to eat at a candlelit restaurant housed inside a white colonial. Two lengths of rope, each tied in bowline knots, hung from the wooden rafters above the table.

"How's the swordfish?" he asked.

"Suspicious."

"What? Why? Why suspicious?"

"You're up to something. I just can't tell what."

"A guy can't take his mom out every now and again?"

"To a fancy dinner like this?" She waved her butter knife. "You never have before."

"Jesus, Mom. That's not even remotely true. Although, in this case, you happen to be right. I have something to tell you."

"You're getting divorced."

"Even better. I'm paying for Green Pastures."

She dropped her knife. "You *are?*"

"I am."

"I love you!" she gasped, like a fish starved for water. "I love you, I love you!"

He reached across the table and took her hand in his. It was so small, he thought, and so cold, the skin like wax paper.

"I love you, too."

"Oh, Scott. Ahmet will be so relieved."

Scott woke the next morning feeling buoyant. It was summer on the Cape, a time for barbecues and blueberries, the air perfumed with the scent of swamp azaleas. He got in his car, which was running like a dream, and drove up to see Colleen. He found her on the front steps, watching her kids play in an inflatable pool. Scott let her talk about the clinic for a while before he said what he'd resolved to say one week earlier. "I don't think we should see each other anymore."

"I thought you wanted me to move to Boston," Colleen said.

"We both know you weren't going to do that."

"I knew that. Did you?"

"Hey, Uncle Scott!" her son Seamus shouted. "Listen to my dolphin sounds!"

"I'm married, Colleen."

"Scree! Scree!"

"So am I." Colleen's husband, Nicky, had developed an addiction to Percocet after falling off a roof he was reshingling. Now he spent most of his time harassing the dancers at Zachary's in Mashpee.

"I have to do right by my wife," he said.

"Is she going to do right by you?"

"Scree!"

"She is," Scott said. He repeated it twice as if casting a spell. "She is. She is."

"The kids will miss you."

"I'll miss them." Colleen's older son, Beckett, was holding Seamus's head under the water. "You should know that this wasn't an easy decision. And believe me, it has nothing to do with you."

"I'm not going to break down and cry if that's what you were hoping for."

"I didn't hope for that, no."

"And if I *was* going to cry, I'd wait until after you left."

Scott got up. "Goodbye, Colleen."

"If your mom fakes sick again, you know where to find me."

As he shut the car door behind him, he wondered, momentarily, if he had made the wrong decision. Who but Colleen could take this news so well and with so much dignity? He admired so many things about her: her pragmatism, her resilience, the way she faced her apparent hardships without complaint. The dank cellar of her sexual imagination. But he had a wife at home and two children of his own, and everything was going to be different from now on.

That night, in bed, Scott asked Deb how she wanted to spend the next thirty years. With Marjorie's down payment finally covered, their only responsibilities now were to themselves. They talked about moving to an apartment downtown and leaving the suburbs behind. They talked about buying a house in the country. Deb knew a woman with a place up in Maine whose chickens produced fresh eggs each morning. "Just think of the omelets!" she said, resting her head on Scott's woolly chest. Or maybe they would move somewhere scenic, like Venice, and become the kind of rapacious expats who wake at sunset to recruit innocent tourists for their demented sexual games.

Joan never entered into these fantasies, which Scott saw as a good sign. Deb didn't mention her, which seemed to suggest that if they *did* move somewhere like Venice, or even Maine, she would leave her girlfriend behind. Scott never sought clarity on this, preferring to keep the name Joan Portafoglio far away from his fantasies.

It wouldn't be long before Carol started asking why the new patients weren't coming in for follow-up exams. Anticipating this, Scott began the slow process of killing them off. Not long after a patient had been randomized, triggering a wave of payment, Scott would tell Carol he'd just been informed that the patient had been hit by a car, or caught the flu, or had otherwise withdrawn from the study.

"Don't you think it's strange?" she asked one afternoon. "The way our patients have been dropping out?"

"Yes," he said. "Strange, but not unprecedented."

She was a few shades darker than she'd been before the trip. When she walked, the beads in her new cornrows clicked. "To enroll all those patients? And then they disappear?"

"I'm telling you, there's nothing to worry about."

"Could you share their phone numbers with me? It might be worth following up."

"The phone numbers are in the eCRFs."

"You haven't granted me access to the eCRFs."

"I haven't?" She was nothing if not trusting, but she wasn't stupid, either. "I'll get those to you by the end of the day."

"I was hoping to look at them now, is the thing."

Carol's best qualities—her thoroughness, her attention to detail,

her near-clairvoyant knowledge of the workings of his practice—
qualities which had literally kept the lights on, like the time she installed a backup generator after snow snuffed the power during a
blizzard in '05—made her, now, not an ally but an obstacle.

"How long have we worked together?" Scott asked.

"Must be around fifteen years."

"If I tell you I'll send you the numbers, I will."

"All I want to do is follow up. Maybe I can get some of them back.
It would be such a shame to see your hard work go to waste."

"You were telling me a few weeks back about the buffer zone."

For the first time since he'd begun mislabeling blood—and that's
all he'd done, stuck the wrong labels on perfectly acceptable blood—
he felt a pang of guilt. He couldn't care less about Braverman's study,
but Carol didn't deserve the treatment she was about to receive.

"That's right," she said. "What does that have to do with anything?"

"Deb gets lunch once or twice each month with the superintendent
of schools."

Her widening eyes told him she understood but couldn't admit to it
yet. "What are we talking about here?" she asked.

"I'm stating a fact, which you can take how you will. Deb has the
superintendent on speed dial. She used to serve on the enrollment
committee. These are just facts that I'm laying out for you." He'd
never thought himself capable of this kind of slick extortion. He felt
as though he were reading lines from a script, as though words leaving his mouth weren't his own. "You don't want your kids enrolled
at . . ."

"Pierce."

"But you'd be happy with . . ."

Carol was shaking. "Lincoln."

"Good."

By August, Marjorie had moved into Green Pastures, where she'd infiltrated a tight clique of women who attended nightly lectures and concerts together. Ahmet, entering his last year of secondary school, was applying to American universities. The Chin twins were set to start first grade at Lincoln.

And then, one night, in the middle of a dinner party, the phone rang and everything changed.

Scott was deposed on an autumn afternoon in a hotel conference room whose only window looked out on the Suffolk County House of Correction. Despite the view, Scott was feeling confident. He'd gone over every detail of his case and concluded that he was in the clear, so long as he didn't incriminate himself. It wasn't even a formal deposition—there were no attorneys present—but what the investigator for the ORI called an "inquiry," which Scott privately thought of as an "inquisition." The investigator was presently struggling to mount a tiny camcorder on a tripod, which Scott took to be a positive sign. The investigator's partner sat in a chair by the door, reading the Sunday comics section of the *Globe*.

"Apologies for the delay," the investigator said, nodding at the camcorder. His voice was high and reedy, almost ingratiating, as if he wanted to be friends with Scott after this was over. "Our equipment is hopelessly out of date."

"They don't give you government guys the good toys?" Scott asked.

The investigator chuckled. "Anything to save a buck."

A minute passed, maybe two—there was no clock in the room—

before a red light on the camera switched on. Then the investigator took his seat. The laminate surface of the conference table was mottled to make it look like marble. A package of Poland Spring water bottles sat between them, encased in plastic.

"What do you say we get this over with?" the investigator asked, sliding out of his suit jacket, a pair of hairless forearms extending from short sleeves. There was something serpentine about the man, Scott thought. His lips were thin, and his head was shaven to the point of sterility.

"Sounds good," Scott said.

The investigator pumped Purell from a personal dispenser. He rubbed his hands together, the sanitizer's squish the only sound in the room. Scott wondered if the camcorder picked it up.

"Would you mind please stating your name for the record?"

"Scott Greenspan."

Scott waited while the investigator pulled a pen from his shirt pocket and scribbled something—Scott could not imagine what—on one of the papers in front of him.

"And your place of business?"

"Longwood Cardiology Clinic."

"Which is where, exactly?"

"Three-twenty Longwood Avenue."

"And that's in Boston, Massachusetts."

"United States of America. Planet Earth."

The investigator smiled, revealing a row of coffee-stained teeth that seemed at odds with his otherwise immaculate cleanliness. "It's just for the record, you understand," he said, as though apologizing for the pro forma nature of the questions.

"Of course," Scott said. "I'm sorry. Let's continue."

"How long have you practiced medicine at that location?"

Scott looked up at the fluorescent light panel above him. "Must be, let's see, fifteen years."

"Is that right? I have it down as sixteen here."

"Fine," Scott said. He wondered why the investigator was asking questions whose answers he already knew. To test his honesty, he supposed.

"And how old are you?"

"Fifty-three."

"Married?"

"Yes."

"Kids?"

"Two. I'm sorry, how is this relevant?"

"Just trying to get to know a little more about you." The investigator shuffled his notes. "I'm sorry. I'll come to the point. Describe for me, if you would, your relationship with Dr. Richard Braverman."

Scott cleared his throat. He'd prepared for this. "Rich and I are colleagues. We're collegial."

"And you served under Dr. Braverman on the Human Outpatient Pericarditis Evaluation study?"

"I was in charge of the Boston site for the HOPE trial, yes."

"I'd like to ask your honest opinion of the trial."

"My honest opinion?"

"Please."

Scott stared into the eye of the camcorder. He imagined Braverman watching on the other side. "My honest opinion is, I think it's bullshit."

"Why?"

"We already have several effective, generic treatments for mild to moderate pericarditis."

"What about severe cases? Are there treatments for that?"

"In theory, patients with refractory or recurrent pericarditis might benefit from a drug trial like this one, yes. But those patients were excluded from the trial by design."

"Excluded? Why?"

"My best guess," Scott said, adopting the gently condescending tone he sometimes used while speaking to his children, "is that the drug didn't perform well in phase two. Or maybe . . ." He looked into the eye of the camcorder again. "Maybe someone's just trying to cash in by selling the public on a pill they don't need."

"Phase two?" The investigator blushed. "I'm sorry, I'm not a physician. Far from it. I got a C in high school biology."

While Scott explained the four phases of clinical trials, he wondered where he would eat after the inquisition was over. He was in the mood for tapas.

"In other words," the investigator said when Scott finished, "you don't believe the study has merit."

"That is a good working definition of bullshit, yes."

"But you enrolled a number of your patients in the trial anyway?"

Scott had seen this question coming. He delivered the answer he'd rehearsed at home. "I had my doubts about the HOPE trial, it's true. But I felt I owed it to Dr. Braverman as a professional courtesy. It's not as though my patients would be harmed by participating."

"And then there's the matter of the princely sum you received for enrolling each patient, is that right?"

He had to laugh. "I'd hardly call it 'princely.'"

"All right. What would you call it?"

"Fair market compensation. Recruiting patients takes quite a bit of time and effort. You have to find the right people, take them through the protocol, and of course carry out the trial itself. That means follow-ups, tracking endpoints and adverse effects—"

"But none of your patients saw the trial through. They all dropped out."

Scott shrugged. "Maybe they didn't see the merit in it, either."

The investigator frowned. He had nothing. He *knew* nothing. Beneath the powerful fluorescent lights, Scott could see the outline of the man's undershirt.

"I guess I'm just surprised that you enrolled so many patients in what you describe as a 'bullshit' study. Especially in light of your history."

"My history? What history?"

The investigator answered without consulting his notes. "I mean the work you did for Dr. Krebs. The research no one could repeat. Help yourself to a water, if you want one."

Scott wanted a water, but not from the investigator.

"Well," the investigator said, "that's neither here nor there. Why don't you talk me through your day on June 13, 2013."

He didn't know why the investigator had mentioned Krebs. To throw him off, somehow? To establish a pattern of fraud?

"June 13," Scott said. "I woke up. Shaved. Made myself some coffee. Went to work. Saw patients." He shrugged as if it had been like any other day. "Probably ducked out early to play tennis."

This last, self-effacing comment did not appear to land with the investigator. "Did you see a patient named Sue Lamb on June 13?"

"I'd have to check my calendar. But if you say I did, I did."

"I'm not saying anything. Only you know who you saw that day."

Pedantic little creep, Scott thought. "I probably saw Sue Lamb, yes."

"Did you ask Sue Lamb if she was interested in enrolling in the HOPE trial?"

"I did."

"And what did she say?"

"I believe she declined."

"But you did enroll a patient in the trial that day, didn't you?"

"I'd have to check my calendar." That was, Scott realized, the second time he had mentioned needing to check his calendar. He resolved not to mention the calendar again for fear of sounding suspicious.

The investigator pumped more Purell into his hands. He coated them from palm to fingertip until the air was stinging with the scent of alcohol. "Let's back up a moment. I want to be sure I have this straight. You saw Sue Lamb on June 15. She declined to participate in the HOPE trial. Correct?"

"June *13*."

"That's right. June 13. So you *do* remember." The investigator smiled. "And according to Dr. Braverman's files, you enrolled a new patient that day. That patient's name was . . . ?"

"I can't tell you that," Scott said, folding his arms across his chest. He leaned back in his chair. "That'd be a HIPAA violation."

A silence fell over the room. Invoking HIPAA was like casting a spell; Scott felt like he had just stepped into a suit of enchanted armor. No matter how much the investigator prodded, he could not compel Scott to give up the names of any patients enrolled in the trial. Without the names, there was no case.

"You're absolutely right," the investigator said. He shuffled his papers again, his lips bent into a frown. "Well, I guess that's all I've got. Thank you for your time, Dr. Greenspan."

"That's it?" Scott asked. "Are you sure?" He was surprised by how quickly the investigator folded. He was almost disappointed.

The investigator shrugged. "By the way, would you say hello to Sue Lamb for me? Let her know I've been praying for her."

"You know Sue?"

"We spoke on the phone."

"You did?"

"Wouldn't be much of an investigator if I didn't! Don't worry, Dr. Greenspan, it's simply protocol."

Scott started to stand but stopped himself. "You said you were praying for her. Why?"

"I'm surprised you don't know, seeing as you're her cardiologist. Sue Lamb suffers from what I gather is a nasty condition known as type two Brugada syndrome. Are you familiar with Brugada?"

Scott nodded.

"Brugada goes by another name," the investigator said. "Do you know what that name is?"

"Sudden unexplained nocturnal death syndrome."

"Very good, Dr. Greenspan. Sudden unexplained nocturnal death syndrome. Sounds scary, doesn't it?" When Scott didn't answer, the investigator asked, "Could you explain what that means in layman's terms?"

"There isn't much to explain," Scott said. "People with Brugada can die in their sleep."

"Just like that?"

"Just like that."

"Sudden unexplained nocturnal death syndrome." The investigator shivered. "Well, I certainly wouldn't want that! Fortunately, I understand that it's quite rare. One in every two thousand people, give or take?"

"That sounds right." For some reason, the camcorder was still on. Scott felt a sudden urge to get out of the conference room as soon as possible.

"It's funny," the investigator said, returning his pen to his pocket. "That patient you enrolled July 13? The one whose name you won't share?"

"*Can't* share."

"Can't share. Of course. We wouldn't want you to violate HIPAA. Then I'd have to investigate you for that!" There were those coffee-stained teeth again, small and sharp and spaced too far apart, like the teeth of a circular saw. "I say it's funny because that nameless patient of yours also appears to have Brugada."

Scott tried not to sound surprised. "What makes you say that?"

"As I said before, I'm no physician. But I learned a few things while reviewing your case. Turns out you can tell patients with Brugada by their EKGs. Apparently, those EKGs will display what's known in your field as a saddleback pattern with two-millimeter J-point elevation—I hope I'm getting this right—and one-millimeter ST elevation with—pardon my pronunciation—a biphasic T wave." He chuckled. "I don't know what that means, to be honest with you. Dr. Braverman tried to explain it to me. He said he thinks you'd know."

Scott was desperate for a drink, but taking a bottle of water now seemed to signal his guilt, somehow. He looked at the camera and wondered if it registered the sweat beading on his forehead.

"Sue Lamb has Brugada," the investigator said. "So does the name-less patient you enrolled on the same day you saw Sue. I wonder what you make of that."

"It could be a coincidence."

"That's what I thought, too!" The investigator clapped his antiseptic hands. "Brugada affects one in two thousand people. So that's one in two thousand multiplied by . . . one in two thousand. Wow. I can't crunch those numbers off the top of my head—I'm not half as smart as you are, Dr. Greenspan—but that seems like a pretty big coincidence."

Despite himself, Scott reached for the package of Poland Spring and pulled it toward him. The plastic was pulled taut over the bottles. He could feel the sweat fall down his forehead as he tried to claw a hole in the plastic. The investigator waited while Scott wrenched a bottle free. He hated the desperate, suckling sound he made as he drank. He wiped away the water dribbling down his chin.

"Maybe they're family," he said suddenly, marveling at his mind's ability to improvise such an ironclad answer. "I run a family practice, and Brugada is genetic. It's entirely possible that the patient I enrolled on June 13 is related to Sue Lamb. Not that I can say without violating HIPAA."

"You have a point. They could be related. But how do you explain the fact that *each of the sixteen patients* you enrolled in the HOPE trial, starting June 13, appears to suffer from Brugada? I mean, what are the chances?" The investigator reached into his jacket and produced a pocket calculator. "One in two thousand times one in two thousand times one in two thousand times one in two—" He frowned over the machine. "Damn thing can't handle a number so small. Budget cuts, right? Like you said before."

Scott reached for a second bottle.

"Unless," the investigator said, "all sixteen patients are related. Why, with that many people, you could start a circus! Do you see many circus families, Dr. Greenspan?"

Scott fought the impulse to grab the investigator by the collar, smash his head against the table until it turned to pulp. Smash the camera, too.

"Here's what I think happened," the investigator said. "I think you drew Sue Lamb's blood without permission. I think you sent that blood, along with her EKG, to Dr. Braverman. And I think you *kept* sending blood, which you got from god knows where, using Sue Lamb's EKG over and over. And you know what? It might have worked—if Sue Lamb didn't have this rare disorder."

The EKGs. The fucking EKGs. He'd been careful, so meticulous and careful, with the blood, but he hadn't thought to check the EKGs. Whatever guilt he carried on account of what he'd done was nothing compared with the annihilating shame he felt now. He tried to retreat inside himself, detach as he did when he was with his mother. But as he approached that inner chamber in his mind, he found, for the first time, that the door was locked.

The investigator pressed a button on the camcorder and the red light went out. "I meet a lot of desperate people in my line of work," he said. "I've met well-funded scientists who fudged figures. I've seen physicians run pain clinics like pill mills. And you know what most of those people have in common? Decency, Dr. Greenspan. Decency. They didn't start with the intention to trick anyone. They didn't set out to commit fraud or overprescribe pills to their patients. They were under pressure, that was all, and bit by bit, things got out of hand. A half-truth here, a compromise there, and pretty soon the whole operation's off the rails. Of course, there are bad actors in the world—I've had the displeasure of knowing some, in and out of my capacity as an investigator—but nine times out of ten, it's just a decent man who cut a corner. Probably he feels bad about it. Maybe even regrets it. So he waits to be found out. He waits and waits. And then, one day, he wakes up and realizes that he got away with it. So what does he do next? Cuts another corner. Who knows, maybe there's a part of him that *wants* to get caught, just to find the line. Just to know there *is* a line." He paused impressively. "That's why I'm here. I'm the line."

The investigator pressed the button on the camcorder and the red light came on again.

"What I'm struggling to understand," he went on, "is why a successful physician such as yourself—a family man with a wife and two kids, his own private practice, in the prime of his life—would draw blood from his patients without their permission and submit that blood to Dr. Braverman, knowing full well that in doing so you were jeopardizing not only the HOPE trial but your own career as well."

Scott muttered something, then took a long swig of water from the second bottle. He had never been so thirsty.

"Dr. Greenspan?" the investigator asked. "Could you repeat that please? As I mentioned before, our tech is hopelessly out of date."

Scott crushed the empty water bottle in his hand. "I was trying," he said, "to be a good son."

The inquiry lasted another two hours, during which time Scott was forced to recount his misdeeds in detail, the investigator interrupting only to make sure he was speaking at a volume loud enough to register with the camcorder. When it was over, the investigator's partner rose from his chair and held the door open for Scott, who stumbled into the carpeted hall as if having just woken from a dream.

He stopped in the hotel café on his way out. He thought he might faint if he didn't put something in his body. At the register, while the cashier swiped his card, he looked over his shoulder and saw the investigator sitting with his partner at one of the low tables. The investigator looked up from his own coffee and waved. His partner stared. Scott thought of approaching them, but he didn't have the strength. The investigator didn't seem so tough now, anyway. It was his job to ask Scott questions. They were all just doing their jobs.

To feel safe, secure, surrounded by the people he loved: that was what mattered now. But as he drove up to the house on Crowninshield Road, he saw Deb's muscular dancer's legs walking out the door, her upper torso and head obscured by the large cardboard box she was carrying. He put the Insight in park and left it idling in the middle of the street.

"What's going on?" he asked, jogging toward her. "Where are you going?"

"I'm going to stay with Joan for a while," she said from behind the box.

"Why?"

She walked past him, heading toward the station wagon parked in the driveway.

"I think I did all right at the deposition. Inquisition. Sorry, inquiry. Soon, this will all be over, and we can go back to the way things were before."

"The way things were before wasn't working."

"Better, then! I promise."

A rust-bitten pickup truck of Freudian proportions pulled up be-hind Scott's car and honked its horn.

"I don't want to have this conversation right now. I just need to get away for a while."

"How long, do you think?"

The truck honked again, and the window rolled down. "Hey, chuck-lehead," called the driver, a red-faced Masshole in a tweed scally cap. "Move your car!"

"You should move your car, Scott."

"I'm not moving anything until we have a chance to talk."

"Would you get the door for me?" Deb asked.

"I'm not going to *help* you *leave me!*" Scott said, as the Masshole in the scally cap climbed out of the truck, brandishing a baseball bat.

"You should really move your car," Deb said.

"I'm not moving anything!"

The Masshole brought the bat down on his windshield.

Scott whipped around at the sound of smashing glass. "Shit," he said. "I just got that back from the shop."

The cabin lights had dimmed and Scott was slipping off to sleep when a flight attendant came on the PA system and asked, first in English, then in German, if there was a doctor on board. Suspended in the air between two distant continents, Scott himself was feeling vaguely ill. He had taken enough Benadryl to knock out a whole family, and his sinuses were bearing on his skull. There was a tightness in his throat, a knot he couldn't swallow, and the dread he sometimes felt, when traveling alone, that he did not belong to any country in particular— a stratospheric Bedouin tearing through the sky.

He picked himself up and stepped over the woman in the aisle seat, her eyes trained on *The Fugitive*, which was playing on the small screen in front of her. His left foot was asleep. He dragged the dead appendage up the aisle, toes pulsing with static, pausing at the wool curtain between coach and business class. Two weeks had passed since the state of Massachusetts suspended his medical license. The wording of the letter was inflexibly precise: after four years of med school and another four in residency, followed by twenty nearly spotless years of service, he was now forbidden from prescribing medication; from performing any and all surgical procedures; from diagnosing, curing, or treating health conditions; from legally calling himself a physician. One small mistake—a minor lapse of judgment—and they had stripped him of both his profession and his purpose. But he could hear a woman shrieking from the far side of the curtain, and despite the risk of legal action, Scott had sworn an oath. He could not sit idly by and let an ailing person suffer. At the very least, he thought he'd take a look.

He swept the curtain aside and peered into business class. A couple of college girls reclined in their recumbent seats, barefoot and flexing their pedicured toes. He couldn't remember the last time he'd flown coach, but the loss of his medical license—and with it, his income— had awoken an ancestral impulse in him, an Old Country instinct for prudence and thrift; for potatoes stashed by the pound in the cellar, diamonds sewn into the seam of a coat.

He looked up and saw what the fuss was about. An enormous, red-faced man a few rows up was asleep on the arm of a woman in a terry cloth tracksuit. His head was resting on her trembling shoulder; a meaty arm lay splayed across her thigh. A flight attendant with long lashes was crouched in the aisle beside them, watching a squat man in glasses check for a pulse. The man, who looked vaguely familiar, said something to the flight attendant that caused her to stand and shuffle off.

"Can I help?" Scott asked as the flight attendant hurried past, but she didn't seem to have heard him.

She returned a moment later with a small cosmetic mirror. The physician—Scott guessed that's what the squat man was—placed it in front of the unconscious man's mouth. Then he rifled through the man's blazer and produced one small orange prescription bottle. The static in Scott's foot had settled, and he inched close enough to hear the physician ask the flight attendant how many drinks the man had ordered. A male flight attendant pushed past Scott, carrying a canister of oxygen hooked to a mask. The physician placed the mask over the man's face and slapped his jowl. The woman in the tracksuit squealed as the man's massive head began to move.

"We're in business, folks," the physician said as business class erupted in applause. "Let this be a reminder to everyone on board that Valium and booze don't mix." He removed his glasses, revealing tiny, deep-set eyes beneath a canopy of wild hairs, and wiped the lenses with a purple cloth. It was then that Scott put a name to the face that for the last minute had seemed so familiar. The beady eyes and unkempt brows belonged to Leonard Amsterdam, an old pre-med classmate of Scott's from Johns Hopkins.

"Scott?" Len said. "Scott Greenspan?"

Scott looked up and pretended to be startled. "Len," he said and extended his hand. "You looked like a pro out there."

"Good to know I haven't lost my touch. I'm just glad the great Scott Greenspan was on call in case I needed backup."

Len had followed Scott around all through senior year. He seemed to believe that they were rivals, somehow, and was determined to unseat Scott from his position at the top of their graduating class. Scott's refusal to recognize Len as a competitor, and his insistence that he didn't really care about grades, only served to strengthen Len's resolve. Actually, Scott cared a great deal, but managed to drive Len mad with envy by giving the impression that he didn't.

"I'm visiting my son in Berlin," Len said after the two men had looked each other over. "After that, I'm heading to a conference in Hamburg. They have me giving some keynote address." He rolled his eyes and flicked his wrist dismissively. "I told them I was trying to cut back on travel, but they kept on insisting. How's that for poetic justice? My grandmother barely makes it out of there alive, and seventy years later, they're begging me back."

"Urology, right?"

"*Pul*monology."

"Of course," Scott said. "My mistake." He delighted in watching the wings of Len's nostrils flare. "How old is Michael now, anyway?"

"Nineteen. And Gideon?"

"He's a junior at Columbia. Biology."

"Getting into the family business, eh? You must be proud."

Things had been strained between Scott and his son since Gideon learned about the scandal. Scott had been the one to break the news, calling Gideon at the start of the semester. Gideon seemed to have taken it well, but Scott hadn't heard from him since. Strange for a kid who used to call a couple of times per week. Scott suspected this change in attitude had to do with Deb, the unflattering story she must have spun for him. For that, he supposed, he could forgive her. What bothered him most was the dawning realization that he'd taken his son's admiration for granted. He'd come to count on Gideon's devotion to him. It had fortified his confidence. He hardly knew who he was without it.

"I am. I am proud. Is Michael studying abroad?"

Len looked out the window at the winking red light on the wingtip. "Actually, he left school last semester. Took a leave of absence, I should say."

It wasn't the boy's fault that his father was an asshole, but after the events of the past few months, it was hard not to take at least a little bit of pleasure in the thought that Len's son, who had probably been pressured all his life by a father who cared only about status and prestige, had ultimately flunked out of school. With all the condescension he could muster, Scott said, "I'm sure he'll find his way back eventually."

A passenger squeezed past them on her way to the lavatory. "That's what his mother and I hope, but I'm not sure. He's making quite a killing as it is."

The hum of the engines and the circulating air made it difficult for Scott to hear. "Excuse me," he said and turned his left ear toward Len. "I thought you said 'a killing.'"

Len explained that his son, Michael, was working as a club DJ in Europe. "It's all noise to me, just one long repetitive thump, thump, thump. But Michael pulls in ten, twenty thousand bucks per night."

The tension in Scott's eardrums tightened. "You said ten or twenty *thousand*?"

"On nights he has gigs, sure. But that's only three or four nights each week. I'm not sure what else he does with his time, but if his Facebook posts are any indication, he seems to have quite a few girlfriends. He plays a lot of fashion shows, apparently." Len shrugged.

"Hard to make the case for med school to a kid who earns what I earn each year in a month! He just bought Barb and me a place on Martha's Vineyard."

The flush of the lavatory toilet hissed behind them. "That's terrific," Scott said through gritted teeth. "You must be very proud."

Len grinned. "Is your lovely wife on board?"

The fasten–seat belt light switched on. "Deb is back at home."

"Aha. Work trip. I should have known. Cardiology conference in Berlin?"

A flight attendant approached them, laid a manicured hand on Len's tweed shoulder, and asked if they would please return to their seats. Len turned, and she withdrew her hand. "I'm sorry, Doctor," she said, her cheeks flushed the same shade of red as her nails. "My apologies. You and your friend take as long as you want."

"You were saying?" Len said. His arms were crossed and his legs were spread apart, straddling both sides of the aisle like a troll whose riddle Scott would have to answer before he returned to his seat.

"No," he said. "No conference." The knot in his throat was expanding in size and starting to choke out his speech. He felt the antihistamines working on his nervous system, a weighted blanket draped over his brain.

"You're being coy," Len said. "Hey, that's all right. Just do me a favor and tell Deb I said hello." He licked his finger and with it suppressed the riot of wild hairs springing from his eyebrows. "And that mother of yours, too."

When Scott shut his eyes and envisioned Berlin, he pictured an abandoned carnival: the park deserted, the rides rusted in place, the smell of spun sugar wafting over a fun house on whose splintered awning was painted the face of a clown with tears in its eyes. He wasn't sure where the image had come from—a documentary on East Berlin, perhaps—but the barred window of his third-story room overlooked a disused Ferris wheel, the cabins spiked with ice, and he was struck by the uncanny, unnerving feeling of having dreamed the city into existence.

It was the cheapest place he could find on short notice. His decision to come to Berlin had not been made with comfort in mind. For sixteen euros per night, he was given one hospital bed in a room that fit four. The white woman with locs behind the front desk said the hostel had once been a treatment center for the criminally insane. Only the graffiti on the wall of Scott's room—BE YOURSELF, in bright bubble letters—helped dispel (or did it?) the air of madness in the place.

Damp clothes were drying on the spare beds by the window. They belonged to a young Australian couple whom Scott had met on his way in. In the last of the beds, someone was sleeping beneath the starchy white sheets, their feet poking out like a corpse in a morgue.

His sleep on the plane had been fitful and he could smell his own sour breath. All he'd eaten since takeoff was a small chocolate pastry, a dense butter bomb, served to him in a plastic pouch by a stewardess in makeup a few shades darker than the pale, mottled skin of her neck. He had been in motion since the cab ride to Logan, and if he stopped now, he feared he would collapse.

A bearded man was playing guitar and singing "Imagine" from a beanbag chair in the lobby. Scott picked up a map from the front-desk woman and headed out into the street. The sky was burning above the park at whose edge the hostel was located. He was far from any urban center, he realized, and checking the map and the street

signs, he saw that it would take him much longer to get to Neu-.
kölln than he'd thought. His knuckles were chapping in the late October cold. In his hurry to leave Boston, he'd left his scarf and gloves
at home.

The morning after Deb moved out, Scott had driven down Route
6, the artery that runs through the arm of Massachusetts. It was Labor Day weekend, Marjorie's last on the Cape, the seawater warm
enough to support hurricanes. Scott sat in traffic on both sides of the
Sagamore Bridge beneath a sky darkening with storm clouds. It had
started raining by the time he arrived, and he found his mother clearing her lunch off the deck. He demanded to see her emails to Ahmet.
When she refused, he snatched her laptop and locked himself in the
bathroom. The young receptionist at his office had shown him how
to track a person's geographic coordinates from their email and IP
addresses. Sitting on the toilet seat, the laptop balanced on his legs,
he tracked Ahmet's location to a tele-café in Neukölln, a southern
borough of Berlin.

Marjorie was pounding on the door, rattling the hook in the eye
latch. "Let me in! Let me in! You have no right!"

"Don't worry, Mom," Scott said. "I'm going to get your money
back."

"It's not my money anymore! It belongs to Ahmet! Anyhow, you're
not exactly destitute yourself."

"Money's tight at home. You know that."

"You have your assets, dear."

"I'm not going to sell my house just because *you*—" He stopped himself. "People prey on old ladies all the time," he said in a measured
voice. "You don't know *who* you're talking to. This Ahmet could be
anyone."

The pounding stopped. A long silence followed before she said, "You think I don't know that?"

Scott looked up from the laptop. "What do you mean?"

"Of course he could be anyone. I'm not stupid."

"So why are you talking to him?"

"I like having someone to talk to, that's all. Someone who likes me and laughs at my jokes."

Rain washed over the roof. Scott felt his moral high ground starting to erode. "You didn't have to send him money, you know."

Even now, he couldn't forget what she'd said next:

"I just thought that's what it cost to keep me company."

It was dark by the time Scott crossed Sonnenallee into Neukölln proper, the streetlights giving dimension to the vapor of his breath. He pressed on past hair salons, corner stores, and cashpoints, the signs embellished with Arabic script. Satellite dishes decorated the balconies of six-story concrete apartment blocks. He turned down a side street to Karl-Marx-Straße, where the sidewalks were dense with street kids and backpackers, tracksuits and unidentifiable tattoos. A little boy sat on the top of a refrigerator that was left out on the curb; its door swung open to reveal a second boy hiding inside. Women in headscarves picked through cartons of fruit.

One hundred fifty thousand dollars. That was the amount his mother had needed to secure her spot at Green Pastures, the amount that had driven him to forge the samples. It wasn't even the money he was after, though he wanted that, too; his own accounts had taken a hit when SOAR came crashing down. It was the principle of the thing. A lonely old woman, a technological illiterate, should not be conned into handing her life savings over to someone she'd met online. Especially if that someone was little more than a phony profile picture and a pair of typing hands. Especially if that lonely old woman had children and grandchildren to bequeath her savings to.

His goal was simple: find Ahmet, or the man posing as Ahmet, and demand his $150,000 back. If "Ahmet" (Scott saw scare quotes in his mind) refused, he would call the authorities. What had happened to his mother was a crime—fraud, in fact—and if he found "Ahmet," he felt confident he could persuade her to press charges.

Failing that, he would exact justice himself, though he hadn't yet decided how.

Scott found the tele-café between a Spielkasino and the striped awning of a restaurant. Beneath a banner for Lycamobile was a sign advertising the shop's services: Internet, Faxen, Telefonkarten. Papers were stuck to the soap-streaked windows, advertising deals in a numerical patois: 20GB + Allnet + 1000. Ortel 12gb Free call. 25GB 20€. This was where the coordinates had led him. A woman on the balcony above him laughed.

The linoleum floor of the tele-café was cluttered with boxed electronics and crates of bottled water sealed in plastic wrap. The kid behind the counter spoke Turkish into an earpiece. He caught Scott's eye and said, "Bier? Zigaretten?"

Scott shook his head. "American. English."

The kid waved Scott toward the counter. "Okay. American. What you want?" He stood before a wall of bejeweled cell phone cases which sparkled in the harsh fluorescent light. Across the small, cluttered shop was a cardboard sign above a white door that read PRIVAT.

"I'm looking for someone."

"Yeah, okay?" The kid behind the counter looked to be about fifteen, with high, arched cheekbones and olive-toned skin. He blinked his long lashes.

"I'm looking for—" Scott began. For a moment, he glimpsed the absurdity of his errand. He beat back the thought with a shiver. "I'm looking for a young man named Ahmet. Or someone *posing* as a young man named Ahmet."

The kid narrowed his eyes. "Is a very common name. Maybe I know. Maybe."

"I know he comes here and sends emails."

The boy smirked. "Buy something."

"Excuse me?" Scott looked up into the round black eye of the security camera mounted in the corner of the shop.

"Buy something. Then we talk."

For a moment, Scott saw himself as the kid must have seen him, as he must have looked to the security camera: hollow-eyed and haggard, white crust around the lips, not exactly the picture of a trustworthy person.

"All right. All right." Scott grabbed a candy bar from the shelf on the counter. "How much is this? I only have US dollars."

The kid clicked his tongue. "Your wallet. Show me."

Scott removed the sole note from his wallet, a one-dollar bill that some previous owner had defaced with a ballpoint pen. George Washington wore a Hitler mustache, and America was spelled with three *K*s.

"This is it, okay? This is all I have."

The kid cocked his chin. "We have machine in back."

It occurred to Scott, as he approached the Geldautomat, that it might be unwise to punch his PIN into a foreign ATM located in a dusty storefront frequented by the young man who had ripped off his mother. But he'd left all sense of reason back in Boston with his scarf.

"Here," Scott said, laying two blue twenty-euro notes on the counter. "Now tell me where I can find Ahmet."

The kid inspected the bills. "Sixty."

"Forty."

"Sixty."

"No!" Scott slammed his fist on the counter. "This is it."

"Okay, okay!" The kid laughed and pocketed the bills. "Your Ahmet. He is in trouble?"

"He tricked my mother into sending him money. He stole from a lonely old woman."

"He stole?"

"He told her he loved her and asked for money for school."

A thin man in dark slacks stepped out from behind the door marked PRIVAT. An unlit cigarette jutted out from beneath the canopy of his thick mustache. He waved sleepily at the kid behind the counter and shuffled out of the tele-café. The papers taped to the door fluttered in the cold.

"He took advantage of her," Scott said as the thin man lit his cigarette out on the sidewalk.

"How?"

"He told her he loves her."

The kid shrugged. "Yes?"

"Well, he doesn't. He doesn't love her."

"You know his heart?"

"I don't give a damn *what's* in his heart. There's a fundamental imbalance of power between them in that relationship."

"Yes. She has money."

"What? No! *He* has the power. He's young, he's technologically literate, and he's flattering a lonely old woman."

"I think she has the power, maybe."

Scott drew a long breath in through his nose and exhaled just as slowly through his mouth. "I'm just looking to talk to Ahmet. The Ahmet that comes here to use the computer."

"She sends much money?"

"Do you know him or don't you?"

"Much money, I think, for you to come all this way."

"Ahmet," Scott said again. "Show me *Ahmet.*"

The door to the tele-café opened again, and the thin man came back in, this time without his cigarette. Leisurely, he crossed the floor of the shop and slipped back through the door marked PRIVAT. For the brief moment that the door was cracked open, Scott could hear the sounds of clacking keys.

"Bring him to me," Scott said.

"Not here."

Scott's language skills were regressing. "You bring Ahmet! Here! Now!"

The kid looked around the empty shop and shrugged.

"Ahmet have money! My money!"

"I think what you say to Ahmet, you say to me."

Scott sighed and made like he was going to leave before lunging across the shop to the door marked PRIVAT. He threw it open before the boy had time to speak.

The room was large, much larger than the storefront itself. Scott stood before a farm of shoddy cubicles that stretched from one sweating concrete wall to another. Each cubicle contained a man at a computer, all lit from above by a bar of buzzing light. The men turned their heads toward Scott in harmony, like a hydra. At first glance, they appeared almost identical, middle-aged and olive-skinned and mustachioed, like the thin man with the cigarette. Any one of them might have been Ahmet. Or maybe they were all Ahmet. Maybe there were dozens of Ahmets, hundreds of them, all in this damp room. And on the other side of the computer screens, dozens or hundreds (or thousands!) of women like his mother: lonely, eccentric, sitting on some savings, willing or even eager to pay for the attention of a young man who didn't exist. It was cruel, it was wrong, it was unconscionable—but before Scott could make his feelings known, he felt a pair of hands on his shoulders and was shortly ejected from the room.

The Australians were getting dressed when Scott got back to the hostel.

"Mate," said the young man, zipping his jeans. "No offense, but you look like shit."

He had wavy blond hair that fell to his shoulders and the easy manner of someone born near a beach. The girl he was with was blond, too, and cherubic, her cheeks flushed with another country's sun. She was pulling a T-shirt over her large, inviting—Scott couldn't help but think *maternal*—breasts.

"He's not so bad," she said, and winked.

This small token of female affection revived him momentarily. He returned to his body; it wasn't happy with him. "I need to eat," he said. "And sleep."

"Do you meditate?" the guy asked, scrolling through his phone.

"Hey," Scott said, falling down on the bed, the springs groaning under his weight. He threw his arm over his eyes to block out the searing industrial light. "My generation *invented* stealing the mystical traditions of the East. I lived in India when I was a kid. Nineteen sixty-nine. The Summer of Love."

"I bet you had servants."

"Everyone had servants."

"Not everyone. Not the servants."

Scott rubbed the sore spot on his arm. On the walk back to the hostel, he'd considered calling the authorities and alerting them to what was going on at the café. A syndicate of scammers—no, a cartel!—busy bilking old ladies for all they were worth. But he wasn't sure if what they were doing was illegal. Ahmet, whoever he was, hadn't forced his mother to do anything. She had sent him money of her own volition. She didn't even want it back. And what if he was wrong? What if it wasn't a cartel at all, but a regular internet café? The problem was, he had no proof. Not really. And the thought of going to the German police and having to explain the situation made him flush with embarrassment. He could picture the uniformed officers smirking as he told them the story. He felt foolish, having flown so far in pursuit of a phantom. He'd been duped, just like his mother.

"What you *need*," the girl said, "is to come out tonight."

Scott lowered his arm from his face. The light bled through his eyelids like they were sheer muslin curtains. "That's the last thing I need."

The girl pouted. "Please? It's my birthday!"

"Is it really?"

"We'll have a good time. I promise." She turned to her companion. "Won't we?"

"Bloody oath. We were just heading out."

"I can't. There's no way. I can barely stand up." Even as he protested, he worried about what would happen once they left him alone.
Very nearly alone. The room's fourth occupant was still asleep.

The girl skipped toward him. "So you *want* to come, but you say
you're too tired." The discomfort of his attraction to a girl his daughter's age was preferable to the discomfort of thinking about the past
twenty-four hours—his impulsive flight from Boston, his confronta-
tion at the tele-café.

Her companion dipped into the open suitcase lying on his bed and
produced a palm-size plastic bag containing three green tablets. "I
reckon I've got something for that."

She gasped. "Oh my god. We have three left? That's a sign. I mean,
that's *perfect*."

He tossed her the baggie and she pressed one of the tablets into
Scott's cold, pink hand. It was stamped with the outline of an alien's
head, an upside-down teardrop with two almond eyes. "What is it?"
he asked.

"Medicine."

"How long does it last?"

The girl extended her tongue—it was a long tongue, muscular and
pink—and placed a tablet on the tip. Then the tongue coiled inward,
and the tablet disappeared. "As long as it's supposed to."

"He might be too old for it," her companion said.

"I'm not too old for anything." He thought of his precious Painkill-
ers, the comfort they provided him, the slow drift of his ego out from
shore as he drank.

He wondered what Deb would say if she saw him now, tossing a
mysterious pill down his throat at the behest of two kids deploying

the most elementary form of peer pressure. But Deb had moved out and, in doing so, renounced the right to say anything.

Scott followed the Australians down to the lobby and out into the cold, quiet night. They led him through a dark city park and beneath underpasses dense with graffiti. The wind pried open the neck of his peacoat. After a few minutes, though, the cold didn't bother him. He felt kindly toward it. His heart was alive and warm in his chest.

"What's this river called?" Scott asked as they crossed a bridge.

"The Spree," the girl said.

Spree! The word was jubilant, and tickled.

He realized that he had never asked where they were going, but before he could, they had arrived. Some young people were smoking outside an apartment complex across the street, purple smoke rising from their cigarettes.

"I'm going to bum a ciggy," the Australian guy said and disappeared into the huddle.

The girl stood with Scott on the sidewalk, cupping her hands in front of her mouth. "I wish he'd quit," she said between breaths.

"One out of every five deaths in the States."

"What are you, a doctor?"

Scott laughed. "That's a much harder question to answer than you realize."

"Maybe he'll listen to you. Guys don't like taking advice from their sisters."

"You're brother and sister?"

She shivered. "I'm freezing. Let's go inside."

He followed her into a crowded salon. There was a bar opposite a stage on which a woman in a long, wavy dress was wailing wordless melodies into a microphone. The light bulbs were red, and there were holes chewed into the surface of the red leather sofas. It looked like a bombed-out brothel.

She sloughed off her coat. "Fuck me dead," she said. "This is where I want to be when the world ends."

"I know what you mean," he said. It seemed to him the coziest place he'd ever been.

"It's coming sooner than you think."

He was too busy taking in the people in the room—a woman in a mesh top, a man in curt leather shorts, a buzz-cut person of indeterminate gender wearing ponytail earrings made from real human hair—to register the meaning of her words.

"Look at this," she said, scrolling through her phone. "'Beirut bombs kill twenty-three. Blasts linked to Syrian civil war.'"

"Terrible," Scott agreed.

He felt the edges of his body start to blur into his surroundings. The molecules that made him up were drifting apart. He watched them float away as he followed her around. When he looked up, he found that he was no longer in the salon but a narrow corridor.

"This must be the throat," she said.

"The what?"

"We just passed through the mouth." She pointed at the pink, perspiring walls. "This must be the throat."

A lone light bulb in a wire cage hung above the door at the far end of the corridor. They followed it and passed through the door into a yellow room. Scott's black dress shoes made a squishing sound. There seemed to be at least a quarter inch of standing water—he hoped it was water—covering the floor. People were dancing and splashing around to the systolic throb of bass rattling a tall tower of speakers. The Australian girl started dancing, too, her head low between her shoulders, both arms extended above her head like a puppet's, each beat a jerk of the strings. Scott stood next to her, nodding along, waiting for the song to change, but the throbbing continued unabated.

A short, dark-haired woman hurried past him. "Carol?" he said, his voice muffled by the music. He was sure it had been Carol Chin, and he hurried after her. She was running through the belly of the club, weaving through crowds of half-naked dancers. "Carol!" he called again, but he couldn't even hear himself.

He lost her somewhere in the colon. She was in front of him, and then she wasn't, leaving him alone in a damp, dark tunnel whose walls were studded with red hemorrhoidal growths. Carol had abandoned him. The Australian girl was gone.

He was alone.

There was a wooden door up ahead on which was scrawled the word SHIT in what looked like shit. All the imaginary creatures of his youth, the terrors that kept him up late at night, were poised to attack him behind that door. Panicking, he turned back the way he'd come, scrambling back up through the large intestine, until a series of small passageways and one heavy door led him to a quiet, warm room. Sheer pink curtains hung from the ceiling; a glowing lantern gave off gauzy light. A neon light fixture read EAT MORE PUSSY in looping cursive. Two women were kissing on a pink sofa while a man in an army jacket sat on the concrete floor in the fetal position, rocking back and forth. Then the man jumped to his feet and hurried out through an archway at the far corner of the room.

Scott followed him past the lantern and through the archway. The walls seemed to be closing in on him, the ceiling sinking as he pressed on. He had to crouch, at first, and then get on his knees to squeeze himself into the narrowing passage, which was padded on all sides with pillows. His heart was in his ears as he crawled on all fours. As he pushed through the curtain at the end of the passage, he saw, backlit by a blinding light, an enormous chicken soaring overhead.

He woke the next morning not knowing where he was. He felt cold, but judging by the damp spot underneath him, he'd been sweating for some time. The cold seemed to be coming from inside him, causing his muscles to contract and spasm. He sat up in a strange bed, the mattress stiff, the sheets coarse as exam table paper. The room took its time coming into focus, as did the view through the barred window. The ice on the Ferris wheel sparkled in the sun. Scott blinked. Berlin, he remembered now. He was in Berlin. He saw the Australians asleep in the bed across from his. Holding each other. Strange. Had they told him they were siblings? Scott was suddenly, profoundly thirsty, the way he had been at the deposition. Inquisition. Inquiry. He dragged his dry tongue along his upper lip. There was a soreness in his jaw, and he realized he'd been clenching his teeth in his sleep.

Adrenaline began to trickle through his veins. Home, he thought. He had to get home. The sooner he was home, the sooner he could start fixing what he'd broken, starting with his marriage. Scott slipped out of the room. The hostel lobby was quiet, empty save for the pair of backpackers checking in. The guy with the guitar was gone, probably sleeping off a night out not unlike Scott's. From his phone, Scott booked the first flight back to Boston, ignoring the frankly unbelievable cost.

He hardly slept on the plane. He rehearsed a speech instead, searching for the words to persuade his wife that he was sorry, his heel bouncing all the way. No sooner had his plane landed at Logan than he called a cab and demanded he be taken to Back Bay. His life was an emergency. There wasn't time to waste.

Joan Portafoglio answered the door. "Can I help you?"

There she stood, his enemy and rival, barefoot in a pink satin robe, on the stoop of an expensive-looking brownstone, a whole head shorter than Scott. She wasn't wearing makeup, and her hair was pulled back in a practical ponytail, but in her brown eyes, now narrowed to a squint, he saw the intensity that he recognized from her publicity photos. Her impressive bust: this, too, he recognized.

"I'm here to see my wife," he said.

Joan appraised him and seemed to find him wanting. "I assume you mean Deb."

"That's right. We have a lot to talk about."

"Well, I'm afraid she's busy at the moment. Making breakfast." Her voice was husky and he didn't like the way she said "breakfast."

"Would you just get her for me, please?" When Joan didn't move, he craned his neck and called, "Deb? Deb! I need to talk to you."

His wife was at the door a moment later, wearing yoga pants that flattered her dancer's figure. Scott felt suddenly nervous, his heart in his throat. He hadn't felt this way since picking up his prom date at her house way back in high school. "Deb," he said. "It's me."

"I see that. What are you doing here?"

"Can we talk? In private?"

Deb looked at Joan, who rolled her eyes before going inside. "Don't let your pancakes get cold," she called over her shoulder.

Deb turned back to Scott. "You look terrible. What happened?"

He'd freshened up in the men's room at the airport, but he supposed that no amount of sink water could mask the effects of two intercontinental flights and one heroic dose of Molly all taken over little more than forty-eight hours. "I just got back from Berlin," he said.

"Berlin? What on earth were you doing in *Berlin?*" The way she said it made it sound like no one in their right mind would ever visit. "And why didn't you tell me?"

Scott blinked. "You wanted me to tell you?"

"Jesus, Scott. What if something had happened while you were away? What if the kids were in trouble? I wouldn't know how to get ahold of you!"

"Please," he said. "Let me explain."

He tried to justify his visit to Berlin, but he struggled to do so without sounding insane. The longer he spoke, the more he wondered if he *was* insane.

"I don't know what to say," she said when he finished. "I guess I'm still wondering what you're doing here."

"I'm here to take you home."

"Scott . . ." She shook her head. "You come here, completely unannounced, looking like you haven't slept in days, and you tell me you're taking me home why? Because you hallucinated a giant chicken?"

"I wanted to do right by my mom," he said. "I wanted to get her money back."

"What about *our* money, Scott? The money you invested without telling me?"

"I made a mistake."

"What did we agree when I stopped dancing? Anything *you* made belonged to *both of us*. We would make our financial decisions *together*. I'm not sure if you've noticed, but raising two kids, cooking five nights per week, and generally keeping this family together is not exactly well-compensated work."

"A lot of mistakes."

"You committed fraud. You jeopardized your career and our livelihood."

"And I'm sorry."

"You disappointed me. Worse, you disappointed our *children*. Do you realize that? What our kids must think of you?"

Scott stared at his shoes, which were still damp from the night before. "I just want things to be like they were before."

"I do, too," she said, her voice small and begrudging. She looked him up and down, no doubt noticing the wrinkles in his eyes and on his shirt. "I just don't think that's possible right now."

Scott stood on the stoop a moment longer, but there was nothing left to say. Defeated, he walked to the corner to hail a cab. In his mad rush to leave Berlin, he hadn't counted on this, the lonely cab ride home to Brookline, scored by the blare of the television screen embedded on the seat in front of him.

When he got back to Crowninshield Road, he found the family home empty. The emptiness shouldn't have surprised him, but it did. Where had everybody gone? Family photos sat propped on the counter like museum pieces in an exhibition on a tribe that no longer existed.

A
Superfluous
Man

•

She was heading down the first-floor hallway when she saw him, a tall, thin man with dishwater hair combed by hand over the high expanse of his forehead. He walked with his shoulders hunched, as if embarrassed by his height, his dark eyes fixed on the floor in front of him. He wore wire-rimmed glasses, and the knot of his tie was tight enough to flush his face. She wasn't sure if he recognized her—it had taken her a moment to recognize him—but when their eyes met, he fumbled his coffee.

"Maya Greenspan?"

William Slate. It had been five years since she'd seen him last, and she could hardly believe she was seeing him now, in a school, no less, whose locker-lined halls resembled those of the school, her school, where they'd met. She might have been seventeen again, standing in a pool of fluorescent light on a newly buffed linoleum floor. A ream of butcher paper was taped to the wall, embellished with children's handprints beneath the words SEE HOW I'VE GROWN!

"What are you doing here?" she asked. Correcting for the note of accusation in her voice, she hazarded a guess. "Dropping off your kids?"

He blinked twice in quick succession, evidently just as surprised to see her as she was to see him. "No," he said. "I don't have any kids. I work here."

A girl in a blue backpack toddled past, the soles of her sneakers lighting up with every step.

"Seems a little young for you, no?"

His Adam's apple bobbed up and down.

"Wait," Maya said. "I didn't mean it like *that*."

It took him a moment to recover his composure. "I'm at the high school a few blocks away," he explained, tugging at his collar. "Sometimes they send my mail here by mistake. What about you? What have you been doing with yourself?"

"Well, I went to college, for one thing," she said, by way of establishing that she was no longer a minor. "I work in publishing now."

"Publishing." His tone suggested interest or contempt, she couldn't tell. "So what are *you* doing here?"

"My boss's daughter left her lunch at home this morning." She held the girl's lunch box in her hand.

William nodded and bit his bottom lip, no doubt wondering, as Maya often wondered herself, how such a bright young woman with so promising a future had wound up running errands for a living.

"I spend most of my time editing books," she lied. It was her boss, Cressida, who did the editing. "I just like to get out of the office. Stretch my legs."

They stood in the hall for a minute and caught up with the halting formality of two people who hadn't expected to see each other ever again. After leaving his post at Maya's high school—that's how he put it, "leaving his post," as though the decision had been his—he'd taken a teaching job in Milton, Massachusetts; he had only just moved to New York. He lived nearby, on the Upper East Side, parts of which had become surprisingly affordable, he said, if sleepy and lacking in good restaurants. She told him that she had gone to NYU to study comparative literature. She had written her undergraduate thesis on the archetype of the Superfluous Man in Russian literature and his counterpart, the Indispensable Woman.

"The Superfluous Man," he said. "That takes me back. But I'm not sure I've heard of—what was it, again?"

"The Indispensable Woman. I coined it myself."

William smiled. "Russian lit. You stuck with it. I'm impressed."

"Well, I had a very influential teacher."

He bowed his head, embarrassed. He seemed not to know where to look or what to do with his hands.

"Listen," he said. "I should probably go. I have class in ten minutes."

"Yeah. I should be getting back to work."

In her hurry to leave the apartment that morning, she'd thrown on the same clothes she'd worn the day before. She wondered if he noticed the wrinkles in her blouse, the run in her tights, the waxy finish on her hair.

"Come on," he said. "I'll walk you out."

A clot of cars had formed on Ninety-First Street, the morning drop-off compromised by the construction on the corner of Park Avenue. The city was installing a docking station for its new bike-share program, clogging the street with concrete barriers bearing the name of the sponsoring bank. Dozens of children, no bigger than their backpacks, tumbled out of cars with tinted windows and cantered down the sidewalk toward the steps where she and William stood beneath two enormous flags. It was a brisk autumn morning, and the flags—one for the country and one for the school, a mother and her children encircled in its emblem—ruffled here and there in the breeze.

"Why don't I give you my number," he said.

"Really?"

He raised his hands to show her—what? That he wasn't armed? "Only if you want. It's your decision."

"No!" she said. "No. I mean, I think that's a great idea."

She took out her phone and scrolled through her contacts until she found his name. She pretended to type as he told her his number, which hadn't changed since he'd first given it to her.

They walked down Ninety-First Street together, parting at the corner, where the construction was too loud for them to do much besides wave and mouth the word "bye." She watched him continue down Park Avenue, playing their conversation back in her mind, trying to remember what she'd said and if any of it had made her sound stupid. But the exchange felt so uncanny, almost like a dream—and like a dream, it was already fading from her memory.

Maya had almost reached the office when she realized she was still holding the lunch box. She didn't have time to turn around, and the Q was running nonstop to Fifty-Seventh Street. Cressida saw lateness as a form of moral weakness, which Maya knew because her boss told her so whenever she was late. Maya, who had missed breakfast that morning, opened the latch of the lunch box, a miniature replica of a Birkin bag. There was nothing inside resembling food; instead, she found pouches of edible goo with plastic caps. Maya was not so starved as to suck down this space-age stuff in public. She did, however, find a grape juice box, which she slurped through a straw until she reached her stop.

Walking through the glass doors of Dunning Kruger Press never failed to fill her with a warm, familiar feeling. The lobby was lined with rare books encased in bulletproof glass, lit from behind as if the prose contained within them were literally radiant. Strolling through the lobby, heels clicking on the marble floor, she felt as if she had come home. When Maya pressed her key card to the reader, the glass panes of the electric turnstile parted just for her.

"What took you so long?" Cressida asked the moment Maya sat down at her desk. Then she raised her hand to her forehead, shielding herself against whatever inadequate excuse her assistant might come up with. "Never mind. Call Marea and set a lunch for one o'clock."

The warm, familiar feeling was gone. "One o'clock."

"And my expenses are overdue."

Cressida had recently been named editorial director after the runaway success of *Dig Deep: How to Be a Bad*ss B*tch in the Boardroom.* She now possessed a nearly boundless budget for lunches and dinners with authors and agents, all of them desperate to do business with the woman who had published what was, by a terrific margin, the biggest book of the summer.

"Sure thing," Maya said. "I just need your receipts."

Cressida had glossy black hair and eyes that seemed to register only displeasure. She wore a black dress that flattered her Pilates-tight figure, and black boots that came up to the pale crescents of her knees. She looked like a charcoal briquette, small and dark and combustible.

"End of day," she said, depositing a wad of crumpled paper on Maya's desk. Then she turned on her heels and disappeared into her office.

"She's so hot," Annette whispered. "I've never kissed a girl in my life—not even in like, the performative way—but I'd literally do anything Cressida asked."

Maya met her eyes over their shared cubicle wall. "You want to do her expenses?"

"Okay, not *that* hot. But she looks great for her age."

Maya smoothed the wrinkles out of the receipts, which were marred by Cressida's careless penmanship. "How old *is* she?"

"You don't know?"

"I don't think anyone does."

Annette was four years older than Maya and had been at the publishing house her whole career. Unlike Maya, however, who couldn't even think about her job without breaking into hives, Annette lived for office gossip and the promise of promotion. With her big, round eyes and rosy cheeks, she looked like an American Girl doll, if Mattel made one that worked in media. "Next time you see her, look at her hands."

"Whose hands?"

Gabe, the editorial intern, stood over them, advertising his considerable height. His father worked at McLuhan, Inc., the media conglomerate that owned Dunning Kruger, and though he was only an intern, he carried himself with the bearing of a boy king surveying his holdings.

"Nothing, Gabe," Annette said. "Just forget it."

"I wasn't talking to you." He turned to Maya. "Plans this weekend?"

"Nothing major."

"Because my improv class has a show tomorrow night. I can get you half-off tickets if you're interested."

"I didn't know you did improv."

"I'm pretty much obsessed."

Maya wondered how many of her colleagues spent their weekends at open mics and kickball tournaments. She'd wanted to be a grown-up ever since she was a child and now, at twenty-two, was depressed to discover that all the grown-ups wanted to be children.

Gabe leaned over her cubicle wall and tweaked the Dostoyevsky bobblehead on her desk. "I've been training for months," he said. "The class is level three."

"Thanks. But I don't really love live comedy." She had been to see some shows when she first moved to New York, none of which left much of a lasting impression. What remained in her mind's eye were the desperate expressions on the performers' faces, their shameless need for approval—a need that made Maya cringe with recognition.

"We're doing a Harold."

"I'm sure whatever that is, it's really funny."

"What if I could get you in for free? The ticket-taker girl owes me a favor."

"I'll pass."

"I helped her move last month," he said. "She didn't know anyone else with a car. I'm pretty positive she'd let you in."

"This is a very roundabout way of letting me know you own a car."

Gabe grinned. "And that I'm a nice guy who helps women in need."

"She has a boyfriend," Annette said. "They've been dating since college. They're practically married."

"Is that true?"

Maya looked up. "I have about a hundred books that need to be mailed out this afternoon."

"If only we had an intern," Annette said.

Gabe put his hands up. "Whoa, whoa, whoa."

"Hold on," Maya said. "I think we *do* have an intern!"

"I just remembered, I'm late for a meeting."

"With who?" Annette called as Gabe hurried off. She rolled her eyes. "He's *such* a dick."

"You know he'll be running this place someday," Maya said.

"So gross. I can't *believe* we hooked up." She cocked her head. "Are you aware that your tongue is purple?"

Maya worked through lunch, typing up a profit and loss statement for a novel that another editor, a preppy blond named Lucy Barnstable, was considering for publication. Official looking though they were, with their percentages and decimal points, the P&Ls, which helped determine what a manuscript was worth, depended on imaginary numbers—namely how many books the house expected to sell—and were grounded less in reality than hope. They were the greatest works of fiction that the company produced.

The task took longer than it should have. Maya was distracted and entered numbers in the wrong columns. She typed "loyalty" instead of "royalty," "unfit" instead of "units." She prided herself on her attention to detail, but she couldn't concentrate on anything apart from William. What were the chances, she wondered, after five years without contact, of running into him now, in a city of eight million?

"It's the story of a mother whose son disappears during the Second Sudanese Civil War," Lucy said at the editorial meeting that afternoon. "As a mom, I felt her pain *right here*." She made a fist and held it over her chest, to show what a small yet resilient thing a heart was. "I'm telling you, I cried for hours after I finished."

"Aren't we publishing an African novel next year?" Cressida asked. "I wouldn't want the two . . . *cannibalizing* each other."

"We bumped it up to fall."

She nodded thoughtfully. "In that case, let's try and preempt. I don't want this one going to auction."

"Maya's already drawn up the P&L."

"Oh?" Cressida shuffled through her papers. "I'm not seeing anything."

Maya shrunk in her seat. "I got a little sidetracked this morning.
It's almost done, I promise."

Cressida let out an audible sigh before turning to her previous assistant, Rebecca Abel, against whom Maya was frequently measured
and found wanting. "Rebecca? What do you have for us this week?"

Myron Maple, an editor old enough to have benefited from the GI
Bill, raised one of his large, spotted hands. "If I may interject," he
said. "All of us are wondering about the rumors."

Cressida cocked her head. "What rumors?"

"You know damn well what rumors." His voice was bitter and
clouded with grit, cigar ash suspended in a glass of tonic water. "The
ones about the Oriental publisher."

"Chinese communications group," Cressida corrected. Even Maya
was impressed with the fearless way her boss talked to men twice her
age. "You're going to have to be more specific."

"There's talk of a buyout, my dear."

"That sounds like a business question, Myron, and this, I'll remind
you, is the *editorial* meeting. Now, if we could please move on. Rebecca?"

Rebecca, who had been promoted from editorial assistant to assistant editor at the intimidating age of twenty-three—she now made
$40,000 as opposed to $35,000 and, more important, could buy her
own books—was considering a "memoir with recipes" from a plus-
size model with seven million followers on Instagram. Malcolm Campbell, the only Black (and sole conservative) editor on staff, announced
his latest acquisition, a retired policeman's account of his years on the

force entitled *Not All Cops*. Ainsley Cranford, one of the last of the old New York WASPs, saw commercial potential in *The Belle of Birkenau*, a star-crossed love story set among concentration camp inmates. Cressida spoke last, concluding the meeting with the happy announcement that Karen Wolfgang, author of *Dig Deep*, was already working on a follow-up, *Dig Deeper*, about the challenges of being a mother while running a Fortune 500 company.

In college, Maya hadn't known that books like these existed; she could never have guessed they kept the industry afloat. All her coursebooks were ex–library editions or had orange USED SAVES stickers on the spine. Apart from her seminar on Walter Benjamin, she had hardly given any thought to their production. Anyway, she didn't plan to work in publishing. She loved school and would have stayed in school forever, first as a grad student and then as a professor, were it not for a shocking and upsetting incident from which she had still not completely recovered.

She was meeting with her thesis adviser, Dmitri, a bearded man with bags under his eyes and a bulbous red nose dotted with enormous pores. He was probably forty but looked much older, with deep-set eyes and graying locks of greasy shoulder-length hair. The meeting had begun pleasantly enough—he seemed to enjoy mentoring a young woman, especially one who had racked up so many departmental honors—but when she informed him of her plans to pursue a PhD, he shook his head so vigorously that dandruff sifted down onto his shoulders. "No," he said. "Don't waste your time."

"But what if I want to teach?"

He picked up the loaf of black bread on his desk and tore some off the end with his teeth. "You don't."

She looked around his office, cluttered with papers, the tall shelf beside him almost toppling with books. A poster of Stalin hung on the wall behind him to scare students who came to complain about their grades. It was exactly the kind of office Maya dreamed of having one day.

"But what if I do?"

"Myshka," he said, "no one wants to teach. Not in the academy, anyway. There is no dignity in it."

"So what am I supposed to do?"

"This I cannot answer for you. But if you want my advice? Go make lots and lots of money."

"I don't care about money," she said. "I want to teach."

"You say that now. But when you have three screaming children? And their teeth are falling out for lack of dental insurance?"

She had heard him give lectures on God and the soul, suffering and redemption, art and revolution. He had never once mentioned dental insurance.

"And if I apply anyway? Would you write a letter of rec?"

He placed one hand over his heart and raised the other. "I cannot, in good conscience, assist in ruining your life."

"One letter. That's all I want. It doesn't even have to be good."

"You are young. You do not know what you want." He tore off another piece of bread and chewed without closing his mouth.

"I know what I want."

"Yes?"

"I want to be like you."

"Like *me?*" Dmitri's body rumbled as he laughed, bread crumbs falling from their perch on his potbelly. Soon, the laugh devolved into a cough, and he raised one enormous hand to his neck while the other groped for the tissue box on his desk. Maya pushed the box toward Dmitri, and he tore two tissues from the top, pressing them over his mouth.

"Dmitri?" she said. "Are you okay?"

He nodded, but his cheeks were turning blue beneath his beard. He made a fist and pounded his desk as though the bread were lodged inside one of its drawers and not his throat.

"Dmitri!"

"No . . ." He pounded the desk. "Dignity . . ."

Then he fell off his chair and died.

It was her first real experience of grief. In novels, people wailed and rent their garments, but Maya was in shock. After alerting the office secretary, she went to her apartment, opened her laptop, and started looking for jobs.

She approached this task with the same ferocious determination that she brought to her academic work. She made a spreadsheet of every publishing house and literary journal in the country and spent the spring semester shooting applications into the abyss. It wasn't until graduation that Maya's exhaustion and grief caught up with her. Standing in the sea of purple robes outside of Yankee Stadium, her father made a joke about converting her childhood bedroom into a home gym, and Maya started sobbing right there in the street. She wept for Dmitri, she wept for her future, and she wept for her childhood bedroom, where her mother had first taught her to read.

It was her grandmother who helped secure the job with Cressida. One of her neighbors in Wellfleet had worked in publishing and helped Maya line up a few interviews, during which she discovered that her facility for feminist interpretations of nineteenth-century Russian literature did not necessarily qualify her to work as an editorial assistant. By the time she interviewed for Cressida, she had learned not to mention her studies and had memorized the names of a few bestselling books she could cite when asked what she liked to read. One of these was *Dig Deep*.

"Really," Cressida intoned skeptically. "Because we've found that the book is doing much better with women of, let's say, *my* demographic. I don't think I've read a positive review by anyone under the age of forty."

"That's weird!" Maya said, forcing a smile. "I found it *very* inspirational."

In fact, she'd found it disagreeable, even insidious, in its insistence that women must become more ruthless, more cutthroat, more *aggressive*, if they were to beat men at their own game. But despite the book's bad politics, a part of Maya *did* want to beat men at their own game without the aid of such squishy concepts as "solidarity" and "fellowship." Deep down, she didn't want a "community." She wanted to win.

After months of unemployment, she was grateful for a job, any job, even one that paid $35,000 before taxes, and while she wasn't naive enough to think she'd be editing the next Turgenev at twenty-two, she harbored hopes of pulling some passed-over talent out of the slush pile. At the very least she'd hoped to work with like-minded colleagues, people who believed, as she did, that literature was more interesting than life, or at least more interesting than money. She was astonished to discover that the publishing industry was a business like any other. The first time she heard books referred to as "units," she almost fell out of her chair.

Her tastes were too idiosyncratic for the industry. She wrote a blistering report on a young adult novel about two terminally ill teens who fall in love; the novel and the film rights both sold in separate six-way auctions. She suggested passing on a self-aggrandizing memoir by an Olympic swimmer, which Cressida went on to purchase for seven figures. After a few weeks, Cressida stopped soliciting Maya's opinion on manuscripts and started sending her on random errands— installing a new modem in her apartment, returning clothes that didn't fit to Eileen Fisher—until Maya was forced to confront the fact that this was punishment for being bad at her job. She had never been bad at anything before.

"Maya?"

"Hm?"

Cressida sat at the head of the conference table, her arms crossed over her chest. "I *said*, did you have anything to add before we go?"

"No." She cleared her throat. "Nothing from me."

Her parents valued intelligence above all other virtues, and Maya prided herself on her academic achievements, which seemed to pre-figure all kinds of long-term success. But despite four years of preschool at her parents' synagogue, fourteen years in a school district consistently ranked among the best in the state by *U.S. News & World Report*, and another four at the nation's largest independent research university, where she devoured the great works of Western civilization, she discovered, after just three months out of school, that she knew nothing about how to live.

"I don't mean to be rude," Cressida said as Maya filed out of the conference room, "but isn't that the same thing you wore yesterday?"

That evening, on her way out of the office, Cressida asked Maya to convert a book-length PDF into a Word doc, a simple-sounding task for which there was, surprisingly, no simple solution and which required Maya to accept the lengthy terms of service on an ugly website called PhantomPDF that was certain to infect her work computer with a virus. She was supposed to meet her boyfriend, Louis, for dinner, but by the time she found him at their usual booth at Wo Hop, she was almost forty-five minutes late.

"You're here!" he said, leaping up from his seat. His thighs crashed against the underside of the table.

"Hey," she said, collapsing into the booth. "I'm really sorry."

Louis rubbed his legs, his face screwed up in pain. "I wasn't sure if you were coming."

"Cressida kept me. What's with the tie?"

He touched the striped tie hanging from his collar. "You don't like it? Because I can take it off."

"No," she said. "It's nice. Just kind of formal."

He loosened the knot. "I'll take it off. No big deal."

"I was only asking."

"It's really no problem."

"I like it!"

By now, the tie hung loose around his neck. "So I should keep it?"

She shut her eyes and pressed her palms to them, provoking an explosion of color against the black backdrop of her eyelids. She loved Louis, but on nights like this she felt burdened by his kindness, his eagerness to please. She knew that she could never be as good a partner as he was, and the fact that this grated on her only served to underscore her relative badness. "Yes. Keep it."

"You look great, too, by the way."

It was one of Louis's most endearing qualities, the way he praised her appearance no matter how she looked—she hadn't showered in days, and the run in her tights now resembled a flesh wound—but right now, she didn't feel like being seen at all. "Thanks, but I have to disagree with you there."

"I mean it," he said.

"I know you do."

They gave their order to a waiter in a pressed blue lab coat, and Louis filled her in about his day. He was earning his PhD in clinical psychology at Yeshiva University, where he served as a research assistant on a study about social relationships among the elderly. Twice each week, he met with old Jewish couples and spoke to them about their marriages.

"What do you think they have in common?" he asked. "These people who have been married fifty, sixty years."

"I don't know."

"Guess!"

"I wouldn't know where to start."

"Age difference? Socioeconomic background?"

"Louis . . ."

"I'll give you a hint: it isn't either of those."

"It's been a long day, Louis. I just want to go home, turn off the lights, and pull the covers over my head."

His face fell. "I thought we'd go for a walk after dinner."

All he wanted was to spend some time with her. What, she wondered, was her problem? Why couldn't she pay him the attention he paid her—the attention he deserved? "I don't know. We'll see."

"I don't mean to push? But I think you'll want to go on this walk."

She closed her eyes and drew a long, slow breath. When she opened them, the waiter had returned with their food.

"Let's see how you feel after you eat," Louis said.

It wasn't long before she was complaining about her job while she worked on her egg roll. She had hoped that working with books would make her interesting—more so than her friends in finance or law— but here she was, droning on about how hard it was to convert a document from PDF to Word. Louis interrupted periodically to ask if she was enjoying her meal, if the temperature in the restaurant was all right, if she thought she might be up for a walk after all.

"I'm fine," she said. "The food is fine. What's with you tonight?"

"Nothing! I just want you to feel comfortable."

When the check came, Louis insisted on paying, though his grad school stipend was even smaller than her salary. As he puzzled over the check, Maya stole a glance at herself in the mirror above the booth. She had never liked the way she looked in profile. There was a notch on the bridge of her nose where it bent like something that had changed its mind. She could see a subtle peak at the center of her forehead—a plugged follicle, the prelude to a pimple. Her skin shone in the unforgiving brightness of the restaurant.

"Let's remember this moment," Louis said.

Her phone buzzed beside the small ceramic teacup on the table. It was a text from William. He wanted to know if she was free to meet sometime the following week.

She looked up from the screen. "What's that?"

"This moment. Let's look around and take it all in."

She set the phone on the red vinyl seat beside her. The room was hot and smelled of frying oil.

"You're blushing," Louis said.

"I'm not!"

"You are."

"You're making me self-conscious," she snapped. Lately, Maya had begun to wonder whether kindness was contingent on comfort. It had been so easy to love Louis in college when her living expenses were paid for by her parents and midterms were the most she had to worry about. Now that she was floundering at work, where she hardly made enough money to live, she found herself taking her aggression out on Louis, one of the few people who loved her unconditionally.

He signed the check and pocketed the pen. "So, how about that walk?"

They left the restaurant and started down Mott Street, past leaking garbage bags and a van tagged with graffiti. Louis talked ceaselessly, nervously, bouncing on the balls of his feet while Maya walked absent-mindedly behind, making plans with William on her phone. He turned to slot himself through the gap between two concrete barriers and into a convergence of streets barricaded with traffic cones, fencing, and chains strung between lampposts. He stopped short at a crowded plaza. It was misting, and he almost slipped on the pavement.

"Maya," he said, after he righted himself, "from the first time we met, I knew that you were someone I could see myself with forever."

She looked up from her phone with a start. This must be what people meant when they described having an out-of-body experience. She felt like she was floating somewhere above herself, watching Louis deliver an impassioned speech, a speech he must have memorized and practiced in the mirror. He was telling the story of their relationship, from their first meeting to the present day. In a way, he said, they had grown up with each other, gone from being kids to adults together. She had shaped the person he'd become, and he could not imagine a life without her. As he spoke, she felt a weight accruing in her stomach, a heaviness where happiness should have been. Then he knelt before her and pulled a blue ring box from his pocket. But when he opened the box, it was empty. She looked up; a small crowd had gathered around them.

"So will you?" he asked. "Marry me? I can't afford a ring right now. This empty box represents a promise. A promise to buy you a ring. And to be with you forever."

She looked past him, past the onlookers, at the enormous cavity in the ground. "You're proposing at the 9/11 Memorial?"

"What? No! I mean, sure, that, too. But no. You don't remember what happened here?"

"A plane flew into a building. Two buildings. Two planes."

"Not that!" He picked himself up. "Sophomore year?"

She shook her head.

"We went out for Chinese and then I got sick? And you said maybe I should try and get some air? So we did, but I still didn't feel very good? So we went to that Starbucks? On Vesey and Church? And I was in the bathroom for a while? But the lock was broken? And you stood by the door and told people it was out of service? So they would leave me alone? And when I was done, we kept walking? And I felt much better? And then do you remember what happened?"

Maya nodded. She remembered now. "You told me you loved me."

"It was right here, right on this spot." Louis was an inch shorter than she was and looked up at her with wide, wet eyes. "So?"

The longer he stood looking at her, the worse she felt. She felt he'd trapped her, without warning, in this enormous question, which had apparently been on his mind for some time and which she'd hardly considered. The egg roll sat inside her stomach like a stone at the bottom of a well.

"I'm sorry," she said. "I can't."

She could tell by the ashen look on his face that he hadn't even considered the possibility that she'd say no.

"Why not?"

"Can we talk about this somewhere else?" She could feel the eyes of the onlookers on her.

"Is it because we met too young?" he asked. "Do you want to see other people? I don't want you to feel like you wasted your best years with me. That I stole them from you."

"Stole them? God, Louis, I don't think that."

"So why won't you say yes?"

"I love you," she said. "I really love you, I do. It's just not a good time." This was the most articulate answer she could give. "I'm not saying I don't want to marry you, okay? I just can't do it right now."

Louis nodded. He closed the ring box and tucked it back into his pocket. He turned to address the onlookers, who now numbered in the dozens. "She said no."

The crowd began to disperse. Someone booed.

"Come on, Louis," Maya said. "Let's go home."

He was quiet on the walk back to their apartment and flinched each time she reached out to touch him, as though she carried some deadly communicable disease. "Hey," she said, hoping to cheer him up or at least change the subject. "Isn't that the guy from *Humans of New York*?"

Louis looked at the photographer across the street. "No," he said, and let out a long sigh. "That's just a white guy with a camera."

"What were you saying about the aging study?" she asked.

"What?"

"At the restaurant. You said those old couples who stayed together all those years had something in common."

"Oh. Right."

"Well?"

"Well, what?"

"What do they have in common?"

Louis stopped outside their apartment and stared across the street, where a college kid was vomiting into a garbage can. "Low expectations," he said.

Maya met William at a lamplit pub a few blocks south of her Midtown office. The bar, which catered to the Broadway crowd, was a favorite among her publishing colleagues, who patronized the place with irony. Maya hoped William would approve.

She was grateful for a reason not to head straight home from work. Louis had retreated inward since the proposal and was logging long hours at the gym; at home, he devoted his free time to day-trading and first-person shooters that he played with unsettling gusto from his gaming chair. She was doubly grateful that the bartender, an extravagantly rouged woman in a black usher's vest, didn't ask for her ID. She didn't want to give William any reason to remember the fifteen-year difference in their ages.

"Club soda and lime," he said when the bartender took his order.

"That's all?" Maya asked.

"I've been sober two years now."

"Oh! Well, congrats." She wished she'd known that before she ordered her drink or suggested meeting at a bar in the first place.

The bartender returned with William's water, and he raised his glass. "To old friends," he said ambiguously. The sound of a piano twinkled from the dining room, accompanied by the smell of fried potatoes. "You work nearby? Tell me about that."

She rattled off her usual complaints about Dunning Kruger. The pay was terrible; the books were worse; her boss forced her to run all kinds of personal errands that fell well outside her job description.

"I thought you said you spent most of your time editing."

"Oh, sure," she said, catching herself. "It's kind of an apprentice-ship model, I guess."

"Do you think you'll stay in publishing a long time?"

She was tired of talking about her job, which she was sure made her sound unbearably boring. "I'm remembering something you said once about 'the so-called culture industry.'"

"What's that?"

"You said—and I'm obviously paraphrasing here—but I remember you said something about how art is made in isolation, and the industries that exist to distribute and market the art rely on the exploitation of cheap labor."

"Oh, God."

"You said that those industries attract young people who forgo a living wage in exchange for the chance to be close to the art-making process."

He shuddered. "Do me a favor and don't ever take anything I say to heart."

"Got it," she said, though it was much too late for that. She remembered every conversation the two of them had. "Are you still teaching English?"

"Yeah. AP Lit."

"I seem to remember you had some very strong feelings about AP classes. About the AP test in general." She could see him reclining in Mrs. Dugan's chair, fingers knit behind his head as he explained how the College Board profited off parental anxiety.

"I had a lot of strong feelings about a lot of things."

"You said literature can't be boiled down to multiple choice. You said—"

"Hey, Maya? I'm sorry, I just can't bear to hear my own words quoted back at me."

She had internalized so many of William's opinions that to hear him disavow them felt akin to a betrayal. "I'm glad you're still teaching, at least."

"I've actually been doing some writing on the side. I'm hoping to eventually shift into that full time."

"What's the hardest part?"

"Of writing?"

"Of teaching."

"Watching students grow up and leave."

The piano faded, followed by a patter of applause. A bald man appeared from behind a black curtain, sat at the bar, and lit a cigarette, though the city had banned them back when Maya was in braces.

"Do you have any roommates?" she asked, straining to keep the conversation alive.

"I live with my wife. She's an actress. Actor. Studies acting."

"Your *wife*?" For the first time, she noticed the gold band around his finger, its millegrain border like microscopic barbed wire.

"I guess you didn't think I had it in me."

Maya became suddenly and unaccountably angry. She had never guessed that William would get married—his invectives against the institution had made a powerful impression on her—and she resented this woman, whoever she was, for making William change his mind. Even the word "wife" sounded wrong coming from him. It was wheezy and prim. It belonged on the shelf, gathering dust with "man-servant" and "petticoat." She didn't understand how someone like William could have something so outmoded as a "wife."

"Has she been in anything I've seen?" she asked bitterly.

"Not unless you're into experimental theater."

"I'm not."

William laughed. "Me neither."

They talked for a while about living in New York, the fate of the subway, and the rising cost of rent. Even more disappointing than the fact of William's wife, or the disavowal of his old opinions, was the way he skirted the past—their past—changing the subject each time she brought it up. He sounded like a criminal trying to live straight, avoiding anything that might trigger a relapse. All that seemed to remain of the man she'd once loved was his handsomeness, which, in light of his marriage, oppressed her.

They left the bar after William's second club soda. The outing had been a failure, that much was obvious. But disappointment implied a set of expectations, and she still wasn't sure what hers had been, even now, as she stepped out into the cold. There were crowds on Fifty-Second Street, shivering outside the lighted marquees.

"So, listen," he said. "I know it's kind of weird between us, but I have a favor to ask."

"You do?" She brightened at the thought that she had something he needed.

"I was hoping you might take a look at this thing I'm writing. Get your professional opinion." He blushed. "I can't even call it a novel."

"Oh," she said, struggling to suppress her disappointment. She didn't know, or couldn't admit to herself, what she'd wanted out of the evening, or even what she wanted out of William in general. But she knew this wasn't it. "I'm only an assistant."

"I thought you were an editor."

It was too late to tell the truth now. "I just don't know how helpful I can be."

"I trust you to tell me if I'm wasting my time."

"You trust me?"

"You're the reason I wrote it in the first place. You gave me the confidence, way back when, to try. It's just taken me a little longer than expected." He laughed. "I guess you're kind of my muse."

This was interesting.

"But if you're too busy, or can't help, I understand. It's a shame, though. I could use a second set of eyes."

She considered this a moment. "So no one else has read it."

"Not yet."

"Not even your wife?"

"Not even her."

"I'd love to."

William smiled as he rifled through his shoulder bag. He produced a bundle of pages cinched at the middle with a straining rubber band. "Here it is! And look, I know it drags in the middle, but I'm hoping you can help me make some judicious cuts."

"Oh!" she said, accepting the manuscript, which was heavier than she'd expected. "I didn't realize you had it on you."

He pulled her close, cradling her head against his chest. "I'm so glad we found each other again."

In college, she had learned that it was bad form to read a book with a writer's biography in mind, but publishing had taught her that the author wasn't dead—would that it were so!—and as she started William's novel on the subway ride home, she recognized stories he'd told her about his childhood. The protagonist, "William," like William, had grown up on a pistachio farm outside Tucson. Like William, he was the sole product of the doomed union between a Raytheon executive and a would-be painter. Like William, he'd developed a drug habit in boarding school, managing through some combination of intellect and privilege to gain entry to UC Berkeley. Like William, he'd dropped out and hitched a succession of rides to Massachusetts, where he lived for a time on a defunct dairy farm in Amherst that had been converted into an anarchist commune. Like William, he'd spent a decade knocking around the East Coast, working as a dishwasher, busboy, dog walker, busboy, punk drummer, petty thief, dishwasher . . .

There had been a time in her life when all she wanted was to know what went on in William's mind. Now she held its contents in her lap. She was so invested in the story, and whether or not she had a place in it, that she almost missed her stop. She kept reading even after she surfaced at the station, stumbling over sidewalk debris, tucking the manuscript into her coat only when she reached the door to her apartment.

She found Louis where she'd expected to find him, cradled in the crook of his gaming chair, firing rounds at virtual Nazis. Maya made her way to the bedroom, where she changed into an old pair of her father's scrubs and slipped beneath the covers with William's manuscript, reading by the light of her phone. When she heard Louis's footsteps outside the door, she shoved the pages underneath the bed and pretended to be sleeping. She didn't want to explain the manuscript and how it had come into her possession. Louis knew virtually everything about her life, but she had never told him about William.

In the morning, Maya picked up where she'd left off, the section where "William" starts substitute teaching. She would have kept reading all afternoon, too, had Cressida not invited one of her authors to the office. His name was Monty Beard and he was an English historian who had written a number of bestselling books titled after turning points in human history—*1517, 1789, 1914*—all subtitled *The Year That Changed the World*. His most recent project was somewhat different, an exhaustive biography of his father, an RAF pilot of no particular distinction, which Cressida had published just to keep him in her stable and which, at 622 pages, was nearly twice the length of *1914*. It had yet to be reviewed by any national newspaper. *Kirkus* called it "a vanity project that got way out of hand." Cressida had ordered the assistants to form a line outside the conference room and lavish Monty with much-needed praise while he autographed their books. It was a heartbreaking spectacle, and Maya felt for Monty until Annette, on her way out of the conference room, whispered, "I think he tried to grab my ass."

"Maya!" Monty bellowed after she walked in, wiping the sweat from his fleshy forehead with a handkerchief. "We meet at last! I would stand, but I'm afraid I can't risk the exertion."

"It's good to meet you, too," she said, recalling the flirtatious emails he had sent her, his unsolicited offers to interpret her dreams. "And, you know, congratulations on the book!"

"Darling Maya, where would I be without you?" He opened a copy of his book and started signing. "It's been a difficult road, but here we are. I feel as though we had served in the trenches together."

You weren't a soldier, she thought. *You were the war.*

"Yes," she said. "It was very difficult."

"What a striking young woman you are," he said, his lower lip moist and quivering. "What a sturdy carriage. Your skin is remarkably elastic, and your eyes! Almond shaped with a Mongolian lid—to say nothing of your nose. I wonder if you've had your ancestry examined. Perhaps there's a little of the Khan in you. The nose, of course, is Roman."

With a flourish of his pen, he completed his inscription, then raised the open book and pressed it to his lips. "Sealed with a kiss," he said and handed it back. It read:

> *for Maya*
> *a beguiling specimen*
> *with love*
> *Monty*

He turned to Cressida, who stood behind him. "Might I take a short interval?" he asked. "I'm afraid I'm due for a piddle."

Back at her desk, Maya pulled William's novel out of a drawer and kept reading. The manuscript was marred with unmotivated flashbacks and basic continuity errors, but she felt compelled to read on for personal reasons. The protagonist was in his thirties now, and teaching at an unnamed school in Massachusetts. Maya's heart raced as she read a scene in which "William" meets an attractive, intelligent, but ultimately sheltered female student in his English class.

William had changed some identifying details—the student character, Mackenzie, was blond, not brunette, with a "small, delicately upturned nose"—but the resemblance to Maya was unmistakable. Conversations in which she had taken part were reproduced in the text, almost verbatim. She was flattered that he had written about her, angry that he had done so without permission, and the clash of these two countervailing feelings produced an irresistible feeling of dread that mounted with each subsequent page.

Late in the novel, "William" sleeps with Mackenzie. When her parents find out, they report him to the school and forbid their daughter from seeing him again. He resigns his teaching post, disgraced but no less in love. After a long night of drinking in his car, he decides that his only option is to kill himself, and drives to a nearby bridge. ("The impact alone would end it all," William had written in one of the manuscript's more arresting passages. "The surface of the water might as well have been concrete.") Just as he's about to jump, Mackenzie shows up to talk him down. She tells him she loves him, that his life is worth living, and together they get in his car and leave Massachusetts with the plan to start a new life in New York.

This wasn't autofiction, wasn't even memoir. This was *fantasy*. William, she realized, overcome with tenderness, had diverged from the truth only once, to write the two of them a happy ending—the happy ending they had been denied in real life.

The vibration of her phone against her desk wrenched Maya from William's vivid fantasy world and back into the drabness of her own. She stole away, still rattled, to the vacant office on the far side of the floor where assistants went to cry and take personal calls.

"Hello?" she said. "Dad?"

"Have you talked to Mom today?"

His voice was frantic, and, apparently, he wasn't wasting time.

"No, I've been at work."

"Good. Because I want you to hear this from me."

"Hear what?"

"She's gone."

Maya shook her head. "What do you mean?"

"I mean, she packed the car and left. I just watched her drive away."

"Where did she go?"

"I don't know. I don't know. With that woman, I assume. Joan Portafoglio. I feel sick just saying her name."

"Why?"

"No one has done more to weaken the position of public schools than Joan Portafoglio."

"No, I mean, why did she leave?"

Scott sighed. "So you know about my problems at work."

A few weeks earlier, her father had called to tell her that he was under investigation for falsifying data in a clinical trial. When Maya asked if he *had* falsified any data, he explained that it was more complicated than that. "You know how some people donate blood, or sell their plasma? That's all I did, really, donate blood. Too much, it turns out." While the details of his case were too technical, too scientific, to explain, he'd assured her that the whole thing had been overblown.

"What does that have to do with Mom?" she asked.

"She says I'm not the man she married. That I committed an abominable ethical whatever. This, from the woman living with another woman! You know she spends most of her time over there."

"She does?"

"Breach. That's what she said, ethical *breach*."

Maya made a fist. It was an old, familiar feeling, this fury, and she welcomed it back like a childhood friend.

"Honey? Can you hear me?"

"I can't believe she said that. I can't believe *she* said *that*!"

"My phone is dying. We'll talk soon, okay? I just thought you should hear it from me. I'm calling Gideon next."

"Of course."

"I love you, honey."

"I love you, too, Dad."

She set the phone down and stood in the empty office. The sun was setting, sending splintered shafts of light through the large windows. When, a minute later, her mother tried to call, Maya let it ring and then called William instead. William, who had never stopped thinking about her. William, who had fixed in fiction what was broken in life. He gave her the address to his apartment—his wife, he said, was in rehearsal that evening—and told her he could be there as early as six.

Rush hour had descended on Broadway. A curtain of steam rose from the sidewalk grates, shrouding the halal carts parked beside Town Cars waiting to ferry executives home. Maya walked north, past bank branches and pharmacies—that was Midtown: medicine and money—before disappearing underground. She took the C train to Ninety-Sixth and crossed the park on foot, dodging tourists and geese and caricaturists and a woman tandem nursing two children at once. The woman cradled a baby in the crook of her arm while a toddler old enough to have laces on his sneakers sucked greedily at her spare breast.

Maya reached William's apartment with ten minutes to spare. Standing there, underneath the awning, she began to worry that she was imposing on him, showing up like this on such short notice. The least she could do—the *grown-up thing* to do—was to buy him a bottle of wine for his trouble. She ducked inside the liquor store across the street and grabbed a bottle of red whose label bore the French brand name in looping cursive. The cashier, a tired-looking white woman in a head wrap, swiped Maya's debit card. The machine answered with a shrill beep.

"Do you have another card?"

In the months between graduating and getting a job, Maya had burned through most of her savings, and the bulk of her publishing paychecks went to rent. She kept meaning to apply for a credit card and kept forgetting. Her wallet, which she'd made out of duct tape, was empty.

"One sec," she said, conscious of the line forming behind her. "I'll be right back. Hold on. One sec!"

She ran out of the liquor store and into the used bookshop she'd passed on her way to William's. At the counter, she pulled Monty's book from her bag. "What can I get for this? I'm kind of in a hurry."

The guy behind the counter wore a black-and-white-striped shirt that made him look like an old-time prison inmate. He turned the book over in his hands. "This looks new."

"Hot off the press."

"We sell *used* books here."

"I just used it. I swear."

He offered eight dollars, which didn't seem fair for a book that re-tailed at $29.95, but she didn't have time to argue with him. He reached into a drawer and procured a slip of paper on which he wrote $8. "You can redeem this whenever," he said.

"Can I get cash instead?"

"Cash value is six dollars."

"*Six?*"

He crossed his arms. "I know what you're doing."

"What am I doing?"

"Brunette? Bangs? Publishing tote? Don't think I haven't seen this little hustle, honey."

Maya's cheeks burned. "Okay, fine, whatever. I'll take six."

"You could've roughed the book up, at least."

"I said okay!"

Cash in hand, Maya hurried back to the liquor store, where, to her horror, she found that the cashier with the head wrap was still waiting and that the line had doubled in size.

"I'm sorry," she said, "I need to pick a new bottle."

Maya put the old bottle back on the shelf and replaced it with one that cost $5.55. The cartoon monkey on the label looked drunk, red spirals swirling in the whites of his eyes. With tax, the wine came to $6.02, but the cashier looked eager to get rid of Maya and forgave her the two cents.

By now, it was nearly six o'clock. A flash of lightning lit up the street. Maya ran to beat the rain. She had just taken cover under William's awning when she remembered that he was sober. A bottle of wine. What had she been thinking? Cursing herself, she ran across the street again. "I need to return this," she told the cashier at the liquor store.

"Get in line," the cashier said without looking up.

There were even more people waiting now than there had been before.

"Can't I just give you the bottle? And you can give me the six bucks back?"

"I'm afraid I can't." The cashier finished with her customer. "Have a nice day, sir. Next!"

"In the time it's taking us to have this conversation, you could have made the return by now."

The cashier finally met Maya's eyes. She was pale, almost anemic, with deep creases beneath her eyes. There were no wisps of hair around her ears, no stray strands sticking out from the head wrap. The woman had the spent expression of the sick.

"Never mind," Maya muttered. "But can I borrow a bottle opener really quick?"

Back beneath the awning, slick with rain, Maya took swigs from the bottle while she waited for William. The wine calmed her nerves and warmed her from the inside. She had just begun to wonder where William was when she saw him jogging toward her in a denim jacket, the shoulders dark with rain. She tossed the half-empty bottle into a trash can on the sidewalk.

"I came as soon as I could," he said.

She saw the truth of this in the rise and fall of his shoulders. Streaks of water fell down his forehead, lumping his lashes into thorns.

"It's my parents," Maya said. "I think they just split up."

There came another flash of lightning, followed by a roll of thunder.

"Come inside," he said.

His apartment was cleaner than Maya had expected. The light through the windows was smoky and gray; the rain dripped in shadows across the parquet floors. She paused a moment before his floating shelves, admiring the haphazard assortment of books: an avalanche of Penguin Classics, a stack of ribboned Everyman editions, the numbered New Directions paperbacks piled on their sides. On the highest shelf of all were books by Dunning Kruger, Trees of Knowledge stamped on the spines in gold foil.

•

Two weeks into Maya's senior year of high school, one of her teachers, Mrs. Dugan, a veteran of the Brookline public school system and
the mother of six middle-aged sons, all cops, collapsed at home one
evening while sorting her collection of Wee Forest Folk. When Mrs.
Dugan regained consciousness, surrounded on all sides by tiny porcelain mice, she found that she had trouble stringing sentences together. In an instant, her adult facility with words had been reduced
to cries for help and crude demands; she sounded more like her three-
year-old grandson than a woman who had taught high school English for the last thirty years of her life.

In those first few days after the fall, a rotating cast of substitutes
filled in, screening whatever DVDs the department had on hand—
Merchant Ivory productions, *Akeelah and the Bee*—until a few concerned parents complained. They worried that their children were
falling behind other students at comparable schools in comparable suburbs. They wanted a permanent sub to teach the assigned
curriculum, and the administration, which existed to appease the
parents, assured them that the hiring process was underway. By
Monday morning, the head dean, Dr. Hollerbach, had found her
replacement.

The replacement was a rangy man in his thirties who instructed
the students to call him by his first name, William, rather than the
more formal Mr. Slate. His dark eyes were interred in a pair of pink
sockets; his cheekbones looked sharp enough to draw blood. He had
enormous hands. He wore black jeans, black boots, and a denim
jacket; if it weren't for the week's worth of stubble on his cheeks, he

might have passed for a mature upperclassman. The four types of conflict were written in faded chalk on the blackboard behind him: MAN V. MAN, MAN V. SOCIETY, MAN V. NATURE, MAN V. SELF.

He picked up the copy of *Crime and Punishment* on his desk, thumbed through the pages, and set it down again. He rubbed his eyes.

"I want you to pay attention to the color yellow as we read," he said. His voice was low and languid like the purr of a sedated jungle cat. "In Russia, yellow was associated with physical and mental illness. An insane asylum was often called a 'yellow house.' Prostitutes carried 'yellow passports,' which contained their medical records. Paper money, in the form of rubles, is yellow. Yellow walls. The yellow sugar cubes in coffee. Yellow faces, bloated from drinking." Beneath the bright light panels, William looked a bit yellow himself. "Now," he said. "Where did you all leave off?"

For the next forty minutes, the students took turns reading the novel aloud. William interrupted only once to comment on Dostoyevsky's "obsession" with prostitutes.

"He saw them as emblems of virtue," he said, "living saints, like Mary Magdalene. He was more interested in redemption than sex." The boys in the back row snickered at the word "sex."

When the bell rang, Maya waited for her classmates to file out before approaching him.

"When is Mrs. Dugan coming back?" she asked.

He was flipping through his battered copy of *Crime and Punishment*, a different edition from the one the students used, which had caused some confusion during class. He kept his dark eyes on the book. "I don't know. Why?"

"Well, Mr. Slate—"

"William."

Maya winced. She respected the authority of teachers too much to be comfortable calling them by their first names.

"I was just wondering if we were going to read the whole book out loud. In class."

"There's no substitute for hearing how the words sound, in my experience. Even in translation. Even when the writer is as bad, on the sentence level, as Dostoyevsky is."

She had never heard an English teacher disparage an author before. "Right, it's just, we usually do the reading at home. *Then* we talk about it the next day."

"Most students don't do the reading at home."

"But won't this just incentivize them not to? If they know we'll cover it in class?"

He met her eyes for the first time. She felt like a hamburger under a heat lamp.

"What's your name?"

"Maya Greenspan."

He massaged his temples. "I have a feeling," he said, "that you're going to make life extremely difficult for me."

Within weeks, a small fan club had formed around William, composed mostly of the boys who sat at the back of the classroom. They talked about how *dope* it was to have a male teacher for once, how *sick* that he never assigned homework, how *baller* that he seemed to be hungover every morning. They bought black jeans and denim jackets and stopped washing their hair. A rumor went around that William had taken them to see *Belle de Jour* at the Coolidge Corner Theatre.

"He goes on these tangents," Maya complained at dinner one night, "that have nothing to do with whatever we're reading. Today it was

fifteen minutes on how there are only three suitable subjects for literature."

"What are the three subjects?" Gideon asked. He was a freshman
then, and Maya had so far pretended not to see him when they passed
in the hall.

"I don't know. Love, death, and I think the third was money."

Deb was sectioning the salmon. "What about family?"

"I think that falls under love."

Scott spooned couscous onto his plate. "Or money."

"The point is," Maya said, "he doesn't even try. He comes to class
completely unprepared. And everyone loves him for it!"

"It's a miracle we can afford subs at all," Deb said.

"How come?" Gideon asked.

"No Child Left Behind."

"Mom's on a crusade," Scott said.

"Excuse me, I am *not* on a crusade, and you shouldn't throw
that word around. But when all our resources are funneled into
testing—"

"Does 'crusade' carry negative connotations?"

"Do two hundred years of religious wars against Muslims carry
negative connotations?"

"That's the problem?" Gideon asked. "Testing?"

"And the proliferation of charter schools."

"What's on this?" Scott asked through a mouthful of fish.

"Ras el hanout. I want to get our palates ready for Morocco."

"I thought charter schools *were* public," Gideon said.

"It's more complicated than that."

"I haven't learned a single thing all year," Maya said. "Except that
the color yellow is important, somehow."

"The problem isn't public schools. The problem is poverty, and the concentration of poverty in certain neighborhoods."

"Geography is destiny," Scott said.

"Don't you mean concentration of wealth?" Gideon asked. "Can you have a concentration of poverty? Since poverty is, like, a kind of lack?"

"Good question."

"Students in public schools today are tackling far more difficult topics in math and science than when we were that age," Deb said.

"Bet you couldn't do my homework," Gideon said.

Scott smirked. "Try me."

"How do you calculate the average atomic mass of an element?"

"That's memorization. Anyone could memorize that. Give me one where I have to *think*."

"So you don't know the answer."

"Is anyone listening to me?" Deb asked.

Maya threw up her hands. "Is anyone listening to *me*?"

She hadn't expected sympathy from her father, who was either too busy or pretended to be too busy to care about classroom politics. But Deb had always kept abreast of the minutiae of Maya's life, especially where academics were concerned. She not only learned the names of her teachers, but took them out for coffee and helped fund their artistic endeavors. She tracked the status of school projects and chaperoned field trips. She was a decorated veteran of the PTA who met for lunch with Dean Hollerbach each week. Maya couldn't understand why she wasn't more interested in the fact that one of her daughter's teachers was utterly incompetent and very likely alcoholic.

"Bon appétit, everyone," Deb said. "I'm running late. Scott, you can put the leftovers in the fridge."

Ever since she started high school, Maya had come to resent her mother's level of involvement in her life. What had once felt like caring now seemed like surveillance; she craved privacy, a life outside Deb's omnipresent gaze. Now that her wish had been granted, however— now that Deb was spending more late nights out of the house and didn't seem to care about her daughter's education—Maya felt adrift.

"Where are you going?" she asked. "We just sat down."

"I have a meeting. At temple."

"It's eight o'clock."

"And?"

"Isn't that a little late?" It occurred to Maya that she was asking the same meddlesome questions, and in the same hectoring tone, that she dreaded hearing from her mother.

Deb rose from her seat and kissed her daughter on the head. "Don't wait up."

Her friends weren't sympathetic, either.

"I don't get it," Zoe said the next day during Spanish. "You're mad because this guy *isn't* giving you homework?"

"¡Silencio!" Señora Hirschberg snapped.

They were crouched in the corner of the classroom with the lights off while the school conducted an active-shooter drill. Zoe raised her shoulders and said, "Lo siento."

"It's not the homework thing," she whispered. "He doesn't seem to *care*. About *anything*."

"So what?" Zoe whispered back. "It's senior year. Pretty soon, your grades won't matter anyway."

"Swear to God, this isn't about grades."

"So what *is* it about?"

"Señorita Okafor!"

Zoe mouthed the word "sorry," but when Señora Hirschberg looked away, she leaned over to Maya and said, "I wouldn't worry about it."

Maya did her best to follow Zoe's advice. Why waste time worrying about William? If he was going to sleepwalk through the year, then so would she.

And then, one afternoon, he crossed a line.

"Do you have a minute?" she asked after class. "Because I think there was a problem with my paper."

William leaned back in Mrs. Dugan's chair. "Maya Greenspan."

She handed him her essay on *Crime and Punishment*. "I think you gave me someone else's grade."

William glanced at the first page. "I don't think so."

"I guess I don't understand what went wrong, then."

"Nothing went wrong. You wrote a good essay. You got a good grade."

"I got a B."

"That's a good grade. I *wish* I'd gotten Bs in high school."

"Mrs. Dugan usually writes questions and comments in the margins to show us where we went wrong. You didn't write anything."

"You know, when I was your age, it was considered extremely uncool to complain about your grade to the teacher."

"I just want to know where I messed up," she said. And then, so as not to sound too disagreeable, she added, "So I can do better next time."

William lifted the first page of her essay and scanned the second. "If you really want to know, I thought your take on the novel was a little . . . sanctimonious. A little judgmental. It's not our job as readers to pass judgment on fictional characters."

"Raskolnikov is a murderer! He killed that old lady!"

"Did you ever stop to wonder *why* he killed her?"

"He's a narcissist. He thinks the rules don't apply to him. He's smart, I guess, so he thinks he's better than other people."

"You never felt like you were better than other people?"

She was aware of her flushed cheeks, her flaring nostrils. "I don't think anyone deserves special treatment," she said.

"So what are you doing here?"

Maya looked at her feet. From the hall, she heard the squeak of sneakers on linoleum.

"Tell you what," William said. "A buddy of mine is giving a poetry reading at the Middle East tonight. Swing by, take some notes, and, if you want, write a few pages about the experience."

It was not unheard of for teachers to schedule strange field trips. There was something of a craze then for "experiential learning," especially where the arts were concerned. The previous year, Maya's acting class had gone to see a production of *Lysistrata* at the A.R.T. in which the actors brandished dildos instead of swords. But she had never been on a field trip alone before.

"Tonight?" she said. "I guess I could take the bus . . ."

"Forget it." He sat up and passed her essay back to her. "You probably can't stay out that late. It's a school night."

She heard this as a challenge. "I'll be there," she said.

"These things get a little rowdy sometimes."

"I'll find a way."

"If you say so. And yes——" He cut her off before she could speak. "It'll count for extra credit."

Maya had met plenty of people in their thirties, but until that night, it had not occurred to her that they constituted an entire generation. They stood on the sidewalk outside the Middle East, a restaurant and rock club in Central Square, their arms sleeved in tattoos. They wore black T-shirts despite the cold, and their jeans were shredded at the knees. The men were losing their hair or going gray at the temples, and some of the women wore slings with babies in them. Maya worried that the bouncer, who had gauges in his ears and a braided goatee, would turn her away. But when she reached the front of the line, he glanced at her ID before drawing *X*s on the backs of her hands in black marker. Then he waved her inside.

She found William standing in the back of the club beside a squat, muscular bald man in a black hoodie.

"Look who it is," he said. "I didn't think you'd come."

"I know," she said, squaring her shoulders. "That's why I did."

William wore a white T-shirt, his collarbone visible where the fabric had frayed. He looked more at home here, more *in context*, than he did at school. She could make out most of the tattoo on his bicep, a goat's head with horns and a bell around its neck.

"This is Maya Greenspan," he said. "One of my students."

The man in the hoodie extended his hand. There were pewter rings on each of his fingers.

"I'm Set."

"What was that?" It was hard to hear him over the chatter of the crowd and the flanging guitar blaring from the speakers.

"Set. The Egyptian god of storms, chaos, and violence?"

"Oh," she said. "Are you Egyptian?"

William leaned close. "His *real* name is Seth."

The man scowled. "How old are you, little girl?"

"Seventeen." She felt a burning on her hands where the bouncer had drawn the *X*s.

"I told you already," William said. "She's a student."

The first poet to read was a witchy-looking woman with enormous hair and a ratty fur coat draped over her shoulders. She read a series of confessional poems with jokey titles like "Breakup Texts from the Moon" and "Watching Reruns of *Law and Order: SVU* and Wishing That Christopher Meloni Was My Dad." Maya wasn't sure if they were supposed to be funny or not. The audience maintained a respectful silence, but William kept snickering throughout.

"I was supposed to headline tonight," Seth said after the poet stepped down, "but you know how it is."

"How what is?" she asked.

Seth's eyes widened as though he had been hoping she would ask this very question. "People think that art making is a meritocracy. The good stuff survives, the rest falls away. But poetry is just like everything else. It's all politics. Who's sleeping with who."

"Why don't you sleep with someone, then?"

William laughed. "See?" he said. "I told you she was sharp."

Seth sighed. "You did say she was sharp."

The blood in her cheeks was running hot. She had never considered the possibility that William talked about her, or even thought about her, outside of school. It didn't seem right that she should exist in his mind when she wasn't around.

"I'm going to grab a drink. Maya? Beer?"

It was unclear whether he was unaware or dismissive of the fact that she was not of drinking age. "That's okay," she said. "I'm good."

She had just begun to relax when she saw, through a blue haze of pot smoke, a woman who bore a striking resemblance to her mother.

"How old are you again?" Seth asked.

"Oh my god," she said. "I think that's my mom."

"Where?"

It might have been another middle-aged woman, she thought, but this one had a dancer's posture and what looked to be a pair of scarab beetle earrings.

"Oh god. I'm so screwed."

"She doesn't know you're here?"

"I'm supposed to be studying. I have a calc test tomorrow."

"I guess the better question is, why is *she* here."

Maya was so surprised to see her mother, and so afraid to be seen by her mother, that she'd almost missed the small, wiry figure with shaggy gray hair standing beside her.

"Whoa," Seth said. "That's Theresa Dunne."

"Is there another way out of here? A back door or something?"

"Her early work was great. A big fuck-you to the academy. Lately, she's become a parody of herself."

Maya searched the room for an exit. "Yeah, well, maybe you should sleep with her."

"I don't think she's slept with a man since the seventies. Does your mom always hang out with famous poets?"

"I've never seen that person before in my life."

"Really? Because they seem close."

The woman, Theresa, was kissing Maya's mother on the mouth.

"*Very* close," Seth said.

Maya felt something stirring at the base of her spine, a cold shiver that crept up her back and into her ears. She felt betrayed, and not only on her father's behalf. She had lived with Deb her entire life and was disturbed by the thought that there were things about her mother she still didn't know. But beneath that feeling was another feeling: envy—at seeing Deb, a woman who had just turned fifty, wanted in the way that Maya wanted to be wanted.

"I'm sorry," she said. "I need to go home."

She slipped through the crowd, tracing a long arc around the back of the club so as to avoid detection by her mother. She pushed through the pair of double doors and hurried down a narrow hall, gasping as she surfaced on the sidewalk. The autumn air was barbed against the back of her throat. She stood at the corner, feeling hopelessly young as she waited, like a schoolgirl, for the bus to take her home.

At home, she shut herself in the bathroom and ran the hot water until steam rose from the sink. She soaped her hands and stuck them under the faucet. She whipped her head around, trying not to scream as she scrubbed the black *X*s from her hands. She took off her clothes, which smelled like pot, and put on a pair of her father's scrubs. Then she forced herself to study calculus until dawn.

When she woke in the morning, the *X*s were gone. The skin on the backs of her hands was pink and puffy where the water scalded it. The clothes she'd worn the night before were buried at the bottom of the hamper. No one would ever know where she'd been or what she'd seen.

Except William.

She stopped by his classroom after school. "I just want to say that I'm all right," she said. "I didn't want you to worry."

The lights were off, and he was tipped back in Mrs. Dugan's chair with his eyes closed. She thought he was asleep until he said, "I wasn't worried."

She stepped inside, and the motion-sensing lights switched on. "Because I left so suddenly. I didn't want you to think something terrible had happened."

William blinked his glassy eyes open. "Something terrible like what?"

"Like maybe I was kidnapped or something."

"You thought I thought that you'd been kidnapped."

"I'm just saying, I'm not your responsibility. If something terrible *had* happened, it wouldn't be your fault."

"I know that. Anyway, Seth told me everything."

"Oh." She shut the door behind her. She wanted to be near him, to be alone with him, to feel special and chosen as she had the night before until her mother ruined everything.

"We don't have to talk about it, if you don't want to."

"Good. Because it's a private thing. A family thing."

"That's what I figured."

"It's just not the kind of thing I feel comfortable talking about with you."

"We really, truly, do not have to talk about it."

"I don't know you very well, and I'd rather not get into something so personal with a stranger. No offense."

"Because it's starting to seem like you want to talk about it."

"With who?" she protested. "My mom knows everyone. If I tell one of my friends, and she tells *her* mom . . ."

"Don't you have a boyfriend?"

"No . . ."

"Really?"

The way he said "really" made her throat seize up. She dropped her backpack and took a seat behind a desk in the front row. "I just don't know what to do. I'd really rather not go home right now."

William nodded. "My parents used to get into these big fights every month. Always on the same day, too. It was the day the credit card bill came in the mail, and after he saw what she had spent, my dad would chase my mom around with a belt. We had a pistachio orchard behind the house, and I would go there to sit under a tree and wait them out. I liked having someplace I could just *be*."

It was, by far, the most personal statement he had made about himself since taking over for Mrs. Dugan.

"Can I stay here?" Maya asked.

He looked surprised, as if he hadn't just planted the idea, like a pistachio, in her mind. "What, here? With me?"

"I can do my homework. I'll be quiet, I promise."

He nodded, chewing his tongue as he thought it over. He glanced at the closed door and back at Maya. "All right," he said at last. "You can stay." Then he leaned back in his chair and closed his eyes.

She spent the afternoon in his classroom, and the afternoon after that. Most days, William either slept or graded papers, but despite this, Maya managed to learn that he had grown up in Cochise County, Arizona, by the Mexican border. His father was a war hawk and serial philanderer known throughout Tucson as the General. He built bombs at the Raytheon plant south of the city; William had grown up in the shadow of the Boneyard, a dumping site for fighter jets arranged in rows on the alkaline soil. He spent his early years three feet off the ground, balanced on the soles of the General's feet as the old man shouted, "Boom go the Falklands! Boom goes Grenada! Boom goes the PLO!" William's mother was a frustrated painter who resented her role as the General's wife. William used to sit for her for hours until she grew discouraged and uncorked the first of the afternoon's bottles of wine. She thought having curly hair was the mark of genius.

The General worried that his wife was "feminizing" his son. When William turned thirteen, he was sent to boarding school, which he said was the formative trauma of his life. It was at boarding school that he discovered OxyContin, where he learned to suck the green gum off the tablets before smashing them into a fine powder he took up his nose. One benefit to being strung out, he said, was that it protected him from Master Jeff, the dorm disciplinarian, who had a predilection for school-age boys but a deep-seated aversion to drug use.

"You know," William would say, "this is the first time I've ever talked about some of this stuff."

Maya felt privileged to have been taken into William's confidence. He made her feel worthy in a way that her male classmates couldn't. Boys her age still quoted *Anchorman* and defaced the terra-cotta soldiers that guarded the school. Whenever she expressed a strong opinion in class, they'd smirk at one another and say, "That escalated quickly!" That she wasn't interested in them didn't make her feel better about the fact that they weren't interested in her.

But William! He made her lists of movies to watch; a number of the titles were in French. He burned her an MP3 CD loaded with songs from his favorite bands: Dinosaur Jr., Big Dipper, the Replacements. She would tell him what she liked and didn't like, and he would tell her what it said about her. "You're smarter than other kids your age," he said. "Smart and ambitious and competitive and driven. You don't have any problem advocating for yourself. Deep down, though, you worry that you alienate people. You're afraid of ending up alone."

It had been a long time since anyone had paid such close attention to her.

William said that every woman should read *Anna Karenina* once every ten years of her life, and for two weeks, she carried the Pevear and Volokhonsky edition with her everywhere she went, bracketing her favorite lines in gel pen, studding the gutters of the pages with stars.

"Have you ever thought about writing a book?" she asked him once.

"The thought's occurred to me, of course, but when you've read as widely as I have, the prospect is more than a little intimidating. I'd want to earn my place on the shelf, you know? The world doesn't need another mediocre novel. It doesn't seem worth the time and effort unless I could be certain it was going to be great."

"I think it would be great."

They talked about culture, history, and politics. Russians, he said, pretended to be cynics, but they believed in the dignity of the human soul. That's why they wrote the best novels. Americans, by contrast, pretended to be optimists, but really, they were cynics to the bone. Barack Obama represented the triumph of identity over ideology.

"My parents love Obama," Maya said. "We have one of his signs in our yard."

"Your parents love the status quo."

William thought that guilt had replaced satisfaction in the hierarchy of American feelings.

One afternoon, Maya asked about his tattoos. The peacock, he explained, stood for immortality. The cypress tree represented rebirth. He found the goat's head design in a book of Soviet prison tattoos. It was used to designate untouchables, the lowest class of prisoner there was.

"I want one," she said. "But my parents would freak out. They're kind of old-fashioned that way."

"Are you sure? You have such beautiful skin."

It was the first time he had mentioned her looks, the first time he had acknowledged that she had a body. She was suddenly aware of the temperature in the room.

"I should probably go," she said, though she wasn't sure if she wanted to or not. "My friend Zoe is playing in the powder-puff game this afternoon."

"You know, I never understood powder puff. It always struck me as kind of sexist."

"How so?"

"When guys play football, it's treated like a real sport. Proper funding, uniforms, scoreboards, the whole deal. But when girls do it, everyone acts like it's a joke. Like it's some sort of novelty act. Right?"

"Right." She hadn't thought of that before. "But it's kind of a whole thing. Everybody goes."

He asked if she had heard of the American psychologist Robert Kegan. "Kegan argued that there are five key stages in adult development. Stage One is the Impulsive Self—that's toddlers and other little kids. Stage Two is the Imperial Self. That's where a lot of your classmates are at. They care about how other people perceive them, but only because those perceptions have consequences for *them*. The majority of adults are stuck in Stage Three."

Maya liked the sound of Kegan's theory. It was a way of making sense of things, a way of classifying a world that seemed to grow more complicated every day. "What's Stage Three?"

"That's the Interpersonal Self. Otherwise known as being a conformist. You get your belief system from outside sources and internalize what other people think of you."

She shifted her weight from one foot to the other. She didn't want to see herself as stuck in Stage Three.

"Stage Four," William went on, "is what's called the Institutional Self. You make your own judgments, separate and apart from other people."

"I feel like I'm already there."

"And you're going to powder puff why? Because it's what everyone else is doing?"

Maya felt he'd trapped her, somehow. "So, okay," she shot back. "I guess you'd say you're Stage Five, right? Whatever that is."

William smiled. "The Interindividual Self. Sad to say, I'm not there yet. I'm working on it, though. Only one percent of adults ever reach Stage Five."

"One percent?" She winced. "That seems impossible."

"You'll get there," he said. "Eventually. So long as you can demonstrate that you have a self-authoring mind."

So she stayed.

She liked being at school after everyone else had gone home. She marveled at how innocent she'd been as a freshman when she'd avoided the bathrooms out of fear that a senior might force her into a stall to do drugs. Now that Maya was a senior, she walked with confidence, feeling very much like the worldly and sophisticated woman she had always suspected she'd become.

Regrettably, she could not spend all her time at school. Every Wednesday afternoon, she went to see a man named Lawrence Lowe in Newton. Mr. Lowe was said to be some kind of genius, a graduate of MIT at twenty whose subsequent research on something called "quantum gambling" was either too brilliant or too baseless to earn him a PhD. In the windowless basement of his mother's house, which doubled as his bedroom—Maya saw the sheeted futon in the corner—Mr. Lowe, a timid but intense man with white, shoulder-length hair and a belt of broken blood vessels below his eyes, taught Maya how to hack the SAT. "Treat the test like a game of chance," he told her, his blue eyes blinking rapidly behind high-index lenses. He showed her how to identify the correct answers in the math section without solving the problems, applying the laws of probability to a test with an even distribution of multiple-choice answers, and how to skate through the reading section by scanning only verbs and proper nouns. When Maya told him that she didn't mind reading the complete passage, the backs of his hands turned red. He seemed to resent the SAT and took Maya's willingness to read its passages personally.

Mr. Lowe's strategy for the essay section involved choosing a topic so thematically rich that it could be applied to any prompt. "You'll have to improvise the body of the essay," he sighed, surrendering to the least hackable section of the test, "but this way you won't waste time wondering what to write about." Maya decided to write about *Hunger*, a Norwegian novel that William had recommended. The novel followed an impoverished writer as he wanders, starving, through the streets of a city called Christiania. It was a dark, dense, and frequently disturbing book—the protagonist periodically refused offers of food, despite nearly gnawing off his own finger—but its unwillingness to yield to obvious interpretations made it perfect for Mr. Lowe's methods. Plus, she could count on William to explain it to her.

"It's the book I would have written if Knut Hamsun hadn't," he said one afternoon. "It describes perfectly the condition of being an artist—that is, a man—at the dawn of modernity. There's no God, no salvation, no hope. Only hunger."

Maya nodded. She wanted to seem like she understood.

"When you finish," William said, "give me a call. We can talk about it."

"A call? But I don't have your number."

"You don't?" William shrugged like it was the simplest thing in the world. "Here, I'll give it to you."

In October, Scott drove her to New York to visit colleges. William had told her that any young person with ambition should live in New York in their twenties, and now she understood why. The city was massive, and, walking through it, she felt her soul expand. After touring Columbia and NYU, she and Scott stopped at the Museum of Modern Art and then ate the best meal of her life at a dingy Chinese place under the Manhattan Bridge.

She felt tenderly toward her father as they walked through the city together. There was kindness beneath his carapace of irony. He didn't deserve what Deb had done to him; more than once she had had to resist the urge to tell him what she'd seen at the Middle East. On the drive home, Scott cued up the album of Bahamian folk tales he had played for Maya when she was young, a souvenir from his time on the Bimini chain. *Once upon a time, it was a very good time / the monkey chew tobacco and he spit white lime . . .*

On returning from New York, Maya noticed for the first time just how small and stifling her hometown was—how provincial. She could hardly believe she'd grown up here, in this neatly circumscribed suburb, where people lived neatly circumscribed lives and nothing interesting ever happened. Everything she had once cared about—grades, parties, college applications—now seemed hollow and ordinary.

"You don't think powder puff is sexist?" she asked Zoe in the bathroom at a Halloween party that fall.

"How is it sexist?" Zoe asked, adjusting her makeup in the mirror. She had come dressed as a Black Sarah Palin, or really it was Tina Fey's impression of Palin, with a sash across her chest that read DRILL, BABY, DRILL. "It's girls playing football. It's the *opposite* of sexist."

"But don't you think it's weird that they only do it once a year? Like it's novelty?"

"That *is* the definition of novelty, yes."

"What's up with you tonight?"

"What's up with *you*? I never see you anymore. You didn't even dress up."

"Yes, I did!" She was wearing her father's scrubs. "Is this because I missed your game?"

"It might not mean a lot to you, but it means a lot to me."

"I'm sorry, okay? I just don't see the point!"

The host of the party, Jason Abdulaziz, an extremely distant relative of the House of Saud, appeared in the doorway. He wore white foundation on his face, a jagged Joker smile scrawled across his lips. "We're playing flip cup. You in?"

"No, thanks," Maya said.

"Why not?" Zoe asked. "You *love* flip cup."

"Not anymore."

Zoe followed Jason, leaving Maya in the bathroom, where she stood for a while, wondering why everyone she went to school with suddenly seemed so *young*, so content to dress up and play drinking games when there was a whole world out there just waiting for them.

William showed her a Boston she had never known existed. He took her to basement shows in Allston, to vegan restaurants in Somerville, to exhibits at the ICA. She stopped doing her homework and read the books William suggested. His car was cluttered with books and crumpled cans of beer. When he dropped her off at home, he parked a few houses away, waiting in the dark with the headlights off until she was safely inside.

She was becoming ever more conscious of his body, the enormity of him, the way he made her feel small and secure. He shielded her from moshing gutter punks at concerts and touched her wrist reassuringly during the scary parts of movies. But she was conscious, too, that he seemed to be keeping his hands within the bounds of the legally acceptable. He never put his arm around her shoulders, never touched her thigh. He had not so much as acknowledged her appearance since complimenting her skin back in October. It was the books he recommended to her, the books she checked out from the public library, their boards stiff beneath the prophylactic plastic, that gave their relationship shape, texture, made it something she could hold in her hands.

But the books were causing problems, too. One evening, Deb knocked on Maya's bedroom door and asked how her SAT tutoring was going.

"Fine."

"Just 'fine'?"

Maya had gone out of her way to avoid her mother ever since she saw her at the Middle East, and resented the fact that Deb could intrude on what was supposed to be her private space whenever she wanted. "Just fine," she said, without looking up from her phone.

Deb sat, uninvited, at the foot of Maya's bed. "I just got off the phone with Mr. Lowe. He's worried about you."

"I'm doing all my practice tests."

"It isn't that. He says he's very happy with your work. He says you're one of the best students he's worked with before."

Maya melted at the compliment. "Well, good."

"It's the essay he's worried about. Not the quality, I gather, but the content. He says you're writing about a book?"

She sat up, propping her back against the wall. "That's right."

"Can you tell me what it's about?"

"It's about being an artist. And the moral bankruptcy of civilization. And what it means to be a man in a world without God."

Deb nodded for longer than seemed necessary. The more she did, the less it seemed to signify approval. "Where did you get it?"

"What is this, the Inquisition?"

"Did a boy give it to you?"

Her mother's powers of perception never failed to amaze her. "What makes you think that?"

"It just sounds like the kind of book a boy might give a girl he's trying to impress."

"No," Maya said, pleased by the thought that William wanted to impress her. "It's for school. Why?"

"I'm surprised they put such a dark book on the curriculum, that's all."

"It's not on the curriculum." She paused, searching for a suitable excuse. "It's extra credit."

"For World Lit? I thought you hated that class."

"*Now* you're interested in what I'm studying?"

"I know I haven't been very available lately, and I'm sorry about that. I just wanted to check in with you."

"By banning books."

"No one's banning anything."

"You're acting like I brought a gun to school!"

"Mr. Lowe was just expressing his concern. If you don't feel comfortable talking with me, I have the name of a counselor who specializes in adolescent development."

"If anyone needs counseling, it's Mr. Lowe."

"He's supposed to be a brilliant man."

"Do you know what we do all afternoon? Math without math. Reading without reading. All he does is show me how to cheat!"

This seemed to surprise her. "Well," Deb said, fumbling to respond, "sometimes, in life, you have to do whatever's necessary, in the short run, to achieve your goals down the line."

"And if he's so brilliant, why does he live with his mom? If that were me, I'd kill myself."

Deb dusted invisible debris from her pant leg. "If that's the way you feel," she said, leaving the sentence unfinished. She left the room and closed the door behind her.

"I'm not going back there," Maya said.

She didn't like fighting with Deb, but the more time Maya spent with William, the more she saw the bedrock of bullshit and rank hypocrisy on which her mother's life was built. She was a family woman who cheated on her husband, a suburban mom who thought herself superior to suburban moms, a dancer who no longer danced. She raised funds for the needy from the comfort of her home. William called it "Starbucks capitalism."

"You give to charity, you buy organic, you support companies with good ethical values. And you do all that without sacrificing very much. It's an indulgence—I mean that in the Catholic sense. It's a way to pay for your own redemption. That's why I get my coffee at 7-Eleven."

He'd lost her there. "How come?"

"Fewer contradictions."

To celebrate the end of the semester, she asked him to take her to get a tattoo.

"Are you sure?" he asked. "I know I'm not exactly the best person to make this argument, but they are, in fact, extremely permanent."

"I know what I want," she said.

He drove her to a tattoo parlor in Allston. On a piece of scrap paper, she scribbled a design and then filled in the text, her favorite line of Tolstoy's:

The guy behind the counter wore a red cycling cap with the brim popped. "Cute," he said. "Did you write that yourself?".

William winked. "She did."

He sat beside her the whole time, squeezing her right hand while her left hung limp beside her. "Breathe," he said. "Just remember to breathe." When it was over, he ran across the street for a bottle of whiskey. She took a long, deep swig to dull the pain in her shoulder.

"How does it feel?" he asked later. He was parked just up the street from her house and had killed the lights.

She moved her shoulder, and the plastic wrap around it crinkled. "Awful."

"Are you having second thoughts?"

"Not at all."

"You were a stoic in there. I'm proud of you." He finished off the bottle they'd been passing back and forth. "Your flight is when?"

"Late tomorrow. We're taking the red-eye to Paris, then changing planes. I don't know what I'm going to do, stuck with my family all week. Stuck with my mom."

"I'll trade places with you. I've never been to Morocco."

"I just don't know what we're supposed to *talk* about for nine days straight." She turned to William. The streetlights cast his face in silhouette. "Why is it so easy to talk to *you*?"

He considered this a moment and said, "Because I'm not your friend and I'm not your parent. I have no reason not to treat you like the mature, young, independent woman that you are."

"You forgot 'pretty,'" she said. "The pretty young woman that I am."

"The pretty young woman that you are."

She was a little bit drunk and in a lot of pain, her shoulder pounding like a second heart. She leaned over and kissed him on the cheek. He turned his head in surprise, and his lips brushed hers. His breath was bitter, a fermented fog, and she could feel his pink tongue muscle its way into her mouth. She was so caught up in kissing him that she forgot to breathe, and with a slight choking sound, she pulled her head away from his. She held still just long enough to realize what she'd done and, in a rush of excitement and shame, quickly let herself out of the car. She skated across the street, slick with ice, and skipped up onto the curb. The front yard of her house was covered with snow, but she could still make out the word HOPE on the campaign sign stuck deep in the soil.

Nothing Maya saw in Morocco—not the mosques in Casablanca nor the Marrakesh medinas—could take her mind off William for an instant. She spent the first few days sealed shut inside her headphones, listening over and over to one of the songs he had put on her CD:

Oh, if you knew how I felt now
You wouldn't act so adult now . . .

Every minute spent apart from him was agony. She felt as though she were carrying him around with her like so much extra luggage.

On the third day, the Greenspans got into a van and drove east from Marrakesh to see some famous gorges. They stopped in the Valley of Roses, at an outdoor strip mall so remote that it seemed to have been summoned from the sand. Scott and Gideon slept in the car, but Deb insisted that Maya come out to shop.

"See anything you like?" Deb asked. The shelves of the shop were packed with pink products: rose-scented soaps, perfumes, and shampoos, bottles of rose water and rose oil.

Maya shook her head. The sooner they left the shop, the sooner they reached the gorges, the sooner the whole trip would be over and she could be with William again.

"You *have* to smell this," Deb said, brandishing a spray bottle.

"I'm fine. I don't want any."

"Is good for the hair!" cried the shopkeeper, a bushy-eyed man in a brown tunic and knit cap. "Is good for the skin! For the heart!"

"You'll love it," Deb said, advancing toward Maya. She pulled the trigger on the spray bottle, sending a rose-scented mist in her daughter's direction.

"Please stop," Maya said. "I just told you I don't want any."

Deb pulled the trigger again, and a second burst of scent sprayed forth. "Come on, Maya. Just *smell* it."

Maya recoiled. "I said *stop*! You never *listen*!"

Deb's cheeks took on the rosy color of the shop. She set the bottle back on the shelf beside her.

"Excuse me," she said, "but you've been in a terrible mood since we got here. And I worked very, very hard to plan this trip."

"I'm in a terrible *mood* because I never wanted to *come.*"

"You smell nice!" the shopkeeper called. "Your boyfriend, he like!"

"It's an enormous privilege to travel like this."

"Yeah, well, I never asked for that privilege."

"Oh!" Deb snapped. "Well! I'm so *sorry* to have *burdened* you with that!"

Maya retreated into her hoodie, counting down the hours until she was back in Boston. She had resolved to lose her virginity to William the next time she saw him. Whether she wanted to because she loved him or because it would upset her mother was impossible to tell. Her attraction to William had become so bound up with her anger at Deb that they seemed to sprout from the same hormone-enriched soil. She could not distinguish one impulse from the other.

Near the end of the trip, at a tannery in Fès, Maya watched from a balcony as the men below dyed animal skins. The skins were treated with cow urine, bird feces, quicklime, and salt before being dunked in large stone wells. The wells contained dyes of different colors. From where Maya stood, the men looked like ants crawling around a painter's palette.

The smell rising from the tannery was pungent, a heady blend of animal flesh and stagnant water. Maya, transfixed by the process and intoxicated by the smell, slipped out of the hoodie that she had worn every day for the past week. The wind on her own dyed skin was wonderful. Her tattoo had chafed and itched against the fabric. Now, finally exposed to the sun, she felt a surge of relief coursing through her, as though she had just set down a backpack burdened with books.

No more than a minute could have passed before she heard her mother's voice behind her.

"Maya! What is *that?*"

"What's what?"

"*That.* On your shoulder."

She froze. "Oh, this? It's a tattoo," she said with all the composure she could muster.

"I see that. I see that." Deb blinked repeatedly, as if trying to wipe the image from her eyes. "But it's not *permanent.*"

"It is."

"Why did you—when did you—you're joking, right?"

"It's not a joke. I'm sorry if the idea of a tattoo is somehow *shocking* to you."

"Shocking! No, Maya, I don't find it shocking. Frankly, I find it unoriginal."

She had expected to be called irresponsible, impulsive, but she had not expected to be called unoriginal.

"You think you're special because you vandalized your body? You think that makes you *unique?* Jesus, Maya. I thought I raised you smarter than that."

"I'm an adult! I can make my own choices!"

"The teenage brain is still developing—"

"Don't give me your speech about the teenage brain. I'll be eighteen in two weeks. *Weeks!*"

"And until then, you're my responsibility."

"You can't handle the fact that *I'm* independent because *your* whole life is built around being a mom! Well, guess what? I don't need you anymore!"

Deb was crying now, albeit softly, in plain view of the other tourists, who had begun to stare. "You might as well have inked a bunch of numbers on your arm."

"Wait a minute," Maya said. "Hold on. Wait a minute. You're making this about the *Holocaust?*"

"My grandparents—"

"No. *No.* You do *not* get to do this."

"My *grandparents*—"

"It has nothing to do with that! Or with them! Or with *you!*"

"You've broken my heart, Maya. You really have."

"At least I'm not cheating on my husband!"

Deb reeled backward, as though she had been shot. She stumbled a moment before steadying herself against the guardrail of the balcony that overlooked the wells. She looked over her shoulder to ensure that Scott and Gideon were out of earshot. In a whisper no less accusatory for its volume, she said, "*Excuse me?*"

"I saw you. At the Middle East. Slobbering all over some *hideous* woman."

Deb went white. All the wisdom and authority had drained from her face. "You don't know what you saw."

"Oh, trust me, I saw plenty."

"And what were *you* doing at the Middle East?"

"It was an assignment. For school."

"Which class?"

"World Lit."

Deb raised her hand to her mouth. "Did *he* do this?"

"Did who do what?"

"Answer me, Maya. Did that, that *teacher*, that new teacher you claim to hate so much. Did *he* take you to get the tattoo?"

"No!" she protested. "I went—by myself."

"I thought you had to be eighteen to get a tattoo. My god. He took you, didn't he?"

Maya flinched. "So what if he did? It was *my* idea!"

"We'll discuss this when we get home," Deb hissed. "And put your sweatshirt on. I don't want to look at that *thing* anymore."

Deb turned on her heels and marched back inside the tannery shop. Maya was left standing on the balcony, above the animal skins and wells of dye, the air perfumed with the scent of piss and stagnant water. The tourists lowered their phones, and then their eyes, like children who have just learned the meaning of shame.

The last two days of the trip were wretched ones. Maya avoided conversation with her mother, avoided eye contact even, so that they were forced to use the men in the family as conversational surrogates. Deb had apparently decided not to tell Scott about the tattoo until they were home, and Gideon was so caught up in his own impressions of the country that he didn't notice anything was wrong. Maya resented him for this. She wanted the support of her younger sibling, the only one who understood how domineering Deb could be. But when he finally realized that something was wrong—this, at the tail end of the trip, while they waited to debark in Boston—she balked.

"I'm fine," she said.

"Really? Because Mom is in a mood, and you two haven't talked to each other in days."

"I don't know what you're talking about."

She wanted to tell him—about William, the tattoo, everything—but she was afraid that he would take their mother's side. She couldn't bring herself to say what she'd seen at the Middle East. It would crush him. Six months earlier, she might have spoken up, but she had done a lot of growing up since then.

"Maybe it's menopause," was all she said.

She woke early on the first day of the new semester and spent an extra hour in the bathroom. She blow-dried her hair and applied a face of makeup until Gideon knocked on the door, desperate for a shower. She watched the clock during first and second period; the minute hand had never seemed to crawl quite so slowly. When the bell rang, she rushed to William's classroom. She paused a moment to smooth her blouse and tuck her hair behind her ears. But when she stepped inside, she found a woman she'd never seen before standing at Mrs. Dugan's desk. She looked to be a few years younger than William, hardly much older than Maya herself.

"Hi there," she said with an idiot's smile. "I'm Ms. Kelly."

Maya scanned the room. "Where's Mr. Slate?"

"You'll have to take that up with Dean Hollerbach."

The following forty-five minutes were torture. Maya fumed as Ms. Kelly read from Flaubert's *A Simple Heart*, pronouncing the protagonist's name, Félicité, as Felicity. But Maya was alone in her misery. Ms. Kelly had blond hair, bright eyes, and breasts like cannonballs beneath her low-cut sweater. She couldn't have been much more than five feet tall, making her shorter than Maya's male classmates, all of whom appeared to have forgotten William entirely. They didn't slouch like they used to but sat up straight as erections, participating more in one class session than they had all year.

Maya texted William under the table, asking where he was and if he was okay. A parade of disasters processed through her mind. Had he drowned? Crashed his car? Or merely caught a cold? Was there something she should do?

"Excuse me," Ms. Kelly said. "I'm going to have to take your phone."

Maya's stomach sunk. She could feel it somewhere down around her bladder. "I'm sorry," she said. "It won't happen again."

"I know it won't," Ms. Kelly said perkily. "Because I'll have your phone. You can get it at the end of the day."

Maya wasn't used to being called out in class. She had a reputation for being a good student, a teacher's dream. Jaw set, she surrendered the phone and spent the rest of the class clawing at the back of her neck. The classroom, which had come to feel like a second home since William arrived, now felt foreign to her.

When, at last, the class concluded, Maya marched to Dean Hollerbach's office. His secretary said that he was on a conference call, but she barged in anyway. She found him at his desk, hunched over a Styrofoam clamshell, a paper towel tucked into his collar.

"I'm sorry, Dean Hollerbach," the secretary said. "I told her you were busy."

"That's all right, Alice. I'll take it from here." Hollerbach was a small, pug-faced man whose reading glasses managed somehow to stay balanced on the abrupt bridge of his snub nose. He waved Maya in as though he'd been expecting her. "Don't you look nice today."

"What happened to Mr. Slate?"

Hollerbach cleared his throat and explained that "some parents" had grown concerned about Mr. Slate's "teaching style" and requested a review of Mr. Slate's record, which was found to contain some "irregularities" that the administration had managed to overlook in their rush to replace Mrs. Dugan, said "irregularities" being worrisome enough to warrant a "thorough investigation," which only confirmed their "irregular nature," and after a long phone call with

Mr. Slate—conducted, Hollerbach complained, during that "relaxing interval" between Christmas and New Year's—the two of them had decided that it would be best to go their separate ways, with Mr. Slate preferring to "resign quietly," which Hollerbach agreed was in everyone's best interest. . . .

The dean's lips were moving, but Maya couldn't hear him. She had imagined every worst-case scenario save for this one. Williams was an excellent teacher, beloved by his students. Why would anyone want to let him go? Who were these concerned parents, anyway?

But as soon as she asked herself, she knew.

Somehow, she made it through the rest of the school day. She felt like someone had cut open her chest and cracked her ribs, leaving her beating heart exposed to the world for everyone to see. She couldn't accept that William was gone, couldn't understand why he hadn't told her, and by the time she saw Zoe for Spanish, she was practically deranged with grief.

"I need to talk to you," she said in the hallway after class.

"I'm late," Zoe said, flanked by two of her friends from the girls' basketball team.

"But it's lunch."

"We have a team meeting. And I'm late."

"Look, I know I haven't been around much lately—"

"Actually," Zoe said, "you haven't been around at all."

"That's what I want to talk to you about! I think my mom got William fired."

"That's too bad," Zoe said, without a trace of sympathy. "I know how close you were."

That night, when Deb came home from work, she found her daughter on the floor, wrapped in the duvet, as though she had fallen out of

bed and stayed there or else thought herself undeserving of the com-
forts of a mattress. Her upper lip was wet with snot, and her eyes
seemed on the verge of rolling out of her head. Deb took off her coat
and got down on the floor with her.

"I hate you," Maya said through hiccuping sobs.

Deb lifted her daughter's head onto her lap and stroked her hair. "I
know," she whispered. "I know."

For all her anger, Maya let herself be held. She had never needed
her mother more than she needed her now.

Maya was more depressed than ever that winter, moving through the
halls of the high school like a phantom. When the last of the plow-
packed snow turned to slush, a kind boy named Kartik asked her to
prom, confessing that he'd had a crush on her since freshman year,
and because she would shortly be moving to New York, where she
had been accepted to NYU—though not Columbia, on account of
her SAT scores—and because he seemed harmless, she said yes. Her
mother insisted on taking her shopping, and Maya submitted, settling on a purple satin dress that Deb liked just to get the ordeal over
with. After prom, at Zoe's house, Maya followed Kartik upstairs and
let him sleep with her for the same reason. At graduation, Marjorie
crowed about how grown-up her granddaughter looked in cap and
gown. "My goodness!" she said. "You're so ma-*toor*."

In August, Maya moved into a dorm on Fifth Avenue, where she
met her roommate, Sadie van den Berg–Slotnick, a raspy, red-haired
girl from the Upper West Side. Sadie served as Maya's guide to the
city, taking her to all the bars that didn't card and eventually buying
them a pair of fake IDs from a gay guy she'd dated in high school.

After years under her parents' watchful eyes in Brookline, Maya was crazed with freedom, staying out late and sleeping through her morning classes. She remained a dutiful student at heart. She made a spreadsheet listing every guy she slept with that fall, with column headings indicating their names, identifying details, general impressions, and a detailed twenty-point ranking system—as if some authority were going to review these notes and give her a grade.

It was difficult, at first, to accept that she wasn't the smartest person in her comp lit cohort. She'd thought of her parents as cultured people—Deb had been a dancer, after all—but her classmates were the sons and daughters of writers, gallerists, composers, painters, and curators, many of whom hailed from New York. They had militant opinions on Shakespeare's "problem plays" and Danish cinema. They spoke with such disdain for the Pevear and Volokhonsky translation of *Anna Karenina*—one boy called it "a *Pevearsion* of literature"—that Maya took to wearing long sleeves to hide the tattoo on her bicep. She considered having it changed to the Constance Garnett translation ("He walked down, for a long while avoiding looking at her as at the sun, but seeing her, as one does the sun, without looking"), but the guy behind the counter at Village Tattoo said it was too wordy. There was no way to fit all that text inside the sun insignia. She asked him to color over it instead.

It was an excruciating session, much more painful than the first, and Maya might not have survived it without Sadie, who gave her a bar of Xanax and hectored the tattoo artist, telling him to take it easy on her friend. The resulting design held no meaning for Maya, but at least now she could bare her arms in class without embarrassment.

One night, near the end of the semester, Sadie procured two tablets of Molly that she and Maya popped on their way to a dim sum parlor that doubled as an after-hours club. They danced awhile near the makeshift DJ booth, boxed in by a girl in gold lamé pants and two shirtless guys in papier-mâché animal masks. When Sadie wandered off to get them drinks, Maya, who had been guzzling water all night, took the opportunity to find a bathroom, where she met Louis Friedman for the first time.

"Is this the line?" she asked.

"It's supposed to be." He pounded the door with his fist and shouted at whoever was inside. "It's the line for the *bathroom*, for people who need to use the *bathroom!*"

Maya giggled. The Molly made her feel gooey and warm. "What are you so mad about?"

Louis stood an inch shorter than Maya, but he cut an impressive figure, with broad shoulders and a brawny torso that tapered to a narrow waist. She had to stop herself from reaching out and touching his arms. "I think some people in there are doing drugs," he said.

She thought it best not to tell him that she, too, was on drugs.

"It's too loud in here," he continued, biceps bulging beneath an ill-fitting T-shirt. "You can't talk to anyone. I can't hear myself think!"

She giggled again. There was something sweet about the sincerity of this well-built boy trying to hear himself think. "I *really* have to go."

"My mom always told me, it isn't polite to make a beautiful woman wait." He pounded on the door and shouted, "Hurry *up*!"

He told her he was studying psych at NYU, which, he explained, probably had to do with the fact that he was an only child. He grew up wondering if other people had thoughts and feelings as confounding as his own. Sometimes life felt like a video game, and he was the only human player. He wondered if it were possible to truly know another person, what went on in their mind. Then he asked her a question she couldn't make out, in part because the music was loud and in part because she was still startled by his use of the word "beautiful."

"Sorry," she said. "I didn't catch that."

"See, this is what I'm talking about!"

The door opened, and three girls spilled out in a fog of glitter. Louis stepped aside to let Maya go first, a small kindness that seemed monumental in the flattering glow of the Molly. But when she emerged a few minutes later, the lights in the dim sum parlor were on, and cops were waving everybody out.

She didn't see Louis again until after winter break when he messaged her on Facebook and asked her on a date. Maya didn't know how to respond. Guys her age texted, they "poked," they danced on you at parties, but, in her experience, they never asked you out.

—Why? she wrote back.

—I guess I want to get to know you.

—I thought you said it was impossible to know another person.

—Let's hope I'm wrong.

The following weekend, over lunch at Wo Hop, Louis peppered her with questions. She talked about her childhood, which had always seemed so uneventful, but the way he listened, his eyes wide, nodding along, made her feel like the most interesting person alive. Maya thought that he would make an excellent shrink.

Louis, for his part, had grown up on Long Island. He spent a lot of time alone, in his black-lit basement, making beats in Ableton and playing *Mortal Kombat* on a mock-leather couch. "I had a pet snake, which lived in a tank, but that basement was kind of like *my* tank," he said. "I remember being thirsty a lot." At sixteen, he got serious. He started going to a gym where he trained in Brazilian jujitsu. Now his goofy grin and chicken legs were all that remained of the scrawny, awkward kid he'd been.

Louis was the man of the house. His father lived in California, where he sold vending machines and sent cards on his son's birthday. Louis was much closer with his mother, who worked at a home for developmentally disabled people and called him every day during her break. "She's my hero," he explained. "She brought me up all on her own. I don't know what I would have done without her." The rapturous way Louis spoke about her made Maya jealous, which Sadie told her later was a sign of true love.

It wasn't long after she started seeing Louis that Maya discovered she had something her sophisticated peers did not: a work ethic. For all their knowledge of bell hooks and the Criterion Collection, they didn't seem to spend much time on their schoolwork. Maya, by contrast, had started logging weeknights in the library with Louis, who turned out to be a dedicated student. She won the freshman essay contest, which her classmates pretended not to have entered.

That November, Louis threw her a surprise birthday party in her dorm's common room. He bought an ice cream cake, taped up streamers, and invited all her friends, even though he didn't know them very well. He spent most of the party with his hands in his pockets, removing them only to collect and dispose of the paper plates that the guests left behind on their way to try their luck at **KGB Bar**. When, late in the evening, a blissfully intoxicated Sadie blacked out, it was Louis who accompanied her to urgent care and sat with her while she had her stomach pumped. Maya insisted on coming, but Louis wouldn't hear of it. "Stay," he told her as he helped Sadie outside. "It's your birthday."

Late that night, when he was back from urgent care, she invited Louis up to her room. She kissed him and unbuckled his belt. But when she pulled her shirt over her head, he froze.

"What's with the tattoo?" he asked.

It had been on her body long enough now that she sometimes forgot it was there. "Oh," she said. "Don't worry about it."

"You know that's a Nazi thing."

"What? I've never heard that before."

"Trust me, I've played a lot of *Call of Duty*. The Black Sun. Satanists use it, too, but mostly Nazis. It was commissioned specifically for Heinrich Himmler. Here," he said, pulling out his phone. "I'll show you."

"I'm putting my shirt on."

"Wait!" He put the phone back in his pocket. "I'm sorry. Forget it."

"I like you, Louis," she said, "but you would be doing me an enormous favor if you never mentioned my tattoo again."

Maya was lying with her head on William's shoulder when he asked if she'd had a chance to read his novel yet. It was a cool, cloudy autumn afternoon, the first autumn of her life that she wasn't starting school, and the breeze through the open window turned her skin to gooseflesh.

"I did," she said and sat up. "Sorry I didn't mention it before. It's been a weird couple of weeks. There's this rumor about a buyout going around."

"And?"

"And everyone is worried about their jobs."

Should a Chinese firm buy the publishing house, Maya would most likely be among the first to go. She had never been an especially good assistant, but ever since she started sleeping with William on her lunch breaks, she had failed to clear even the low bar of competence. She'd already missed one editorial meeting, her desk was a mountain range of manuscripts, and the number of unread emails in her inbox had recently broken four figures.

William propped his head up. "I *mean*, and what did you think of the book?"

"I'm not exactly objective," she said, swinging her legs over the side of the bed. "Given how close I am to the material. Not to mention the author."

"But it must have made *some* kind of impression."

As an admission of William's feelings for her, the novel had made an enormous impression. But as a work of art? She wasn't sure. There was a kind of charisma to the prose, which was by turns swaggering and sensitive; it was the same charisma William had exhibited when he'd taken charge of Mrs. Dugan's class. At the same time, the subject matter itself—the love affair between a male teacher and his female student, told without irony, from the teacher's perspective; the detailing of cigarettes smoked and whiskey drunk; the valorization of an especially louche brand of bachelorhood—seemed hopelessly out-of-date. So, too, did the swaggering style, however much there was to admire in it. It was precisely the kind of novel, she thought, that might have been published to some acclaim a couple of decades earlier. It might have even squeaked by five years earlier, had he written it when they'd first met. She rolled her tights up over her knees and tried to think of something truthful she could say. "I'll tell you one thing, I couldn't put it down."

"Really? You mean it?"

"I almost missed my stop on the subway. True story."

He let his head fall back on the pillow. "I can't believe it. You don't know what this means to me, Maya. I've hardly slept since I gave you the novel. But to know that you loved it . . . You did love it, didn't you?"

"What you need to do now is to give it to someone who doesn't know anything about you. Someone with a fresh perspective."

"But I want *your* perspective. Your professional opinion."

She sighed and smoothed the folds in her skirt. "You're right. I loved it. Really, it's great."

"Thank you, Maya. I don't know what I'd do without you."

"Well," she said, planting a kiss on his head, "you'd better figure that out, because I have work. And so do you."

"Stay," he pleaded. "Just a little bit longer."

She thought of the manuscripts stacked on her desk, the stark disappointment in Cressida's eyes. "Okay," she said, unzipping her skirt. "But quick, because I *really* have to go."

"What's the rush?"

"There's a marketing meeting I can't miss."

"You don't *really* want to leave me for a marketing meeting."

She laughed as she peeled off her tights. "You're right," she said. "I really don't."

Sex with William was a kind of time travel. He made her feel like she was still in high school, minus the insecurities and inhibitions. When she was with him, she remembered how she was at seventeen, wide-eyed and sincere, hungry to take on a world that she was certain had been built with her in mind. He made everything seem possible again.

In bed, he wasn't stilted like he had been at the bar. He relaxed into the William she'd known once, the William she remembered—and when she pulled off her underwear and parted her knees, he looked grateful just to be alive.

Every so often, however, he would call to say that something had come up. A staff meeting, a parent-teacher conference. His wife running lines in their apartment. From the vacant office on her floor, she'd try to keep him on the phone.

"Did you think about me?" she asked him once. "Back then?"

He paused a moment before he said, "You were seventeen."

"So? I know some guys are into that. Teens or whatever. It's called— not pedophilia, but—"

"Can you not use that word around me?"

"Ephebophilia."

"Let's avoid anything that ends in '-philia.'"

"Did you, though? Think about me?"

And here he paused again before he said he had to go.

Those were the days that frightened Maya most. It was only when he canceled their meetings that she realized how much she'd come to depend on them.

Her loneliness was so acute that one afternoon, a few weeks into the affair—she couldn't believe that she was engaged in something so literary as an *affair*—Maya picked up the phone when her mother called. "Hello?"

"Hey! Hi! I'm glad I caught you!"

Deb's eagerness made Maya shudder. "I'm at work."

"I'm guessing from your tone that you've been better about taking your father's calls than you have mine."

"We talk."

"And I'm guessing he told you I'll be living with my friend Joan for a while."

"It came up." She was determined not to let her mother think for a moment that the move had affected her.

"Did he happen to mention *why* I moved out?"

"Is this why you called? To talk about Dad?"

"Actually, no. I wanted to know if you'd heard from Gideon."

It had been a few weeks, at least, since Maya had seen her brother. New York was big enough that sometimes she forgot they lived in the same city. "I've been busy."

"I can't imagine how hard this must be for him."

"I'm glad you're worried about one of us."

"Excuse me," Deb said. "That is totally unfair. I've been trying to reach you for weeks."

"Like I said—"

"You've been busy. Fine. I'll be brief. I'm calling to ask you to talk to your brother. Better yet, invite him over. Let me know if he seems all right to you."

"You want me to, what, spy on him?"

"What I want is for you to look out for your brother, who thinks the world of you, by the way. There are things he'll say to you that he won't say to me. And yes, I do worry more about him, but that's because you're much more mature. He needs me to worry about him. You don't."

Maya resisted the pull of her mother's praise. "I doubt he's free, anyway."

"I'm only asking you to extend an invitation. I'm asking you to spare two hours of your life to check on your little brother. Make sure he's okay. I'd do it myself, but I don't live in New York. I need you, Maya. Will you help me? Please?"

It was a testament to her mother's powers of persuasion, her skillful deployment of flattery and guilt, that Maya went ahead and texted Gideon, inviting him to dinner. She didn't think he'd come, especially on such short notice, but when she opened the door that evening, there he was, standing next to Astra, bearing a bottle of wine. Maya recognized the monkey on the label.

"Glad you two could make it," she said, accepting the bottle. "You didn't need to bring anything."

Astra shrugged. "It wasn't expensive."

Gideon stepped inside and traced a slow, winding path around the living room, running his fingers along the floral sofa, the oak bookshelf, the back of the green wing chair. He knelt to examine the coffee table, a circular slab of glass supported by flaking iron legs. "Is this *all* Mom and Dad's old furniture?"

The color rose in Maya's cheeks. She was proud of her apartment, which she'd filled with the furniture her mother had displaced when she redecorated. Her friends' places were invariably furnished with functional pieces from IKEA or secondhand stuff salvaged from the sidewalk. When they came over, they would comment on how nice the apartment looked, how *adult*. She crossed her arms. "Not *all* of it, no."

"Is that my old desk?"

"That's my dining room table."

Gideon stuck his hands under the surface of the table, squinting as he felt for something. A moment later, he pulled out a wooden tray. "My computer keyboard used to live right here."

"Wow," Astra said. "A family heirloom. Beautiful."

Louis emerged from the bathroom a few minutes later and entertained their guests while Maya prepared a pan of sodden stir-fry. The scum on the burner and the scarcity of silverware only served as additional reminders, if she needed any, that she lacked her mother's gift for hospitality.

"What are we talking about?" she asked as she came into the room. They sat elbow to elbow around the small table, which could hardly fit four plates and the serving bowl.

"Gideon was telling Louis about his lab work," Astra said.

"We inject the eggs with hormones," Gideon said. "After they hatch, we see which ones develop feather-pecking syndromes. It's an indicator of anxiety."

"You probably think of psychology as a 'soft science,'" Louis said, "but there's a wealth of new research on managing anxiety among the elderly that I'd love to tell you about."

"He studies mice, not people," Maya said. Her guilt about turning down Louis's proposal had hardened into resentment over the past few weeks. Her guilt about fucking William was too great to consider.

"Actually," Astra said, "he studies chickens. Because eggs?"

Growing up, Gideon had fallen in love approximately once per month. The objects—and that's what they were to him, Maya thought, objects—of his affection could be classmates, cousins, and, frequently, her friends. It was clear to her, even then, that these were more than crushes. They were infatuations, obsessions, as all-encompassing as they were destined to fail. He probably wouldn't have known what to do if his feelings *were* reciprocated. It wasn't even their bodies he wanted, or not only that. He seemed to be seeking himself in these girls, adopting their interests and mirroring their manner of speech, trying their personalities on for size. Maya had liked his first girlfriend, Nina, whose seriousness seemed to cure him of his worst tendencies. She wasn't so sure about this one. Astra was nice, but maybe too nice for her brother. She thought he needed someone *less* supportive, someone who could put him in his place.

"I can speak for myself," Gideon said. He turned to Louis. "I study chickens. But I *am* more interested in human subjects. I'm thinking of leaving the lab, actually."

"I didn't know that," Maya said.

"The chickens in their cages depress him," Astra said, rubbing her boyfriend's back. "Right, baby?"

Gideon bristled. "How many times are we going to talk about this?"

"About what?"

"About information I share with you in confidence."

"There's nothing wrong with being sensitive to other people's pain! It's why you'll be such a good doctor."

"Other *chickens'* pain," Louis put in.

"I'm thinking of leaving," Gideon said, "because I need some experience working with patients to put on my med school application."

"How's the essay going, by the way?" Maya asked, trying to lighten the mood. Her mother, she had to admit, was right. There *was* something going on with Gideon. He seemed more irritable than usual, and she thought he'd loved his job at the lab.

"The essay is kind of a sore subject," Astra said.

"Like, for instance," Louis interjected, "did you know that anxiety is more common among the elderly than young children?"

Maya cut him off. "*Is* that interesting? Sorry, Astra. You were saying?"

"It's not a sore subject," Gideon said. "I'm happy to talk about the essay. I'll talk about anything."

"I thought you said you hit a wall," Astra said.

"Astra! How many times!"

"I'd be happy to read it and give you some notes if you need a second pair of eyes," Maya offered.

"I didn't hit a wall!"

"Calm down," she said. "It's okay. I guess Dad could give you better advice, anyway."

Gideon muttered something Maya couldn't hear.

"What was that?"

"I *said*, I don't want his advice."

"Why not?"

"I don't know, maybe because he's disgraced himself and the entire medical profession?"

Maya tensed instinctively. She felt that *she* was under fire, somehow, as though Gideon were attacking *her* work performance and not their father's. "Disgraced? What do you mean? He made a mistake."

"A mistake? A *mistake*? Is that what he told you?"

"Gideon is trying to put up some boundaries between himself and the toxic people in his life," Astra said.

"And yet he's talking to our mom," Maya said.

"Can I pour anyone more wine?" Louis asked. "Or maybe . . . less?"

"What did Mom ever do?" Gideon asked.

"You mean apart from ditching Dad for her girlfriend?"

"What girlfriend?" Astra asked.

"Joan Portafoglio."

Astra shook her head. "No one has done more to weaken public schools than Joan Portafoglio."

"She has her reasons!" Gideon cried.

"Wouldn't be the first time," Maya said. She thought of telling Gideon about the Middle East and poured the syrupy wine down her throat to stop herself. She wiped her lips on her sleeve. "There's a lot you don't know about their marriage."

"Sounds like there's a lot *you* don't know," Gideon grumbled.

She stared at him in disbelief. As kids, her brother had always deferred to her. She wasn't used to seeing him stand his ground, and she didn't know how to respond.

"What's in this?" Astra asked, setting down her fork. "It's very, um—chewy!"

"Chicken," Maya said through her teeth.

Later that night, after Gideon had left, Maya lay in bed, watching car headlights sweep the ceiling.

"This day-trading stuff is interesting," Louis said. He was sitting up in bed beside her, scrolling through his phone. "Don't get me wrong, it's extremely predatory, and a lot of people could lose their shirts if they're not careful. But if you know what you're doing—and I think I do—you could walk away with a nice little nest egg."

"I can't believe my brother's siding with my mom," she said.

"It's totally free to sign up. Which, again, predatory, but I've been making out okay."

"And did you hear the way he was talking to Astra?"

Louis put down his phone. "Yeah," he said. "You shouldn't treat people that way."

"What's that supposed to mean?"

"What's what supposed to mean?"

"The way you said that sounded like an accusation."

"I'm agreeing with you!"

"You're clearly still upset about the proposal."

"Of course I'm upset! I asked you to marry me, and you said no! Do you have any idea how embarrassing that was?"

"*You* were embarrassed?" She sat up. "What about *me*?"

"What about you. What about you." Louis shook his head. "I'm going to clean up in the kitchen."

Maya turned over and listened as he shut the door behind him. She pulled the covers over her head, wishing—and hating herself for wishing—that she were in William's bed and not her own.

Maya might have spent even more time with him that fall had senior editor Myron Maple not succumbed to cancer. Myron, a member of the silent generation, had been characteristically quiet about his condition, telling only the first of his four ex-wives. The other three read about it in the *Times* along with his colleagues at the publishing house. "The man was a legend," Gabe said when he came by Maya's cubicle to share the news.

"Hardly," said Annette. "He was a total dinosaur. I heard he used to sleep with all the women working under him."

"*You* slept with someone working under you."

"Your dad owns the company, Gabe. You're basically my intern *and* my boss."

He shook his head. "The last of the old guard to go."

That afternoon, Cressida made an unusual request. She wanted Maya to clean out Myron's office, sorting through his personal effects and preserving anything that might be of value. It was far too sensitive a task for his assistant, who had been hired only a few weeks earlier and had her hands full planning a memorial service for a man she hardly knew. When Maya asked what Cressida considered valuable, her boss stared at her with eyes like burning coals until she saw herself out.

She spent most of September sorting through Myron's effects, during which time she discovered that Gabe was justified in calling the old man a legend. He'd been in the industry for seven decades, during which time he had worked with Pulitzer Prize winners and Nobel laureates, editing bestsellers and the avant-garde alike. She found carbon copies of letters to Cormac McCarthy in which the two men argued about punctuation. She found a very early draft of *To Kill a Mockingbird* in whose margins Myron had written, "Too racist?" She found the fifth known photograph of Thomas Pynchon, which Myron had apparently been using as a bookmark. This was the kind of work she could get used to, conducting what amounted to scholarly research in an archive she had all to herself. During her lunch breaks, as she unbuttoned her blouse, she shared news of the day's finds with William: a cigar box signed by Gabriel García Márquez, a bullet-riddled copy of a book by Richard Ford. William, sounding like his old, opinionated self, told her that the death of a man like Myron Maple represented the country's cultural decline, a sacrifice of standards smuggled under the guise of populist accessibility. "They don't make men like that anymore," he said, in the same wistful tone that Gabe had used when he first broke the news of Myron's death. Maya, whose taste was unfashionably canonical, saw where he was coming from. She'd have liked to be a white man in the seventies, too.

Maya had almost finished culling Myron's office when she found a shoebox perched atop his bookshelf. Standing precariously on his swivel chair, she took the shoebox down and set it on his desk. When she opened it, she found that it was full of letters to Myron, all of which appeared to be composed by the same person. The ink was fading on the oxidized paper, but Maya could make out enough telling phrases to see why he had saved them. These were *love letters*. Maya picked one up and stared at the signature, which was no more legible than the rest of the letter, trying to work out why the awful handwriting was so familiar. It was only when Cressida emailed about her expenses that Maya realized where she'd seen the signature before. Blushing, she put the letters back in the box and smuggled them back to her desk.

"Find anything good today?" asked Annette. "First edition copy of *Lolita*? Restraining order from Elizabeth Hardwick?"

Maya was not in the mood to make jokes. Despite his apparently infamous affairs, there were plenty of people who had cared about Myron; the shoebox was proof of that much, at least. At the end of the day, she slipped into Cressida's office and left it on her chair.

Myron's memorial service was held in an auditorium beneath a glass dome at the New York Public Library. The room was packed with editors from Dunning Kruger and writers Maya recognized from the dust jackets of the books she'd devoured as a teen. She stood at the back with the other assistants, behind the neat rows of chairs they'd arranged, watching the writers and editors greet one another with stiff handshakes and solemn nods. Malcolm Campbell gave the eulogy.

"Where's Cressida?" Annette whispered.

"I don't know," Maya whispered back.

"Do either of you know Myron's assistant?" Gabe asked.

Annette shook her head. "But she did an amazing job putting this together. I hope they assign her to another editor. It's not her fault Myron died."

"It can't be easy, coming to work in the morning, not knowing if or when they're going to let you go."

"Leave her alone, Gabe."

"I'll bet it's a very vulnerable time for her." He stood on his tiptoes. "Is that Don DeLillo?"

Maya excused herself to the restroom. She was no less awestruck than her fellow assistants to be standing in a room of literary luminaries, but there was something unseemly about the irregular ratio of colleagues to family members, glad-handing to grief. She shut herself inside a stall and started texting William her impressions of the service. This was an unexpected side effect of the affair, the ability to be in two places at once, the compulsion to describe her experiences at the same time she was experiencing them. She wondered if that was how it felt to be a writer, condemned to the public restrooms of the world while everyone around her went on living.

Maya had been texting for a couple of minutes when she became aware of the woman in the stall next to hers. She was letting out a low, watery whimper, the kind of sound you'd expect a wounded animal to make, and Maya felt embarrassed just to hear it. When she bent to get a better look, she thought she recognized the black boots.

"I swear it was her," she told William later as they meandered through the Midtown Barnes & Noble. "I wanted to say something, but I didn't know what. I've never seen Cressida smile, much less cry. I didn't even think she had it in her."

"First they came for the indie bookstores," William said, "and I said nothing, because I was not an indie bookstore."

"All those people paying their respects, and the only one who actually *felt* anything was stuck in the bathroom by herself."

"Then they came for the big corporate chains . . ."

"I mean it, William. I've never seen someone so alone."

He pulled a volume from the shelf in front of him and turned it over in his hands, assessing its weight. He flipped through the pages as if stress testing the binding, before putting it back. "I wonder what Myron would have thought of my novel."

"Yeah, well, now we'll never know."

"I think he would have liked it. Don't you?"

"I guess."

"The important thing is that a new generation of editors takes the reins. Don't you think?"

She was still thinking about Cressida. "Uh huh."

"I was actually going to ask if you'd considered . . ."

"Considered what?"

William laughed. "Buying my novel, of course!"

"Oh!" she said, taken aback. "I guess I hadn't thought of that before."

"But it's good, right? You said yourself that it was good. You said you loved it. You couldn't put it down."

"I'm not allowed to buy books," Maya said, defusing the panic that was ticking inside her. The prospect of working with William in a professional capacity made her sick. It was bad enough that she was cheating on Louis, but to enter into a working relationship with her lover? Or whatever he was? She'd never been happier to have so little power. "I'm too young."

"Your boss, then! Do you think he might go for it?"

"*She*—"

"Excuse me."

"—doesn't usually buy fiction."

"But if the book is as good as you said it is, I'm sure she'd make an exception."

"That's not really how it works." He seemed hurt, so she said, "What I *can* do is write you up a reader's report."

"That sounds great. How long will it take, do you think?"

"Well, I'd have to read the book again."

"You tore through it the first time."

She felt trapped between the shelves. "I'm sort of slammed right now, but I could try next week. Then I'll write up my notes, which could take another week—"

"I don't want you to do anything you're uncomfortable doing. I never have. Have I?"

She remembered the cautious placement of his hands during all those arthouse films. "You've never made me uncomfortable," she admitted.

"Forget I said anything."

"It's not that I don't *want* to help. It's just . . . my boss is kind of going through a lot right now. I'm just not sure the time is right." She also wasn't sure what the editor of *Dig Deep* would make of the story of a man whose affair with a teenager finds them both living happily ever after.

"Message received. Seriously, this conversation never happened." He looked around the store. "I can hear my stomach rumbling, and it's getting kind of late. The ball and chain is undoubtedly wondering what's keeping me. I'll say this for her, she's an excellent cook."

Maya felt him slipping away. She wanted to help, she really did. It wasn't William's fault that he was out of fashion. And she was the one who'd persuaded him to write in the first place! His success seemed to depend entirely on her.

"You know what?" she said. "Why don't I send it to my boss. Not making any promises, of course."

He turned away from her. "I don't know."

"Seriously!" she said, appealing to his denim-clad back. "After all you've done for me. This is the least I can do."

He looked over his shoulder. "Don't do it for me. I only want you to do this if you believe in the book."

"I believe!"

When William turned around again, he was holding his cell phone. "I just sent you the Word doc."

It wasn't until the subway ride home that she started to regret forwarding the manuscript. She wasn't about to risk her reputation on a novel in which she was a character. She didn't want to invite the bull of her affair into the china shop of her career. She resolved to email Cressida as soon as she had service and tell her not to bother with the novel after all. On second thought, that might not be necessary; Cressida had never trusted her taste and had no reason to do so now. She probably wouldn't even open the attachment. But when Maya got off the subway and surfaced on the sidewalk beneath a sky the color of cheap red wine, she saw that Cressida had written back. She thanked Maya for the manuscript, which she promised to read over the weekend—Myron's death, she wrote, with unusual openness, had gotten her thinking about the importance of mentorship—and which she'd already shared with the rest of the staff.

Cressida started Monday's meeting with an announcement that their parent company, McLuhan, Inc., was officially in talks to sell Dunning Kruger to Beijing Mobile, a Chinese telecom company. "I'm sure you all have questions," she said in a steely voice that bore no trace of grief, "but for the time being, I can only tell you that we intend to operate independently of Beijing Mobile, without Chinese interference, and that we will remain, in a very meaningful sense, an American company. We will continue to publish conversation-defining books from a wide variety of voices, but we will do so with the support and distribution channels of the world's second-largest economy."

With that, Cressida knit her fingers and looked around the conference table as if daring her colleagues to express their dissent. She fielded questions for the next few minutes, but Maya was too nervous about William's novel to pay close attention to the conversation. If Cressida hated it, as Maya thought she would, her future at the company was shot. But if Cressida actually *liked* the manuscript, Maya would be tasked with editing the man she was already sleeping with on company time, which seemed, at best, like a bad career move.

"Now," Cressida said, "let's see what's on the docket. Maya? Would you like to lead off?"

Maya sat on her shaking hands. "I have this novel in from an old friend," she said, trying to sound noncommittal. "I thought it was . . . interesting. I'm eager to hear what everyone thinks."

"Can I start?" Lucy said, tucking her hair behind her ears. "The opening was strong, and I thought the mom was great, but apart from her, I didn't see myself in any of the characters."

"I couldn't agree more," Cressida said. "We're asked to pity—what's his name, William?—but it's almost impossible to do so when so many of his problems are his own fault."

"All good points," Maya said, relaxing her shoulders. She pulled her hands, damp with sweat, out from under her legs. Now she wouldn't have to work with William, and she could tell him that she'd honestly tried. "I'll let him know we won't be pursuing it further."

"Who's the hero here?" Lucy asked. "I mean, who am I supposed to be rooting for?"

"It's a lot to ask a reader to spend three hundred pages with someone so unpleasant," Rebecca said.

"Got it," Maya said. "I'll let the author know."

"We should talk about the student-teacher thing," Rebecca said.

Her comment piqued Malcolm's interest. "What student-teacher thing?"

"There's a very upsetting section near the end where the protagonist seduces one of his students."

Lucy shivered with disgust. "A seventeen-year-old. A child."

"I don't know if I'd call her a *child* . . ." Maya said.

"I kept waiting for the author to acknowledge that what the character was doing is wrong," said Rebecca, who had recently published a successful novel about a woman who slaughters, cooks, and eats her ex-boyfriends.

"I'm not sure he *does* know," Lucy said. "He named the character after himself!"

"What about the girl?" Malcolm asked. "Is she game?"

"We're told that she has some problems at home, which I guess explains why she's susceptible to his advances."

"Damaged goods."

"Exactly. Her entire life is a cliché."

"No, it isn't!" Maya blushed and lowered her voice. "I agree that we could have seen more of Mackenzie, but personally, I found her interesting."

"That's fine," Lucy said. "But she still lacks dimension. The author—and I know he's a friend of yours, Maya—but in reducing Mackenzie to a stereotype, the author essentially denies her personhood."

"Students have crushes on their teachers all the time."

"That's my point. We've heard this story before."

"Speaking of Mackenzie," said Rebecca. "Did anyone else find it weird how she just goes along with it? I mean, isn't she supposed to be smart? Isn't that her entire personality?"

Cressida crossed her arms. "A stronger woman would have stood up for herself."

"Too bad she didn't read *Dig Deep*," Rebecca said.

"I just think," Maya said, making a fist under the table, "that we should all stop and think about what we were like at that age. What we would have done in her shoes. You read the novel, right, Annette? Don't you agree?"

Annette looked briefly at Maya, then at Cressida. "Speaking for myself?" she said quietly. "I wouldn't have let that happen to me."

"She *marries* him," Rebecca said. "And we're expected to believe they live happily ever after."

"Well?" said Maya, tears welling in her eyes. "So what if they do?"

"She was raped!" The word fell like a gavel in the room. "I'm just saying. The girl was seventeen when they hooked up. Technically, that's statutory rape."

Cressida picked up the papers in front of her and shuffled them against the surface of the table. "I keep asking myself: How would this play in China?"

After the meeting, Maya retreated to the vacant office and cried without exactly knowing why. She felt a rush of tenderness toward her younger self. She wanted to cradle that girl's head in her arms.

She found Gabe at her desk when she got back. "Idiots," he said. "They're all a bunch of idiots."

"Thanks," she said, still blinking back tears. "I actually didn't like the manuscript, either."

"Fucking China. I mean, what the hell is my dad thinking?"

"I didn't think everyone would hate the characters so much."

"Maybe it's time to jump ship. This is a dying industry."

"We shouldn't reject the book because it's controversial. We should reject the book because no one wants to read it!"

"Or I could learn Mandarin."

"What are you talking about?" Maya asked.

"What are *you* talking about?"

The door to Cressida's office opened. "Maya?" she said. "Can I see you for a minute?"

"Nice knowing you," Gabe said.

Maya walked into Cressida's office and closed the door behind her. If she could quit before Cressida fired her, she thought, she could preserve whatever scraps of her dignity remained. "Before you say anything," she began, "I want you to know that I've given it some thought, and I've decided to—"

"Sit."

Cressida took a seat behind her desk. Her skin was smooth and elastic in the natural light that poured in through the picture windows. There was a wall of books behind her, with the jackets facing out beside pictures of her with Salman Rushdie and Obama.

"I remember the first book I tried to buy," she said. Her voice was softer, more wistful than Maya was used to. "A weight-loss book by a California fitness guru. *To Live and Diet in L.A.* Much to my dismay, my bosses wouldn't bite. They were brilliant, most of them, with tremendous careers, but they were behind the times. Out of touch. They were, to be frank, simply too *old* to know what worked and what didn't. We wound up passing, and a different house bought the manuscript. They sold more than a million copies."

"So you're saying I *should* buy the novel?"

Cressida furrowed her brow, and for a moment, her forehead erupted in folds. "Of course not. It's extremely offensive. What I'm trying to tell you, Maya, is that I know what it's like to be young in this business." She opened the drawer of her desk and produced a small white envelope. "I want you to have this."

Maya accepted the envelope and opened it. Inside was a silver American Express card with the words DUNNING KRUGER PRESS embossed on the surface. It seemed to be made of metal, rather than plastic, and sat cold and heavy in her hands.

"This, Maya, is a company card. Consider it a vote of confidence. A passport to the next phase of your career. You can expense meals and drinks—up to a point, of course. I want you to start taking young agents out. Go to readings. Go to parties. See what's new. Dig deep."

"I thought you said we had to tighten our belts."

"The Chinese are going to do a number on this place. But those of us who make the cut will flourish."

"At the risk of sounding ungrateful, why me? Annette has been here longer."

"Annette has never brought a manuscript to my attention. She's a competent assistant, but she doesn't have what it takes to make it as an editor. She's too timid. She's too *nice*. You, on the other hand, are a terrible assistant. But I liked the way you handled yourself back there. You're tough. You have ambition. You remind me of me." She swallowed. "And I appreciate the work you did on Myron's office."

Maya shook her head in disbelief. "I don't know what to say."

"Say, 'I'm going to acquire a number of franchisable multi-platform properties that will perform well in the Asian markets."

"I'm going acquire a number of franchisable multi-platform properties . . ."

"That will perform well in the Asian markets."

"In the Asian markets. Right."

"Good. Now get to it."

The overhead lights burnished the brushed steel surface of the credit card. "Thank you," Maya said, slipping it into her pocket. "I won't disappoint you."

"Better not."

Maya felt weightless as she walked back to her desk. After months of floundering at work, months of wondering why she seemed so out of step with her colleagues, why she struggled with the simplest administrative tasks, wondering what on earth she was qualified to do if not read and evaluate books, she had received the exact kind of affirmation that had been missing in her life since she left school. The credit card, like the good grades she had earned as a student, made her feel like a person of value and worth.

"What was that all about?" Annette asked.

Maya looked over the cubicle wall at the so-called friend who had left her hanging in the meeting. "Not much. Got a company card."

"You *what*?"

Maya flashed the Amex. "She said she sees herself in me."

"Congratulations," Annette said softly before excusing herself and hurrying toward the vacant office where Maya had cried fifteen minutes earlier.

Maya started working harder than she had in years. She scheduled drinks with young literary agents, trading useless gossip from her office in exchange for useful gossip from theirs. She subscribed to *Granta*, *n+1*, *Tin House*, *ZYZZYVA*, and *Ploughshares*, and put the subscriptions on the company card. She trawled for talent in the New Directions catalog, the Graywolf catalog, the Counterpoint catalog. She read five years of O. Henry and Pushcart Prize anthologies. She followed *Publishers Lunch*. She attended grad student readings at the New School and haunted the Lillian Vernon house at NYU. She drank white wine in plastic cups served by too-beautiful interns at *Paris Review* parties. She joined the company softball team, where she played catcher and led in RBIs, helping deliver a long-sought-after victory against Simon & Schuster.

One consequence of all this work was that she hardly had any time left to see William. She let his texts sit unanswered for days, and when she did write back, she could honestly say she'd been too busy to respond. She remembered a passage from *Dig Deep*, in which a recently divorced Karen Wolfgang wrote about the joys of being "married to your job." On first read, Maya had winced at the wording, which sounded to her like corporatist rhetoric dressed up as female

empowerment. Now she felt Wolfgang was onto something. The
Amex couldn't stroke her hair or make her come—though she did
feel a stab of pleasure when she swiped it—but the confidence it gave
her almost made him redundant.

After avoiding William for a few weeks, during which time Maya
acquired her first manuscript, a young adult novel about a levitating
orphan, Sadie invited her out to the Hamptons. It was early November, and cold—Sadie's family would shortly close the house down for
the season—but Maya was desperate to get out of the city, away from
William and the mess she'd made of things with Louis. She caught
the Jitney after work one Friday and debarked at the medical spa that
marks the Water Mill stop.

"Aah!" Sadie squealed. "I haven't seen you in *forever.*"

"I missed you, too," Maya said. She'd been so consumed by William, and by work, that she hadn't spoken to Sadie in months. "I'm
sorry if I've been a little out of the loop."

"Please," she said. "You have literally nothing to apologize for."

It was a short drive to Sadie's Hamptons house, which, like its
neighbors, was hidden from the street by an imposing wall of hedges.
Maya had never understood why people in the Hamptons took pains
to hide such stunning property, but now, as they pulled up to the
porch, she saw the appeal in keeping life at arm's length. The hedges
blocked the view in both directions.

They were greeted on the porch by Sadie's father, Geert. "Maya
Greenshpahn!" he said. "My dotter from anotter motter!"

"Dad," Sadie said. "You're embarrassing yourself."

Geert had what Maya thought of as a European face, with pink
skin, narrow lips, and a nose like a church bell. With his rectangular

glasses and sparse blond hair, he looked like he belonged negotiating farm subsidies for the EU, not cutting throats in commercial real estate. His calves were hairless beneath his madras shorts.

"It's good to see you, Mr. van den Berg," Maya said.

"Tell us, Maya, vere are you living now?"

"I'm renting a place in the Lower East Side."

"Not Brooklyn? I hear all de youngshters live in Brooklyn."

"My boyfriend and I both work in the city."

"Have de youngshters dishcovered Brownshville yet? I vould like to shnap it up before dey do."

"Daddy," Sadie said. "No talking business on vacation."

He pulled his daughter close and kissed her head. "She ish alvays reminding me who ish really in charge."

Maya dropped her things inside and followed Sadie out to the backyard. It was too cold to swim, so they sat by the edge of the pool with their legs in the water, numb to their knees, and before long Maya was talking about William. She hadn't realized how desperate she was to tell someone, anyone, about the affair.

"First of all," Sadie said when she had finished, "big congrats on the promotion."

Maya shrugged. "It's just a company card."

"Are you kidding? I'd *kill* for a company card. I'm trying to negotiate a raise right now, but my boss is being a total dick about it."

"Don't you work for your dad?"

"And he's being a dick! As for the affair . . . I guess the body wants what it wants. My poli-sci professor told me that."

"In what context did that come up?"

Sadie smiled. "Never mind. But so, what about Louis?"

"Things have been pretty awkward between us since I turned down his marriage proposal."

"You *what?*"

"He asked me to marry him, and I said no. I think he's been mad at me ever since. *I've* been mad at me ever since."

"Why did you say no?"

"I don't know, because we're too young? Because it's a huge commitment? I thought you of all people would back me up on this."

"You don't want to lose what you have with Louis. Trust me. Anyway, it's not about who you're with," Sadie said. "It's about what you build together. My poli-sci professor told me that one, too."

"I can't believe what I'm hearing."

"I'd kill for a guy like Louis. Any guy, really. Girls like me went out with the Bush administration. Nothing says 'Iraq war' like big tits and flat asses. Thanks, Obama."

"You think I should have said yes."

"Do you love him?"

"Of course I do."

"Last I checked, he loves you, too." Dead leaves floated on the surface of the water, rocking gently on the ripples Sadie's kicking feet produced. "You're lucky, you know. No one's ever loved me like that before."

Geert grilled four enormous steaks for dinner that his wife, Sheri, served on beds of leafy greens. He circled the table, refilling Maya's wineglass while Sheri reminded her to save room for dessert. Maya wondered what it would be like to belong to Sadie's family; to enjoy, without guilt, all the pleasures of her privilege. To love and be loved by people who conserved their generosity just for her.

She got her answer early the next morning when she was violently evicted from her sleep by the most vicious hangover of her entire life. She spent the next hour on her knees before the toilet, trying to expel the poison she had poured into herself. Her head was buried in the bowl when William called.

"Hello?" she croaked, recoiling at the smell of her own breath.

"Hey," he said. "I'm outside."

She squinted at the light streaming through the bathroom window. It seemed to be composed of tiny glass particles; she could feel each one pricking her eyes. "I'm not at home. I'm in the Hamptons."

"I know," he said. "I'm outside."

Maya sat up, and the room sat up with her. Her neck felt too soft to support her head, which had apparently received a lead injection overnight, and when she opened her mouth in front of the mirror, she found a yellow fungus growing on her tongue.

"Are you coming out?" he asked. "Or should I ring the bell?"

The thought of William waking her hosts helped dissipate the fog of her hangover. "Don't do anything," she said. "I'm coming out."

After vigorously brushing her teeth, and her tongue, she dragged herself downstairs and out the front door, where she found William waiting on the gravel drive. He looked out of place in the manicured morning, with his chapped hands and stubbled cheeks, the faded denim jacket on his shoulders.

"Nice place," he said.

"What are you doing here?" she asked, her voice throttled with phlegm.

"What do you mean? You told me to come!"

She motioned with her hands for him to keep his voice down. "I have no idea what you're talking about."

He handed her his phone. There, on the screen, was irrefutable proof that she'd not only asked but begged that William come to see her. She had even sent him Sadie's address, a remarkable feat considering the many misspelled texts that preceded it. Her stomach sunk.

"You shouldn't have come," she said. "I was drunk."

"How was I supposed to know that you were drunk?"

"These are the texts of a severely incapacitated person."

"I thought maybe there was news about the book."

Maya swallowed. She would have to tell him sometime. "Actually," she said, "there is."

"Really?"

She pursed her lips. "I'm sorry, William."

His cheeks flushed, and his eyebrows knit together. He looked like he couldn't decide whether to be angry or defensive or ashamed. "Your boss didn't like it? Why not?"

Sadie's dog, Darius, had deposited a large yellow turd just a few feet away. She suppressed the swell of acid in her throat. "I can't get into it right now."

"Was it the ending? Does he want me to change the ending?"

"*She* just didn't think—" Maya stopped herself. "This really isn't the best time, William."

"It's cold," he said. "Let's go inside. I want to know everything she said. And I want to know everything you said back."

"It's not my house, William. I'm a guest here, too. I can't just invite people over."

"But that's exactly what you did."

"I'm sorry, but you can't come in. I'll call you when I'm back in the city, okay?"

"I took a cab out here, Maya," he said, raising his voice. "I've been on the road for hours. Not to mention the three hundred dollars it cost me. Six hundred, with the return trip. And now that I can't count on an advance . . ."

If she stood there any longer, she was certain she would puke. "Okay," she said. "Here's what we're going to do."

She let herself back into the house, turning the knob slowly, wincing as the door wheezed open. When she returned, she held Cressida's Amex between her fingers.

"What's this?" William asked.

"Take a cab home. On me."

"I'm not taking your money, Maya."

"It's not my money. It's a company card. Take a cab, take a bus, take a helicopter. Whatever gets you back. I don't want to wake up Sadie's parents."

William weighed the card in his hand. "She really didn't like the book?"

Birds had started singing in the woods behind the house, insistent in their optimism, loud enough to wake a light sleeper. "She liked it, William. We all liked it. Okay? It was just too edgy to publish. Too raw. You know how risk averse publishers can be."

"Okay," he said after a moment. "Call me when you get back to New York."

Maya waited until he'd cleared the archway carved into the hedges before she went back inside. She tiptoed up the stairs, not wanting to wake her hosts, but when she got to her room, she found Sadie lying sprawled across her bed.

"Was that him?" Sadie asked.

"Was what who?"

"I have a very big window in my room, you know. With a wonder-ful view of the driveway."

Maya flopped down on the bed beside her. "Yeah, that was him."

"Eek!" Sadie squealed. She seized her phone. "What's his name again?"

"William Slate. He's not on Facebook."

"Is this him?" Sadie held up her phone. William had apparently made a LinkedIn profile. The photo wasn't flattering. He was wear-ing a sweater over a shirt and tie and seemed to be squinting behind his glasses. Maya scrolled down the page. Her heart skipped when she saw, under the heading EXPERIENCE, the name of her high school.

"Yeah," she said. "That's him. You're fast."

"I've stalked a lot of guys." Sadie took the phone back. "You said he was married, right?"

"Yeah, but I don't know her name or anything."

"Mackenzie, maybe?"

Maya froze. "What makes you say that?"

"I ran a reverse image search on his LinkedIn photo, and this came up. It's from some girl Mackenzie's Instagram."

On Sadie's screen, Maya saw a picture of William at the beach—he looked all wrong, pale and skinny in his swimsuit, set against the soothing backdrop of the sea—with his arm around a much-younger-looking woman. A blond woman with what could only be described as a "small, delicately upturned nose."

Sadie scrolled. "Studies acting at Tisch," she said. "Went to Milton Academy. Hey! She's from Massachusetts, too!"

Further scrolling confirmed the suspicions that had already started churning in Maya's stomach: that William's wife was named Mackenzie; that she had been his student at Milton Academy; and that she, not Maya, was the basis for the love interest in his novel. This last blow was delivered with such force that it threatened to split Maya's skull. She trained her thoughts on the smaller, manageable disappointment of not having been able to uncover it herself.

"I tried to find her online, too, but I never could."

"Maybe, subconsciously, you didn't want to find it."

Maya swallowed. "Right."

"Are you feeling all right? Your skin is, like, completely yellow."

"Give me a second," Maya said. She walked briskly to the bathroom down the hall and threw up.

She'd hardly settled into her desk on Monday morning when Cressida called her into her office. "It's been brought to my attention that there have been some unusual charges on your company card," she said, without inviting Maya to sit.

"I had to take the bus back from the Hamptons," Maya said. She hoped that Cressida could relate to this particular problem. "I'll reimburse the company, of course."

"The bus I could imagine myself overlooking, but I'm seeing a charge for the Bridgehampton Inn & Restaurant? The Duck Walk Vineyard?"

"Vineyard, you said?" She wondered if William had fallen off the wagon.

"It sounds like you had quite the weekend."

"You don't understand," Maya said. "That wasn't me!"

"You weren't in the Hamptons this weekend?"

"I *was*, but I didn't make those charges."

"So the card was stolen."

"Exactly," she said. "I was mugged."

"In the Hamptons."

Clouds were massing in the sky outside. "I know it sounds strange, but you have to believe me."

"I'd really love to," Cressida said. "But last week, I stopped into my local bookstore and found this." She picked a copy of Monty's book off her desk. "Autographed and everything."

Maya swallowed. "That's not mine."

"So it's inscribed to a *different* 'beguiling specimen'? You're supposed to be buying books, Maya. Not pawning them off. That's the whole point of the company card."

"I sold it *before* I got the company card."

"So you did sell it! Well, that's one mystery solved. On to number two. Where's the Amex?"

"It was stolen. I swear. You have to believe me."

"Because we've just established your reputation for honesty."

"I should probably be getting back to work," Maya said.

"Don't bother. You're fired. And at your next job? If you pawn company property? Maybe don't do it in your boss's neighborhood."

A woman from Human Resources who looked even younger than Maya was waiting at her desk with a cardboard box. "This is so weird for me," she said. "Usually, they fire people at the *end* of the week."

The subway ride seemed to take longer than usual. When she surfaced, she saw that it had started to rain, the drops hard and cold against the nape of her neck. She took out her phone and called her mother.

Deb answered on the second ring. "Maya! Hi!"

"Hi, Mom."

"What's wrong? Are you at work?"

"I'm all right."

"Are you okay, honey? You don't sound like yourself."

Maya steadied her voice, which had started to shake. "I'm fine. Just a head cold is all."

"I'll order a thing of chicken soup to your apartment. You shouldn't cook if you aren't feeling well."

"You don't have to do that, Mom."

"I'm sending the soup. You don't have to eat it, but I'm sending the soup."

"Thanks."

"What's going on?"

"Nothing," Maya said. "I just wanted to hear your voice."

It was pouring by the time Maya got to her apartment. When she let herself in, she found, to her surprise, a paper cone of roses on the counter. Louis stepped out from the bedroom. "Those are for you."

Maya wiped the wet hair out of her eyes. "For me? Why?"

"I'm sorry about how I've been acting lately."

"*You're* sorry?"

"I put you on the spot when I proposed. I shouldn't have. And ever since, I've been acting like a jerk."

She looked around the living room. "Where's your gaming chair?"

"I disassembled it and brought it back to the store. The guy gave me a really hard time, too, but I told him I was writing a piece about customer service for *The New York Times*. Pro tip: you can get away with anything in this city if you tell people you work for the *Times*."

She felt a spasm in her chest, and she started to cry. "Oh, Louis," she said. "You didn't have to do that."

"You like roses, right? I wasn't sure about your favorite flower, and the guy on the subway only had roses, but he said they're romantic, which I obviously know, but—" He looked up at her. "What's the matter?"

She spoke haltingly through hiccuping sobs. "I'm . . . *hic* . . . the . . . *hic* . . . one . . . *hic* . . . who . . . *hic* . . . should . . . *hic* . . . be . . . *hic* . . . sorry!"

"Why? You didn't do anything wrong."

Maya fell to her knees. "Marry me," she said.

The
Resettlement
Committee

•

Freezing rain had been falling all month, boring holes in the banks of smog-licked snow outside the synagogue. Deb ducked beneath the Damoclean icicles dangling from the roof, avoiding eye contact with the two security guards standing sentry on the front steps. (She objected to the presence of the guards, and their guns, which, if anything, made her feel *less* safe each time she stepped inside the building.) The synagogue, one of Boston's oldest, was a limestone edifice with four ionic columns and a soaring atrium that humbled every soul that passed beneath it. Black-and-white portraits of disapproving rabbis frowned at Deb, who was not in need of further humbling, as she hurried down the hall. She found the rest of the Resettlement Committee sitting around a large wood table in the library. Their chatter died out as Deb entered the room, so suddenly that she wondered if they'd been talking about her.

"I'm sorry I'm late," she said and sat next to Gail Sacks, who poured her a glass of red wine.

"Don't worry, honey," said Yotam Brav. He lifted a pair of tortoiseshell glasses off his head and placed them on his nose. "You know we'd never start without you."

Deb had founded the Resettlement Committee after Maya left for college and she realized, with a start, that her days as a full-time parent were numbered. She devoted most of her free time to the committee, organizing canned food and clothing drives for immigrants newly arrived to the city. For the past year, she'd worked exclusively with the Nassers, a Syrian family displaced by the civil war. The Nassers' case was complex—it was the first time Deb had worked with refugees as opposed to immigrants—and the committee members met each month to update one another on their progress.

The Norman Goldlust Memorial Library was the pride of the synagogue, with a vast collection of books in print and on CD—more than half of the congregants were over sixty-five, a demographic that had not yet abandoned compact discs—and a special section on adolescent health, which featured such titles as *Welcome to the Red Tent* and *Pimples on My Punim*. Deb draped her coat over the back of her chair. "Avital?" she said. "What's the latest?"

"I'm afraid I don't have any news since last month's meeting," squeaked Avital Oberbrunner, a mousy woman who ran the only tearoom in Boston authorized to serve Mariage Frères. "The Nassers are still at the UNHCR camp in Jordan. We're waiting on the Department of Homeland Security to finish vetting them."

"What's to vet?" Yotam scoffed. "They're refugees!"

Avital hung her head. "I know. I'm so sorry."

"Don't apologize, Avital. It's not your fault."

"I can't believe we still *have* a Department of Homeland Security," Gail said.

Yotam snapped his fingers in agreement. "Remember the color-coded threat levels?"

Karla remembered. "Whenever Bush was falling in the polls, they'd raise it to red. Scare us all into submission."

"I could never keep track. Orange, amber, crimson, scarlet—"

"Maroon!" Avital cried, joining in the fun.

"Vermillion—"

"Burgundy! Merlot!"

"Easy, Avital. Now you're naming wines."

"All right," Deb said. "Let's focus up." She usually looked forward to the monthly meetings of the Resettlement Committee, but it had been a long day—a long five months, really—and Deb was exhausted. Her contacts were dry, and her bra was digging into her back. These were petty grievances compared with those of, say, the Nasser family, who had been living in a refugee camp for eight months, but knowing of the Nassers' troubles didn't help alleviate Deb's. It was a problem she'd encountered countless times in her years of civic service, the problem of relative suffering. "Yotam, where are we on the apartment front?"

"Excuse me," Karla said. "Before we dive in, I wanted to bring something to the committee's attention."

Deb rubbed the corners of her eyes. "What is it, Karla?"

"I was listening to NPR the other day, and I heard a very unsettling story that I feel is pertinent to the committee." She took a slow, deliberate sip of wine, relishing the rapt silence of her audience before setting down the glass. "There is, apparently, a conspiracy theory taking root in some extremist circles. The theory holds that Jews are colluding to bring immigrants to America, leading to the replacement, and eventual destruction, of the so-called white race."

Avital gasped. "That's exactly what *we* do!"

"No, it isn't," Deb cut in. "We help people in need. We aren't 'replacing' anyone."

"But we *are* a group of Jews colluding to bring immigrants to the US," Karla said. "I stand by the work we do here, of course, but I thought this was something we might want to get ahead of."

"First of all, I'd hardly call this 'colluding.' Second, I don't think it's wise to waste our breath on this ridiculous idea. Conspiracies are like fire. They need oxygen to spread. Now, if we could just—"

"I heard the story, too," Gail said. She looked apologetically at Deb. "I wonder if we might at least consider a rebrand? Starting with our name."

"What's wrong with the name?" Deb asked.

"I've always felt 'resettlement' sounded a little sinister."

"'Committee' is sinister, too," Yotam said. "Très Soviet."

Deb rubbed her eyes. "We don't have time for this."

"How about if we were called something nice? Something like, I don't know, Friends of America?"

"Friends *in* America would be more accurate," Gail said.

"Hands Across America?" Avital suggested.

"I'm pretty sure that's taken. Anyway, we're reaching out to people overseas."

"Hands Across the Water, then."

"Like the Paul McCartney song?"

"Enough!" Deb snapped. A custodian in the hall outside the library looked up from his work. "I don't care *what* we call ourselves. I'm pretty sure the Nassers don't care, either. Now we can sit around all day coming up with names, or we can help this poor family find a home. Okay?" She cast her eyes around the table. "Good. Now, if I'm not mistaken, Yotam was going to tell us about apartments."

Yotam, a real estate broker, said he'd found a few properties for rent in Roxbury but couldn't take any concrete steps until he knew when the Nassers were due to arrive. "The landlords won't wait around forever," he said, "and we don't have the funds to pay rent on an empty apartment."

"Roxbury?" Karla said, wrinkling her nose. "We can't do any better than that?"

"What's wrong with Roxbury?" Deb asked. Not content to disrupt the meeting once, Karla was apparently going for a new personal record.

"I'm just worried it isn't entirely *safe*."

"Safer than Syria," Yotam said. "Safer than a refugee camp."

"Send me the addresses, Yotam," Deb said. "I'll check the apartments myself."

"You don't have to do that, Deb."

"It's really no problem." She trained her eyes on Karla and narrowed them. "I'm not going to send a family of refugees to live in a neighborhood I wouldn't feel comfortable visiting myself."

"It isn't that," said Gail Sacks.

There it was again, the sense that they'd been talking about her. "So what is it, then?"

"You've just seemed so . . . *busy* lately. We don't want you to feel overwhelmed."

"Who says I'm overwhelmed?"

"Please," Yotam said. "You and Scott split what, four months ago? Five? We're just trying to be sensitive to the fact that you might have your hands full at the moment."

"What does my husband have to do with the Resettlement Committee?"

"Nothing, Deb. Nothing at all. But with all that's going on in your personal life—"

"My personal life is fine, thank you."

"—and your finances—"

"What about them?"

"—exploring your sexuality—"

"My *what*?"

"If you needed a break, we'd understand," Karla said. "You're a human being, after all. You're not Wonder Woman."

"I *am* Wonder Woman!" Deb shouted, slamming her fist on the table. Her glass tipped, splashing red wine across the surface. Mortified, she jumped out of her seat and snatched a roll of paper towels from behind the checkout desk. "I'm so sorry," she said, mopping up the mess while the rest of the committee looked on. "I don't know what came over me."

"We were talking before you got here," Karla said, "and we think that it might be best for everyone if we switched things up a little bit."

Deb made a fist around the sodden paper towel. "Switch things up how?"

"As in, maybe it's time for a change. Time for someone else to take the lead. Until things on your end are a little more . . . *stable*."

Deb had founded the committee on the democratic principle that leaders must be elected, not appointed, though she had chaired it with unanimous support since its inception.

"Oh?" she said. "And who exactly did you have in mind?"

Karla cocked her head. "Well! I hadn't thought of that. I suppose *I* could take over, if no one else objects. And, if elected to a leadership position, I promise to appoint a subcommittee to look into a rebrand. War with white supremacists is the *last* thing we need."

"Seconded!" Yotam said, then caught himself. "Wait. Was that a formal motion? Do we need someone to second?"

"We have a protocol for this," Avital said. "But I can't remember what it is."

"What about term limits?" Gail asked. "Did we establish term limits?"

"It's in the bylaws."

"We have bylaws?"

Yotam ran a hand over his head. "Surely *one* of us remembers how this works."

Deb dropped the last of the paper towels in the wastebasket. "I remember."

"Well?" Karla said. "What's the protocol, then?"

It was one thing for Karla to stab her in the back. It was another thing to ask Deb where she kept the knives.

"I'd be happy to tell you how the process works," she said.

"Tell us!"

"According to section three of our bylaws," Deb began, referring to documents that didn't exist, "a committee member must formally announce her intention to run for a leadership position five weeks—excuse me, *nine* weeks—before a vote is held."

"But we meet monthly," Karla said.

"That's right. So we'll hold the vote in, let's see . . . March."

"March? The Nassers could be here by then!"

"And who better than you, Karla, to greet them?"

Karla crossed her arms. "I'm going to look up those bylaws."

"Of course," Deb said, nodding in the direction of the library's record room. "They're in the archives. Shouldn't be too hard to find."

She drove home in a rage. It was Deb who had founded the Resettlement Committee and Deb who had recruited its members, including Karla. It was Deb who had written to the State Department, and it was Deb who had emailed back and forth with the officials at the UNHCR. She had tapped every resource at her disposal to ensure

that the Nassers' application for asylum was approved by the Department of Homeland Security. To lose that momentum now was
unthinkable. Her bit about the bylaws would buy her some time, but
now she had less than three months to get the Nassers to Boston,
install them in a cozy apartment, somewhere *safe*, and provide for
them such a wealth of American opportunity that Yotam, Avital,
and Gail would have no choice but to grant Deb a second term.
The prospect of losing her leadership of the committee after losing,
in a sense, her husband and her home only added to Deb's feeling
that her life, so peaceful only six months earlier, had taken up arms
against her.

She was still cursing Karla when she parked outside her house. All
December, the city had shone white, but the snow that lined her lawn
now looked like soiled toilet paper. Here and there, patches of grass
poked through, pale and starved for sun. One of the front steps was
lacquered with ice, and she made a mental note to salt it later.

"I'm home!" she called, closing the front door behind her. As a
touring dancer, Deb had grown accustomed to crashing on strange
couches and sleeping in her car, going so far as to develop an exercise
routine that could be done from the passenger seat. She was reluctant, at first, to purchase a house, the commitment embodied by all
that brick and timber, the fixedness of the future it seemed to suggest.
But then she'd seen the house on Crowninshield Road, the Queen
Anne with its squat columns and cross-gabled roof, the fresh coat of
cheery yellow paint. It was everything she'd wanted in a house: sin-
gular yet stable, eccentric yet secure, the kind of place that made you
wonder what kind of interesting people lived inside it.

"What are you doing here?" her husband asked.

Scott stood before her in a pair of sweatpants and the tattered

Pfizer T-shirt he refused to throw away. He held a sunny orange cocktail in his hand, a little blue umbrella bobbing at the surface.

"What do you mean, what am I doing here?"

Scott shut his eyes for a moment. When he opened them, he seemed surprised to discover that she was not a figment of his imagination. "I didn't think you lived here anymore."

The color drained from Deb's cheeks. She'd been so consumed with work, with the synagogue, with Karla, that instead of driving to Joan's apartment, where she lived, she had come instead to the house that she'd abandoned along with Scott back in September.

"I'm so sorry. I must have made a mistake."

He raised his right eyebrow. "A mistake."

"Oh god, this is too embarrassing. Honestly, I didn't mean to barge in on you like this."

"Well, you're here now," he said and raised his glass. "Can I make you a drink? Stop & Shop had cream of coconut on sale."

Deb still couldn't believe her mistake. "Sure," she said. "If you really don't mind."

She watched Scott pour, with scientific precision, the rum and the juice into a measuring cup, crouching to check the quantity against the hash marks. She saw him suddenly as a little boy, playing with his very first chemistry set, and the thought of that boy, discovering for the first time the joy of discovery itself, made her heart ache.

He poured the contents of the measuring cup into a cocktail shaker and then into a glass of crushed ice. Before handing her the glass, he rooted around in the pantry until he found a cocktail umbrella.

"Thanks," she said and took a sip. A streak of color flashed across her tongue. "Scott! This is *good*! Really takes your mind off the weather."

"Exactly."

"Have you heard anything about your license?" she asked. "I don't mean to ask a loaded question. I just wondered—I do wonder—how you've been holding up."

He took a long, slow sip, as though the cocktail contained the resources required to answer her question. "The good news, though 'good' is a relative term, is that it doesn't look like the FDA's criminal investigation office is going to get involved. But they're likely to take me off the registry of physicians who can conduct clinical trials. So even if I *do* get my license back, my research career is effectively finished." He looked away from her. "Carol left."

"Oh, Scott. I'm so sorry."

"I fucked up. I *know* I fucked up. But I didn't do anything physicians don't do all the time in other parts of the world. Everyone knows that. Big Pharma knows that. Bribery, fraud—these things are baked into the system. For the FDA to hound me like this . . ." His hands were shaking. He set his drink on the counter. "You know where they get their money? The FDA?"

"The federal government."

"That's half their budget. *Half.* The other half comes from charging fees to drug companies. They're *funded by the industry they regulate.* And guess who sits on the advisory committees? Consultants for drug companies! It's no wonder half of Cape Cod is hooked on OxyContin!"

"I didn't mean to upset you."

"Remember all the trips we used to take? Remember Big Sky?"

"I twisted my ankle on the slopes," she said, buried momentarily in an avalanche of memories. "You rode down the mountain on the lift with me. I remember how funny it felt, the two of us in that chair, going down the mountain in the wrong direction. Everyone was staring at us on their way up."

Scott was not in such a sentimental mood. "You know who paid for that trip? Johnson & Johnson!"

"Karla tried to sabotage me today."

Her statement succeeded in disarming him. "She did?"

"She wants to take control of the Resettlement Committee."

"But that's *your* committee!"

A smile flickered across her lips. She could still count on Scott to take her side. "The Nassers, the refugee family I've been working with, are stuck in Jordan," she explained. "Unless their applications are approved, and soon, the rest of the group is bound to vote her in on the grounds that I'm not doing enough. Never mind all the work I *have* done. Never mind that at this point it's out of my hands."

"The Nassers are doomed if Karla takes over."

"Thank you! I know!"

"You know what you could do is call my mom."

"Marjorie? Why?"

"There are a lot of ex-diplomats at Green Pastures. Ex-ambassadors. It's the place where foreign policy goes to die."

"You think she knows anyone from the State Department?"

"She plays mah-jongg with the State Department every Tuesday. It's a whole scene over there. I spent an hour on the phone with the former deputy managing director of the IMF."

"Why?"

"He's worried about his upcoming heart transplant."

"What did you tell him?"

"I said I thought you had to be heartless to work for the IMF."

She set her empty glass on the counter, next to a pile of mail. "I should probably get going," she said. "I'm sorry, again, for barging in."

"You're leaving?"

"I don't want to intrude, and besides, it's been a long day as it is."

"Last I checked, you can't intrude on your own house." Scott pursed his lips. "I miss you, you know."

"I miss you, too." A part of her felt compelled to stay—it was, as Scott said, her house, too, and it felt more inviting, more familiar to her, than Joan's apartment—but she was afraid of what might happen if she did. It seemed likely that if she moved back in with Scott, she would find herself stranded in the quagmire of secrecy and betrayal that had caused her to leave in the first place. What's more, it would prove her to be the fickle, flighty woman that she worried she was, someone who skipped from one set of problems to another, and that was not a person she could bear to be. "I really should go," she said, turning away from her husband's plaintive expression. She pushed open the storm door. "Thanks again for the drink."

The wind had picked up and started to squall, forcing Deb to drive well below the speed limit as she navigated Boston's narrow, snow-packed streets. She was doubtful that Marjorie's friends could help her—they were retired by virtue of their living at Green Pastures, a facility which, on account of its cost, had only caused her family grief—and even if they could help, she didn't particularly like the thought of being in her mother-in-law's debt. But with the Nassers stuck in Jordan, and Karla plotting to depose her, she felt she had no other choice.

"Deborah!" Marjorie cried, so loud she might have been sitting in the passenger seat. "What a happy surprise!"

Deb held the phone away from her ear. "It's good to hear your voice, Marjorie. Is this a bad time?"

"It's never a bad time, dear. The girls and I are just watching *Property Brothers*."

"I'm happy to try again later," Deb said. She was already regretting having called.

"I always have time for my favorite daughter-in-law."

"Your only daughter-in-law. How are you, Marjorie?"

Deb drove in silence, watching the road, while Marjorie talked about life at Green Pastures: her social rivals, her death-obsessed roommate, the "woman doctor" she suspected of flirting her way into residents' wills. The flurries came fast, great swarms of snow that rode the currents of the wind like a plague of locusts.

"I need to ask you a favor," Deb said during a brief lull while Marjorie paused to catch her breath. "I was just talking to Scott, and he mentioned—"

"Oh! Oh! You two are talking again?"

"We never stopped, Marjorie."

"So you changed your mind and took him back?"

"First of all—"

"Or are you still shtupping that Italian meatball?"

"Marjorie!"

"You know he misses you. He calls me all the time. He says, with tears in his eyes, 'I miss my wife.'"

Deb wondered momentarily if this could be true. "This isn't why I called."

"I'm sorry, dear. How can I help?"

Stalled by the crawl of Back Bay traffic, Deb explained the situation with the Nassers. "I know it's a long shot, but I wouldn't ask if it wasn't serious."

"That much, I believe."

"Don't do it for me. Do it for the Nassers. They've been through enough as it is."

"I'll talk to some people. See what I can do. My friend Fern here had a long career at the UN."

"Thank you, Marjorie. You don't know how much this means to me."

"But I am going to ask something in return."

"Oh?"

"I've never asked you for anything before, but I need to ask you something now."

She had done Marjorie a million favors, but no matter. "Of course," she said. "Anything."

"I'm asking you to forgive my son. Whatever happened between you two is not my business—though I do have a few theories of my own—but there is nothing, *nothing*, that cannot be overcome by two people who love each other. I know that I can be difficult sometimes, but I want you to hear me all the same. Dr. Greenspan is a good man. He's miserable without you. So please, for his sake, for the children's sake, for mine, I'm asking you, Deborah, to forgive him."

Deb pulled into a parking spot in the public alley behind Joan's apartment. "I'm sorry, Marjorie. I can't promise you that."

"No, no. You can't promise that. But you'll try. Please, dear, tell me you'll try."

From the alley, she could see up into Joan's apartment, the lighted window glowing in the dark.

"Yes, Marjorie," she said. "I'll try."

For twenty-five years, her mother-in-law had seized every opportunity to blow up her marriage, unleashing an arsenal of slights and provocations directed at Deb's self-esteem. She didn't understand why Marjorie had changed her mind, especially now that she and Scott had separated. Maybe Marjorie was putting Scott's wishes before her own. Maybe he really was miserable without her.

Deb let herself into Joan's apartment—double-checking that this was, in fact, Joan's apartment—dropped her bag and dragged herself into the living room. "You would *not* believe my day," she said, collapsing onto the sofa, the white cushions soft as clouds.

"I was starting to worry about you, Greenspan," Joan said, pacing back and forth before the decommissioned fireplace. The only daughter of a retired Army Ranger, Joan called DeLuca's on Newbury Street "the commissary" and referred to her intimates by their last names. "Help me with something. What sounds better: 'underserved' or 'underprivileged'?"

"'Underserved.'"

"'Kids' or 'children'?"

"Always 'children.' Why?"

"I'm a guest on *Terry Gross* tomorrow," Joan said, brandishing a glass of red wine. "Her people got in touch this morning. She wants to ask about the academy, school choice, whatever. But I don't think that's the reason she reached out, given the little, er, *incident* we had last week. It's going to be a bloodbath. I'm preparing for the worst."

"A bloodbath? Terry Gross?"

"Don't underestimate Terry. She's a killer."

Victory Academy, the network of charter schools that Joan had founded, was modeled on the military rigors of her childhood. The school day started at "0500 hours" and was scheduled to the second. Students didn't walk down the halls; they marched. The academy eschewed plaid skirts and blazers in favor of olive-green dress shirts and slacks. Joan's standards for behavior, in and out of the classroom, were no less exacting. Victory students did not speak unless spoken to and punctuated their sentences with "sir" or "ma'am." Children who did not meet these expectations were swiftly and summarily expelled.

In response to critics who found her methods punitive, Joan pointed to the numbers. Ninety-six percent of Victory students achieved proficiency in math, according to the last year's MCAS results, as compared with 39 percent of Boston's public school students. The stats for other subjects were equally impressive. Over the past five years, Joan had collected million-dollar donations from Fidelity, Aramark, and Staples—this, in addition to the taxpayer-funded grants from the Department of Education—which enabled her to pay for a robust PR effort. You could hardly open the *Globe* or the *Herald* without happening upon a puffy profile of Joan or an op-ed in favor of "school choice."

Shortly after Deb moved in, Joan had taken her on a tour of the flagship Victory Academy in Dorchester. Deb had heard stories about students made so anxious by Joan's rules that they vomited on their way to school. She'd read reports on the poor rates of teacher retention, and she was wary of words like "scalable" and "monopoly," which stunk of corporate interference. She was both disappointed and relieved when she walked through the halls of the academy for the first time. Disappointed because the school was so much cleaner and quieter than any public school she'd seen. Relieved because the woman she had left her husband for was not the demon Deb's friends in the Massachusetts Teachers Association made her out to be. When she looked into the classrooms, she saw first graders (first graders!) sitting up straight, facing forward, their fingers knit together on their desks. The teachers spoke to them like adults—Joan, who had no children of her own, found the singsong lilt of baby talk infantilizing—and the kids answered in kind. "The moral of the story," Deb heard one girl declare, "is that people are never happy with what they have. Which is why you should never give a mouse a cookie. Ma'am."

The discipline on display was unlike anything Deb had seen before. After more than two decades of parenting in Brookline, where she had encountered every cutting-edge, creative, child-centric curriculum on offer, she wondered now if something more rigorous—militaristic, even—might have been a better strategy. Joan's approach was undeniably seductive, with its spotless halls and stylish uniforms, and though it ran counter to everything Deb held dear, she was presently estranged from her husband and losing her grip on the group that gave her life outside her family any meaning. She was ready to reconsider everything.

The "incident" to which Joan had referred concerned a video recorded almost four years earlier that had recently resurfaced online. The video depicted, or appeared to depict—Joan was careful to use words like "appeared" and "alleged" when discussing the clip and asked that Deb do the same—a white teacher berating a Black student as the student scrubbed the brick facade of a school with a sponge. This was—allegedly—not an uncommon punishment for students who violated the uniform policy. Nevertheless, Joan had been on the defensive for days, supplying the press with overlapping and contradictory excuses. The video was old; the video lacked context; the teacher had been fired. She had not, as yet, settled on which story served her best.

"Do you think Terry will ask about race?" Joan said now. She stopped pacing and paused over the plants on the mantel. Joan's place was packed with potted plants: aloe vera, devil's ivy, strings of pearls—shocks of green in the clean, white apartment. She rubbed the glossy leaf of a money tree between her fingers. "What if Terry asks about race?"

"You have a white woman screaming her head off at a Black boy while he does manual labor. As punishment. At school. So, yes, I think Terry will ask about race."

"It's bad optics, is what it is. I have plenty of parents—most of them immigrants, by the way—who say that they approve of our disciplinary system. It reflects the way they raise their kids at home." Joan chewed the inside of her cheek. "I should be focused on the new academy in Mattapan. Not some stupid cell phone clip from a million years ago!"

Perlman staggered into the room, mewing as he rubbed his cheek against the corner of Joan's couch.

"Poor thing," Deb said, stroking his head. "Does he seem sick to you?"

"I need to tread *very* carefully around the racial stuff."

"Has he been eating your plants again?" Deb sat up and squinted at the palms of Joan's enormous bird-of-paradise, searching for holes and jagged edges. "Some of these might be toxic."

"How should I know? He's your cat."

"*Our* cat."

"I'm sorry if I have more important things on my mind right now than what Bernstein—"

"Perlman."

"—has eaten! I happen to run the biggest charter school network in the state. I've got parents up my ass, unions up my ass, and tomorrow I have to go on *Terry* fucking *Gross* because half of Boston thinks I'm running a plantation!"

"Meow," Perlman said.

"They're calling me Joanwall Jackson!"

"Don't you know what a dog whistle 'discipline' is?"

"I don't see why *I* should have to throw away my plants when *Perlman* is the interloper—"

"And please don't call Perlman an interloper when he lives here. I walked away from everything to be with you, Joan. I don't think it's asking too much for you to make a minuscule sacrifice and get rid of any plants that might be toxic to my cat. *Our* cat. And for God's sake, it isn't called *Terry Gross.*"

"Of course it is."

"Terry Gross is the host! The show is *Fresh Air!*"

Apart from the health and safety of her family, there was nothing more important to Deb than education. Her mother had dropped out of college to raise Deb and spent the rest of her life making up for those lost semesters. In the evenings, after cooking dinner and clearing the table and washing the dishes, she would retire to the salon, which other families called the living room, and make her way through Janson's *History of Art*, circling the "key works" and modeling studious behavior for her daughter. She attended lectures and screenings at Harvard and hosted a monthly book club at which she was invariably disappointed to discover that none of her friends had finished *Lady Chatterley's Lover.* Deb's father, a menswear salesman at Filene's, was never so deferential as when in the presence of a university professor. He regarded his physician neighbors on Pill Hill not with envy but respect. "I don't know from Shakespeare," he'd say to Deb, "but *this*"—and here he would tap her forehead—"is your ticket."

Her parents were part of the postwar exodus of Jews who left the city in search of superb public schools, and it was at one such school that Deb decided to devote her life to dance. They didn't understand why such a stellar student as their daughter would make her living with her body, not her brain, but after months of bitter conflict, a compromise was struck: Deb would study dance, but not at a conservatory. That was how she wound up at the University of Iowa, where dance was considered one of the liberal (as opposed to fine) arts. She had never been west of Washington, DC, before and marveled at the fields that flanked the highway on the ride from the airport in Cedar Rapids.

Most of Deb's classmates were descended from the Scandinavians who had settled the state. They had legs up to their ears and moved in ways that she couldn't. She quit coffee; she stretched; she bought supplements from a health food shop in Coralville. Her legs remained disproportionally short. She wasn't built for ballet or even modern dance. For the first time in her life, she was confronted with a problem that could not be solved through sheer force of will. She spent that first winter in a deep depression, watching her classmates through a window webbed with ice as they shuffled through the snow in short skirts. That they were not only long-legged but beautiful, with blue eyes and abrupt noses and flowing blond hair that called to mind the phrase "amber waves of grain," only served to complicate her all-consuming envy.

She considered changing majors. She considered dropping out. What was a Jewish girl doing in Iowa, anyway?

She stuck around just long enough to take a class in choreography. It was the perfect fit for someone like Deb, who discovered she loved directing others even more than she loved dancing herself. Enthroned in the booth of a black box theater, separated from the stage by chairs arranged in rows, she ruled over her peers with the iron will of Ayatollah Khomeini, whose rise to power in Iran coincided with Deb's in the Iowa dance department. After graduation, most of her classmates moved to Chicago, but in June of that year, Deb's father had a stroke.

She returned to Boston to help with his care, where she danced for a decade, surviving on saltines and stipends before retiring to raise her children.

"I think you should own up to the video," she said now. "Come forward and apologize."

"Everyone thinks I'm this cold, uncaring woman. Like I get some sick thrill out of punishing kids. But you *know* me, Deb. You know how hard it is for me when I don't feel supported!"

"You're not the only one."

"Maybe we should schedule a couple's massage."

Joan was an early convert to the gospel of self-care, which for her meant massages and milk baths and bottles of Sancerre. "Caring for yourself is not self-indulgence. It's self-preservation," she liked to say, quoting Audre Lorde through an exfoliating mask.

"It's the Resettlement Committee," Deb explained. "That's the one thing in my life I can control. The one thing I have any say over. If I lose that . . ." Her heart caught at the thought of it.

"Is *that* what you're so stressed about?"

"Meow!"

"Among other things, yes."

Joan laughed. "And here I thought something *really* bad had happened."

"It may not mean a whole lot to you," Deb said, "but I founded that committee. It sure as hell means a lot to me. And I'll bet it means a lot to the Nasser family, too."

"Baby," Joan cooed, "I'm on your side. I'm just wondering if your many talents might be put to better use somewhere else. The Resettlement Committee has, what, a half dozen members? What's your annual operating budget?"

"We don't have one. We fundraise for whatever we need."

"Jesus. No wonder you're a wreck." Joan lowered herself into the seat of a plush white recliner, draping her arms over the chair's. "Imagine how much good you could do at a place with millions at its disposal."

"Such as?" When Joan didn't answer, Deb looked up and saw her smiling. It was a moment before she caught the meaning of the smile. "I appreciate the offer, Joan, but I can't work for you."

"Why not?"

"Meow!"

"For one thing—and don't take this the wrong way—but you and I have different ideas about education."

"I knew it."

"Knew what?"

"You don't believe in my mission."

"That's not true."

"You never have!"

Deb rubbed her eyes. They were supposed to be talking about the committee, but Joan had managed, as always, to turn the topic back to the academy. "I sent my kids to public schools, you know."

"You paid their tuition in property taxes."

"Meow!"

"You aren't hearing me," Deb said. "The committee is the one thing that I can call my own."

"You're turning down a position of real influence because, what? Because of pride?"

Deb had lost the plot of the argument, which followed its own Portafoglian logic. "You'd get sick of me," she said. "Seeing me at your office every day and then at home on top of that?"

"No, I wouldn't," Joan assured her. "Why? Would *you* get sick of *me*?"

Deb straightened her spine, adopting a defensive posture. "That's not what I said."

"I love you. Ergo, I want to spend as much time with you as possible. If you loved me, you'd feel the same. Anyway, it's not like we'd *share the exact same office.* You'd have your own cubicle and everything."

"Meow! Meow! Meow!"

"A cubicle! How generous."

Perlman sat up and started pumping his head, trying to coax something out of his throat.

"Oh my god," Joan gasped. "I see what's happening here. You're afraid that if you work for the academy, you'll be stuck with me forever. You won't be able to leave."

That wasn't the sole reason Deb declined the offer—among other things, she had no interest in charter schools—but the prospect of being pegged to Joan did make her uneasy. "That's ridiculous," she said. "You're being paranoid again."

"You hesitated just now."

"No, I didn't."

"I can hear it in your voice. You're going to leave!"

Perlman pumped his head.

"I never said that, Joan."

"But I can hear it! In your *voice*!"

Deb knew just how difficult it was to reason with Joan when she got like this. All the qualities that made her a successful CEO—her ego, her ambition, her ruthlessness, her paranoia—also made her difficult to live with.

Perlman hacked and coughed something up. Deb, grateful for the distraction, leaned forward to see what it was. Beneath the cat, on the carpet, was a small brown clod. Nestled in the clod was a shard of scarlet silicone, glowing like an ember in a pile of ashes.

"That's disgusting!" Joan shrieked.

"It must be something he ate."

"Just clean it up before it stains the carpet."

"Wait a second," Deb said. "I know what it is." She looked up and saw that Joan now recognized it, too, as a half-digested fragment of the dildo that Perlman had disfigured two weeks earlier. Both women started laughing uncontrollably.

"Jesus," Joan said, wiping her eyes. "That's too much."

"Don't lift a finger. I'll clean it up."

"I'll get it. He's my cat, too, like you said."

Deb allowed herself to sit back in her chair. "I'm sorry," she said. "I don't know why we fight like this."

"I hate it."

"I do, too."

Joan got up and planted a kiss on Deb's forehead. "Let's never fight again."

As Deb watched Joan walk toward the kitchen, she could hear her practicing for her interview under her breath. "The truth is, Terry, we're the last hope for underprivileged kids in Massachusetts. Underserved. *Underserved.* Underserved *children.*"

For a woman who kept a meticulous calendar, Deb hadn't seen her fifties coming. She was so preoccupied with raising two teenagers and with her commitments to the high school and the synagogue that when she came home one summer evening five years earlier to find a crowd of people shouting, "Surprise!" she turned around to see who they were talking to. Surely it couldn't be her birthday *again*. But there was Scott, clutching a bottle of champagne in one hand and a gold balloon in the other. Behind him hung a banner that read I DEMAND A RECOUNT! She pretended to be pleased, and wore a smile all night, but after all the guests had left and Scott had gone to bed, she ripped the banner from the wall and tore it to pieces. She didn't want to turn fifty any more than she wanted the back pain, mood swings, and loss of bone density that were her body's birthday presents. It occurred to her, standing over the scraps, that she'd spent the past quarter century caring for other people. She had cared for her father after his stroke, cared for her mother after his death, cared for Scott throughout medical school, and cared for her children their entire lives. She felt it was time that she did something for herself—which was how she wound up taking a poetry workshop with Theresa Dunne.

Earlier that spring, a profile of Theresa had run in *The New Yorker* beneath the gently condescending headline "A Poet (and Pipefitter's Daughter) Gets Her Due." The piece was published to coincide with the reissue of Theresa's first book, *Stick and Poke*, a collection of narrative poems—she called them "prose Polaroids"—about growing up in Fall River, Massachusetts. On account of the profile, Deb knew a great deal about Theresa before they ever met. She knew, for instance, that Theresa was the daughter of a union rep (UA Local 77) and a housewife who didn't understand why her youngest daughter didn't want to play with dolls. She knew that Theresa had attended Catholic school and that her father sometimes pulled her out of class to watch the men in hard hats build the Braga Bridge, an enormous green structure linking Providence, Rhode Island, to the whaling city of New Bedford. ("It cemented this idea in me," Theresa told the journalist, "that Fall River was a place you passed through to get to somewhere else.") She knew that Theresa cited as her primary poetic influence not the Beats, nor the New York School, but the nineteenth-century mill girls who worked in the hulking red factories along the Quequechan and sang protest songs when their wages were cut: *Isn't it a pity, such a pretty girl as I / should be sent to the factory to pine away and die?* She knew that Theresa had run away to Boston after high school, where she cut her hair and passed for a man in order to work the construction jobs that funded her early poetic efforts. She returned to Fall River only once, when her sister was murdered by a self-styled Satanist who ran a coven out of the Freetown State Forest, an event that inspired her 1981 collection, *Barbara: An Exorcism*. It was the most sensational crime to occur in Fall River since Lizzie Borden butchered her parents in 1892.

Theresa's tough charm was apparent on the page. She spoke colorfully about Fall River ("This is a city whose official slogan is 'We'll try'") and the days when she donated plasma to pay rent ("Best job I ever had"). She seemed to goad, tease, or flirt with the journalist, sometimes all at once ("It's funny, you writing this profile of me. I've been trying to get you people to publish my poems for thirty years"). Deb was so taken by Theresa's tone, at once easygoing and tenacious, that she ordered her most recent collection, *Sex with Eleanor Roosevelt*. She hadn't read much poetry since her kids had outgrown Shel Silverstein, but Theresa's work was approachable: short poems composed of short lines with very little in the way of abstraction. Theresa's great subject was the female body, and Deb was inspired by the frankness with which she addressed life after menopause. Even the titles, like "Elegy for My Pelvic Floor," suggested that Theresa didn't care what the reader, and especially the male reader, thought of her.

Deb was a feminist, of course, as were her friends, but that didn't mean they weren't embarrassed by their bodies. How liberating it must be, Deb thought, to transcend the customs of her class, to care nothing for appearances nor reputation. *Sex with Eleanor Roosevelt* shattered every taboo concerning life as a middle-aged woman; reading it, Deb felt that Theresa had cracked her skull open, scooped out all of her forbidden thoughts, and arranged them, artfully, on the page. No sooner had Deb finished the book than she signed up for Theresa's class at Harvard Extension in the hopes of learning something from this unconventional woman who seemed to live for no one but herself.

It was plain from the first day of class that Theresa resented having to teach at the precise moment that her career was taking off. She told her students that she expected to become very busy soon and lamented the fact that Harvard was paying her only $4,000 for the course. In any other instance, Deb would have found this behavior unprofessional, but because she was already convinced of Theresa's brilliance and because Theresa framed her complaint in the language of the labor movement, Deb found herself nodding along in agreement. It didn't hurt that Theresa was handsome, with deep lines in her leathery face and shaggy, shoulder-length hair. She looked less like a poet, as Deb imagined them to look, and more like a gunslinger from a Western film. She wore a suede vest with the buttons on the right side. A bolo tie cinched the collar of her denim shirt.

Theresa paid no special attention to Deb—or any other student, for that matter; she could hardly be bothered to learn their names— until Deb approached her on the last day of class and confessed to being an enthusiastic admirer of her work. "I can't say I've been reading you for very long," she said, "but *Sex with Eleanor Roosevelt* was a revelation."

Theresa looked up from her phone and narrowed her eyes in a squint of appraisal. Then she asked what Deb was doing later on.

What followed was one of the most wonderfully spontaneous evenings of Deb's adult life. After attending a reading at the Grolier Poetry Book Shop in Harvard Square, she and Theresa and a group of grad students got drunk on scorpion bowls at the Hong Kong Restaurant before flocking to the dance floor upstairs. There, a slightly drunk Deb closed her eyes and whirled with such graceful abandon that when she opened them again, she was surprised, and not the least bit flattered, to discover that a circle of admirers had formed around her.

"You never told me you could move," Theresa said as they stumbled out of the restaurant.

"I never got the chance," Deb said. Embarrassed, she pulled her eyes out of the tractor beam of Theresa's gaze. "I used to dance."

Theresa laid a calloused palm on Deb's blushing cheek. "You still do. You just did."

Deb ordered herself to step back. "My husband is probably wondering where I am."

"Wanna bet?"

"I really should go. Thanks for a great class."

Walking to her car, she checked her phone for the first time in hours. She hadn't told Scott she was staying out late, and expected to find at least a few missed calls. She winced in anticipation of a wave of guilt. But her home screen was empty, save for the family photo that served as her digital wallpaper: the four of them smiling on the Spanish Steps in Rome. It seemed like centuries ago.

Walking to the car, she assessed her sobriety and found that she could put one foot in front of the other. It wasn't like her to drive after having a few drinks, even if she thought she could, but she didn't want to have to explain herself to Scott. His silence that night seemed smug, somehow. Apparently, he wasn't worried about her. He trusted her—she knew that—but maybe he took her for granted, too.

Deb kept busy the next few weeks, making dates with old friends from her dance days and driving to New Hampshire on the weekends, where she channeled her confusion of feelings for Theresa into canvassing votes for Barack Obama. One night, after a long day of knocking on doors, she found Scott in the living room, reading *Sex with Eleanor Roosevelt*, and felt so exposed he might as well have been reading her diary.

"'Labial Song,'" Scott said.

"Where did you find that?"

"'Lolling lips, no longer plump—'"

"Scott . . ."

"'Clytemnestra, estrogen—'"

"Scott!"

He laughed and set the book aside. "I can't believe anyone reads this stuff. I can't believe anyone *publishes* it."

Had she not been so embarrassed, she might have murdered him. "Any idea whose it is?"

"I guess Maya must be reading it for class."

"Give it here," Deb said. "I'll make sure she gets it back."

Scott used the book to swat her hand. "Who's her English teacher this year, anyway?"

"Dunlap," she said through gritted teeth. "Cathy Dunlap."

"Does this Ms. Dunlap have a husband?"

"I think so. Why?"

"I'm just saying. *Sex with Eleanor Roosevelt?*"

The fog of her embarrassment had burned away, exposing the anger behind it. "So?"

"Let's just say her husband is in for a rude awakening."

Deb's interest in women traced back to adolescence, when she'd fixated on Lynda Carter's legs while watching *The New Adventures of Wonder Woman*. It didn't occur to her then that her infatuation with those shapely Amazonian thighs—to say nothing of the flesh that bounced beneath her breastplate—was anything other than typical. Television, paperbacks, porno mags, comic books, billboards, art films, even oil paintings: all of culture seemed to celebrate the female form. This made an intuitive kind of sense to Deb. She was attracted to boys, she had crushes on boys, but they weren't beautiful; their bodies weren't fit for art.

She knocked on doors all across the Granite State, smiling until her cheeks stung, talking herself hoarse about Iraq and the collapse of Lehman Brothers, affordable healthcare and net neutrality. She block walked until her blisters bled, punishing herself for her inability to stop thinking about Theresa. Once, a bearded biker answered the door, his sunburned arms sleeved in tattoos, a pewter snake around his ring finger. He threatened to shoot her if she didn't leave the property. Just as Deb was backing away, a petite man in a pink shirt with paisley contrast cuffs came up behind the biker, kissed his cheek, and asked Deb for a pamphlet.

Driving through the country, the hills ablaze with color, she remembered that a friend of hers from high school, Eve Coughman, had moved to a town in Vermont near the New Hampshire border.

Deb decided, on a whim, to look her up; she remembered hearing that Eve had left her husband for a woman. She pulled into a park and ride off the highway and tried to sound natural as she explained that she just happened to be in the area and was Eve free that afternoon? She was.

Eve lived in a renovated farmhouse a few miles south of Quechee Gorge, a fertile cleft in a rock formation just below the belt of Route 4. She greeted Deb at the door with a hug, looking unusually well-preserved for fifty. Her skin was pink, her eyes lively and intelligent. Apart from the shock of white through her dark hair, she looked just like Deb remembered her. Her partner, Val, was out hiking with friends, so they would have plenty of time to talk.

They caught up for an hour over meatless sandwiches. Eve was at the same pediatrics practice where she'd worked since earning her MD from Dartmouth, though she'd never had children of her own. "I've seen too many sick kids," she said, "and I've seen what that much worry does to parents." Lately, however, she'd considered adopting.

"So what changed?" Deb asked. They had moved from the dining room to a screened-in porch with a view of the White Mountains.

"All credit goes to Val. I never thought I wanted kids before. But I can see myself raising *her* kid, if that makes sense. Maybe it sounds silly."

"It doesn't sound silly at all." Deb had been waiting patiently for just this moment. "How did you two get together, anyway?"

"It was the most incredible thing," Eve said. "I belonged to this Reform synagogue in Lebanon, a few miles east of here. I only really went on holidays. But then our cantor retired, and they hired Val. Suddenly I found myself going every week, staring at this woman with the soaring voice. We started spending time together—first at synagogue and then other places around town. I wanted to be around her all the time. We were friends, very close friends. At least, that's what I told myself. I'd never been attracted to a woman before. Now I realize I was falling in love."

"Did you tell your husband?"

"Not until I was sure of how I felt. Even then, I wasn't ready to give him up. Give *it* up—I mean my life." She set down her wineglass and looked left, then right, as if to confirm that there was no one listening in. In a low voice she said, "We tried an open marriage for a while."

"You *did?*"

"I don't recommend it. Not for straight couples."

"Why not?"

"Straight men." Eve laughed. "I shouldn't say that. Barry did his best. But the jealousy, his jealousy, got in the way. He didn't say as much, but I could tell. I told him he was free to explore. I encouraged it. He never did. I think he wanted to wait out what he thought was a phase with a clean conscience. But I could tell the jealousy was eating him up."

"And when you left?"

"He was very supportive. Almost too supportive. I sometimes wonder if he's worked through his anger."

"So he was angry."

"I certainly hope so. He has every right to be. I think that if I'd left him for another man, he would have lost his temper. This was different. It's almost like he didn't know how to react. Sometimes I wonder if he believes, deep down, that I'm going to come back."

Scott, too, had a habit of suppressing his anger. Deb could see him responding the same way. "And you were never interested in women before?"

"I don't know that I'd say I'm into women now. I'm into Val. I don't think there's a name for that."

"But you're happy? I mean, you think you made the right decision? You don't have any regrets?"

This, it turned out, was one question too many. Eve stared through the porch screen as though she hadn't heard it. After a long moment, she clapped her hands. "So. Can I send you home with something? A slice of pie? There's a stand down the road that sells excellent pies."

"No, thank you. I should probably get going." A pang of disappointment resounded through her body. What had she wanted from Eve, anyway? Affirmation? Insight? Kinship? Permission?

"It was great to see you, Deb," Eve said. "I'm glad you called."

"Lunch was lovely. Thank you. And I'm glad, too."

Standing at the door to Eve's farmhouse, certain that they'd never speak again, she forced herself to ask one final question. "Is it different?"

"Is what different?"

The wine had sapped the moisture from Deb's mouth. "You know. *It.*"

Eve looked at Deb a moment, her expression changing from one of surprise to sympathy, maybe even understanding. "Yes," she said. "It's different."

"In what way?"

"It's less transactional, somehow. Less *economic.* I don't know how else to say it. I can't even tell you why. But to me, at least, it doesn't feel so *productive.* It's not about making anything."

"And it's—better?"

"I've always found that the most valuable things in life are the least productive. Do you know what I mean?"

"I do." It was the reason Deb loved dance. "Well, thank you again."

"Good luck," Eve said as Deb started toward her car. "Whatever you decide. Although, in my experience, it's not up to you. What happens, happens. It's liberating that way."

It had never occurred to Deb to open her marriage. Open marriages belonged to another time, an age of wife swaps and key parties that Deb, still a child in the 1960s, was always grateful to have missed. The phrase itself, "open marriage," sounded like a paradox, an oxymoron, no more sensible than "civil war" or "open secret." At the very least, it was a contradiction—but an intriguing contradiction. An open marriage, she imagined, was a kind of controlled chaos. A liberation within limits. It appealed to the two apparently irreconcilable women inside her: one who craved security, one who wanted to break free.

The notion stalked her through New Hampshire, a stitch in her side as she stopped to catch her breath at a Dunkin' Donuts in Manchester. Why *shouldn't* it work? Why *couldn't* she have everything she wanted? She didn't have to break the rules. She could rewrite them.

But there was so much at stake. Her husband, her children, the sterling reputation in Brookline that she had built and burnished. To enter into such an arrangement required an unthinkable amount of faith—blind, irrational faith. But then again, so did marriage. Monogamy was like a religion, and before Theresa, Deb had been a true believer. More than that: a zealot. An extremist who would sooner blow herself up than question her God. But what was wrong with asking questions?

A week later, in the afterglow of the election, she asked if Scott wanted to sleep with someone else.

He was sitting on the living room sofa, reading *The Voyage of the Beagle*. It was a Saturday evening, and neither of their children was home. "Is this a trick?"

"No, it's not a trick."

He removed his glasses, wiped the lenses on his shirt, and put them on again. "I only have eyes for you."

"Be serious, Scott. Just for a minute. We've been married a long time."

"If I say I don't want to, you won't believe me. But if I say I do . . ."

"I won't take offense."

"You promise?"

"Promise."

Scott sighed. "Yes, I've wanted to. Sleep with other people. But no more than any other red-blooded American man. And of course, I never would."

"What if you could?"

"I can't."

"I'm saying—what if you could?"

"What's the catch? There has to be a catch."

"The catch," she said, "is that I can do it, too."

She proceeded to explain, in an offhand tone, the logistics of a possible arrangement that she had carefully planned out in advance. "It's not that I don't love you. Quite the opposite. I love you so much, I want you to be happy. As happy as you can be. And I want you to want that for me."

"Am I not . . . 'satisfying your needs'?" She could hear the quotation marks in his voice, the irony masking his discomfort.

"You satisfy my needs," she said, addressing him without quotations. "You satisfy the needs I have *from you*. But what if I have other needs? What if you have them, too? Needs we don't know about?" He didn't seem convinced, so she continued. "You're my best friend, my co-parent, my sexual partner. My financial support! It's too much to ask of one person."

"You think I can't handle it?"

She put a hand on his thigh. "You can handle it. You *have* handled it. But that doesn't make it right."

"It *is* a lot to ask," he admitted.

"This isn't going to be easy," she said. "In fact, it might be very hard. But if anyone can make it work, we can. Don't you think so?"

His tongue probed the inside of his cheek. "If we *did* do this—and I'm not saying we should—but if we did, how would it work?"

Deb had already prepared a list of rules. The list was a sort of safety precaution, a means of managing potential fallout. Bumpers on the bowling alleys of their lives. She had never been comfortable playing a game until she knew the rules.

Talking with Scott, she got them down to three:

1. they would tell each other about their respective partners,

2. they wouldn't sneak around, and

3. they wouldn't fall in love with anyone else.

All this talk of imaginary lovers diverted the flow of blood within their bodies, and soon they were lying panting on their Persian rug.

They amused themselves at the idea of other couples they knew opening *their* marriages. The thought of Karla Cantor at a hotel bar in a
little black dress made them weep with laughter.

Deb waited a week before she got in touch with Theresa. She was
on tour, she said, reading at bookstores and galleries and wherever
else would take her, sleeping on couches or in her car. Deb tried to
hide the disappointment in her voice. She had gone to great lengths
to make herself available to Theresa, and now she would have to wait.

Theresa returned from her tour on a Thursday. Deb blew off a
meeting of the Resettlement Committee and met her at the Midway
Cafe in Jamaica Plain. When she arrived, she found Theresa sitting
at a table with friends. This was the first of two impediments to inti-
macy that threatened to ruin the evening. The second: it was kara-
oke night.

Deb was determined to overcome these obstacles, and, with an assist
from Sam Adams, she did. By the end of the night, she and Theresa
were on the elevated stage singing Joni Mitchell's "River."

She walked Theresa back to her apartment and accepted her invitation to come upstairs. The place was a mess, and there was nowhere to sit except for a futon behind a pair of parted French doors.
Deb was looking around, trying to find something to compliment in
the apartment, when Theresa said, "I know why you're here."

The first time Deb pressed her lips to Theresa's, she felt like her
body was heaving an enormous sigh. There was a comfort in her soft-
ness, her sameness, a sense of recognition Deb had never felt with
Scott. When, a few minutes later, she put her hand between Theresa's
legs, she was shocked by how warm and how wet this weathered-
looking woman was. Theresa took Deb's hand and guided her fingers,

her thumb on Deb's wrist, bucking to the rhythm of her pulse. Deb was surprised by how comfortable she felt. There was something uncannily familiar about Theresa. She knew her lover's body like she knew her own. Then it was Theresa's turn. She slid beneath the covers of the futon, where she transformed herself into an enormous tongue.

Deb had always had trouble believing men when they told her she was beautiful. She never knew if they meant it or if they were just trying to sleep with her, and wanting to sleep with someone didn't make them beautiful. But Theresa was a woman, and an artist at that. She understood beauty. When she called Deb beautiful, Deb believed her.

They were holding each other, breathing hard.

"I've never slept with a woman before," Deb said.

"You still haven't," Theresa replied.

Deb didn't understand. Maybe sex meant something else between women, she wasn't sure.

Theresa registered her confusion. "I never thought of myself as a woman."

"So what are you?"

Theresa shrugged and swung her legs over the side of the futon. "Call me what you want," she said and scratched her ass. The skin was wrinkled like clothes left too long in the dryer. "In my own mind, I've always been a cowboy."

They spent at least one evening each week together, getting drunk at bookstores and cemeteries. They went to readings at Café Algiers and concerts at the Middle East. Over the course of her marriage, Deb had become convinced of a certain version of herself. Of all the personalities she might manifest, she told herself that this one—the stalwart wife and devoted mother—must have been the truest. Now she wasn't sure. She was living the life of an artist again, the life she'd abandoned when she had kids. She was delighted to discover it was right where she'd left it.

Despite her close ties to the labor movement, Theresa didn't do a lot of work. Her days began at 2:00 p.m. and consisted largely of watching trash TV and eating takeout. She went out almost every night. That this routine reliably produced one poem per week—and that the poems were *good*—only made her more of a mystery to Deb, who, in her days as a dancer, had adhered to a rigorous rehearsal schedule. She didn't understand Theresa's lifestyle any more than Theresa understood hers, the meetings she attended, the meals she prepared. "I'm not the one who told you to have kids," Theresa said.

There was also the problem of Theresa's fame. Wherever they went, Theresa was bound to run into someone she knew: a student, a colleague, an ex. She had exes in Cambridge, in Somerville, in Brighton. Exes in Arlington, Medford, and Boston. They couldn't even step foot in Jamaica Plain. Deb knew she had no right to be jealous, but she was.

Theresa lived just south of Inman Square on the second story of the rent-stabilized building she had lived in since leaving Fall River. One night, Deb found her there in the company of an attractive, barefoot girl who could not have been much older than Maya. "This is Deja," Theresa said by way of an introduction. "We're assembling my archive." The apartment was even messier than usual. The floor was littered with cardboard boxes, spiral notebooks, photographs, and stacks of paper.

"I didn't know you had an archive," Deb said.

"People pay a lot of money for a poet's papers," Deja said. She had long legs and braided hair extensions. Her toenails were lacquered in sparkling red polish, and her jeans were shredded beyond repair.

"Deja is a freshman at Tufts," Theresa said. "She was kind enough to invite me to read to her class."

Deb narrowed her eyes. "So someone made an offer on your papers?" she asked.

"Not yet. Not formally, at least. But I want to get things in order for when the day eventually comes.

"If I were a university library? I'd *totally* buy your stuff," Deja said.

"You, my dear, get to look for free."

"Forgive me," Deb said, "and maybe I don't know how this works, but isn't it a little bit presumptuous to think that a university would want your papers?"

"Who *wouldn't* want her papers?" Deja asked.

"I'm not saying they *wouldn't*, just that it seems a bit, I don't know, self-aggrandizing to work on the assumption that they would."

Deja leaned toward Theresa and whispered, "I don't like her."

"Oh, Deb's all right," Theresa said. "She just doesn't understand what it's like to be an artist."

"I'm an artist," Deb said.

"You *used* to be an artist."

The statement confirmed the fear that had been dogging Deb for weeks. "I had to raise my kids," she said.

"My point exactly. *You* have kids, and *I* have an archive. Anyway, I need the money. Not all of us married rich doctors."

"Theresa . . ."

"I don't remember making plans to see you tonight."

A few weeks later, she found a pair of pink panties on Theresa's bedroom floor, the name DEJA printed on the iron-on label. They were the same labels she used to mark her kids' clothes when they went to summer camp.

She felt like a girl again, a beginner in a grown woman's body; her shoulders were sore from sobbing. Theresa had betrayed her, but hadn't Deb betrayed Theresa, too, every night she slept beside Scott? Her guilt polluted her grief, made it hard to breathe. She needed something to do to take her mind off Theresa, and so, once the physical agony subsided, she started planning a family trip to Morocco. She spent hours on TripAdvisor, perusing five-star reviews of travel packages and initiating correspondences with different guides. They would drive from Casablanca to Marrakesh and on through the Atlas Mountains, stopping at every casbah and valley and village of note along the route to Fès, and then Rabat, and then back to Casablanca. They would visit every sight worth seeing *if it killed them.*

Deb was surprised by how sullen Maya seemed throughout the trip. She was reminded of when Maya decided she was too old for bedtime stories. Deb had cherished those evenings, just before she went to sleep, when she would climb into bed beside her daughter and read from *Strega Nona* or Singer's *Stories for Children*, and later, *Little Women* and *Harriet the Spy*. But when Maya was eight, she decided that she didn't need Deb anymore. "No, thank you," she said one night with complete civility. "I think I'll read by myself from now on." On one level, this was a triumph—Deb had successfully instilled a love of books in Maya—but she knew, as her daughter closed the bedroom door behind her, that a chapter of her life was closing with it. That was how Deb felt in Morocco, like there was a tall, impenetrable door between them that Maya had decided to close.

Then she discovered the tattoo. That night, at the riad in Fès, she lay awake wondering exactly what Maya had seen and how to address it. The easiest thing was not to address it at all, and given everything already going on—namely that a faculty member at the high school had been grooming her daughter—that was what she decided to do. She emailed Dean Hollerbach from the riad to let him know that the school employed a predator, and if he wasn't dismissed before the new semester started, she would pull her support from the Innovation Fund, which, she reminded the dean, had brought in close to a million dollars the previous year.

It was only when Deb came home after work to find Maya sobbing on her bedroom floor that she understood the consequences of her decision. She had never seen a child of hers in so much pain. She got down on the floor beside her daughter, and soon she was sobbing, too, as she told herself—silently, over and over—that sometimes you had to hurt your children to keep them safe.

One night in April, while Scott was out with some drug rep from Bristol Myers Squibb, Deb dug a sleeveless black dress out of the closet and drove to the Fairmont Copley Plaza. She sat at the bar and nursed a glass of white wine, waiting with both excitement and dread to see if someone would approach her.

Deb had been with Scott so long that she'd forgotten how to be alone. The simplest things had become difficult: how to sit, how to stand, how to hold herself in public. His body had always provided the necessary context for hers. She was too used to being beside him.

As she shifted on her stool, trying to find a comfortable position, a squat, balding man with gleaming white teeth took the seat next to hers. He said his name was John ("last name Doe, ha ha") and that he was in town for an inflatable pool toy convention. A few drinks later, she followed him to his room upstairs, where he heaved and grunted and called her mommy before expending himself on the duvet.

Deb was too tipsy to drive and spent the night. When she woke the next morning, John was gone. Only after she had showered and treated the duvet with cold water and a stain remover did she notice the set of ten twenty-dollar bills fanned out on the bedside table next to a handwritten note. WE NEVER TALKED $$$, it read. HOPE THIS IS ENOUGH.

At first, the sight of the money offended her. Despite her open marriage, Deb was not so liberated as to approve of sex work—the phrase had always sounded strange to her ear, "sex" being both synonym and antonym for "work"—and she was insulted to have been mistaken for a prostitute. But the more she thought about it, the more she felt that John Doe *did* owe her something for the time and effort. Deb pocketed all but two of the bills, which she left on the table for housekeeping.

Deb didn't meet Joan until a few years later, at a conference at the Seaport World Trade Center, a converted maritime cargo facility overlooking Boston Harbor. The conference, sponsored by Fidelity, featured "thought leaders" from a variety of disciplines delivering ten-minute talks about their work. From her seat in the dim amphitheater, Deb, who never passed up an opportunity for self-enrichment, listened to bite-size lectures on gene therapy, compost, and the neuroscience of hugs.

Joan was the last speaker in the morning session. She stalked the stage in pink high heels, the sole concession to color in an outfit composed of a navy pantsuit over a white T-shirt cut low enough to intimate a pair of ample breasts. America's public schools, she said, were

broken, and proceeded to cite dispiriting statistics about the Boston
public school system in particular. Thirty-two percent of K–8 students
were failing at science. Twenty-seven percent were failing at math. A
quarter wouldn't finish 'high school. Charter schools, on the other
hand, were publicly funded but privately run, which enabled them to
experiment and innovate, much like a startup. Joan's Victory Acad-
emies, to take one example, were inspired by her childhood on army
bases. She then cited a series of more encouraging statistics. Ninety-
six percent of Victory students went to college. Victory students routinely outperformed those in public schools in nearby districts on state
exams. When her ten minutes were up, she thanked the audience and
encouraged them to visit her online at victoryacademy.com. Walking
out, Joan received a standing ovation.

After the lecture, the group broke for lunch. Deb found Joan outside the amphitheater, standing by the buffet amid a mob of admirers. "Excuse me," Deb said from the fringes, "but I wondered if you
wanted to address the concern that charter schools are not held accountable to the same standards that public schools are."

"We hold ourselves accountable," Joan said. She was shorter than
she'd seemed onstage, even in heels. She had big brown eyes and a
strong jaw; up close, she looked a little bit like Lynda Carter. When
she smiled at Deb, as she did now—it was a private, rather than a
public, smile—her upper cheeks pouched considerably.

"I'm sure *you* do," Deb said, diplomatic as ever, "but what about
reports of charter school executives embezzling money from parents?
To take just one example."

"You don't have to answer that, Joan," someone said.

But Joan did answer. "The key word here is 'choice.' We have to
empower parents to choose what school is right for their little ones. If

your grocery store doesn't carry cold-pressed juice, what do you do? You go somewhere else. All we want to do is give families a few more places to shop. And maybe—just maybe—that first grocery store, facing stiff competition, will start stocking cold-pressed juice after all."

"Forgive me, but a school is not a grocery store, and an education is not a cold-pressed juice."

Joan's cheeks pouched again as she dipped into the pocket of her blazer and passed Deb a business card. "This hardly seems like the time or place. Why don't you drop me a line and we can continue this discussion?"

Joan later confessed that she hadn't expected to hear from Deb again. But she did, later that night, in a lengthy email Deb composed refuting each of Joan's arguments point by point.

The following week, at the Starbucks on Newbury Street, Deb and Joan engaged in a passionate argument about the merits of charter schools and the state of education in general. They disagreed on so much and resolved so little that they decided to meet again the following week, and then the week after that. One afternoon, they talked for so long that the staff began sweeping and putting up chairs. Joan proposed moving the conversation to her place.

Unlike Theresa's triple-decker, which had the air of grad student housing about it—the smell of molding cheese inside a pizza box, the loneliness of a stray can of beer—the inside of Joan's brownstone was immaculate, with sheer pink curtains and polished hardwood floors and walls so white Deb had to squint. There were houseplants everywhere: palms reaching out from white ceramic pots, vines suspended from the ceiling in a cascade of green. Joan stepped out of her heels and lost four inches. "This is it," she said, wiggling her toes.

"Joan, my god. Your apartment is gorgeous."

"No husband, no kids," she said. "No compromise." She strode bare-foot into the kitchen, with its sparkling subway tile, and opened a bottle of rosé. "You were saying?"

Deb was so impressed with Joan's apartment that she almost forgot what they'd been talking about. "I was saying, you can't commodify an education."

"Says who?"

"Says me."

"Is that right?" Joan wrapped her arm around Deb's waist.

Deb stooped so their lips were level. "That's right."

Joan was just as stubborn, just as driven, as Deb was. Deb felt the same spark of recognition that she had with Theresa, the shared understanding of what it meant to be a woman in the world. Deb had never met anyone so similar to her before, but where she had devoted her life to unprofitable—or nonprofitable—causes (her children, her dance career, public education), Joan had succeeded in the private sector. Her elegant apartment was like a portal to the life Deb might have lived had she not been hamstrung by her moral high ground—or her family. Joan encouraged Deb to indulge, to take it easy, to seek out pleasure for herself. After half a lifetime of uphill battles—trying to dance despite her legs, raising money for a school system plagued by budget cuts—she finally let herself be selfish.

And Joan could be tender, too. She treated Deb better than Deb treated herself, surprising her with spa days and sterling silver brace-lets for no special reason. Scott, by contrast, had a standing order with a local flower shop, presenting Deb with the same bouquet on her birthday, their anniversary, and Mother's Day. He seemed proud, and not at all embarrassed, to have this arrangement "down to a sci-

ence." Joan took a special interest in Deb's dance career, too, asking
question after question until Deb started to feel as impressive as Joan
seemed to think she was. Unlike Scott, for whom she'd played the role
of housewife so long that she sometimes forgot she had more to offer,
Joan made her feel special, a woman with a purpose.

But if the affair with Theresa carried a whiff of transgression—her
first lover in years, and a woman at that—she soon found herself in a
rigidly domestic arrangement with Joan, cooking and cleaning for
lack of anything else to do. What's more, she now depended on Joan
for money in precisely the same way she had depended on Scott. Every meal that Joan paid for, every bill she signed reminded Deb that
she was not making material contributions to the household to which
she belonged. Living with a woman as successful as Joan only made
her feel less accomplished by comparison. Standing next to her at
galas and black-tie dinners, watching Joan charm money from the
pockets of her many admirers, she couldn't help but wonder what she
herself was worth.

"Do you think they made it over?" Deb asked, watching weary passengers stagger through the automatic doors beneath a sign marked
ARRIVALS. Beside her stood a stocky, short-haired woman in a
snowsuit—a caseworker with the Jewish League of Greater Boston.
"Maybe they missed the connection in Munich."

The caseworker let out a hearty laugh. "You worry too much.
They'll be here."

Deb had been working for more than a year to bring the Nassers to
Boston, and she could hardly believe that they were finally here, not

three weeks from the day she'd placed the call to Green Pastures. It was a cold and cloudless February night, the stars above the airport frozen in place; across the bay, the skyline looked more crowded than ever, as though the buildings were huddling together for warmth. If something had happened to the Nassers, she thought, she would never be able to forgive herself. The stream of passengers slowed to a trickle. Her heel bounced on the floor.

Deb had once known a dancer who conceived of a strategy for coping with performance anxiety. Before going onstage she would roll the straps of her leotard over her shoulders and light a cigarette. Then she'd press the lit end against her exposed skin and try not to scream while her eyes welled with tears. Deb watched the dancer do this on two or three occasions before she finally asked her about it. So long as she was focused on the pain, the dancer said, her mind was centered. She was thinking about her skin, the smoke, the smell of burning flesh. Anything but the performance ahead of her.

Deb was regretting her decision to quit smoking when the doors slid open to accommodate a luggage cart. She recognized the person pushing it as Khalil Nasser, a short, balding man of about forty with heavy-lidded eyes and a graying goatee. He was slimmer than he'd looked in the photos from the camp, and there were dark circles underneath his eyes. He paused beneath the ARRIVALS sign, prompting Deb to raise one of her own. This sign was made of cardboard and read "Welcome to America" in English and Arabic; the caseworker had helped with the translation. Khalil spotted it and started toward her, followed by his wife, Fatima, and their daughter, Amina, who looked to be about seven years old. Deb was surprised by Fatima's outfit, a denim jumpsuit with a leopard-print hijab. But what had she expected? A tattered burqa? Rags? She'd worked with immigrants before, but never refugees, a distinction that seemed significant before. Now, she wasn't sure.

The caseworker made introductions in Arabic, pausing to pronounce Deb's name in English, a stubbed toe in the rapid patter of her speech. Somehow, despite all her preparations, which had involved enrolling the Nassers in English classes, Deb hadn't thought much about the language barrier. When she envisioned this moment, as she had done a hundred times, she always pictured herself conversing with them. "I'm sorry about the weather," she blurted, just to have something to say. Did it snow in Syria? She felt stupid for not knowing.

The caseworker helped Khalil load his luggage in the back of Deb's car while Fatima attended to Amina, who was crying. "Is there something I can help with?" Deb asked.

"She wants to sit on her mom's lap," the caseworker explained. "They don't really do car seats in Syria."

The caseworker spoke to the Nassers in Arabic while Deb drove into the city. Her inability to comprehend the conversation made her feel suddenly small-minded and provincial. Apart from college, Deb had lived here all her life, rarely venturing beyond the bounds of Route 128, which ensnared her like a golden lasso.

She thought of the stories she'd grown up hearing about her ancestors' arrival in America: the long passage by steamship, the stew of languages at Ellis Island, the chalk marks etched on the shoulders of the sick. Despite what must have been a miserable experience, the stories were always told with a romantic wistfulness, and Deb wondered if the Nassers would one day tell their story with that same wistfulness, recounting with no small amount of romance their ride in the back of her sedan.

In the back seat, Fatima clucked her tongue.

"What was that?" Deb asked the caseworker. "What's wrong?"

"Someone at the camp in Jordan told them that their rent would be covered for a year. I just had to let them know that we can only pay for three months. That's actually more than most of my clients get, thanks to your fundraising efforts." She sighed. "They don't know how good they have it, relatively speaking."

Yotam had secured one half of a duplex on a dead-end street just south of Dudley Square, where the rooftops were all decked with satellite dishes. The paint was peeling, and the TOW ZONE sign on the sidewalk was stooped like a junkie, but it was cozy and the best he could do on short notice. Parking in front of the house, Deb noticed the streetlamp out front, the dull, yellow light illuminating little more than the pebble-strewn pavement at the bottom of the post.

Do you really want me any brighter? the streetlamp seemed to say. *Look at the cracks in the concrete. Look at the weeds. The hypodermic needles in the vacant lot next door. Is that what you want them to see? No! Would you let your daughter live in a house like this? No! You could have done more. You should have done more!*

Deb shivered as she stepped out of the car, avoiding the Nassers' eyes as she climbed the wooden staircase and opened the door.

Fatima gasped. She dropped the bag she was holding and wrapped her arms around Deb, who was no less stunned than the Nassers. She had forgotten just how thoroughly she and the rest of the Resettlement Committee had prepared. They had furnished the house with secondhand pieces, and the gently worn quality of the furniture only served to make the place feel lived-in, the frayed threads on one arm of the sofa suggesting a succession of family cats. They had stocked the linen cabinet and filled the fridge with food. A bowl of apples and bananas sat on the counter by a basket full of gift cards to local businesses.

Khalil, who had been quiet in the car, said something under his breath.

The caseworker laid a hand on Deb's shoulder. "He says he only ever dreamed of a house like this."

Deb had never known such relief. With renewed excitement, she set about showing them the house, gathering strength with each subsequent gasp. After the tour, Fatima took notes as Deb explained, with the help of the caseworker, the business of running an American home: how to salt the drive, where to set the bins on trash day, the meaning of the different settings on the washer-dryer. She was thrilled to be of use and shared with Fatima all the tips and tricks she'd learned in twenty-five years of housekeeping, like running lemon rinds through a smelly garbage disposal or scrubbing scratches off wood furniture with shelled walnuts. Amina ran from room to room, jumping on the furniture.

After a while, the caseworker yawned. "It's getting late," she said. "I'm sure the Nassers are exhausted."

"I know this is a lot to take in," Deb said, pausing to let the caseworker translate, "and I don't want to keep you up all night. I'll come by tomorrow to see how you're doing. In the meantime, if there's anything you need, my number's on the fridge."

"Thank you," Fatima said. "Very much."

Deb brightened. "You speak English?"

She pinched the air like you would a child's cheeks. "Little," she said. Cocking her head in Khalil's direction, she added, with a touch of exasperation, "He, not so much."

"Well, there's never been a better time to learn."

It was almost midnight when she left the Nassers' new house. The street looked brighter than it had before. Snow sparkled in the vacant lot beside the house; a pool of warm, buttery light spread from underneath the lamppost. She could hardly believe that this was the same streetlamp that had taunted her on the way in. Standing in the cold, she felt hopeful for the first time in months.

"You did a mitzvah," the caseworker said when Deb dropped her off in Jamaica Plain. "You should be proud."

"Well," Deb said, "I can't take *all* the credit. I have the support of a wonderful community behind me. The Jewish League, of course, has been a great help. I don't know what I would have done without you tonight. I don't speak Arabic, and it's been about a hundred years since Hebrew school, but to my ears, you sounded like a natural."

The caseworker smiled, reached for the door handle, and then drew back. "Do you want to come upstairs?" she asked. "Celebrate with a drink?"

"What, now?"

"It's not every day we welcome a new family to the city." The caseworker laid a hand on Deb's knee. "That seems like cause for celebration to me."

Deb was flattered—and confused. How did the caseworker know she slept with women? She wondered at the imperceptible ways she might have changed since moving in with Joan. "I should probably be getting home," she said, removing the hand from her knee. "My partner"—that word, still so new, tasted bitter on her tongue—"is probably wondering where I am."

"Hey, no problem. I respect the urge to merge."

As Deb watched the caseworker walk toward her apartment, she wondered if she should have accepted the invitation. Not because she was attracted to the woman, but because she thought that she *should* mark the occasion somehow and because the prospect of another argument with Joan at this late hour was enough to make her dread driving home. She pulled up the text thread she shared with her children and typed out a message conveying the good news. Then she sat for a while in her car, a current pulsing through her veins, until she decided to drive home. But she blew through the intersection at Beacon Street, turning left toward the old house on Crowninshield Road. Scott answered the door in shorts and a T-shirt.

"Deb?"

"I'm sorry," she said. "I hope I didn't wake you."

"Just taking a turn on the rowing machine." His shirt was soaked with sweat, and the muscles in his arms twitched.

"You're wondering what I'm doing here. Can I come in?"

His face betrayed no particular feeling as he held the door open for her.

"Mix me a drink?" she asked.

"Yeah, okay."

She sat on one of the stools by the kitchen island. "I don't know what Marjorie did," she said while Scott prepared a pair of cocktails, "but the Syrian family arrived today. I was just over there, helping them get settled."

"That's good news. You should probably give her a call."

"I will. But I wanted to thank you first. It was your idea for me to call her to begin with."

"In person?" He handed her a glass. "At midnight?"

She drained the glass in a single sip, the alcohol surging through her system. She had been so nervous for the Nassers' arrival that she hadn't eaten anything since breakfast. "I talked to Maya yesterday. She might come home for Passover after all."

"Oh yeah?"

"It was a brief call, but at least she picked up. I'm hoping, if she comes, that we can talk about this wedding. It's never too early to start looking at venues. I thought the arboretum could be nice. I can understand not wanting to get married in the same place as your parents, of course."

"I was so scared it was going to rain. I must have checked the weather report a hundred times."

"But it didn't."

"And you were worried about your dress."

She set her empty glass aside, smiling at the thought of the dress, all that nervous energy for nothing. It had been a perfect day. "I'll bet it's somewhere upstairs."

A moment passed before she saw the spark of understanding in his eyes. "I could help you look," he said.

"I could use your eyes."

He followed her upstairs. She could feel his eyes on her, warming her back. She hadn't been in her old bedroom in months, and she was stunned by the sight of her clothes in the closet. They seemed to have been waiting patiently for her return.

"Here it is," she said.

"I wonder if it still fits."

She unbuttoned her blouse and let it fall to the floor. Then she reached back to unclasp her bra before stepping out of her skirt. As Deb undressed, she felt as though she were shedding not just her clothes but her history, their history, so that when she finally turned

around to face her husband, wearing nothing but her scarab beetle
earrings, she did so as a stranger, someone yet to be discovered.

The Nassers were settling in nicely. Twice per week, Deb drove them
to the language center in Somerville where Khalil and Fatima took
their English classes. They hadn't found jobs yet, but Deb was confident that something would come along, especially once their language skills improved. Amina, who was enrolled at John Winthrop
Elementary, was already halfway fluent, her child's brain soaking up
the words she learned in school. Deb volunteered to watch the girl
while her parents were in class. She'd been feeling a bit bereft of purpose ever since the Nassers arrived. She was thrilled that they had
made it, of course, and though this achievement ensured Deb's re-
election, the Resettlement Committee had not yet decided on its next
undertaking. Deb was desperate for something to do to fill her days,
especially if that something involved Amina. The girl reminded her
of Maya, headstrong and opinionated. Whenever Deb complimented
Amina's appearance, she replied, "I'm not beautiful. I'm *bright!*"

Deb brought Amina to all the old haunts: the puppet theater, the
Children's Museum, the aquarium. Watching her explore these places,
Deb ached for a time when her own children had been that age—
when she had seen the world through their awestruck eyes. She'd
always loved being a mother, almost so much that it embarrassed her.
She was a competent dancer, a pretty good cook, the dedicated chair
of the Resettlement Committee. But as a mother, she excelled.

One evening, when she'd exhausted all other ideas, she drove Amina to the Boston Dance Complex, a studio space run by a former
colleague, Lisa Vayntrub. The brick building, which had once been

a foam factory, occupied an entire city block in a neighborhood that Deb no longer recognized. When Lisa first found the space, back in 1986, Winter Hill had been a blue-collar, crime-ridden slice of "Slummerville," the yards replete with garden gnomes and bathtub Madonnas. Deb had witnessed her fair share of shakedowns in those days, and twice contracted tetanus from rusty nails left out on the sidewalk. But Whitey Bulger didn't live here anymore, having taken up residence in federal prison, and the rent had skyrocketed since. Walking toward the building while she held Amina's hand, Deb noticed not one but *two different apiaries* in the front yards of homes across the street from the Complex. She didn't mourn the gangsters, but she missed the Madonnas. They had always looked so serene, so forgiving.

Deb dropped Lisa's name at the front desk. The smiling young woman seated there, most likely a dancer herself, showed them to the studio space that Lisa had promised would be free that evening. A class was letting out when they arrived. A dozen limber bodies spilled from the studio, patting themselves dry. When the room had cleared, Deb showed Amina inside. All at once, she was overcome with a warm, familiar feeling. She knew this space, or at least others like it. The mirrored wall, the ballet barre, the boom box in the corner. The smell of sweat.

"What are we doing here?" Amina asked. She scowled and planted her hands on her hips, aping an adult posture of consternation. Probably something she'd picked up from her parents.

"You'll see," Deb said as she rolled her neck.

She crossed the studio floor and sat on the bleachers. Lisa had said that there would be a cord to connect Deb's phone to the boom box. She searched in vain for a few minutes before deciding that someone from the last class must have taken it. Deb dug her tongue into the pocket of her cheek. She didn't know where else to take Amina, who was sitting in the center of the studio, legs splayed out in front of her, slack with boredom.

Deb rested her hand on top of the boom box and wondered what to do. She supposed she could show Amina around Somerville, though she wasn't sure what would be open at this hour. Resigned to an evening of aimless wandering, she started to stand, when the lid of the boom box, responding to the pressure of her touch, opened like an oyster. The pearl: a compact disc with the words "Jock Jams" scrawled in blue Sharpie. Deb exhaled, her shoulders sinking with relief.

"All right, Miss Amina," she said. "On your feet!"

For the following hour, they moved their bodies to "Whoomp! (There It Is)" and "Tootsee Roll." Amina flailed about, waving her arms over her head with a confidence Deb admired, even envied. What the girl lacked in technique she more than made up for with enthusiasm. Watching Amina surrender herself to the music, Deb remembered seeing, at sixteen, the Joffrey Ballet on a trip to Chicago with her parents. The dancers wore red skirts and bell bottoms, twisting to the Beach Boys before a wall of graffiti, their bodies swaying as if riding an invisible surf. That night changed the way she thought about movement forever. The world, she realized, was kinetic. Choreographed. Sidewalks, satellites, flight patterns, traffic lights: they told people when to move and where, directing the great folk dance of urban life.

Deb's own career was predicated on dancing for pay, raising funds for studio space, and selling tickets. Her highest aspiration then was to be *professional.* But now, dancing to the syncopated claps of "It Takes

Two," she wondered if, in fact, professionalism was the problem—
that to love something was to do it for free.

At the end of their hour, Deb carried an exhausted Amina to the
car, where the girl promptly fell asleep. She was still sleeping when
Deb pulled up to the language school.

"Sorry I'm late," Deb said in a quiet voice. She nodded at Amina
in the back seat. "We had a little too much fun, I think."

"Thank you, Deb," Fatima said. She wore white jeans that flared
at the ankles and a Mickey Mouse sweatshirt that Deb recognized as
having once belonged to Avital's son. "Was she trouble for you?"

"Oh, my goodness. Not at *all.*"

Deb was glad to have to mind Amina. There were days when it felt
like the Nassers were all she had to bind her to the world beyond her
broken family.

Khalil climbed into the front seat and Fatima got in back. He
mumbled something to his wife in Arabic. Fatima translated.

"He says that one day we will repay you."

Deb waved away the offer. "Really, Fatima. The pleasure is all
mine."

Khalil spoke again.

"He insists," Fatima said. "If you ever need us, you understand, we
are here."

Joan had been especially sour since her spot on *Fresh Air.* She claimed
to have been "dismembered" by Terry Gross, who "wasn't fooling
anyone" with her "fraudulent warmth," stashing pointed questions
in her cozy affect "like a teddy bear stuffed with razor blades." Joan
had been in a rage these last two months, having dismissed Deb's

suggestion that she apologize for the "incident." She'd decided to double down instead. She went so far as to track down the teacher who had shouted at the boy in the viral video and hired her to serve as an assistant principal at the new academy in Mattapan. It was never enough for Joan to thwart her rivals; she had to spite them, too. This was, after all, the same woman who had tattooed "Si vis pacem, para bellum" on her bicep in a font better suited to the phrase "Live, laugh, love."

Deb could hardly claim to be surprised when Joan shot down her plan to host Passover at the house on Crowninshield Road. Joan was unwavering in her conviction that this was the first in a series of maneuvers that would end with Deb moving back in with her husband. Deb swore on her children that this wasn't the case. She hadn't even seen Scott since that night they had slept together six weeks earlier— not that she said this to Joan. She spoke instead of the importance of tradition, of communing with family and friends over brisket, of renewing the ties that bound them to the past. She spoke of the trials of the ancient Israelites and the plates her grandparents had smuggled out of Poland. She spoke of the spa weekend she'd booked for Joan at Canyon Ranch.

"Fine," Joan said, folding her arms. "But I'm getting an oxygen facial. And I want to see a hypnotherapist."

Deb kissed her cheek. "Anything you want."

As soon as Joan left town for Canyon Ranch, Deb set about preparing for the ritual meal, preparations that had become rituals unto themselves. She planned her menu and made a grocery list. She bought boxes of Streit's matzah and bottles of Gold's horseradish and the kosher Coca-Cola with the yellow caps. She stopped into the Israel Book Shop on Harvard Street, not because she wanted to buy anything, but because it was always mobbed this time of year, and the crowds gave her that hallowed feeling that she was part of something larger than herself.

Nothing was so sacred to her as gefilte fish. The recipe originated with her grandmother, and Deb considered the process of preparing it an act of ancestor worship. First, she washed the bones, head, and skins of the whitefish, which she wrapped in cheesecloth and dropped into a pot of salted water with chopped carrots and onions. Once the broth was sufficiently flavorful, she removed the cheesecloth, sliced the fish into strips, and fed them to the meat grinder on the Kitchen-Aid. Next, she mixed the ground fish with onions and eggs and a little salt and pepper. This mixture was the basis for the fish balls, which Deb then dropped into the simmering broth. By the time she finished, Joan's immaculate apartment, redolent of rattan reeds in lavender oil, stunk like a kosher fish market. It was a wonderful smell, as far as Deb was concerned, but she wasn't sure Joan would agree. She left the windows open to air it out.

The following evening, she hosted the usual crowd at the house on Crowninshield Road. Along with the Cantors, Sackses, Selzers, and Steins, she'd invited the Waxmans, the Oberbrunners, and Yotam Brav, who brought with him a beautiful Dominican boy who looked to Deb like he'd just cleared the age of consent. She was thrilled to discover that the Nassers had come, too, and made a point to introduce them to those guests who were not on the Resettlement Committee. But she was most excited to see Maya, who arrived with her fiancé on her arm and a modest moonstone on her ring finger. It was almost enough to make up for the fact that Gideon, citing school, had stayed behind in New York.

"The Hebrew term 'Pesach,' or Passover," she began, after every-

one had taken their seats, "means 'to leap, to bypass the normal order.' The word 'seder,' on the other hand, comes from a Hebrew root
word meaning 'order.' The phrase 'Passover seder' is a paradox: an
order that facilitates the transcending of order. A kind of liberation
within limits."

It occurred to her with a start that the speech she was delivering now—the speech she delivered each year with such sincerity it
sounded like the first time—bore more than a few similarities to the
speech she had given herself and then to Scott when they first opened
their marriage. That was what she'd wanted all along, she thought.
An endless seder. Continuous transcendence. She blushed, embarrassed by the breadth of her appetites.

Someone coughed. She had lapsed into silence.

"What Deb is trying to say," Scott said, "is that tonight, we transcend the normal order." He looked at her, his eyebrows raised in
earnest. "Is that right?"

"That's right," she said, relieved that he had come to her rescue.
"Tonight, we transcend."

Perlman, whom Deb had brought at Scott's request, mewed his approval.

Apart from Marty's routine heckling—"Why on this night do we
drink four glasses of wine? On all other nights, my wife cuts me off at
two"—the evening proceeded without interruption. Scott broke the
middle matzah, Maya read the Four Questions, and soon everyone,
including Fatima, whose English had improved since she'd started
language classes, was taking turns telling the story of how the Israelites
came to be slaves in the land of Egypt. When Gail Sacks recited the
Ten Plagues, she replaced "blood" with "climate change" and "frogs"
with "Mitch McConnell." Amina ran off to hunt for the afikomen.

The only moment of discomfort came during dessert when a drunk Marty Selzer started blustering about the ancient Israelites. "I've gotta hand it to 'em," he said. "Forced to leave their homes . . . pursued by hostile forces . . . starting their lives over from scratch. Can you imagine?"

A brief silence followed before Fatima said, "Yes."

"I'm not talking about material goods. I'm talking about psychological trauma. Leaving behind everything you've ever known."

"Yes."

Marty, who had apparently forgotten that the Nassers were refugees, cocked his head in confusion. "I'm talking about the Israelites."

That was when Deb intervened. "Marty?" she said. "Would you mind clearing the table?"

"I'm trying to make a point here, Deb."

"And I'm asking you to clear the table."

"To know that you can never go back . . ."

"Marty."

"That the home you left no longer exists . . ."

"Found it!" Amina stood in the foyer, holding a ragged rectangle of matzah wrapped in white cloth.

Deb, grateful for the interruption, waved her over. "Good job, Amina! Maya, what's the going rate for afikomen?"

"When I was her age?" Maya shrugged. "Five bucks."

"Adjusting for inflation?"

"Six fifty," Marty said. "I'd recommend starting a retirement fund."

Scott bent to whisper something in Amina's ear. "Whatever you do, don't give that guy a cent."

Marty calmed down after Deb served tea and coffee. Maya went hunting for her old beading kit, and when she found it, she showed Amina how to make a bracelet. Louis talked politics with Larry Sacks while Fatima befriended Yotam's date. Khalil ate two helpings of gefilte fish. Deb received countless compliments about her cooking; even Karla Cantor confessed to being impressed by the brisket. Apart from the fact that Gideon hadn't come home, the evening was everything that Deb had hoped it would be.

Later, after everyone had left, she stood over the sink, scrubbing dishes. "Have you thought any more about venues?" she asked and passed a plate to Maya. "There's a place in Chestnut Hill, the Waterworks Museum, that has a kind of funky, industrial feel."

"It's too early for that, Mom."

"And the ring? Is it permanent or just a placeholder?"

"*Mom.*"

"I'm sorry! I'm excited!"

Maya slotted the plate into the dishwasher. "Gail told me Talia lost her job."

"Talia Sacks is not exactly a model citizen. Remember when she drove her car into the reservoir?" Deb shook her head. "How she wound up working for the Anne Frank Center, I don't know."

"There are lots of reasons people lose their jobs. It doesn't make you a bad person."

"No, of course not. But between you and me, I think Talia was fired."

"So?"

"So she must have done *something* wrong."

"I'm just saying that society tends to associate unemployment with some kind of moral failing, and personally, I don't think that's fair."

"Since when are you such good friends with Talia Sacks?"

Louis came into the kitchen before Maya could answer. "So, we have a slight problem."

"What's that?" Deb asked.

He nodded in the direction of the yard. "Take a look."

Deb met her daughter's eyes before they went to the window. Squinting past the glare, Deb saw Perlman on the lawn, his back arched in a defensive stance, his tail puffed up to twice its regular size. Standing a few feet away from him was a wild turkey. Its feathers were dark, almost black, with an oily luster, its pink head pecking in Perlman's direction. The bird was coming toward the cat, one claw foot at a time, looking as though it had walked out of prehistoric times and onto her family's front lawn. Scott stood a safe distance from the turkey, waving his arms.

"Scott! Do something!" Deb shouted.

"Too dangerous!" he shouted back. His voice was muffled through the pane of glass.

"Dad's right," Maya said. "Those things are vicious. I knew a girl who got her eye pecked out."

The turkey was in striking distance now.

"Somebody, please!" Deb cried.

Louis lunged toward the counter. He reached into a Tupperware container and picked up a ball of gefilte fish. Then he ran outside and whistled. When the turkey looked in his direction, Louis chucked the gefilte fish across the street. The turkey pursued it with considerable speed, allowing Scott to scoop up Perlman and run him back inside.

"Louis!" Maya threw her arms around his shoulders. "You're a hero!"

"Is Perlman all right?" Deb asked.

Scott set the cat down. "He's fine. A little spooked is all. Thanks,

Louis. That was real quick thinking. Who knew turkeys could tolerate gefilte fish?"

Louis nodded. "Not a problem."

"You have my permission to marry my daughter."

"Dad . . ."

Deb bent to pet Perlman, who was shivering with fear. "Well, that's probably my cue to take him home. Or—not home, but—you know what I . . ." She felt the heat rise in her face. When had the simplest things become so complicated? "Louis, I really can't thank you enough. You saved the day."

At the door, Scott asked if Deb wanted to stay. "It'd be nice, I think, to spend some time together. With Maya here. Anyway, I could really use your help with Louis. The kid's a ball of nerves. He keeps calling me 'sir.'"

"I'd like to," she said, "but I don't want to confuse her. Maya, I mean. I don't want her to get the wrong idea."

A few weeks earlier, in a rare fit of good humor, Joan had written a check to the Nassers to be put toward their rent while they looked for work. It was a startling display of generosity from a woman not normally given to charity, but Deb understood the gift to be for her benefit as much as theirs. It was, in a sense, a romantic gesture, an acknowledgment of what mattered most to Deb. So despite the fact that Deb wanted to stay with Scott—to prolong, even for another hour, the illusion that nothing in her life had changed—she felt she owed it to Joan to leave.

"Maybe tomorrow, though!" she added. "I could swing by on my way back from the gym."

He nodded slowly, his lips forming a thin, slanted line. "You can come back anytime you want."

It was tempting, especially on a night like this, to think she could stop time and rewind it, the way she had when she scrutinized tapes of her recitals, her limbs jerking backward behind the bars of static until she paused, her body poised at the start of the routine before she had made any mistakes. But Scott had betrayed her just like he'd betrayed his patients, and she wasn't sure if she could trust him again.

Joan wouldn't be back for two more days, and Deb dreaded the emptiness of her apartment, which had never quite felt like her own. Her books and furniture were still at the old house, and Joan was too meticulous, too stubborn, to give Deb any say in the decor. But as she made her way inside, she soon discovered that the apartment wasn't empty at all. Her son was sitting at the dining room table.

She cupped her hand over her mouth to keep from screaming. "Gideon?"

"Hey, Mom." There were hollows in his cheeks, the bones more pronounced than usual. He looked pale, the olive coloring squeezed out of his skin. "I was starting to wonder if you were coming back."

"What are you . . . How did you know where to find me?"

"I looked up your girlfriend's address online."

"Joan is not my girlfriend."

"Then what is she?"

The shock of finding him was still fresh. She hugged him, holding his lean body close. "I wish you'd told me you were coming home," she said. "We had our seder tonight."

"I know."

"How did you even get in?"

"You left the window open. All the windows, actually. I came up the fire escape."

Deb put a pot of water on the stove and sat across from her son at the table. She asked why he'd missed the seder, why he wasn't at school, and, repeatedly, if everything was okay. What he told her over the course of the next half hour was so unexpected, so confusing, and above all, so alarming that later, in bed, she would lie awake wondering how well she really knew him. In a voice at once gentle and resigned—he sounded less like her twenty-year-old son than a mortician patiently explaining funeral rites—he told her that he'd broken up with Astra, left his job at the lab, and (here she almost spat up her tea) dropped out of college altogether.

"You dropped *out?* With six weeks left in the semester?"

"I guess I just stopped seeing the point." He raised the teacup to his lips with maddening composure. "This is a good thing, Mom. You'll see."

The news mingled with the lingering smell of gefilte fish to form a single, nauseating sensation. "When did this happen?"

"Few days ago."

"Why didn't you tell me? Why didn't the *school* tell me?"

"FERPA."

Of the many ways a son can let a mother down, Deb could imagine none more piercing, none more grievous than this. "I would love for someone to explain to me why my son, a National Merit scholar who won first prize at his seventh- *and* eighth-grade science fairs, has decided, without consulting his mother, that he's too good for a college education."

"I don't think I'm too good for anything. I just don't think college is the right fit for me. Anyway, Dad did those science fair projects."

"What did I do wrong?" she asked. "Tell me. I want to know what I did wrong."

"I swear, this has nothing to do with you, Mom."

"What about your classes? What about your friends? For God's sake, Gideon, what about med school?"

"I don't want to go anymore."

"What about Astra?"

Gideon was quiet for a minute. Then, without meeting Deb's eyes, he said that he didn't see the point in dating someone when even the best marriages were bound to fail.

Deb gripped the table to steady herself. "This is what's going to happen," she said. "You're going to call Columbia first thing in the morning. You're going to apologize. And then you're going to beg them to take you back."

"I'm sorry, Mom, but I'm not doing that."

"Dad and I paid for your tuition already, so yes, that's exactly what you're doing to do."

"You aren't hearing me. I'm never going back."

"Okay," she said and pushed her chair out. "Get your coat. We're going over to the house. You can explain this to your father."

"I'm not doing that, either."

"Fine," she said, pulling her cell phone from her bag. "I'll tell him myself."

"Wait! Stop!" There was no trace of anger in his voice, only fear. "Please, Mom. I don't want him to know."

"In what universe do you drop out of college and expect me not to tell him?"

"A universe in which the two of you aren't talking."

A rush of self-recrimination overcame her. If only she hadn't moved out, she thought, if only she hadn't opened her marriage, if only she'd emphasized his education more, if only she'd emphasized his edu-

cation less, if only she'd accepted his limitations, if only she'd refused to accept his limitations, if only she'd talked more, if only she'd
listened . . .

"He's going to find out one way or another," she said. "Honestly,
Gideon, what were you thinking? Do you have any sort of plan whatsoever?"

His shoulders were hunched, his hands tucked between his legs.
He looked helplessly small, like a kindergartener on his first day of
school, not a college junior on his last.

"I was thinking I might stay with you for a while."

Joan was none too pleased to come home from Canyon Ranch to
discover that Deb's son had moved in while she was gone. She might
have made more of a fuss had she not received a phone call that morning, in the middle of her sound-healing workshop, informing her that
a district judge had dismissed the complaint of racial bias lodged by
local activists after her *Fresh Air* interview. Joan, aglow with the good
news (and three days of salt scrubs, zip lines, and reiki), granted Gideon
use of the guest room until he got back on his feet. Besides, she said,
the next few months would be busy. With the law, if not justice, squarely
on her side, she could now devote her time to establishing the new
academy in Mattapan.

Deb was grateful for Joan's understanding while she tried to figure out what to do with Gideon. When she asked if he wanted to
come with her to work or to a meeting of the Resettlement Committee, he shrugged and said he "didn't see the point." He refused her
suggestion to speak with a therapist, refused her offer to walk with
her through the Fens. She could hardly believe that this sullen young

man was the same boy who used to catalog plant species at the pond sanctuary after school. The hollows in his cheeks made him look like a hostage. He took his meals in his room when he ate anything at all.

It wasn't until she left town for a weekend that she realized just how precarious this new arrangement was. Maya had invited her to shop for wedding dresses, and Deb wasn't going to pass that up, even if it meant leaving Joan alone with Gideon. She'd spent the past month watching Amina while Khalil and Fatima went to English classes and job interviews. She was happy to do it, but privately, she felt that she could do with a vacation.

They spent the weekend popping in and out of bridal shops, making stops at Russ & Daughters and Veselka, where they debriefed over bagels with lox and stuffed cabbage. It had been a long time since Deb felt so close to her daughter, and she was pleased to be reminded just how prudent and mature a young woman Maya was and how lucky to be starting a marriage with a clean slate.

She felt so close, in fact, that when Maya asked after Gideon, Deb couldn't bring herself to lie. From her seat outside the changing room, she told Maya everything.

"So he dropped out of school," Maya said.

"That's right."

"And he moved in with you."

"Right again."

"And Dad doesn't know."

Deb had agonized about what to tell Scott and whether she should tell him anything at all. He'd probably find out eventually, if and when Columbia refused his next tuition payment, but in the meantime, she told herself that this was payback for his investment. If Scott could divert family funds in secret, surely she could "forget" to mention that their son had dropped out of college.

"I think it would be better for everyone involved if Gideon took responsibility and told Scott himself."

"Well," Maya said, after a minute, "I guess this is probably as good a time as any to tell you that I lost my job."

"You *what*?"

The door to the changing room opened, and Maya stepped out. Deb was so stunned by the sight of her daughter that for a moment, she forgot what they were talking about. The dress was sleeveless, exposing arms so smooth and so pale that they resembled porcelain. Maya's tattoo was smaller than she remembered. The hard, flat plane of her chest, which had been the cause of so much anguish in her teenage years, was perfectly suited to the lace bodice. In the mirrored wall behind her, Deb could make out a trail of white buttons tracing her spine.

"So?" Maya said, clutching her own wrist. "What do you think?"

"Oh my *god*," gasped the sales associate, a tall man with a floral pocket square in his blue blazer. "You look *gorgeous*."

"He's right," Deb said, catching her breath. "You look beautiful. I'm sorry, I'm just not used to seeing you like this."

"Look at Mom tearing up!" the salesman said. "That's always a good sign."

Maya regarded herself in the mirror. "It *is* pretty. But I don't know." She turned, examining herself at different angles. "It's exactly the kind of dress I thought I wanted, but now that I'm wearing it, I'm not sure."

Deb dabbed at her eyes with a tissue, folded it, and placed it on the bench beside her. "I'm sorry, honey. You get that from me."

"Get what?"

"Always wanting something slightly better. Never being satisfied exactly where you are."

Despite the fact that they didn't buy the dress, and despite Maya's news about her job, Deb regarded the trip as a success. She had raised a mature and intelligent young woman, and she was proud of her daughter, no matter what the future held. But when she got home, she found Joan in such a state that she regretted having left.

"I don't mind him sleeping here," she said in bed that night, "but he spends all his time in the apartment. In that *room*. I hardly saw him once the whole time you were gone. What's wrong with him, anyway?"

"There's nothing wrong with him," Deb said, defensive. "He's just going through a phase. Anyway, I thought you'd be glad that he stayed out of your way."

"And the way he looks at me, with those big, blank eyes . . ."

"If you were a parent, you might understand."

"You wouldn't believe what he's got in that room."

"You were in his room?"

"It isn't his room! It's mine! Now let me explain."

The previous morning, while Gideon showered, Joan slipped into the guest room where she found, among the dirty clothes and duffel bags, a number of alarming items on his desk: a passport, a SIM card, a first aid kit, a flashlight, a pack of razors, spare batteries, a power adapter, a roll of toilet paper, an English to Hebrew pocket dictionary, an English to Arabic pocket dictionary, a wad of foreign currency (she wasn't sure what kind), and, most concerning of all, the bottle of Drano she kept under the sink.

"Why is that concerning?" Deb asked.

Joan lowered her voice to a whisper. "If you mix Drano, water, and aluminum foil in a plastic bottle, the chemical reaction can cause an explosion."

Deb would have been more outraged had she found the charge even remotely credible. "You think my son is building a *bomb*?"

"Have you seen the beard he's been growing?"

Over the past few weeks, Gideon's cheeks had darkened with hard, creaturely hairs. He looked less like a hostage now than he did a hostage taker, the kind who wrote manifestos and recorded home movies from a basement or a cave.

"I'd hardly call that a beard," Deb said, though she couldn't explain what Joan had found, the odd inventory on his desk. "Maybe he's going camping."

"In the Gaza Strip? I'm telling you, Deb, the kid fits a profile."

"What kind of profile?"

"Disillusioned kid drops out of college, moves in with his mother, grows a beard . . ."

"Jesus, Joan."

"Starts studying Arabic . . ."

Deb turned over in bed. "I'll talk to him tomorrow. Okay?"

"Let's hope that whatever he's planning, he isn't planning to do it tonight."

Though Deb didn't think her son was building a bomb, she did scan the *Globe* on her phone the next morning and was relieved not to find news of any attacks. She was doubly relieved when she stopped by the guest room after breakfast and found that he had shaved his beard. "Can I come in?" she asked.

The room was even bleaker than she'd imagined. In addition to the dirty clothes crumpled on the floor, there were stains on his sheets and empty soda bottles and a wastebasket brimming with tissues. She opened the blackout curtains, and the room flared with light. Dust motes hung suspended in the air.

"I had a nice weekend with your sister," she said, scanning the room. There, on the desk, were the items Joan had mentioned, the passport and the flashlight and the pocket dictionaries.

He sat on the bed, wearing boxers and a white T-shirt, squinting against the glare. "Did you find a dress?"

"We didn't," she said and picked up his passport. "Going somewhere?"

He cleared his throat. "Actually, yeah. I've been meaning to tell you. I'm going to go to Israel."

"Oh! . . . Why?"

"I don't know. I'm just thinking it might be good for me. You're always saying I should get out of the house."

"You don't have to go *that* far."

"The trip is free for anyone between eighteen and twenty-six. Anyway, it only lasts a week."

"Well, if it's only a week," she said, surveying the items on his desk, all of which suddenly made sense. All but one. "What's the Drano for?"

He stroked his chin. "I clogged the sink in the bathroom," he said. "When I shaved."

As a girl, Deb had gone door to door raising money for the Jewish National Fund. She'd been raised to believe in the need for a Jewish state and tried to impart that belief to her children. In recent years, however, she'd come to feel unsettled by the occupation, and guilty for not feeling unsettled sooner. The country's slide into right-wing authoritarian rule made Deb feel as though she'd been physically attacked by her own family. Now she could hardly think about the place without bothering the wound. Israel didn't seem any safer for the Jews than Brookline did. There had never been a suicide bomb in Brookline, and you could get pretty good falafel there, too. She didn't know why Gideon wanted to go or what he expected to find when he got there. Then again, there was nothing for him in this room, and seven days in the company of other college students might make him rethink his decision to drop out. At the very least, he'd get some sun.

She drove him to the airport two weeks later.

"Be careful," she said as she saw him to security. He'd wanted to say goodbye on the curb, but she had insisted on coming inside. "You don't have to do anything you don't want to. If they try to wrap you up in tefillin, or something like that, and you don't feel comfortable, you can say no."

"I know."

"Stick to bottled water. Keep your eyes peeled at all times. And don't take any public buses, okay?"

"I'm pretty sure we have a private bus."

"You aren't going to Gaza, are you?"

"Mom."

"Should we check the itinerary? Just to make sure?"

"*Mom.*" He wrapped his arms around her. "I'll be fine."

She could feel the echoes of her body's trembling in his. "I'll be standing right here to meet you in a week."

He let go (why did they have to let go? She could have stayed hold-ing him forever) and started toward security. Deb waited to see if he would turn around and wave, but he kept his head forward, advanc-ing through the line, which was moving at a brisk pace. She shut her eyes against the tears clouding her vision, but when she opened them again, he was gone.

His departure had the desired effect of easing tensions between her and Joan, who did little to hide her happiness at having the apart-ment to herself again. She made comments about how *clean* the place was, how suddenly *spacious*, and stressed the importance of *letting the apartment breathe.* Deb didn't disagree. As much as she missed him and worried for his safety, she took a guilty sort of pleasure in knowing that, for these seven days, at least, he wasn't her responsibility.

At the end of the week, Joan threw a cocktail party to celebrate the new academy in Mattapan. Deb expected teachers and administra-tors, mostly; she wore a simple black dress with minimal makeup. But the guests who began to crowd the apartment at five were so well-dressed and so outrageously successful that she felt like a mere accessory, no more valuable than the plain gold band that encircled Joan's bicep. She met "the most influential VC in Massachusetts," ex-mayor Menino's "most trusted adviser," and a man Joan intro-duced as "the single best reporter on the education beat that the *Globe* has ever employed." Then Deb heard herself described as "a pioneer in modern dance, the Boston Balanchine" and suddenly saw through the veil of glamour that Joan had draped over the evening.

"That's amazing," said the young woman standing next to Deb. "Do you still dance?"

The question rankled Deb. In it she heard an implication that the moment she stopped dancing, she ceased to be a dancer and in turn a person worth talking to. "As it happens," she said, "I was never very good."

"She's being modest," said Joan.

Deb thought it best to change the subject. "What do you do?" she asked the young woman.

"I'm the new assistant principal," she said, and suddenly Deb realized she'd seen her before.

"Whatever happened to him?" Deb asked. "The boy from the video?"

The young woman's smile wilted.

"Deb's had a few too many drinks," Joan interjected.

"You're here, at this beautiful party," Deb said. "It makes me wonder where he is."

"Deb, darling. I think your phone is ringing."

She was about to object, when she realized Joan was right. She could hear the fragile Philip Glassian piano riff looping from her cell phone on the counter.

She took the call in the guest room.

"Good news," Scott said. "I've got my license back."

"Your medical license?" She sat on Gideon's unmade bed.

"No, my liquor license. Of course my medical license!"

"That *is* good news. I'm really happy for you, Scott."

"Is that all you have to say?"

"I'm sorry," she said. "I'm just taking it in."

"I won't be able to enroll patients in clinical trials, but it means I can practice again."

"No more trials? Will that be enough?"

It wasn't clear, even to Deb, what she meant by this. Enough money? Enough work? Enough happiness?

"It's never enough," Scott said. "But it's something."

"When will you go back to work?"

"Monday. I'll have to notify my patients, of course. If I still *have* any patients."

Deb let herself tip back onto the bed. She was happy for him, but she was envious, too, of how readily he seemed to be able to return to their old life.

"So?" he said. "When do you want to move back in?"

"Who said anything about me moving in?"

"Come on, Deb," he said. "I'm doing my best here."

The ceiling fan spun madly overhead, and she had to shut her eyes against the creep of nausea. She felt compelled to tell him about Gideon but didn't. "It's not that simple, Scott."

"I thought you had a nice time at Passover."

"I did."

"And before that, when you came over—"

"I did."

A crash came from the other room. Deb sat up with a start. She heard a patter of applause; someone whistled. One of the guests must have dropped a glass.

"What's that sound?" Scott asked. "Are you watching a movie?"

"No," she said, as her heartbeat slowed. "We're having a party."

The next morning, Deb drove to the airport to pick up Gideon. She parked in the cell phone lot and went inside, standing in the same spot where she'd dropped him off, the same spot where she'd waited for the Nassers. It struck her that for all her trips to Logan lately, she hadn't been on a plane in ages. She couldn't remember the last time she'd left the country, much less the state. She wondered what it said

about her that she spent so much time at the airport but never wound
up going anywhere.

Just last week, she'd attended a Fourth of July party at the Nasser
house. The crowd was modest, mostly people who had helped get the
Nassers set up, among them Karla Cantor and the caseworker, but
Fatima's spirits were high. She had planted small American flags
throughout the yard and seemed eager to show off her improved
English. Khalil, by contrast, struck a sullen, unsmiling presence and
went inside long before the party had ended. Fatima confided to Deb
that he was having trouble adjusting to his adopted country, whereas
she felt it important to embrace her new home. They were having
fights about Amina lately, how Syrian she was going to be; Deb could
hear, in the upward lilt of the girl's speech, that she was already becoming an American.

The double doors by the ARRIVALS sign opened, and a fresh wave of
passengers poured out. Some wore yarmulkes, and others were in
black suits and top hats with sidelocks. She thought about Scott while
she watched for Gideon, their conversation from the previous night.
It wasn't that she didn't want her old life back, but it would never
be quite the same as it was, and anyway, there were so many compli-
cations.

The atrium was beginning to empty as the passengers, having collected their bags, filed out of the airport. A young Orthodox woman
in a long skirt with tights came through the doors, pushing a baby in
a stroller. There were bags beneath her eyes and an enigmatic stain
on her blouse that Deb recognized from her days as a young mother;
she used to have that very same stain on all her blouses. She recognized the look on the woman's face as well. It was the look of a woman

who hadn't slept in days, whose child had been screaming for so long that her ears didn't register the sound. Deb watched as the woman walked toward baggage claim. She wished she could tell the woman not to worry, tell her that her child would grow up healthy and strong, but when she turned to find her own child in the crowd, she saw that the double doors had closed for good.

Emotional Justice; or, The Cure for Ambiguity

●

JULY 2014

S hellfish, dander, latex, dust mites, peanuts, pollen, cashews," the girl next to Gideon said. She'd been talking since the bus left Tel Aviv, and though he nodded periodically to look like he was listening, his eyes were trained on the ponytail in front of him. The desert sun was sinking, and the warm light through the window set the brown hair ablaze with iridescence. "I've never been stung by a bee," the girl went on, "but I'm probably allergic to that, too. One time my dad got stung? By a bee? And went into anaphylactic shock. His skin broke out and his throat swelled up. Shellfish and latex, I got from my mom."

The ponytail was secured not with a hair tie but with the hair itself, wrapped at the nape in a beguiling knot.

"See that?" the girl said, pointing out the window. Her apple cheeks were shining, and her semi-rimless glasses formed a single dark brow above her eyes. "That's the separation wall. The West Bank's on the other side."

The photos Gideon had seen online promised fertile plains and rocky peaks, celestial skies and cerulean seas. Bikini-clad coeds slathered in mineral mud. The State of Israel, they seemed to suggest, was the sort of place a guy could go to figure things out; where he might, in the words of the tourism site, "unearth the roots of his soul." But Ben Gurion had looked like any other airport, with a duty-free and a

Pizza Hut, and, upon boarding the bus, Gideon was disappointed to discover just how barren the country seemed to be. The highway ran on without end, bordered on both sides by the parabolic curves of telephone wires. There were no buildings for miles, but if he craned his neck, he could see a concrete barrier flickering in and out of view from behind a veil of trees.

"It's a violation of international law," she said. "I'm going to ask Moshe about it."

He inched away from her. "I'm not sure you should."

"Someone needs to say something. We can't pretend it isn't there."

"Can't we?"

"It's our duty to speak up. If not us, who? If not now, when?"

"Maybe once we're off the bus?" Gideon looked at the ponytail and wondered how its owner felt about the wall, and how strong those feelings were, and, finally, how he might avoid supporting or opposing it until he knew the strength and character of those feelings. "It's a complicated issue, and I don't know too much about it, but I feel like once we're off the bus, and you can talk to Moshe on your own, in private, you might have a better chance. . . ."

Her hand was already in the air.

"Moshe?" she said. "Moshe? I have a question."

The tour guide, Moshe, stood at the front of the bus. He was stocky, with a head like a massive slab of stone, his eyes concealed behind wraparound sunglasses. A small, redundant microphone was clipped onto his collar. "Yes?" His voice fizzed through the speakers that were mounted overhead.

"Are we going to get a tour of the West Bank?"

He cupped his ear. "Speak up!"

"I *said*, are we going to get a tour of the West Bank?"

"No. No." He shook his head. "No. We will not have time to take you to Judea and Samaria."

"Why not?"

"Every trip there is one troublemaker. You, Shelby, are the trouble-maker!"

Gideon shrunk in his seat. Some of the students on the bus had met before, back home, at their campus Hillel Houses or Chabads. Some went all the way back to summer camp. But Gideon had come alone, and no one knew him yet. He didn't want anyone to get the impression that he and Shelby the troublemaker were friends.

"I'm only asking questions," she said.

Moshe's square pecs bounced beneath his T-shirt. "The wall is for safety."

"Whose safety?"

"Yours. Where we are going can be dangerous. This is why we have Dov." He gestured to the back of the bus, where a young soldier sat on a bench alone. He balanced an assault rifle between his legs.

"What about the war in Gaza going on right now?"

A guy across the aisle turned to Shelby. "If you're so obsessed with the wall or whatever, you can get off the bus and go see it yourself." He smoothed the silken fabric of his basketball shorts. "You can't sign up for a free trip and spend the whole time bitching."

"I'm not the only one," Shelby said with less conviction. She prodded Gideon with her elbow. "Right?"

The girl with the ponytail turned to see what was going on. Her face was heart shaped, with a wide forehead and narrow chin, the curve of her cheekbones sloping down to her lips. But it was her eyes, small and dark like the barrels of a gun, that made his blood bounce. He was ashamed just to be looking at her and incapable of looking anywhere else.

"Well," he started, "I don't know about *that* . . ."

The guy across the aisle shook his head. "There are people who would kill to sit where you're sitting right now, bro, and believe me, they'd be much more grateful."

"I didn't say anything!"

It was no use. The boy kept shaking his head, and so did Shelby, united for a moment in their disappointment. The girl in front of him smirked and turned around, her ponytail swishing behind her.

Gideon retreated to the comfort of his phone. Even with his international SIM card, however, he didn't have service out here on the highway. His most recent text was from his mother, asking if he was safe. She'd been hectoring him like this since April, ministering to him like he was a mental patient—as if dropping out of college made a person crazy. But he hadn't been crazy when he left Columbia. Confused, maybe. Crazy, no.

He hadn't planned on moving in with her. In that first rush of freedom following his big decision—though at the time it hadn't felt like a decision at all, more like an inevitability—he thought he'd go backpacking somewhere. Maybe South America. He imagined himself sipping ayahuasca tea beneath the thatched roof of a jungle retreat while his ego dissolved like wet tissue paper. Or maybe he would pick up some new skill, like driving stick, or get a job doing something with his hands, like construction. Earn a living off the sweat of his brow. But he couldn't afford a ticket to Portland, much less Peru, having paid restitution to the university for the so-called damage he'd inflicted on Dr. Park's lab. He didn't have a car, whether stick or au-

tomatic, and his roommate, or rather former roommate, Dewey Suss-
man, said his hands were way too soft to work construction. He couldn't
even go home because his mother had moved out, and he'd hardly
spoken to his father since Scott lost his medical license. So he moved
into the guest room at his mother's new apartment, where he'd spent
the past three months trying to work out what to do now that he
wasn't in school anymore. By the time he made up his mind to visit
Israel, that initial rush of freedom had diminished to a trickle, and
the guest room had come to feel like limbo itself.

Israel had been his roommate's idea. Dewey was a good-natured
slouch with slurry speech, the son of a psychoanalyst single mother;
he moved through the world with the artless confidence of a kid who
never had a father to compete with. In the pages of the parenting
guide *The Joys of Boys*, written by his mother's colleague Rosa Gittel-
man, Dewey, referred to throughout the text as "D," was described as
"a gentle youngster with poor coordination, more likely to trip over
his own shoelaces than he is to find himself in a backyard brawl." But
Dewey had apparently undergone quite the transformation in the land
of milk and honey. "I have three words for you," he said when he got
back from his trip, a few months before Gideon dropped out, "Jews
with guns. You haven't lived until you've seen so many Jews with guns.
I'm not just talking Desert Eagles, either. I'm talking Uzis. Sniper
rifles. Semiautomatics. Guns made in Israel. Jewish guns. FUBU,
dude!"

"I didn't know you were so into guns," Gideon said.

Dewey fingered the Star of David hanging from his neck, a souvenir he'd picked up from a mystic in Tsfat. "And the women. The
women. I use the word advisedly. They're nothing like the uptight girls
we have here."

"You met someone?"

"Tall women. Tan women. Women with guns! Did you know how hot a language Hebrew is?"

"I didn't."

"As soon as the plane touched down, all the anxiety I've lived with my whole life just . . . *evaporated*. In Israel, you know where you stand. You know who's good and you know who's bad. You know what's right and what's wrong. It's like they found the cure for ambiguity."

"Isn't it, like, famously complex?" Gideon asked. "The whole political . . . situation?"

"That's what I used to think, too. But thinking?" Dewey tapped his temple. "That's the root of the problem. Over there, no one sits around and wonders what to do. They just *do*."

Gideon had never given much thought to Israel before. He'd never thought a lot about Judaism, period. Jews were to Brookline what Mormons were to Salt Lake City, so ubiquitous as to hardly merit mention, and he hadn't encountered any of the oppression that, according to his social psych professor, was crucial to the formation of one's identity. His mother was involved with the synagogue, of course, but his father was a self-described "secular humanist," and long before Gideon knew the meaning of the term, he'd decided that's what he was, too. Listening to Dewey wax poetic, however, he wondered if his father was mistaken. After all, he'd made mistakes before.

"Wow," he said. "Sounds amazing."

The Star of David twinkled. "I don't think I'll ever be the same."

Gideon leaned his head against the window, searching for some greater significance in the scrubby expanse of desert and finding nothing but a yellow road sign that read, incredibly, DANGER OF DROWNING. He watched the wall flicker in and out of view until it peeled off from the highway and was gone. A guy behind him said, "I was here a year ago, with a different group? We had a soldier guarding us named Shira. She was really hot and super into me. We flirted the whole trip, and on the last night? We hooked up. She's the reason that I'm here. I came all this way to find her."

It was dark when they reached the kibbutz, a network of single-story stone and stucco buildings encompassing a vast green lawn lined with palm trees. Gideon had read about life on kibbutzim with interest in the days before his flight. He liked the thought of sharing money, of living off the land, and was intrigued by the concept of communal parenting; he wondered how he might have turned out if, instead of two parents, he'd had hundreds. But the cafeteria in the kibbutz looked like the one from his high school, with yellow light fixtures, linoleum floors, and a vending machine with an OUT OF ORDER sign taped to the glass. The room smelled like steamed brussels sprouts, and the speech they heard during dinner was hardly inspiring.

"In the eighties, everyone thought we were doomed," explained the slick young man in acid-washed jeans who introduced himself as the CEO of the kibbutz. He wore a graphic tee that read BELIEVE beneath his blazer. "The shekel was worthless. Debts were through the roof. So why are we here? How did we survive?" He raised his arms to heaven. "Privatization! Our assets are managed by professionals now. The more you work, the more you earn. No more sharing under-wear. Now we have a waiting list one hundred names long. People are desperate to live here, desperate."

Shelby raised her hand. "You don't practice collective ownership?"

"Not anymore."

"In what sense, then, is this a kibbutz?"

"Ignore her," Moshe said. "This is our troublemaker, Shelby."

The CEO laughed. "You are thinking of the old way. My grandfather's way."

Shelby shot Gideon a look across the room. Why, he wondered, had she chosen *him*? Couldn't she find someone else to commiserate with? It wasn't even that he disagreed with her—he'd expected more from the kibbutz, too—but he never would have said so out loud. He shuddered at the thought that they had anything in common.

"I thought everyone worked the land together," Shelby said.

"And now we have a fitness center, complete with Olympic-size pool."

After dinner, Moshe asked the group to form a circle and instructed everyone to share their names, where they were from, and what they hoped to get out of the week.

"I will begin," he said, in a voice so deep it might have belonged to God himself. "I grow up in the north, near Haifa. After military service, I work on a kibbutz, like this. For eight years now, I have been leading trips. What I hope is that you will all renew your connection to the Jewish homeland."

"Eight years?" asked a guy in khaki shorts and boat shoes. "Don't you get tired of it?"

"No."

"What do you make?"

"Eh?"

"I mean, what are they paying you to do this?"

Moshe set his jaw. "Watching your connection is my reward."

"Never mind," the guy said, pulling out his phone. "I'll look it up on Glassdoor."

The first student to introduce herself was named Abby. "I'm from

LA," she told the group, "but don't let that intimidate you. My older sister met her husband on one of these trips."

"Thank you, Abby," Moshe said. "And what do you hope for this week?"

"I just told you. My older sister met her husband here."

Moshe pulled a sleeve of Peanut M&M's from the pocket of his cargo pants. "This reminds me. If you are single, you get the green M&M. If you have boyfriend, girlfriend, whatever? Red M&M. And if you are somewhere in between? We have the yellow M&M. We do this to avoid confusion."

"Confusion about what?" Shelby asked.

"Trust me. In a few days, you will want to know. You will be saying, 'Thank you, Moshe, because now I know.'"

"Know what?"

He smiled. "Who is free and who is not."

Later that night, in a room that resembled the kind you might find in a business hotel, Gideon logged on to the kibbutz wi-fi, ThePromisedLAN, and pulled up Astra's Facebook page. She'd changed her relationship status to single, as expected, but she'd also deleted every photo he was in. He'd never broken up with anyone before and was surprised to find just how sick it made him feel, the way his guilt compounded his grief. He'd left her like he left Columbia: all at once, in a fit, no looking back. Her last update, posted hours earlier, read, "The past is a foreign country. —Proverb."

He was overcome with sympathy. He'd spent so much of his life pining after girls, then licking his wounds when they turned him down or left, that he actually found himself siding with Astra, the more heartbroken of the two of them. He identified more with her than he did himself.

———

In the morning, Moshe led the group up Mount Bental, a dormant volcano that overlooked the Golan Heights. Silhouettes of soldiers had been cut out of sheet metal and were propped up all around the peak.

"You are standing on important real estate," he said. "The Syrians used to drop shells on Israel from here. Bam, bam, bam, bam! What else could we do but take it back?"

The sky was clear, the blue fading into white at the horizon, but a battalion of clouds was closing in from the west. The breeze cooled the sweat under Gideon's arms. A small crowd sat nearby in canvas chairs, eating orange slices and peering through binoculars, watching for explosions across the border.

Moshe passed around his own binoculars. When it was Gideon's turn, he looked out on the blasted landscape beyond the patchwork farms below, straining to see something special, something awesome, some sign that this improbable country still had the power to inspire.

"Find yourself yet?"

He lowered the binoculars. The girl with the ponytail was standing next to him.

"What do you mean?" Gideon asked.

"Last night," she said. "At the kibbutz. When Moshe asked what you wanted out of the week, you said you came to find yourself."

Blood rushed to Gideon's cheeks. He'd thought it sounded profound at the time, but hearing her repeat his answer in a gently mocking tone made him want to throw himself off the edge of the volcano. "So far, all I can see is yellow dirt."

"Let me look."

He passed her the binoculars. Her name was Bari, he remembered, and she was from Buckhead, a suburb of Atlanta. She was even better looking up close, the straps of her sports bra visible beneath her baggy tank top, her calves sculpted by lilac leggings. As she scanned the horizon, he noticed what looked to be a jar of Skippy peanut butter in her backpack, the blue cap flashing like a tongue from inside the puckered mouth of the drawstring.

"Israel made the desert flower," Moshe was saying. "From nothing we grew olives, oranges, pears . . ."

"Sorry," she said, lowering the binoculars. "I can't find you out there, either."

". . . if you look closely, you will see the dairy farms—dairy farms, from nothing!—where we process milk and cheese . . ."

"Jesus," she whispered. "This guy's got such a hard-on for Israel."

Gideon looked over at Moshe holding forth. He wished he had even an ounce of the man's conviction. "Maybe it means a lot to him," he said.

"I had one of those magical oranges for breakfast. Guess what?"

"What?"

"They taste exactly like the oranges back home."

Her tone was beginning to bother him. "Why are you here," he asked, "if you hate it so much?"

Abby from LA interrupted them before she could answer. "I'm having a party in my room tonight," she said, lowering her voice as if disclosing state secrets. "But be chill, okay? I'm not inviting everyone."

Bari glanced at Gideon and shrugged. "We won't tell."

"Do you think Dov would come if I asked him?" Abby asked. Dov was leaning on a guardrail, shapeless in his uniform. The olive fatigues swallowed up his legs, rippling at the ankle, where they tucked into his boots. His eyes were sleepy behind his wiry glasses. A cigarette drooped from his lips. His assault rifle was slung across his back.

"Why wouldn't he?" Bari asked.

"Oh god. I'd be too embarrassed." She blushed. "I want to have his Jewish babies."

"I bet they'd come out wearing glasses."

"With little bitty machine guns!"

"Seriously?" Gideon said. "*Him?*" He didn't see what Abby saw in Dov, but he suspected it had to do with the gun, the authority it conferred on an otherwise skinny and bespectacled Jew.

"Are you gay?" Abby asked.

"No," he said, perhaps too insistently.

"Then, I'm sorry, your opinion doesn't matter."

From the Golan Heights, they drove south to Masada, a sort of fortified mesa where hundreds of Jews were said to have killed themselves rather than succumb to slavery at the hands of the encroaching Romans.

"What bravery," brayed Moshe, staring out at the Dead Sea. He turned to face the group. "You are very fortunate to breathe this air, you understand. Most who know Masada know only the miniseries."

"What miniseries?" Abby asked.

"With Peter O'Toole?" Moshe seemed surprised they hadn't heard of it. "Ah, well. Better you are here in person. The series is a travesty."

"They gave it the Hollywood treatment, huh."

"The series is not Hollywood *enough*! The courage of those men as they faced certain death . . ." Moshe looked like he might cry. "No film can do it justice."

"I thought Jews weren't allowed to commit suicide."

Moshe had an answer ready. "It is not suicide. First the men kill their wives and children, then each other."

"Oh." Abby furrowed her brow. "But there had to be a last man standing, right? Unless the last two somehow killed each other at the exact same time?"

"Excuse me?" Shelby said. A collective groan resounded through the group. Gideon had groaned, too, involuntarily.

"Yes?" Moshe asked.

"Not everyone was killed."

"Say again?"

She looked at Moshe from beneath the brim of her bucket hat, which had a flap in back to guard her neck against the sun. Where the rest of the group were cultivating tans, Shelby wore a long-sleeved shirt and polyester pants. Her rubber shoes had articulated toes.

"Some of them went into hiding. At least that's what I read. Which means that some Jews—maybe even some of us on this trip—are descended from the ones that hid. Are you saying they were cowards for not killing each other?"

Moshe frowned. He seemed stumped by her question, and struggled to formulate an answer that wouldn't undermine his authority. "Maybe," he said, "they did not know about the plans for suicide. Maybe—how do you say?—they did not get the memo."

Shelby sat with Gideon on the bus ride back to the kibbutz.

"I don't care what Moshe says," she told him. "We aren't getting the whole picture."

Gideon sighed, preemptively exhausted by the conversation. "How so?"

"What he told us at Masada doesn't check out. Most scholars think the story was fabricated. Or at least wildly exaggerated. And have you seen the map he's working with? The West Bank isn't even on it."

"So?"

"So we can't trust anything he tells us!" She seemed unable to control the volume of her voice. "My cousin works for an NGO in Jerusalem. He thinks he can connect me with some Palestinians."

"Sounds fun."

"Right?" she said, mistaking sarcasm for sincerity. "I knew you'd understand."

He was relieved and not entirely surprised to find that Shelby wasn't at the party that night. In fact, she might have been the only one Abby hadn't invited. The room was packed, and it took Gideon a minute to find Bari, who was sitting on the edge of Abby's bed, a beer bottle sweating in her hand. She wasn't wearing her ponytail anymore, and her dark brown hair fell in waves over her shoulders. He sat beside her.

"I meant to ask you earlier," he said. "What's with the peanut butter?"

"What peanut butter?"

"I thought I saw a jar of peanut butter in your backpack."

She turned away from him. "It's nothing."

"What do you mean?"

He watched her throat pulse as she took a long swig of beer.

"You really want to know?"

"I do."

"That's not peanut butter in there," she said and wiped her lips. "It's my brother's ashes."

Gideon sat in stupefied silence for a long moment before he spoke. "I'm sorry, what?"

"I came here to scatter them."

"You didn't."

Bari narrowed her gun-barrel eyes as if searching for something in his. "Never mind. Forget I said anything."

Someone lit a cigarette and the room fouled with smoke. A couple of drunk girls were singing "David Melech Yisrael."

"I'm sorry," Gideon said. "You can trust me. Go on."

"So my dad owns an insurance company," she said, the searching look still in her eyes. "It's actually one of the most successful firms in the South, and my dad doesn't just own it. He founded it, too. He started selling car insurance to put himself through college. After that, he worked his way up at Crawford & Company before he struck out on his own. But no matter how successful he was? And even though he had hundreds, maybe thousands, of employees underneath him? Every time we went to a party—it could be a dinner party, wedding, bar mitzvah, whatever—he'd try to sell the other guests insurance. Most people get into the business for financial reasons—it's a pretty stable industry, you know, recession-proof—but for my dad? Insurance is his life."

But years of selling policies had made him panicky. His world was one of car crashes and cancer diagnoses, house fires and hurricanes. Persuading customers to fear freak accidents was his job, and losing his wife to late-onset Tay-Sachs disease only sharpened his sense of the world as a place where disaster was just as likely to strike the human body from within as from without. He parented in what Bari called the paranoid style, insisting not only on helmets and kneepads for bike rides but on curfews and hourly calls to check in. When Bari and her twin brother Isaac turned sixteen, their father started administering monthly drug tests. "If my dad had his way," Bari said, "he would have locked us in a padded cell forever. Not because we were crazy. Just to keep us safe."

His plan backfired in Bari's case. Rather than respect her father's wishes, she devised creative ways of asserting independence. She mixed cough syrup with Sprite and got drunk off the concoction from the confines of the bathroom before going out, and made a point of behaving as recklessly as possible before coming home to beat his curfew. Bari's father held Isaac to an even higher standard. His dream was for Isaac to run the company, which he'd named Berman & Son while his son was still in diapers. That his daughter might be interested in the family business must never have occurred to him, but that was fine because, by the time she left for college, the last thing she wanted to do was sell insurance.

"Did your brother want to sell insurance?" Gideon asked.

Bari shook her head. "They fought about it constantly," she said. "Isaac wanted to go into the military. That's why he enlisted in the IDF."

"Not the US Army? Why?"

"It's not like we were super observant or anything. He just thought he'd see more action in Israel. Turns out, he was right."

"What happened to him?" Gideon asked.

"Killed in combat. Six months ago."

"I'm sorry."

The words were like sand in his mouth. He'd never known any-one his age who'd lost a sibling, much less to a war, and suddenly the world depicted in *The New York Times*, which his parents read religiously—the world of car bombs, coups, assassination attempts—seemed much closer to him than it ever had before.

"It was stupid, what he did. But I understand. He enlisted for the same reason I spent so much of high school fucked up. Growing up like we did, you start to seek out danger. I think he wanted to put himself in harm's way."

He wondered what she meant by "fucked up." What she meant by "danger." He pictured Bari, drunk to the point of incoherence, being pushed into a bedroom by a pair of football players. He shuddered at the thought.

"They were going to bury Isaac here, in Israel, but my dad de-manded that they send the body home. He fought with the Israeli government about it. Eventually, he won, and they sent his body back. My dad had him cremated. I'm not sure what he planned to do with the remains, but I know what my brother would have wanted."

"What's that?"

"A military funeral. I can't give him that, but I can scatter his ashes on Mount Herzl with the other lone soldiers."

He understood now why Bari was so dismissive of Moshe's booster-ism, and why she'd come to Israel anyway. "Did you ever forgive him?" Gideon asked.

"My dad or my brother?"

It hadn't occurred to Gideon that Bari's brother might need to be forgiven. "Your dad."

"No way. When we talk at all, which is basically never, he refuses to acknowledge that Isaac is dead."

"So he's in denial."

"I wish. It's more like he won't admit Isaac ever *existed.*"

"What happens if you mention him?" Gideon asked. "What does he say?"

"He says he doesn't know any Isaac. He says he doesn't know who I'm talking about."

Gideon envisioned his own funeral, a soldier's funeral, complete with taps and a twenty-one-gun salute. A large crowd had gathered, everyone in black, and there was much weeping and rending of garments. He saw his mother and his sister standing by the coffin, but he couldn't find his father anywhere.

"So what about the peanut butter?" he asked.

"It was the only way to get him through security."

He nodded, recalling the increasingly enigmatic questions he'd been asked at the airport. Had he packed his own bag? What was the purpose of his trip? Did he know his Hebrew name? Did he belong to a synagogue? Which one? Was he sure that he was Jewish? Had he taken a genetic test? If not, how could he be certain? Would he like to change his previous answer? Why had he claimed to know something of which he wasn't certain?

Bari reached behind her head and pulled her hair over one shoulder. "So what made you want to come here?" she asked. "And don't give me that crap about finding yourself."

Gideon motioned for her beer, took a long sip, and handed it back. He'd never told anyone about his father's fraud before, nor his parents' open marriage, and did his best to describe them to her in the same disaffected tone that Bari had employed while telling him about her own family. The more cynical he sounded, the more control he felt over his circumstances. A distance was opening up between himself and the events of the past few months, insulating him from pain.

"Hold on," Bari said when he had finished. "I'm confused. Why, exactly, did you drop out of college?"

"I didn't want to lead the same life as my parents."

"Right. But you didn't have to *drop out.* Isn't that a bit . . . extreme?"

He gave a noncommittal shrug. "Yeah, well," he said. "I don't care."

"Huh." She tossed her head back and drained the beer, condensation wetting her lips. "Kind of seems like you're cutting off your nose to spite your face."

His cheeks burned with embarrassment. He thought Bari would have been impressed by his not caring.

"So what about you?" he asked to change the subject. "What do you want to do with your life?"

She let out a bitter laugh.

"What's so funny?"

"Nothing. It's just that no one's ever asked me that before."

Just then, there came a heavy roll of thunder, the sound of the sky ripping open at the seams. Everyone in the room held still, as the sound—not thunder, Gideon realized, but a rocket—passed over the hotel. Bari grabbed Gideon's wrist, and she kept it there a minute until Abby broke the silence.

"Hey, guys?" she said. "Just FYI? The beers cost ten shekels each. You can Venmo me tomorrow."

Gideon loved like an occupying force, with no regard for proportionality. The first woman to find herself on the receiving end of his romantic offensives was Ashley O'Boy, the teacher's aide in his fourth-grade class. Ms. O'Boy, a pretty bottle blond with black eyebrows, was charged with looking after Gideon's classmate Phillip Pollard, who knew the tech specs for every kind of airplane ever made but couldn't tie his own shoes. It was Ms. O'Boy's job to intervene when Phillip disrupted class by shouting, "I did it all for the nookie! The nookie! So you can take that cookie! And stick it up your—" Gideon was too young to know what "nookie" meant, but he would forever associate the word with Ms. O'Boy, whose cheeks flushed red whenever Phillip said it.

He was not the only fourth grader in love with Ms. O'Boy, but he was the only one who wrote her poems, which he left in her cubby, even after she asked him to stop. One morning, Gideon's fourth-grade teacher, whose name (unlike Ms. O'Boy's) he'd eventually forget, sat on the rug instead of in her usual chair and told the class that school was canceled for the day because someone had flown an airplane into a building in New York. Two airplanes, actually, she said. Two buildings. Gideon burned with envy as Phillip buried his head between Ms. O'Boy's breasts, shoulders heaving as he wept for the decimated plane. Gideon still thought of Ms. O'Boy every time he took his shoes off at the airport.

A few years later, he fell in love with romance novels in the dim, musty bedroom of his dead grandmother's house. Deb had come to sort through her things and tasked Gideon with boxing up the old books in her room. The carpet, he remembered, smelled of kitty litter; a cardigan was draped across a rocking chair. A twig struck the window, and he jumped. He hurried to the bookshelf and started pulling titles, stacking them inside a cardboard box to take his mind off the eerie atmosphere in the house. There was a row of red *World*

Book encyclopedias, arranged alphabetically and missing J–K; a copy of Janson's *History of Art*; and a *Norton Anthology of World Literature*. On the shelf below sat the complete Steinsaltz Talmud, the worn, jaundiced jackets like a mouth of rotting teeth.

He'd boxed the encyclopedias and was starting on the Talmud when he saw a set of books hidden behind it. Pastel paperbacks with veiny spines. They had titles like *Caress and Conquer,* and on the covers—the covers!—he found couples conjoined in passionate embraces. The men were shirtless, with muscles where Gideon had never thought muscles could grow, rippling up their sides and down their backs. The women wore dresses that fell off their shoulders and crept up their thighs at the very same time in defiance of the laws of gravity. Behind the women were landscapes stocked with castles and horses, or raging seas whose spray fell, sparkling, on heaving breasts. Waterfalls, brigantines, white-columned plantation houses. Tentatively he reached for *A Pirate's Pleasure.* An hour passed before his mother called upstairs to check on him. He had made no further progress with the Talmud.

He put the novels back where he had found them. The soft-core covers were one thing, but if someone were to catch him reading—actually look past the covers at the printed text—they'd see the real reason his grandmother had tucked the books away. They'd find Gideon engrossed in a world of *writhing bodies,* a vast verbal landscape of *moist kisses* and *probing hands.* They'd find him reading about *sodden loins* and *steely intrusions, stiff nipples* and *tingling breasts,* all that *gasping, sliding, thrusting, trembling, panting, pulsing, throbbing, clenching, shuddering,* and *gushing.*

It wasn't just the gerunds. His mother wouldn't mind if he read romance novels; she would only have objected to their literary merit.

He worried instead that the books would endorse her view that he was *sensitive*, the kind of fey, delicate boy who cried when he went away to sleepaway camp and picked daisies in the outfield during Little League games. In sixth grade, there was nothing worse than being *sensitive*. So he started bringing the books home in batches, storing them in the back of his closet, reading them only after his parents had gone to sleep.

He passed the next few weeks in a state of ecstasy, accompanied by fops, dandies, and overbearing governesses, men in starched cravats and tasseled boots, women dressed to stun in see-through muslins. He traversed Scottish moors and Irish hills, Texas ranches and Louisiana shipyards. Most of the books took place on at least two continents. The ambition impressed him. The scope. Here were people willing to cross oceans for love.

He wanted more. The Putterham library didn't have a wide selection, and anyway, he shared an account there with his parents. His solution was to visit the New England Mobile Book Fair.

The New England Mobile Book Fair was neither mobile nor a book fair. Housed in a sprawling former tennis racquet factory and lit by long, dangling industrial fixtures, the Book Fair was a labyrinth of cheap pine shelves, the cement floor crowded with boxes of books. It was a nine-minute drive from Gideon's house, but without a car, it took two buses and a train. He didn't mind the trip; it was part of the adventure. He might have been sailing a schooner after pirates in pursuit of the woman he loved.

The best thing about the Book Fair was not that the books were sold at wholesale prices or that he could sit on a footstool between the shelves and read, undisturbed, for hours. What he liked most was the way the store was organized, though "organized" wasn't quite the right word. Instead of sorting through his inventory, the owner, a Harvard-educated chemist, grouped the books by publisher to save time. The system, if it could be called a system, was perfect for Gideon, who couldn't have cared less about authorship. It didn't matter to him that the author of *Her Shining Splendor* hadn't written *Stolen Spring*. What mattered were the houses. Avon. Harlequin. Silhouette. These were the names he looked for on the spines, stamps of consistency and quality.

It was at the New England Mobile Book Fair that he discovered there were other kinds of romance novels than those his grandmother had read. Some had ghosts or dragons. Some were set in outer space. Some involved time travel or murder. Some involved time travel *and* murder. Some of them—and this was the most thrilling discovery of all—some of them took place in the present-day United States! In those novels, lovers were kept apart not by civil war or shipwrecks, but by their own ambitions, hopes, and fears. The heroines had jobs and cars and mortgages and kids. There was still plenty of glamour in the form of black-tie dinners, Napa Valley vineyards, and ski lodges in Aspen, but the point was that the stories were contemporary. Romance wasn't consigned to carriages and ballrooms. It was not the sole domain of knaves and damsels in distress. Love was just as likely to strike a journalist on Capitol Hill, a socialite in Hollywood, or a cowboy on a California ranch. A twelve-year-old boy in a suburb west of Boston.

More than the exotic locales, more than the sex scenes—which, while titillating, could not compete with porn, readily available on LimeWire and Kazaa—he loved romance novels for their sense of *emotional justice*. It wasn't that the stories were predictable (they weren't) or that they all had happy endings (and so what if they did?), but that the characters were rewarded for their goodness and devotion. They may face tropical storms, bouts of insecurity, or the collective scorn of beachside towns, but there was never any doubt that the central characters would wind up together. You could feel the momentum on every page, the couple moving slowly but inexorably closer. It was almost scientific, a forgotten law of Newton's, the rule that governed true love: two bodies meant for one another can't be kept apart.

It wasn't until he met his first girlfriend, Nina, at a STEM-based summer camp for high school students that he tried to put the law into practice. Nina was short, with brown eyes and shoulder-length hair, the daughter of two physicists from Ukraine. She had become a minor celebrity by virtue of being one of the few girls at the camp, which was held at UMass Amherst, and for the bright red lipstick she wore daily. Gideon could hardly believe his luck when the two of them were paired for a robotics challenge. They grew close over the course of that week as only teenagers can when confined to a specific time and place. On their last night together, they stayed up all night talking until, somewhere around three in the morning, she asked if he wanted to sleep over. He did. After she switched out the lights, he slipped out of his shorts, grateful to be wearing boxers, not briefs, and climbed into bed beside her. She lay on her side, turned away from him, and for the next forty interminable minutes, he inched ever closer until her back was flush with his stomach and her thigh touched the head of his erection, which throbbed in time with his heart. He lay there for another hour, her body pressed to his, wondering if and when he could kiss her or stroke the budding breast just north of his knuckle.

Suddenly he wasn't sure about those *probing hands*. What if she was asleep? Would that constitute assault? He thought of the advice that his father had given him a few years earlier: "If the girl is drunk, don't do anything. If she's unsure or looks ambivalent, don't do anything. Don't do anything with anyone you don't trust. Trust is important. If you don't feel comfortable talking about the possibility of pregnancy, or disease for that matter, you're not ready, so don't do anything. If you're ever uncertain about what she's thinking, *just don't do anything*."

They stayed in touch after camp, and by October, he told her he loved her. She didn't say it back, but that was okay, because she showed him that she loved him in lots of other ways. They texted all day, in between (and sometimes during) class, and called each other as soon as school let out. He kept his grades up to keep his parents off his back, but everything else in his life—his parents, his friends, the Academic Decathlon—spun like satellites around Planet Nina, incinerating in the atmosphere. One weekend, her parents drove her up from New Jersey to see her brother, a sophomore at MIT. Nina had dinner with Gideon and his parents. Afterward, he borrowed Deb's old station wagon and drove her to the parking lot behind his elementary school. He killed the engine but kept the headlights on, and plugged his iPod into a cassette adapter, which he slid into the slot on the dash. He'd searched the internet for the best slow-dance songs of all time and made a playlist out of all the tracks that appeared on more than three different sites. His plan was to dance with Nina in the headlights, a gesture he hoped she'd find sufficiently romantic to want to get back in the car and have sex. But when he looked up from the iPod, she was already taking off her shirt. He was disappointed to have to skip the dancing part, which he had worked so hard to prepare, but as she drew him inside her, he remembered thinking, *Oh! So* this *is what all those songs are about.*

Gideon drove to see her every few weeks and would have done so more often, but it was four hours each way, and he didn't have his own car. Nina didn't even have her license. He couldn't understand why she put off driving school, especially now that they were "doing long distance," or why she told him to take a few months to think before he bought a car of his own. They didn't have a few months. The summer lay in wait like a land mine up the road. When college acceptance letters arrived in March, and he found out that he'd gotten into Columbia, but she had not, he told her he would turn the offer down. He would take a gap year, apply all over again, wherever she decided to go.

She broke up with him a few weeks after that. He shouldn't plan his life around someone he'd known less than a year, she said, and besides, he'd worked hard to earn that acceptance letter, and she wouldn't be able to live with herself knowing she'd denied him that opportunity. "You'll love New York," she insisted, "and there, you don't even need a car." He sobbed so hard he pulled a muscle in his shoulder, and when his mother came to comfort him, she said that the first time was always the hardest and that nothing would ever hurt so much again. It wasn't what he'd hoped to hear. His life before Nina was colorless by comparison. He *wanted* to feel this way again.

Now, when he peered through the scope of his longing, it was Bari that he saw between the crosshairs. She was worldly, despite living in Atlanta all her life, and he was awestruck by the fearlessness with which she expressed her opinions. She objected to the shower scene in *Schindler's List*, for instance, because—and she said this, in front of everyone, when Moshe asked the group about their favorite Holocaust films while they waited in line for Yad Vashem—it was "wrong to milk a moment like that for suspense." More than that, he envied Bari's devotion to her brother and his wishes. She'd obviously found herself a long time ago.

A strange thing happened at Yad Vashem. The group had just finished their guided tour and were wandering the grounds, half-dazed, arms raised to shield their eyes from the sun. No one seemed to know what to say, least of all Gideon, as they walked through the cobblestone plaza dedicated to the gentiles who had risked their own lives to save Jews from extermination. The memorial had shamed him, even though he hadn't done anything wrong. It seemed to mock the scope of his ambitions, belittle the size of his concerns. How could anything in his puny life matter when compared against the Holocaust?

He found Bari standing before a wall engraved with names. He went to stand beside her, hoping she'd been saving some pointed remark that would help put some distance between him and that empty feeling. But Bari only stood there, reading the names. Maybe, he thought, she was feeling puny, too. Maybe he could say something to dispel that feeling for the both of them. He brightened at the possibility that *he* could help *her*. He was feeling better already.

"What a waste of space," he said. "All this real estate set aside for non-Jews. Were they afraid they wouldn't sell as many tickets unless they included everyone?"

Bari turned and gave him a quizzical look. It was clear his comment hadn't come off as intended.

"I'm just saying, isn't this memorial supposed to be for us? Feels like pandering."

"I don't know," she said. "Risking your life to save others seems worth celebrating to me."

Gideon agreed and slunk away, cursing himself. He couldn't even get cynicism right.

After touring Yad Vashem, they visited a vast, open-air marketplace where Moshe let them roam free for an hour. To shop so soon after contemplating the millions dead seemed offensive at worst and a failure of planning at best, but Moshe insisted they stick to the schedule. The brief bus ride between activities was silent, strained by the occasional question pertaining to practicalities like when and where they would eat lunch. Gideon took his cues from Bari, bowing his head when she bowed hers and rolling his eyes only when she'd done it first.

When they reached the market, she pulled Gideon aside. "I'm going to do the thing now," she said. "The thing I came here for?"

"Right. Got it."

"You don't have to come."

"I want to, if I can."

She gave a tight, appreciative smile. "Good. Just follow me."

He trailed her through the crowded stalls. Vendors shaved shawarma off spinning metal spits and scooped dried fruit into bags. A man shook hands with a shopkeeper over a counter bearing bricks of halva. After a few minutes, they surfaced onto a pavilion, where two teens in jean shorts and yarmulkes were break dancing.

Walking beside her, or rather just behind her—she moved fast, and with purpose—he was seized by the desire not to be near her but to *be* her, to feel the summer sun on her skin, to taste the inside of her cheek as she chewed it. He wanted to feel her heart, not his, beating against her drum-tight chest.

They continued down a sunny street of sandstone buildings, Stars of David carved above the jutting concrete balconies. "We should probably get back soon," he said. They'd been walking for forty minutes now, though it felt like longer, one block of beige buildings giving way to another. The sun was high, and he'd given up wiping the sweat from his brow.

"Almost there," she said, without looking back.

Finally, they reached the military cemetery at Mount Herzl. He followed her while she scouted for locations, eventually settling on a small plot of grass at the top of a hill. She reached into her backpack and pulled out the jar of Skippy peanut butter.

"I'm going to need some privacy," she said. "You keep watch. If you see anyone coming, just cough."

"But what if I actually have to cough?"

"Don't."

Gideon stood guard at the head of the path while Bari performed a sort of private funeral. His thoughts drifted to Nina, who died suddenly (drunk driver) six months after they broke up. He was surprised when her parents asked him to be a pallbearer, but he was honored, too, and tried to appear appropriately solemn. He lost his composure when he saw how small the casket was. He couldn't believe it was really her in there.

After the funeral, at Nina's parents' house, he stood alone, snacking on cold cuts in the kitchen. He'd never met her friends nor her extended family, and the memories the other mourners were sharing involved people and places that weren't known to him. He felt ashamed to have helped carry the casket. He'd loved her, but as he eavesdropped on their conversations, he wondered if he'd ever really known her.

Eventually, he came out from behind the kitchen island and paid his respects to Nina's father, a stocky, snub-nosed man who looked much older than his age. The fire that usually burned behind his eyes was reduced to a dim pilot light.

"You want to hear something?" he asked, palming Gideon's head. "I used to call her Ladybug."

"I didn't know that."

"The night she died, a ladybug landed on my shoulder."

Gideon nodded, not knowing what to say.

"Now, every time I see a ladybug, I know it's Nina, watching over me."

Gideon's stomach dropped. Not because he believed, as her father did, that Nina had been reincarnated as an insect, but because he could only imagine what kind of loss would drive a man like Nina's father, a physicist and former boxer who had hopped the Iron Curtain, to superstition.

He looked up. Two guards were coming up the hill. Behind him, Bari was kneeling on the plot of grass. He coughed, but she didn't seem to hear him. He coughed again. She didn't move.

"Cough!" he shouted as the guards approached. "Cough!"

Bari's eyes widened in alarm. She got up, and they hurried down the back of the hill, walking as fast as they could without arousing suspicion.

"Did you do it?" he whispered.

"Yeah," she said. "It's all done."

The path down the hill spat them out onto the street, where they took cover behind a sandstone wall. She wrapped her arms around him. "Thank you, Gideon," she said, her shoulders heaving, her mouth pressed right up to his ear.

———

The trouble started that evening in the hotel ballroom, where a jowly expat with one slow eye stood before a glass window stained with two Lions of Judah and implored the group to join a bone marrow registry. "DNA is the code of life," he said, "and Jews are one of the most distinct genetic groups on earth. We've survived all these years in exile by remaining close to one another, and that closeness has resulted in a particular set of genetic features. We are linked to ancient times and to each other by these features—the Jewish chain of life. Forget culture, forget faith. This, in the end, is the thing that makes us Jewish: a shared genetic code."

"I'm going to be sick."

Gideon turned in his chair. Abby was holding her hand over her mouth. Her skin was sallow, her hairline hemmed with sweat. "I'm sorry," she said, and she kept saying it, "I'm sorry," as she got up from her seat and fled the ballroom.

"Where is Abby going?" Moshe asked.

The man pressed on with his presentation. "The Talmud says that if you save one life, it is as if you have saved the whole world."

A kid from Kentucky named Wyatt tapped on Gideon's shoulder. "Do I feel hot to you?" he asked.

Gideon felt his forehead. "You're on fire."

"Sheket bevakashah!" Moshe barked.

"Excuse me," Wyatt said, starting for the exit, but before he reached the doors, he threw up on the carpet.

"Please," cried Moshe, "we only want for you to swab your cheek!" But by then, a great exodus was underway, from the ballroom to the bathroom, as the group broke off in six different directions. Only Bari and Gideon remained in their seats.

It wasn't long before Gideon determined that the cause of the outbreak must have been the restaurant where Moshe took the group to lunch while he and Bari were walking back from Mount Herzl. The rest of the group was too sick to sleep, and they were still sick at breakfast the next morning. They were sick on the bus ride to the Bedouin camp and they were sick as they mounted the depressed-looking camels that carried them miles into the desert. The smell of the Bedouins' dinner, stewed lamb, only made it worse, and Moshe was forced to cut the meal short and quarantine the group in a large goat's hair tent.

Later on, in a large brass bed, Gideon lay awake, listening to the eerie chorus coming from the quarantine tent. It was cold in the desert, too cold to fall asleep, so he slipped out of his tent and headed toward the campfire, where some Bedouins were strumming pear-shaped guitars, the light undulating on their faces. He could see Bari's tent on the far side of the campfire. He wondered if she was awake.

He'd been warming himself for a few minutes when he looked up and saw Shelby coming toward him. She sat down and hugged the blanket draped across her shoulders.

"Are you feeling okay?" he asked.

"I think the worst of it is over. But I still have the chills."

"That's good."

"Everyone in our tent is hooking up. It's disgusting."

"I thought you guys were sick."

"It isn't stopping anyone." She fixed her eyes on his. "I'm going to walk off the trip tomorrow."

"What do you mean?"

"We're passing back through Jerusalem to pick up some more soldiers on the way to Tel Aviv. I'm going to meet my cousin, the one with the NGO." Shelby scooped some sand and let it fall through her fingers. "I don't get why Moshe won't talk about the conflict. There's literally a war going on *right now.* Sixteen people were killed at a school in Gaza."

If he were a character in a romance novel, he would stride confidently to Bari's tent, where he would find her waiting for him. According to the laws of emotional justice, they would make love in the moonlight, their virtue at last rewarded.

"Walking off means I'll forfeit my ticket home. When you leave a trip like this, that's the end. You're on your own. They can't protect you."

"Uh-huh."

"Do you want to come with me?"

"I don't know." He got up. "Probably not."

"Where are you going?"

It couldn't have been more than thirty feet to Bari's tent. He stood at the threshold a minute before peeling the flap open and stepping inside. There was just enough light from the fire outside for him to see Bari lying on her stomach. He crept closer, but as he reached out to tap her shoulder, he sensed something moving behind him. Instinctively he dropped to the ground and rolled beneath the bed.

"Who's there?" Bari asked, her voice thick with sleep. The bedspring sagged as she turned over, brushing against Gideon's stomach. He was pinned between the bed and the sand at his back. He could see a pair of combat boots coming toward him.

"It is Dov. I hope I do not wake you. I think I see someone come into your tent."

"You did?"

"I am positive. If you permit me, I will search the tent."

"What's to search?"

"Around. Outside. Under the bed."

Gideon suppressed a gasp.

"Do you need your gun for that?"

"Of course."

He considered speaking up, and making his presence known, but in the time it would take to explain himself, Dov could unload a couple hundred rounds.

"You don't know hand-to-hand combat?" Bari asked.

"Of course! I know Krav Maga."

"What's that?"

"A self-defense technique. Preemptive strike. Repeated blows."

"Sounds harsh."

"Also situational awareness. We must be aware of our surroundings. At all times I am seeing who is near me, counting all the people in the room."

"My brother was a soldier," Bari said after a moment.

"I know. I have heard of him. He is very brave."

"Was." The weight shifted on the bed again. "I want to know what they teach in basic training. I want to know what he knew."

Dov sat on the edge of Bari's bed. The spring sunk and pressed into Gideon's cheek.

"In Krav Maga," Dov explained, "we target the most sensitive areas. Eyes, neck, throat, face. Groin. I show you."

The weight shifted on the bed.

"Like this?" Bari asked.

"Like this."

Trapped beneath the bed, Gideon had no choice but to listen to the grunts and moans coming from the other side of the mattress. His mind filled with pictures of *probing hands* and *writhing bodies*. All the scenes from his childhood reading recurred to him, the *stiff nipples* and the *sodden loins*. The *groping*, the *gasping*, the *gushing*. After a few endless minutes, one of them rolled over, and Gideon was able to squeeze out from underneath the bed. In the flickering light of the fire, muted by the walls of the tent, he saw Dov, targeting Bari's most sensitive areas.

Gideon army crawled out of the tent, swallowing the curses accumulating on his tongue. His need. His fear. His diffidence. His doubt. The ache in his legs as he picked himself up. The sky was thick with clouds, and the bundles of stars still visible between them, as though the sky were falling, one point of light at a time. Shelby sat alone, shivering beside the fire. The Bedouins had turned in for the night, and from across the campground, he could hear the quarantine tent, the moans of retching and sexual pleasure, the body's answer to illness and love. From where he was standing, they sounded the same.

Gideon sat next to Shelby on the bus the next morning. He couldn't bring himself to look at Bari; he couldn't even stomach his reflection in the window of the bus. Hiding under Bari's bed had been humiliating. His behavior *all week* had been humiliating. That was what desire did to a person. It turned him inside out.

It was a short drive back to Jerusalem, where Moshe stopped to pick up more soldiers who would accompany the group for the duration of the trip. "In Tel Aviv, we will see Silicon Wadi," he said while they waited for the soldiers at the rendezvous point, a parking lot across from a gate to the Old City. "You will see why they call Israel the start-up nation!"

"Okay," Shelby whispered. "It's time."

"Are you sure about this?" Gideon asked. It hadn't bothered him the night before, but now he felt bereft at the thought of losing Shelby.

"I can't keep going with a clean conscience."

"All right," he said. "Do what you have to do."

Shelby closed her eyes and exhaled before getting up and standing in the aisle of the bus. "Excuse me, everyone," she said. Most of the other passengers were sleeping, new couples sharing headphones or cuddling underneath their coats, as if conjoined at their upset stomachs. "This is really hard for me, but here goes. This trip is supposedly a gift—"

"It is," Moshe said.

"We were told, or I was told, that this trip was an opportunity to learn about our culture. But every time I try and ask Moshe a question, he shuts me down. I'm standing here to say I won't be silenced anymore."

"I am disappointed," Moshe said. "This is disappointing."

"Like I said, this is really hard for me, because of all the bonds I've formed the last few days." There was a quiver in her voice that only Gideon could hear. "I consider you all the best friends I've ever had."

"If you leave, you leave," Moshe said. "But we do not have time to hear your speech."

"Okay." She was shaking as she reached for her backpack.

Gideon got up from his seat. "I'm going, too."

The outburst surprised him as much as anyone.

"You are?" she asked.

"I'm with Shelby," he said, allowing himself to look at Bari for the first time all morning. He felt her beauty like a bullet in his side.

"Shelby is a troublemaker," Moshe said. "You, Gideon, are a good boy."

He could taste the splash of acid at the back of his throat. "Anyone brave enough to come with us, now's your chance."

No one moved. Bari blushed and looked at her lap.

"Ah!" Moshe said, peering through the windshield. "Here come reinforcements."

Gideon followed Shelby down the aisle, the temperature rising in his head. They collected their bags from the belly of the bus just as the rest of the soldiers climbed aboard. "Shira!" someone cried. "Baby! I've *missed* you!"

"Thank you," Shelby said after they had crossed the street. "That meant a lot to me."

He could hear his blood pumping in his ears. "Don't mention it."

They dragged their suitcases through the corridors of the Old City, the plastic wheels kvetching against the cobblestones. The more they walked, the narrower the corridors became. He felt like the world itself were closing in on him.

"My cousin said he'd meet us at the Temple Mount," Shelby said, consulting her phone. "If we turn left—although, wait . . ."

Gideon wiped the sweat from his brow. "I can't do this."

"One step at a time. First, we'll meet up with my cousin—"

"I'm not coming, Shelby. I'm sorry. I just can't."

"So what, then?" she asked, an edge of anger in her voice. "What are you going to do?"

Shelby's voice grew fainter as he started toward the bus. The Old

City seemed to expand, sprouting stalls and archways everywhere he turned. Shadows stretched across the cobblestones, casting the corridors in strange, forbidding darkness.

Night had fallen by the time he surfaced on the street. He stood in the empty plaza where the bus had been. Across the busy intersection, a row of windows glowed like candles on the Sabbath, lighting street signs in a language he didn't understand.

•

The deli counter at the Stop & Shop on Harvard Street is not exactly known for courtesy, much less compassion, but that's where I first saw selflessness in action and decided what I wanted to do with my life. I was five years old then, with a limited capacity for encoding episodic memory, but I remember that afternoon like it was yesterday. We were standing, Dad and I, in the line behind the counter, most likely in a pool of cool, fluorescent light; I was holding the paper ticket with our number on it. Other sensory details: the smell of honey-baked ham, the hum of the electric meat slicer. The dull thud of a body on polished concrete. I looked up from the ticket. A woman in front of us was lying on the floor, lemons spilling from her upturned cart. Dad was at her side in seconds. (At the time, I assumed she'd had a heart attack, what with Dad being a cardiologist and all, but on the car ride home, he told me that she'd fainted.) He unbuttoned her collar and loosened her belt for reasons that would become clear to me later, but my failure to grasp what was happening just then—I didn't understand why he seemed to be taking off her clothes—only made the scene more compelling. When, maybe twenty seconds later, she came to, the rest of the customers started applauding like they'd seen a magic trick, or mira-

cle. The guy behind the counter called Dad a hero, and we took a couple pounds of Boar's Head home for free.

That was the day I decided to become a physician. I even started my own practice at the baseball diamond after school, establishing an office in the dugout, where I dispensed Flintstones vitamins to my classmates. (Unfortunately, one of my patients OD'd and developed a bad case of diarrhea, thus bringing a premature end to my first stab at a medical career.) I stayed interested in science throughout middle and high school, but it wasn't until my freshman year at Columbia that I was able to pursue this longstanding goal of mine in earnest. After taking a seminar on epigenetics with Dr. Harold Park, a real pioneer in the field, I started volunteering in his lab, assisting in his studies of transgenerational epigenetic inheritance in livestock. Building off one of Dr. Park's previous studies, in which he demonstrated that the offspring of livestock with elevated levels of corticosterone (CORT), a stress-related hormone, were more likely to develop feather-pecking syndromes than the offspring of parents with reduced basal CORT levels, we began injecting chicken eggs with CORT to simulate prenatal stress. Dr. Park says I'm not allowed to disclose our findings here until they're published, but suffice it to say that parental stress plays a decisive role in determining the phenotypical outcomes in their offspring.

I'm fascinated by the idea that the environment in which certain creatures, oviparous or otherwise, are conceived might alter their genetic expression, and I remain grateful to Dr. Park for allowing me to continue assisting him in this work. But in my sophomore year, having worked with chickens for a few semesters, I realized I was eager to treat actual people. (This desire to work directly with human patients is not, by the way, incompatible with my interest in epigenetic research.

Psychiatrists have already begun investigating what they're calling the transgenerational transmission of trauma. We all know that Nazis tattooed numbers on their victims' forearms, but is it possible they also "tattooed" some kind of chemical coating on their victims' chromosomes?) In order to pick up some clinical experience, I shadowed Dr. Ruth Goldberg-Reddy of Mount Sinai, a primary care physician specializing in family medicine. Dr. Goldberg-Reddy taught me the importance of communication—of explaining, in layman's terms, what's wrong with a patient and why she prefers one treatment to another—especially when it comes to longitudinal care. "An informed patient," she says, "is an empowered patient," which seems to me pretty logically sound.

This past summer, I shadowed Dr. Cal Christopoulos at the National Institute of Environmental Health Sciences in Raleigh-Durham's Research Triangle. Dr. Christopoulos, detecting (I think) my desire for more stimulating, hands-on work, agreed to oversee my senior capstone project, which will bridge the gap between my interests in epigenetics and family medicine. If toxins like DEET and BPA—to say nothing of trauma itself—can induce transgenerational effects, who knows what else our parents have unwittingly passed on?

Such was the state of Gideon's application essay when, eight months before he left Columbia, his parents called to inform him that his father was under investigation by the Office of Research Integrity for manipulating data in a clinical trial. It was only a rough draft, and a partial one at that, but he was pleased with what he'd written so far and felt confident that, with some revisions, it would round out what was already shaping up to be a formidable med school application. He planned to complete the essay during winter break while Astra was visiting her parents in Palm Beach and his roommate, Dewey, was in Israel. He was so sure of his ability to pull this off—the partial draft had taken only a few hours—that he spent the first week of his vacation tying up loose ends. He washed his bedsheets for the first time since September. He purged the fridge of wilted produce. He read the pop science book his sister had sent him six months earlier, a "history of humankind" far too sweeping to be scientifically sound, and then, as a way of showing her his gratitude, and in the hopes of repairing their relationship—they hadn't seen each other since that disastrous dinner party at her apartment—he invited her and her fiancé, Louis, to dinner at an Ethiopian place in Harlem. He toasted their engagement over bottles of imported beer, all of which made him feel exceedingly mature, and, in that flush of maturity, he apologized for his behavior the last time he'd seen them.

"No, *I'm* sorry," his sister said.

She seemed more mature to him, too. She was the first person of his generation he'd ever known to get engaged.

"How does it feel?" he asked, sincerely wanting to know.

Louis looked at Maya, and the two of them smiled, then shrugged. "We've been dating for a while," she said, hooking her arm in his, "so it's not that strange. But it definitely feels different."

"Good different?"

He saw his sister soften, the edges of her expression sanded down. "Definitely."

They looked happier together than Gideon had ever seen them. Growing up, his fantasies had always skewed marital, and he could think of no warmer feeling than binding himself to someone for eternity. He felt ashamed of this, of course—in high school and even college it was the quantity of girls bedded, not quality, that counted—but

Gideon was never more at peace within himself than when he had a girlfriend. Someone to ground him, give him context, remind him who he was.

It was a while before they turned to the subject of their parents. After Louis told a story about meeting Marjorie on Skype—two minutes into the call, Marjorie had asked if Louis thought that his father's absence during his formative years was the reason he wasn't "more conventionally masculine"—Gideon mentioned building her a birdhouse, and the strange conversation he'd had with his father while putting it together.

Maya almost choked on a mouthful of flatbread. "A *what?*" she said after she swallowed.

"An open marriage. It was weird. He seemed to want to, I don't know, bond with me about it?"

"I'm literally speechless. I don't know what to say."

"He had this whole moral he wanted to teach me about not taking Mom for granted. He said they were ending it, though."

"That explains why Mom and Joan got together like they did."

"Only three to five percent of species mate for life," Louis said. "Most birds are only socially monogamous. They raise offspring together but have flings on the side."

"Wait," Maya said. "I'm still processing this."

"People used to think swans mated for life. They're a universal symbol of romance. When they face one another, their necks make a heart shape. But it turns out they cheat on each other, just like humans. They divorce."

"Everything is clicking for me now."

"What do you mean?" Gideon asked.

"When I was in high school, I saw mom kissing some woman."

"You *did*? Was it Joan?"

She shook her head. "But it really messed me up for a while."

"Why didn't you tell me?"

"I didn't tell anyone. I didn't tell Dad! But I guess if they had an open marriage . . ."

"It doesn't make it okay. Does it?"

"It makes it *make sense*. God, I hated Mom for that kiss. For a while there, it was all I could think about."

"That's funny. I guess I don't think much about Mom. I guess I *do* take her for granted. It's Dad I think of as, like, a whole person."

"Really? I'm the total opposite."

He swelled with love for his sister. She was the only other person on the planet who knew what it was like to be raised in the hothouse of their childhood home, straining under the weight of their parents' expectations.

"I feel five pounds lighter," Maya said. "Just being able to talk like this. Clearing out the cobwebs, so to speak."

Louis raised his glass. "To clearing out the cobwebs," he said.

At the end of the meal, Gideon hugged them both and left the restaurant feeling renewed.

But when he got home and opened the Word doc, he was disturbed to discover just how *wrong* the application essay felt. Dishonest, even. There was something artificial, almost affected, in the writing itself. When he read the text aloud, it sounded soulless, the literary equivalent of "Jingle Bell Rock," which had been blaring from a shop across the street all afternoon. His clever turns of phrase sounded clunky. Stories that had once seemed cute now made him cringe. He could hardly believe he'd written the thing. It seemed to be the work of someone else entirely.

He remembered how his father had broken the news by phone at the start of the semester. In an earnest, even sheepish voice, Scott had explained that he'd made a few missteps at work and that he had some things to clear up with the ORI. When Gideon asked what he meant by "missteps," Scott said he was forbidden by law to discuss specifics. The important thing was, he regretted his actions, and no one was hurt. It was just the kind of thing that happened, sometimes. Looking back, Gideon might have been more concerned, but at the time he almost felt honored that his father was opening up to him like this. It was a new side of Scott that Gideon was seeing, more vulnerable, sharing news not only of his successes but his failures. Gideon appreciated his forthrightness and his candor, his honesty in admitting his mistakes. If anything, he ended the call more impressed with his father than he'd been before.

It was only when his mother called, later that night, that Gideon became aware of the full extent of his father's so-called missteps. Scott hadn't made an innocent mistake. Far from it. He'd *deliberately* manipulated data to enrich *himself.* For all Gideon knew, that money— literal blood money!—was paying for his college tuition. And what would it mean for his medical career, now that the family name was tarnished? The thought that he was tainted by his father's mistakes made him physically ill. These fears, like a family of parasitic worms, had taken up residence inside his body, where they were beginning to lay eggs.

Had that been all, Gideon might have found his way, eventually, to forgiving his father. But to mislead him like Scott had a few hours before, and to do so under the guise of honesty—that was unforgivable.

He struggled to assimilate this information in the weeks that followed. That his father was capable of such a betrayal—not only of his patients, but of his son as well—seemed so at odds with the man Gideon knew and revered, he concluded that either Scott had changed, or he'd been wrong about him all along. Gideon preferred the first of these two interpretations, as it spared him from feeling stupid, but it didn't really matter either way. Even school seemed pointless to him now. He couldn't focus on class, and started skipping, getting stoned with Dewey back at their apartment instead. He was horrified to realize how much mental real estate his old man occupied, and endeavored to fill the space with smoke.

Now, revisiting the essay four months later, he found he could hardly even look at the thing. He took a drag on a joint to steady himself and watched the wind push a flurry of snowflakes through the window, where they vaporized in the rippling heat of the cast-iron radiator. He considered sending the draft to Maya, who had once offered to give it a look, but he worried she would only affirm his suspicion that the whole thing would have to be chucked. Anyway, she seemed overwhelmed as it was. She and Louis were trying to plan their wedding, which, she'd said, was proving to be more stressful than anticipated. So he set down the joint and picked up his phone and called the only person on the planet on whom he could depend for unconditional support.

Deb answered on the second ring. "Are you all right?"

"I'm fine," he said, startled by the sheer power of her intuition. "Can't I just call you to say hi?"

"I'm sorry, sweetie. Of course you can. But would you do me a favor and turn the music down?"

"What music?"

"I'm getting quite the earful of 'Jingle Bell Rock.'"

"Oh, that. It's coming from outside. I'll close the window."

"Why on earth do you have the window open?"

"It's a thousand degrees in here."

"It *is*?"

"I told you before, Mom, I don't control the heat in my building."

"You need to talk to your landlord about that."

"I know." He strained to shut the window, which was stuck, the
wood frame swollen from the radiator's moisture. "I'm closing it."

"Do you know how much heat goes to waste every winter?"

"I do not."

"I can't remember the exact figure, but it has to be a lot. They did
a whole piece about it on NPR today."

"*I'm closing it*," he said. Only she had the ability to get on his nerves
like this in a matter of minutes. The window slammed against the
sill, and he collapsed, exhausted, into his chair. "So?" he asked, a
trace of irritation in his voice. "What else is new?"

"Oh, just the usual catastrophes. Karla's getting on my nerves, and
I haven't heard from the Syrian family in weeks. I told you about
them. The ones in the refugee camp? Let's see . . . I downloaded a
mindfulness app. For my phone? That was Joan's idea. She thinks I
could stand to be more *centered*, and she's right. But I really can't stand
the guy's voice. It's very grating, and doesn't do much to calm me
down. Oh! And Perlman has fleas. At least I think he does. I have
these little red bites on my back. Joan thinks it's a rash and I should
see a dermatologist. I said I should see a vet!"

She had been such a monumental figure in his youth, as robust as the cast-iron radiator currently hissing with heat, but when he spoke to her now, from a distance, in New York, her life sounded terribly small. He realized he'd forgotten to laugh. "Good one, Mom."

"In happier news, Joan's planning a New Year's party at the apartment. I hope you know that you're invited. You could be my date!"

"That's a little too overtly oedipal for me."

"Well, her door is always open. I guess I should say *our* door. What about Passover? Are you coming home then? Not that I know what I'm doing yet, or where . . ."

"I don't know, Mom. I can't plan that far ahead."

"It would mean a lot to me if you were there."

"I'll do my best." He wondered if it was even worth mentioning the essay, now that she'd succeeded in making him feel guilty about skipping a holiday he hadn't yet skipped and that was still four months away. "Though I'll need to finish my med school application essay first."

"That's right! Your essay! When can I read it?"

"Well, that's the thing," he said. "I'm not really sure if what I wrote is working."

"I don't believe that for a minute. You know you've always been hard on yourself."

"I have?"

"Absolutely! A perfectionist in all things. I'm sure you're just holding yourself to a high standard. Don't let the perfect be the enemy of the good!"

A warm feeling flowered in his chest. "Maybe you're right."

"I know I am."

They talked for another minute or two before Gideon said he should be getting back to work. The call had succeeded in restoring his confidence, and he was eager to reread the essay with fresh eyes. He made it as far as the second paragraph before a bead of sweat slipped from his forehead to the keyboard. The temperature had shot up since he'd shut the window. He stood and tried to lift it open, with no luck, so he crouched below the window by the radiator and pressed his palms against the underside of the rail. Still stuck. The more he strained, the more he sweat, so he rose from his crouch and peeled off his shirt, which he used to wipe his forehead, then his neck. This seemed to help, if only slightly, so he proceeded to pull off his jeans as well, his hands shaking as he fumbled with the belt buckle. He sat down and started the essay again, but his head was so hot he could feel his brain boiling inside his skull. He wiped his palms on his bare legs. His heart was skittering around inside his chest like a lab rat in a labyrinth.

He reached for the phone on the desk.

"Nine one one," the dispatcher said, "what's your emergency?"

Use the space provided to explain why you want to go to medical school.

The first responders found him in the hall outside his room, lying on his back, in his boxers, his chest rising and falling rapidly. The dispatcher's voice crackled through the earpiece of the phone that lay on the floor beside him.

"Panic attack," one of the EMTs said, sweeping a flashlight over his eyes. "You'll be fine." She propped Gideon up while her partner checked his pulse. Two cops, fat and thin, watched from the doorway.

"It wasn't a panic attack," he croaked. His mouth was dry; he licked his lips. "I overheated."

"Have you been under a lot of pressure lately?" the EMT asked.

"No more than normal."

"What constitutes normal?"

"I'm premed."

"Next time you have a panic attack?" the fat cop said. "Don't call 911."

"It wasn't a panic attack."

"Especially not on Christmas."

"I know what a panic attack is. I overheated."

"You should listen to him," the EMT said, rolling her eyes. "He's premed."

The spring semester, and the many obligations it entailed, spared him from having to think about his application essay. He was taking six classes for eighteen credits on top of the three nights each week he worked in Dr. Park's lab. What little time he had left, he spent with Astra, though that, too, had become an obligation, like injecting a batch of egg yolks with corticosterone or putting in an hour in the weight room at Dodge.

He wondered what had changed since that first time he saw her, the only student sprawled on the South Lawn, so myopic that she'd failed to register the KEEP OFF signs at the corner of the green. When he told her that she would get in trouble if she didn't move, she looked up at him with her enormous, liquid eyes and said, "I won't." There was something so guileless in the way she said it that Gideon decided to lie down next to her. Her legs were long, and she looked a little malnourished, the blue veins visible beneath her pallid skin. His heart was working overtime, as if pumping molasses, but the rise and fall of her pale belly put him at ease. She seemed to be visiting earth from some distant planet.

That planet, he later learned, was California. Her parents, a half generation older than his, had comprised a folk duo in the late sixties celebrated for their radiant, sun-drenched harmonies and art nouveau album covers. Their first LP, *Turtledoves and Fertile Loves* (1968) earned them a place among the luminaries of Laurel Canyon and recurring invitations to Mama Cass's slumber parties. They were summarily expelled from the scene a few years later when they wrote "Kids Today (Just Wanna Be True)," a folk tune for True filtered cigarettes. The ad campaign, and its attendant licensing agreements—their attorney, Sammy Simchowitz, worked tirelessly to ensure that Astra's parents retained partial ownership of the song—was so successful that they never had to work again. Astra professed to hate "Kids Today," but selling out might have saved her parents' lives. While many of their former friends in Laurel Canyon were dying of drug overdoses, Astra's parents were making sound investments and flirting with right-wing politics. Presently, they lived in Palm Beach, having reached the terminal stage in the life cycle of a baby boomer.

He'd never met anyone like her before, a girl who drew intricate mandalas for fun and spelled the word "magic" with a *k* on the end. When a spider took up residence in Astra's bathroom, she refused to kill it and even had its likeness tattooed on her foot. She floated through the world as if enfolded in a bubble, glowing with absent-minded goodwill. The way she writhed with pleasure in bed, like a woman possessed, was so staggeringly sexy that he had to stare at the Tame Impala poster on the wall above her headboard because he couldn't bear how beautiful she was when her narrow hips thrusted and her pale arms thrashed and she succumbed to an ecstatic fit, lost to a private world that he could only glimpse from the outside. He'd been certain that he loved her then, with unambiguous, Israeli certainty—but now, nearly two years later, he wasn't sure.

Without telling his parents, he decided to spend spring break at his grandmother's cottage on the Cape. When Astra asked if she could come, he said she couldn't, citing the need to write without interruption. But because he had no means of getting to the Cape, and Astra had a car, he changed his mind. So long as she didn't expect much from him. He was going to be busy. He had a lot of work to do.

By the time they reached the Sagamore Bridge, the landscape had become reassuringly familiar: the pitch pines flanking the two-lane highway, the marquees advertising motels and lobster huts. The fishing boats perched atop roadside trailers. The brackish funk in the air. He felt suddenly hopeful about the coming week. He figured he could finish the essay in a few days and take the rest of the time to relax. Flocks of cormorants flew overhead in a V formation, an arrow guiding him toward his future.

He'd never come to the cottage on his own, without family, and was almost surprised to find it empty. He worked on kick-starting the water heating system while Astra unpacked. It was dark by the time they were done, and Astra suggested they go into town for dinner.

"Okay," he said. "But only because it's late. Tomorrow morning, I have to work."

Astra raised her hand to her head in a salute. "Aye, aye."

"I mean it. The next few days, you're on your own."

He woke early the next morning and, after shaving, put a pot of coffee on. Then, with Astra still asleep, he set up a workstation in the semifinished garage, laying out a legal pad and pen for taking notes, setting up a space heater, running an ethernet cord in from the cottage. He poked around until he found a chair whose seat was high enough that he loomed over his laptop; he wanted to feel as though he were dominating the essay and not the other way around. Finally, with everything arranged just how he liked it, Gideon double-clicked the document. He sipped his coffee while he waited for it to load. The space heater glowed like a mind afire with ideas. He adjusted the size of the window, then the brightness of the screen. Finally, he scooted forward so that the table touched his navel, locking himself in place.

Squeezed between the table and the back of his chair, he realized that his bladder was full. He told himself that he would have to wait it out. Only after he'd written one new paragraph would he reward himself with a trip to the bathroom. But he couldn't focus, he was fixated now, imagining his spinal cord relaying signals from his bladder to his brain stem and back again. He pushed back his chair, relieving some of the pressure, and went back inside the cottage. He sat on the toilet, resting his elbows on his knees, and wondered what to write. Something was stirring inside him. The acid from the coffee, maybe, scalding his stomach. The fried scallops from the night before. He waited while the scallops swam through his system, surfing the peristaltic waves in his colon before dropping into the bowl beneath him. He wondered why his shit smelled different here. Maybe it was all the salt in the air. He made a mental note to look it up later.

At last, having emptied both his bladder and his bowels, Gideon was ready to work. He installed himself at the desk in the garage, but before he got too comfortable, he noticed that his coffee mug was half-empty. Half-full? Either way, he'd better fill it up before he *really* got going. Back in the cottage, he found Astra in the kitchen, wearing one of his father's Pfizer T-shirts; blue veins ran up the backs of her legs. She'd dyed her hair silver during winter break, and for a moment, he thought she was his grandmother.

"You're up early!"

He nodded. "Whatever it takes."

"Making progress?"

"Uh-huh."

"Good!" She stepped forward and kissed him on the cheek. "I'm going to read out on the deck."

"If you get hungry later, don't wait up. You can go ahead and have lunch without me."

He refilled his mug and returned to the garage, where he slipped the metal hook on the door into the eye latch before returning to his seat.

Use the space provided to explain why you want to go to medical school.

He could hear Astra's feet on the floorboards inside. He felt her presence in the cottage as a kind of reproach. He imagined her stalking the house, bored out of her skull, waiting for him to finish. Like it was *his* responsibility to entertain *her*. When *she* was the one who'd insisted on coming! He shook his head. It had been a big mistake to bring her. Gideon got up from his chair, arched his back, and lay on the futon to gather his thoughts. He was still on the futon when Astra knocked and asked if he'd be joining her for dinner.

The next few days were no different. He couldn't find a comfortable position at his desk; his body kept making fresh demands of him. All the while, he pictured Astra in the cottage, waiting like a proctor for him to finish. One afternoon, when his confidence was at its lowest ebb, he went out and found Astra reading on the deck. She was bundled in a puffer jacket underneath the branches of the apple tree that Scott had planted shortly after Gideon was born.

"What are you reading?" he asked.

"Tibetan Book of the Dead. Did you know that individuality is a delusion?"

It was a tall, attractive, healthy-looking tree with toothy leaves and a broad trunk of flaking bark, but its roots had grown deep enough to penetrate the septic tank, rendering the apples too toxic to eat. The branches were studded with buds and white blossoms that belied the poison coursing through them.

"News to me."

"Are you hungry? I was just going to make some lunch."

"I guess."

"Yay!" She stood up. "I'm thinking sandwiches."

Her jacket rose as she bent to pick a fallen apple and he noticed, for the first time, a black spot on her lower back, just above her waist. It was roughly the size of a quarter and seemed to have some dimension to it, raised above the rest of her skin.

"Have you always had that?" he asked.

"Had what?"

"That thing. On your back."

She furrowed her brow and looked over her shoulder. "This?" she asked, touching the spot with her finger. "It's a beauty mark. You never noticed it before?"

Far from being beautiful, it seemed to him like a stain on her otherwise unblemished body. It was strange that he hadn't noticed it before, but now he couldn't stop staring. "Have you ever thought of having it removed?"

"My dermatologist looked at it once. She said as long as it doesn't change in size or color, I'll be fine."

"Right," he said. "That's why I was asking."

She smiled at him. "You're so observant. Always looking out for other people. That's why you'll make such a good doctor."

On Saturday, Astra suggested that they drive to Provincetown for dinner. Gideon begrudgingly agreed. He wasn't getting any work done anyway. He sat beside her, stewing, as she drove up Route 6, passing signs for ceramics studios and farmers' markets, rehab facilities and sober houses. He felt like a little boy again, dragged along on one of Deb's errands.

Commercial Street was as crowded as he'd ever seen it, and they walked shoulder first, carving through the congestion until Astra found the restaurant where she'd made a reservation. The wood-paneled pub had a nautical theme, with sea creatures cut into the stained glass shades of the Tiffany lamps hanging over the tables. A few minutes after they ordered, the lamps dimmed, and a spotlight landed on a ratty velour curtain on the far side of the room. The curtain parted to the sound of steel drums, revealing what appeared to be a stocky woman in a sparkling aquamarine gown. She wore a pair of plastic seashells on her chest.

"Good evening, P-Town!" she said in a low, husky voice. "My name is Ariel the Not-So-Little Mermaid, and I'm going to be keeping you all company this evening." She cleared her throat. "Excuse me if I sound a little hoarse, I was out late last night and swallowed too much sea . . . water!"

Gideon leaned over the table. "What is this?" he whispered.

"It's a drag show," Astra said.

"I see that. But why are we here?"

"I fucked a fisherman once," the drag queen said. "He promised me a lobster dinner, but all I got were crabs!"

"You've been working so hard. I thought you could use a break."

"I agreed to go out to dinner. A nice, quiet, relaxing dinner. That's all."

"Do you want to leave?"

"We *can't leave*," Gideon said. "She'll single us out. She'll make fun of us for leaving, and she'll single us out."

"I slept with a sailor, too," the drag queen said. "After a minute, he stopped and asked how he was doing. I told him he was doing about three knots. 'Three knots?' he said. 'What's that supposed to mean?' 'Well,' I said, 'you're knot hard, you're knot in, and you're knot getting your money back!'"

"She won't 'single us out.'"

"Of course she will! That's what drag queens do!"

"Excuse me, honey? What do we do?"

He looked up with a start. The Not-So-Little Mermaid was walking toward him as briskly as her gown allowed. "Nothing. I'm sorry."

"Look at you, pinker than a salmon's pussy! What's your name?"

"Gideon," he muttered.

"Gideon! I knew I recognized you. You left your Bible in my hotel room last night."

The color rose in his cheeks. "Ha ha," he said, trying his best to sound game. "My bad."

"Is this beautiful creature right here your girlfriend, Gideon?" she asked.

"Yeah."

"What a catch! How'd you reel her in?"

"I don't know."

"You got a house?"

"No."

"A job?"

"No."

"A car?"

"No."

"My goodness, Gideon! You must have a big dick!"

He laughed uneasily until he realized she expected him to answer.

"Well, do you?"

Gideon's breaths grew short and shallow. The hairs on his fore-arms stood at attention. What was he supposed to say? If he answered yes, said he did have a big dick, he'd look like an arrogant jerk, and the drag queen would see fit to take him down a peg. But if he said no, he'd embarrass both himself *and* Astra. Worse, he didn't even know *how* big it was. He'd seen smaller in locker rooms and gym showers, but he'd seen bigger, too. *Much* bigger. As his thoughts began to quicken in time with his heartbeat, he realized that the longer he waited, the more likely Astra was to answer for him, and he wasn't sure if he wanted to know what she would say.

Before he could respond, the drag queen said, "Holy mackerel! I'm just messing with you!" and moved on to the next table.

Gideon was silent for the rest of the show, but after dinner, on the drive back to Wellfleet, he complained about the treatment he'd received from the drag queen. "I understand comedy," he said. "I have a sense of humor. But making fun of people isn't *inherently* funny. It's just *mean*."

"I thought it was funny," Astra said.

"Okay, fine, I don't have a job. I'm in college!"

"It was just some stage banter."

"I'm twenty-one years old! Am I *supposed* to have a house? Am I *supposed* to have a car?"

"I have a car."

"And why, of all people, did she have to pick on *me*?"

"You *were* talking during her set."

"Like I'm supposed to have my whole life figured out already!"

Astra pulled off the road and into a parking lot abutting a beach. "Let's take a walk," she said. "You're all wound up."

Grumbling, he let himself out of the car and followed her down to the water's edge. Astra took off her shoes and started walking, her feet squishing against the wet sand. Farther down the beach, a group of men in orange jumpsuits picked up garbage with mechanical claws.

"Is there something you want to talk to me about?" Astra asked. The night was cold, her pale feet blue in the moonlight.

"Like what?"

"I don't know. You just seem a little distant lately."

He stubbed his toe on a pill bottle half-buried in the sand. "Yeah, well, my plate is pretty full right now. We can't all be film majors."

She stared up at the starry sky. "That's what I mean. You never used to say things like that."

"I'm sorry. But this essay is due in a few weeks, and—"

"It's not the essay. You've been acting weird for months. I know you've had a hard time, ever since your mom moved out . . ."

He bristled. "No, I haven't."

". . . but that doesn't mean you can talk to me that way. Whatever's going on with you, I want to help, because—ow!" She lifted her left foot. Something jagged was protruding from the sole.

Gideon stared at her foot. "You stepped on a piece of glass."

"Oh my god. Oh my god. . . . What do we do?"

He blinked. "I know *exactly* what to do."

He picked her up and carried her back to the car. He expected to feel chivalrous, but he didn't. There wasn't time for feeling anything. He was a man possessed by duty. He drove the remaining few miles to the cottage, where he found a sewing kit in the linen closet and ran some green thread through the eye of a needle. He put a pot of water on the stove, turned the heat on high, and washed his hands. Then he knelt before her foot, which was propped up on an ottoman, and slowly removed the shard of glass. He held it up to the light. The glass had a greenish tint.

"Beer bottle, would be my best guess."

She flexed her toes. "I'm not so sure about this."

"Don't worry. I used to practice all the time with my dad's old suture kit." He swabbed the wound with alcohol while he waited for the water to boil.

"Practice on what?"

"Chicken breast."

"Oh my god."

"Their skin is a lot like ours. You'd be surprised."

He sanitized the sewing needle in the pot of boiling water before returning to her side. The glass had lacerated the layer of fat beneath her skin. He pushed the sewing needle through the skin as Astra winced. Then he twisted his hand so that the tip of the needle appeared once again on the other side of the wound. Tugging on the tip, he dragged the green thread across the opening.

"Gideon!" she cried.

He held the loose end of the thread between his teeth. "Don't you trust me?"

"Of course I do."

"Didn't you say I'd make a good doctor?"

"Well, sure, but—"

"Weren't those *your words exactly?*"

It was an intoxicating feeling, stitching her up, knowing that he alone would make the difference between a clean wound and one that was infected. He felt sharper, more focused, than he had in months. This, he thought, was his calling after all: practicing medicine—not writing essays about it. When he finished, he wrapped her foot in a brown Ace bandage like it was a birthday present.

The next morning, as he packed his duffel bag, he decided to start the essay from scratch. He would scrap the Stop & Shop anecdote and replace it with a paragraph about Astra's foot. He would write about the difference between thinking and doing, between learning and life. He'd spent his whole life preparing for medical school, but it wasn't until he'd performed a procedure himself, removing a foreign body from a human foot, that he understood the power and the burden of holding someone else's health in his hands.

He heard a car pull up the seashell drive. When Gideon went out to see who it was, he found his father's Insight sitting there, a web of cracked glass in the windshield.

Scott got out and stood behind the open door. "Gideon?"

They hadn't seen each other since September. "What are you doing here?" Gideon asked.

"I came to get a few of Grandma's things."

"Right." He felt light-headed, the craggy shells beneath his feet fucking with his balance. "What happened to your car?"

"You should see the other car."

"Really?"

Scott shook his head. "I had a little run-in with this Masshole."

Gideon nodded. "And Grandma? Is she okay?"

"Actually, no. I don't think she's going to make it up this year."

"Why not?"

"She can't make the flight to Boston. Not anymore. Even if she could—even if I drove her up myself—she couldn't manage alone. I offered to hire live-in help, but you know Marjorie. She's very proud when it comes to her independence."

Gideon nodded. "So what's wrong? Is it her back?"

"Her back, her shoulders, her knees . . ."

"And we're sure she isn't just exaggerating?" It was always easier, talking like this, not as father and son but as physician and apprentice.

"I'm positive she's exaggerating. On the other hand, she's eighty-one years old, and her body just doesn't work the way it used to. If she's in half as much pain as she says she is—"

"We have to take her seriously."

"If not literally."

"Right."

Scott came out from behind the car door and closed it. "It's funny, having lost my dad so young, but I kind of always figured that she'd be around forever."

Gideon swallowed the knot in his throat. "I know what you mean."

"Dying doesn't sound like something she would do."

"In my mind, she's indestructible."

"We should head out if we're going to beat traffic," Astra called from the doorway. "Oh! Whoa! Hey, Dr. Greenspan!"

"Hello, Astra. You know you can call me Scott."

"We, um, stripped the beds," she said. "Clean sheets are in the linen closet."

"Thank you, Astra. I'm sure I'll figure it out." He furrowed his brow. "What happened to your foot?"

"Beach glass," Gideon said. "I stitched her up."

His father's thin, almost imperceptible, lips slanted. "Why don't I take a look at your handiwork," he said after a moment.

"That's all right," Gideon said. "I have it under control."

"I wouldn't mind," Astra said to Scott. "If you're offering."

"It's *under control.*"

Scott nodded, wearing the look of silent disapproval that Gideon knew so well. "I won't keep you kids any longer."

"Good," Gideon said. "I mean, Astra's right. We should hit the road."

He helped her to the car and got in after her.

"Drive safe," Scott said. "And, Astra?"

"Yeah?"

"Don't put too much weight on that foot."

The following morning, back in New York, Gideon started rewriting the essay. When he wasn't in class or Dr. Park's lab, he was in his apartment, fine-tuning his prose, paying special attention to the first paragraph—the scene in which he came to Astra's rescue. Two weeks later, he completed what he considered to be a quality piece of writing, a superlative personal statement to serve as the keystone to his application.

He and Dewey were high and watching *The Fly* when Astra came over a couple of days later, complaining that she'd lost all the feeling in her foot. She sat in the swivel chair she'd scavenged from the sidewalk and laid her foot on Gideon's knee. When he peeled back the brown bandage, he was surprised to find that the skin around the stitches was inflamed.

"That's normal," he said, trying to suppress the uncertainty in his voice.

"Are you sure?"

Dewey leaned forward. "It looks like a diseased football," he said drowsily.

"Her immune system is fighting off infection."

Astra sat up. "It's *infected*?"

"I'm saying your foot is *fighting off* infection."

"I think I should see someone about this."

"You *are* seeing someone, remember? You're seeing me."

"You're not a doctor!"

"I'm premed!"

"Dewey's prelaw! That doesn't make him a lawyer!"

Gideon looked to Dewey for support, but his roommate had fallen asleep. Dewey's tongue, incandescent with Dorito dust, lay lifeless in his open mouth.

"Wrap it up," he said, nodding at her foot. "You have to keep it clean, or else it won't heal."

The next day, after his virology lecture, Gideon walked across campus to the tall concrete building that housed Dr. Park's lab. A group of students stood on the sidewalk outside, the same students that he always passed on his way in, holding signs that read CURIOSITY KILLS and ANIMALS ARE PEOPLE TOO. One young man wore a yellow chicken suit, complete with a red tail and strap-on beak. Someone else, in black robes and a skeleton mask, made stabbing motions with a prop syringe. "Excuse me, sorry," Gideon said, squeezing through the barrier of bodies blocking his path.

"What if we put *you* in a cage?" someone shouted after him.

"Bawk bawk!" clucked the chicken.

It was true, what Astra had told Maya about the chickens making him depressed. It wasn't so much that the chickens were caged, but that they didn't seem to *realize* they were caged. They knew something was wrong—that much was clear from the panic in their eyes—but they didn't know what, and that, more than anything, was the true source of his sadness. Astra had asked him once why he didn't quit the lab and join the student protest. The fact was, he didn't object to animal testing any more than he objected to animals being killed for food. Not on principle. He was just too cowardly to do it himself.

After checking in with Dr. Park, Gideon prepped a batch of eggs for injection. He sat in front of a computer and commanded the device that Dr. Park had patented—an inverted bed of needles suspended from the ceiling—to descend onto a tray of twenty eggs. The chickens in cages on the far side of the lab watched the needles pierce the eggs and then withdraw. Gideon inspected the shells for breakage before placing them in the incubator.

He took his lunch break in Riverside Park, where he met Astra on their usual bench, and they talked for a while about her thesis project. Her plan was to stitch together clips from Woodstock with contemporary car commercials that licensed those same songs. She was describing the difficulty inherent in creating seamless sound collages from live and recorded audio when Gideon noticed that the bandage wrapped around her ankle was white.

"Did you do that yourself?" he asked.

"Did I do what?"

"Your foot." He bent to get a closer look. "Did you buy a new bandage or something?"

"Yeah," she said. "I bought a new bandage."

"Where?"

". . . student health."

He shook his head in disbelief. "You went to *student health*? Astra, that clinic is totally unreliable. All they do is give STD tests. And they can't even do that right! Dewey went once and got a false negative."

"The woman I spoke to seemed to know what she was doing."

"Did you tell her I didn't have a suture kit? I could have done it better if I had a proper suture kit."

Astra bit her bottom lip. "She, um, actually took the stitches out."

"She took them *out*? That's proof they don't know what they're doing! What if the wound reopens? What if it gets infected?"

"She said my foot was already infected. She said I was lucky she caught it in time. She said if she hadn't—"

"I can't believe this! You don't trust me at all!"

"Please lower your voice," she said.

"Not when you go behind my back and *betray me* by seeing someone at the student health clinic!"

"Calm down, Gideon. You're acting like I cheated on you."

"Yeah, well, in a way, you did!" He crushed the empty brown paper bag in his hand and got up from the bench. "I'm going back to work."

"Sit down!" she snapped, raising her voice for the first time since they'd started dating. "Don't you get what's going on?"

"Why? What's going on?"

"Did you ever stop and wonder why you can't write your essay?"

"I *can* write my essay! I *did* write my essay!"

"That maybe this is all about your dad?"

"I wrote about your fucking foot!"

"And maybe you don't actually want to be a doctor?"

"This is bullshit," he said, shaking his head.

"It's nothing to be embarrassed about. Everyone I've ever met is either running away from their parents or trying to become them."

"It's not that simple!"

"Isn't it?"

"If I'm so bad at what I do, maybe you should dump me."

She looked up at him with wide, patient eyes. "But I don't want to. Is that what you want?"

His heart started skittering inside his chest again. A scarlet rash rose to the surface of his trembling hands.

"I don't know," he said. "Maybe. I don't know."

He turned on his heels and made his way out of the park. He was shaking so violently he hardly noticed the glaring red hand across Riverside Drive. A car nearly clipped him, honking as it passed. He ran across the street, dodging SUVs and buses, and kept running once he reached the other side. He blew past the protestors outside the building, taking shelter in the familiar sterility of the lab.

It was dark. Dr. Park was out to lunch. Standing alone in that windowless room where he'd passed the last three years of his life, he noticed, for the first time, just how oppressively claustrophobic it was. Menacing, even. Dr. Park's device looked like an instrument of torture. The chickens stared at Gideon through the bars of their cages, their beady little eyes locked into his. *Help us*, they seemed to say. *Help us understand why you're out there and we're in here.* If he stacked the cages, he could carry four of them at once, and he did, his sneakers squeaking on the linoleum floor as he waddled down the hall. He backed into a door marked EMERGENCY EXIT, his arms aching from the cumbersome weight of the cages. He didn't hear the alarms until after he surfaced on the sidewalk, but by then, he had already set the birds free.

———

Ernie Power was a combat photographer with a swashbuckling style. At six foot three, his brown cheeks snowy with stubble, he stood out among the white, college-aged clientele at the budget hostel on Hillel Street. He looked like a revolutionary, a guerilla general, clad in black with combat boots, a bandolier of film canisters strapped to his chest. Though he'd grown up on the South Side of Chicago, his accent was impossible to place, as though each of the countries he'd visited in his career had left a faint impression on his speech.

"Gaza was a shit show," he told Gideon the first time they met, adjusting, with beringed fingers, his black beret. "I was shooting this girl—shooting photos, I mean—whose parents had been killed in an Israeli airstrike. The building where they lived was still standing, but just barely. One whole side was missing. You could see inside it, like a dollhouse. They were trying to evacuate the building, and this girl, six years old but with eyes like my grandmother's, wouldn't budge. Old eyes, you know, full of terrible wisdom. And I'm standing there, taking her picture, and it occurs to me that any minute a slab of concrete might fall and crush us both. So what do I do? I throw her over my shoulder, like a sack of flour, and I run. I mean, I run as fast and far down the street as I can. When, at last, I turned around again, the building was gone. A pile of rubble, enveloped in dust." He slipped his finger through a silver hoop earring and tugged hard as if to remind himself of the pain he'd so narrowly avoided. "My critics claim I've lost my objectivity. But what was I supposed to do, watch her die on principle? Just because I've got a camera? I've made plenty of mistakes in my life, but at least I didn't sit back and do nothing."

The two weeks before Ernie checked into the hostel were among the loneliest in Gideon's life. He passed the days in Aroma, a wi-fi-ready coffee shop near the hostel, so as not to tax the diminishing data on his SIM card, searching desultorily for jobs in Jerusalem and refreshing Astra's Facebook page. She'd stopped posting proverbs and was using the platform to update her friends on her attempts to adopt the domestic shorthair that lived in the alley behind her apartment. In one photo, Astra held it in her lap, one hand on the mangy fur of its chest, the other scratching behind its tipped ear. A strange discomfort shot through Gideon's stomach, an unpleasantness he couldn't place until he realized, with a stab of self-loathing, that he was jealous of a feral cat.

In the evenings, he walked around the city, feeling helplessly lost among the Orthodox children chucking stones at passing cars and the Christian tourists rubbing their scarves on the Stone of Unction. They seemed so certain of themselves and their beliefs, and this certainty appeared to protect them from the crushing solitude that bent Gideon's back. He dreaded dinner—dreaded deploying his grade school Hebrew to request a table for one—and took to eating in the upper deck of the two-story McDonald's on Shamai Street, where at least the menu was in English, the food inexpensive and familiar. Even there, however, he was reminded of his loneliness, watching another single diner, a nun, nibble contentedly on the contents of her Chicken Party Bucket. She didn't look half as depressed as Gideon. She had her god to keep her company.

Growing up, whenever he'd found himself at loose ends, Gideon had turned not to God, but to his father. He rarely made a move without consulting Scott, whose authority was absolute, solid as a golden dome. But over the past year, he'd lost faith in his father and in just about everything else. Now he drifted through the streets like some benign dybbuk, a soul without a home. One night, without intending to, he wandered into a Hasidic neighborhood, past shops selling framed portraits of prominent rabbis and signs admonishing women for their immodest clothes. An old man in a ubiquitous black suit approached and asked if he was Jewish. Gideon, suspicious of the question, said he wasn't. "Are you sure?" the man asked. "Not even your mother?" Gideon shook his head. The man smiled, apparently relieved. "Come with me." Gideon followed the man into his dark apartment, where a woman sat on a long leather sofa, surrounded by children on both sides. "Please," the man said, "would you turn on the lights?"

Two weeks in Jerusalem and Gideon had become a Shabbos goy.

Apart from the old man in the suit and the pretty girl who worked the counter at Aroma, he hadn't spoken to a soul until Ernie arrived at the hostel. Ernie must have seen how lonely Gideon was, smelled the stink of solitude clinging to his skin. Hardly had the photographer unpacked before inviting his bunkmate to a Russian bar on Jaffa Street. There, he told the story of his life, which he delivered in a disaffected, but not indifferent tone of voice and embellished with dramatic hand gestures. He told Gideon about growing up on the South Side and his chance encounter with a battered copy of *How the Other Half Lives*, which inspired him to lift a camera from a local pawn shop. He'd cut his teeth at the Warehouse, shooting the Chicago house music scene, until one night, juiced on cocaine, he was visited by the ghost of Jacob Riis. "There he was," Ernie said, "in his three-piece suit, looking at me from behind those wire-framed glasses like I was letting him down. Two weeks later, I was on a plane to Alaska to shoot the *Exxon Valdez*."

For five consecutive nights, Ernie took him to the bar, bought him drinks, and told him stories. He'd been to South Sudan, Rwanda, and Iraq. He'd covered genocides, civil wars, and occupations. He appeared to be possessed by the same sense of purpose that had once driven Gideon in school; but where Gideon pursued good grades, Ernie chased atrocities. He had a special sympathy for sex workers and had once freed a girl from a trafficking ring in Patpong. "I bought her for four US dollars," he said. "I felt awful about paying her captors, of course, but I kept thinking about the life she would have led had I not intervened. I drove her to a nearby school, paid her tuition, and told her she was free to do what she liked. Though I suppose, for a minute there, technically speaking, I was the owner of another human being."

"What did it feel like?" Gideon asked.

"Horrible." Ernie shook his head. "It was the most horrible feeling in the world."

It was hard not to love Ernie, at least a little bit, with his sonorous voice and wide-angle eyes, his willingness to buy another round, and then another, as he unspooled the endless yarn of his career. The more incredible his stories, the more perfunctory his tone, as though he'd happened upon some war crimes on the way to the store. The drinks weren't half as intoxicating as the stories, the intensity with which the photographer spoke, his sense of purpose, the mission that made his eyes light up like a pair of lanterns. It was the same light that Gideon saw behind the eyes of the faithful as they poured out of tour buses, trained on something greater than themselves. But as much as he loved listening to Ernie, he couldn't help but hear the stories as a kind of reproach, a judgment on his own cowardice. He felt bad about abandoning Shelby and believed that by not crossing into Palestine, he'd missed his chance to do something meaningful.

Something true. He was tired of hiding beneath the bed of Experience while other, more adventurous souls rolled around on the mattress, sweating through the sheets. And no one had sweat through more sheets than Ernie Power.

It was Ernie who showed him the beheading video. It was their fifth night in the Russian bar, and Ernie, unruffled by his many vodka sodas, asked if Gideon wanted to see what history looked like before the historians had cleaned it up. In the clip, which Ernie pulled up on his phone, a man knelt before a barren landscape. He might have been a Buddhist monk with his shaved head and flowing orange robe, but he was, in fact, a journalist from Massachusetts and a prisoner of a terrorist organization that called itself the Islamic State. One of its members stood beside the journalist, wearing a black robe and a balaclava, brandishing a knife. Gideon, half-drunk, watched with fascination and terror as the man in black placed one hand over the journalist's mouth. Then he raised the knife like a champagne sabre and uncorked the journalist's head.

Gideon had seen videos like this before when, in middle school, his friend Dan Franken-Atlas first played him "The Pain Olympics," a series of extremely violent videos culminating in a clip of a man cutting off his penis with a kitchen knife. He spent hours sitting in front of Dan's computer, the chunky desktop monitor radiating heat as if the machine itself were ashamed. At first, he watched only to prove that he could; the ability to stomach sickening content, from scenes of self-mutilation to coprophilia, suicides, and public executions, was a kind of currency among his friends in seventh grade. But there was something alluring about the videos, too. They gestured to a world beyond Brookline, beyond the mute safety of his childhood. After his parents had gone to sleep, Gideon would creep downstairs to the family computer and sit before the malevolent glow of the screen until his eyes clouded over.

"These guys," Ernie said, "just took control of Mosul. They're moving into Raqqa, too."

"That's terrible," Gideon said, though he wasn't sure where those cities were exactly. The clip upset him, but it excited him, too, to think how close he was, geographically, to the extreme acts depicted in the video.

"I've been emailing with this Kurdish group," Ernie said, lowering his voice so no one else would hear him. Gideon felt lucky to be let in on the secret. "What do you know about the Kurds?"

"A little," Gideon lied—he knew nothing—"but not much."

"The Kurds are the largest ethnic minority in the world without their own country. They mostly live in Turkey, Iran, Iraq, and Syria, where they've been second-class citizens for decades. Now that the country is up for grabs, they're trying to carve out an autonomous region. A Kurdish homeland. I want to get there before anyone else does."

"How are you going to do that?"

"Unfortunately, it's just about impossible to go without enlisting in the Kurdish militia fighting with the Syrian Democratic Forces."

"That's too bad," Gideon said, trying not to sound relieved. The past five days had been his happiest in weeks. He couldn't stomach losing Ernie, the first real friend he'd made in Israel.

"So I've decided to enlist."

Gideon looked up from his glass. "You're leaving?"

"I'm a transient," Ernie said in his sibilant voice, rubbing his thumb and forefinger together as if to suggest an affinity between himself and the breeze blowing through the open door. "I don't have a house. I don't have a mortgage. I don't actually *live* anywhere. Everything I own, I carry with me. Such is the life of a professional witness."

Gideon was crushed. "When do you go?"

"Two days from now. I've got a plane ticket to Sulaymaniyah, Iraq. After that, I'm in the hands of the YPG. That's the People's Protection Units. The Kurdish militia. I'm very curious as to how they plan to sneak me into Syria. They have a training camp called the Academy somewhere in the northern part of the country."

"We should probably settle up," Gideon said, signaling the bartender.

"One more drink," Ernie insisted. He lifted up his black T-shirt, revealing a white scar twisting up his torso like the snakes on the Staff of Hermes emblazoned on the sides of ambulances. "I haven't told you how I got *this*."

The next morning, Gideon walked through the fog of his hangover to Aroma, where he bought a small coffee and sat at a table, watching the cute girl behind the counter. She tossed her bangs with a jerk of the neck as she stood before the espresso machine, her delicate fingers working the knobs. He thought that if he asked her out, and she said yes, he'd be able to tolerate Ernie's departure. And even if it didn't work out with the girl, even if they shared one disastrous date, her yes would give him the confidence to ask someone else, and he could sustain himself that way, leaping from one person to another, never staying alone for too long. He could ask out every girl in every coffee shop in Israel! But when, after much deliberation, he at last approached the counter, he was met by a muscular man in a tank top, and by the time he managed to explain that he didn't want to order anything, or rather had already ordered, and wanted instead to speak to the man's female colleague, who couldn't hear them over the espresso machine, a line of impatient Israelis had formed behind him, and the girl was looking at him with such indifference that it seemed to violate his human rights. He apologized and ducked out of the shop, leaving half a bready croissant on the table.

He stood in the street, ashamed and still hungover. He wandered for a while until he found himself in the Old City, drawn like a fugitive to the scene of the crime; the pocked, irregular bricks beneath his feet made him remember Shelby. Her broad, guileless face, her eyebrows bunched behind her glasses as he started to back away. As he abandoned her. He wondered where she was, if she'd stayed in Palestine or flown home. He wondered where home was for her. Probably she'd told him, but he didn't remember. He wanted to write her, to apologize, explain—but why? So she would forgive him? He didn't deserve her forgiveness or her friendship.

He stopped for lunch at a small café inside the Old City. A laminated poster was plastered on the wall, flashing white where the paper was wrinkled. The text at the top of the poster read, in English, WHAT YOUR WAY OF EATING HUMMUS SAYS ABOUT YOU, and below there were six illustrations of six different hands dipping pita into six different platters of hummus. Gideon looked at his own hands and then back at the poster. His method most resembled illustration number three, "The Jerk." DINER BEWARE, the text below the illustration read, THIS PRICK WANTS ALL THE TOPPINGS FOR HIMSELF.

He had just paid the bill when the thought occurred to him to leave with Ernie. It was, he saw now, with perfect clarity, the best opportunity to redeem himself, not to mention his only means of leaving the country. His hostel had cost most of his meager savings, which were already hurting from the $4,000 he'd paid Columbia for "destroying campus property"—that is, the chickens—pursuant to §16b of the undergraduate handbook. He'd forfeited his ticket home when he walked off the trip, and he didn't want his parents to have to bail him out. The time had come for him to prove himself on his own terms. He was determined to perform at least one heroic act before returning to the comforts of home, such as they were.

That night, at the Russian bar, he put the idea to Ernie.

The question seemed to startle him. "You're kidding."

"I'm not," Gideon said.

"Don't you want to, I don't know, talk it over with your parents?"

"I'm over eighteen. I don't need to talk anything over."

"I'm not exactly champing at the bit to grant such a spontaneous request," Ernie said. "This shit is dangerous. You have to think about it."

"Didn't you jump on a plane after that dream?" Gideon asked. "The one about Jacob Riis?"

"I did. But that was to shoot an oil spill."

"So?"

"So an oil spill never cut anyone's head off."

This line of argument wouldn't work on Gideon. The danger of the mission was part of its appeal, and anyway, he didn't really think he'd be beheaded, not with Ernie by his side. The photographer had seen so much and turned out fine.

"I thought you of all people would appreciate a little spontaneity," Gideon said.

Ernie shook his head and laughed. "You really want to come with me to Syria?"

"I do."

He felt the weight of the statement on his tongue. The words were

matrimonial, wedding him to Ernie, until death, or Kurdish independence, did them part.

"I'll have to email the militia. See if you can get a ticket."

"Right."

"I'm not sure they can deliver. This is very short notice."

"I understand."

"So I'll email the militia."

"Good."

A smile carved Ernie's lips. "Okay, then," he said and signaled for
another round. "Let's go to motherfucking Syria."

Hope

·

AUGUST–SEPTEMBER 2014

S cott had never seen inside a prison before and was surprised to discover just how familiar the facility in Norfolk felt. With its cinder block dormitories, baseball diamond, and manicured quad, the campus could have passed for a public university's were it not for the enormous concrete wall encompassing the grounds. His supervisor told him that the wall, twenty feet tall and crowned with barbed wire, had been constructed, like the rest of the prison, by the inmates it would come to house, an irony Scott never failed to appreciate each time he passed through the fortified gate to carry out his court-mandated community service.

The supervisor, Dr. Christian Treat, was a few years shy of forty, with wavy hair, ruddy cheeks, and a buoyant disposition for a full-time prison physician. He'd spent the first ten years of his career in private practice, he explained, before his group had gone bankrupt. He actually made *more* money in corrections than he would have in a for-profit hospital. The hours were better, and the benefits, too, plus: free malpractice insurance. When Scott asked if he ever felt unsafe treating murderers and sex offenders and the like, Treat smiled and pulled out a small black device, the size of a cell phone, from his pocket. This was his personal panic button, and in his five years at Norfolk, he'd never pressed it once. In fact, he felt safer here than in some city clinics and found that the prison population, on the whole, was kinder and altogether more civilized than many patients on the outside.

Scott soon discovered this fact for himself. He enjoyed his weekends in Norfolk, attending to common colds and stomachaches, acid
reflux brought on by the canteen food, and toenail infections contracted in the prison shower. He liked the routine nature of the work,
his patients' manageable maladies, the gratitude they showed him as
he wrapped their bruised hands in bandages and dispensed ibuprofen in small paper cups. The politics of career advancement, of publishing papers and conducting clinical trials, had no place here. All
Scott had to do was help people, make them feel a little better. That
much he'd learned how to do in medical school. That much he was
capable of.

Only once did he face a patient whose problems exceeded his abil-
ities. The man was tall and potbellied with a coppery beard, a black
sun tattooed on the back of one hand, an iron cross inked on the other.
Despite his imposing appearance, however, he blushed when Scott
asked what was wrong. Then he pulled down his orange prison-issue
pants, revealing a padlock around the base of his purple, oxygen-
starved genitals. He'd just come from a conjugal visit with his wife—
at least that's what it was supposed to have been—who was apparently
still upset with him for fucking her sister. Could the Jew doctor help?

It seemed Scott's destiny to inspect the stricken sex organs of other
men. This was not the fate he would have chosen for himself, but it
was one he supposed he could learn to live with. He cocked his head
and examined the lock, along with the genitals inside it, trapped like
little prisoners inside their cell. "I'm not sure what I can do for you,"
he said, feeling a surge of unexpected sympathy for the man's purple
penis, if not the man himself, "but I think we'd better call a lock-
smith."

Scott lingered at the end of his shifts, asking Dr. Treat if he needed any help and asking the same of the half dozen physician assistants on staff at any given time. He invented small tasks to keep himself there, such as cleaning his examination room, anything to postpone the hour's drive back to Brookline, which he made in silence and smelling faintly of formaldehyde. The prison had come to feel like home, whereas his home—solitary, quiet—felt more and more like a prison.

When he wasn't at Norfolk, he spent as much time as he could at his Longwood office to stave off the loneliness of the empty house. The hallways and examination rooms seemed to be in slightly different places than he remembered, and in the evenings, he wandered the halls, half-lost, as in a dream, waiting for someone to appear around the corner and explain the mystery to him. Waiting for Carol Chin. She was working at a tech startup in Palo Alto, a company that specialized in "biomedical informatics," according to the brief but not unfriendly email she'd sent Scott at the start of the summer. It wasn't easy managing the team of twentysomethings who had founded the company in their freshman year of college, but she was used to dealing with difficult personalities. Whether she was referring to Scott or their patients, he wasn't sure. Either way, she said she wasn't angry with him anymore. In fact, she was happier than ever.

He missed her. The person he'd hired to replace her, a fleshy woman with a wrist brace and a *Sailor Moon* wall calendar, was forever leaving early or calling in sick, or taking personal days to attend comic book conventions. He was lucky, at least, not to have lost too many patients over the course of the past year. Two or three of them had left for other practices, but by and large, they didn't seem to have noticed he was gone. Those who did felt that Scott had been unfairly suspended. They wouldn't, they couldn't, they *refused* to believe that the man to whom they'd entrusted their health for the past twenty years had betrayed them. He kept waiting for someone to confront him, to ask point-blank what he'd done. No one did. The thought depressed and comforted him in equal measure: no one cared.

At the end of August, just before Labor Day weekend, Scott visited his mother at Green Pastures. By then, he hadn't spoken to his wife in two weeks, not since that terrible morning she called to tell him that his son had dropped out of college and, after a few months of living with Deb, decamped to Israel. The news came as such a shock that Scott was rendered speechless. She must be mistaken. She must be joking. None of it made any *sense*. How could Gideon leave Columbia without his knowing? Why Israel? And why hadn't he come home? According to Deb, who was apparently in sporadic contact with their son, he'd signed up with an NGO to advance the cause of peace between Israelis and Palestinians. This didn't make any sense, either. Gideon had never expressed any understanding of, much less a passing interest in, Middle Eastern politics. When he finally wrapped his head around the thought—when he realized, at last, that Deb wasn't kidding—he unleashed such a torrent of anger that, later, he had to conclude it must have been lying dormant inside him for years. He couldn't remember most of what he said, possessed as he was by the anger, but he did remember how he'd ended the call and was certain that Deb remembered, too.

Marjorie, whose health prevented her from traveling, took her misery out on him. "It makes me sick just to think of it," she said, "you, all alone in that enormous house, rattling around like a walnut in a shell. What do you *do* all day?" For once, however, her hectoring didn't bother him. He felt he could see her for what she really was, a lonely woman who had never learned how to love. It wasn't his mother talking, anyway. It was the loneliness talking *through* her. In his own loneliness, he could hear it now.

•

After exchanging emails with the People's Protection Units, Ernie managed to get Gideon tickets from Tel Aviv to Sulaymaniyah, Iraq, via Istanbul, an itinerary that bewildered airport security.

"I cannot stop you from leaving," a burly El Al agent flecked with eczema said, staring at Gideon with suspicious eyes. "But you will not find it so easy if you try to come back."

Ernie's placid manner put Gideon at ease. He flirted with the flight attendants and told war stories, his ironic inflection like a Kevlar vest protecting him against the shrapnel of post-traumatic stress. "I was in the Congo once," he said, sipping a Bloody Mary from a plastic cup. "This was during the second civil war. I was walking back toward my hotel when I saw some soldiers killing time by the side of the road. Sharing a cigarette, that kind of thing. Cleaning their guns. A few of them were kicking a ball back and forth. I remember feeling safe. I'd seen these guys do terrible things, but for the moment, everything was peaceful. Then I realized it wasn't a ball. It was a human head. They were kicking *a human head*."

"Were you afraid?" Gideon asked.

"Could I get another one of these, hon?" he asked the flight attendant. He took another sip and smacked his lips. "In loud environments— I'd say we're at about eighty-five decibels right now—tomato juice *tastes* better. Not just tomato juice; anything umami. Our taste perceptions depend on the sensory inputs of our surroundings. About ten years ago, I was staying at the Sheraton in Baghdad. Suddenly, the building shook. I saw a massive fireball outside my window. Insurgents had fired rockets at the hotel."

"I've stayed at a Sheraton before."

"Luxury hotels are soft targets. Multiple points of entrance and egress, constant flow of traffic. You can find floor plans and photos online. They often house diplomats and contractors. And of course, they're symbolic of Western affluence."

Gideon nodded studiously. "Of course."

"After the blast, soldiers opened fire from the roof. It was deafening. I had to sit tight while they evacuated the civilians on the floors below me."

"What did you do?"

He drained the contents of the cup and set it down, a gritty residue clinging to the plastic. The ice cubes had holes in them. "What could I do? I opened up the minibar. They had a Bloody Mary mix, and let me tell you, with the sound of bullets hammering the air? I've never had a better drink. You sure you don't want anything? This might be the last booze you have for a while."

Gideon declined. He wanted to stay sharp. Maybe if he kept his body pure—empty, clean, free of toxins—his mind, and thus his motives, might be pure, too. He wanted to face the coming adventure with courage and clarity of heart.

"You'll be empty, all right," Ernie said. "You're going to shit your brains out."

They were met at the airport in Sulaymaniyah by a man in an Ed Hardy T-shirt with a smiling skull design and the words LOVE KILLS SLOWLY above it. He drove a white Toyota Hi-Lux pickup with dirt encrusted on the fenders. When Gideon got inside, Ed Hardy handed him a black bandanna. The last thing he saw before blindfolding himself was the card clipped to the car's sun visor. It was a picture of a young man around Gideon's age, in military fatigues, set against a yellow background, a red star printed in the upper-left-hand corner: a martyr for the People's Protection Units. When, after half an hour, Ed Hardy stopped the car and they took off their blindfolds, Gideon's heart bucked. They were parked outside a Sheraton.

It didn't seem real, his being in Iraq, a place which, to Gideon, had existed exclusively in black headlines and scrolling chyrons. Ernie didn't seem concerned. He was a calming presence, stretching as he got out of the truck, joints popping as he rolled his neck like an athlete preparing to take the field. Gideon tried to mimic Ernie's movements, his attitude, the slack in his limbs. He felt better when he did. By relaxing his body, he could short-circuit his brain, convincing it that there was nothing to worry about.

Ed Hardy helped them check into their rooms, which were booked under false names. These were the names they were to use from now on. Henceforth, Ernie was no longer Ernie. He was "Kochar." Gideon was "Amraz." They were not to share their given names with anyone, not even their comrades. Not even Ed Hardy, who explained, in halting English, that they were in the process of being reborn. Whatever mistakes they'd made in the past were meaningless. The struggle for independence was all that mattered now.

They changed hotel rooms three times that night. For security purposes, Ernie explained. In the last room, Ed Hardy delivered a passionate lecture about women's liberation as it related to Kurdish independence. Western capitalism, he explained, had reduced women to commodities exploited by the patriarchal nation-state; women as a group could be understood to be a colony of sorts. The only solution was to create a stateless democracy in which power flowed from the ground up, rather than from the top down, with women as equal participants. Gideon listened intently. Far from being foreign, these ideas were the logical extensions of the values that his parents had instilled in him. The Kurds were trying to create the kind of place that Brookline professed to be, the kind of place that the kibbutz professed to be: a free, open, tolerant society. He burned with questions: How would such a nation participate in global markets? What was the relationship between misogyny and imperialism? And historical materialism: What *was* that? His mind felt like the plasma globe at the Museum of Science, blue filaments of thought surging from a hot electrode.

"All this you will learn at the Academy," Ed Hardy assured him.

"When will we get there?" Gideon asked.

"Soon. Very soon."

Then something unsettling happened. After sunset, Ed Hardy left Gideon with Ernie and advised them to get some rest before the long drive the next morning. Gideon, who was still getting used to his new name, rolling it around like a gumball on his tongue, waited until Ernie's breath slowed before he let himself fall asleep.

A few hours later, he woke with a start to the sound of Ernie's voice. He couldn't make out what the photographer was saying, save for a few stray words: "No . . . can't . . . please . . ." Ernie's long, muscular body was rolling back and forth on the bed. Gideon switched on the lamp above the bedside table. There were dark stains on Ernie's shirt and on the sheets beneath him. Beads of sweat were rolling down his smooth bald head. "Help me! Help me!" Ernie cried, his voice high and fragile as glass.

The next day, they put their blindfolds on again and boarded the truck. They drove for a long time, too many hours to count, until they reached the banks of the Tigris River. The sun had set some time before, and it was darker here than anywhere he'd ever seen. There were only the headlights of their truck, wobbling on the surface of the water. A second pair of headlights flashed ahead of them, some distance away, on the opposite bank. Gideon imagined that his mother was in the other car, come to pick him up from school. She would ask about his day, his friends, his homework, if he was hungry. The thought of her waiting there sustained him as he skipped across the water on an inflatable raft, but when he reached the other side, he found a man in military fatigues waiting for him in her place.

"Congratulations," Ernie said as they climbed out of the boat, the water saturating their shoes. "You've just crossed the Syrian border."

It was dark enough now that they didn't need blindfolds. The man in fatigues drove until they reached what appeared to be the literal end of the road. Gideon had never seen anything like that before, a road just stopping in the middle of nowhere, as if the people charged with paving it had given up. The man in fatigues left the car where it was, strapped on a busted-looking pair of night vision goggles, and motioned for them to follow him. They hiked for hours, single file, carrying heavy packs. The man in fatigues walked slowly to avoid setting off a land mine.

The mention of land mines made Gideon nervous. Until now, all the danger he'd encountered had come in the form of Ernie's stories, all of which had ended in his safe return. But this was a story without an ending yet. The desert night was cold, and all Gideon had to keep him warm was his adrenaline—which, while abundant, was a finite resource. He felt himself growing tired, the tips of his toes turning numb.

A few hours into the walk, his heart stopped. He had stepped on something. Something solid and irregular. In an instant, he saw his own death staring back at him—a welcoming shadow, a beckoning wraith.

Gideon looked down. Beneath the sole of his waterlogged sneaker was not a land mine but that most ubiquitous piece of American detritus: a crushed can of Diet Coke.

At sunrise, they reached the Academy, an enormous compound surrounded by a cinder block wall. It stood alone in the barren moonscape, but somehow Gideon hadn't seen it coming; it had all the hazy majesty of a mirage. He exhaled as he passed through the tall iron gate that admitted them into the compound. He was finally going back to school.

•

Scrapping the wedding solved the problem of paying for it. Maya's parents had offered to cover the reception, but Louis's mother insisted on paying for half, and there ensued a series of tense negotiations between Deb Greenspan and Patty Friedman, communicated through the proxies of their children, who were saddled with the task of translating, and toning down, their mothers' more explosive sentiments. Patty, Maya learned, was no less stubborn than her mother, but their inability to settle on a budget gave her something to bond over with Louis. They stayed up late, forgoing wedding planning to share stories about the indomitable women who had raised them. She'd never felt so close to Louis as she did then, trading tales from their childhoods, the two of them utterly fascinated by each other. She didn't recognize the person she'd been this past year, the person who had taken someone as loving as Louis for granted.

Maya was having money troubles of her own. After Cressida cut her loose, she made a few attempts to find similar jobs, but publishing is a small industry, growing smaller by the day, and after she ruled out properties owned by Beijing Mobile, there were precious few literary imprints left, and fewer still who hadn't heard about her firing. She interviewed for an assistant editor position at a company that published how-to books as well as calendars and puzzles, but the job—$45,000 with two weeks' vacation—went to a woman with a PhD from Syracuse.

She didn't know what she would have done without Louis. After Maya lost her job, he pulled his money out of the day-trading app, which was enough to cover Maya's half of the rent for six months.

"I can't take this," she'd said. "It's your money. You made it."

"I didn't really 'make' anything. It's smoke and mirrors. Besides, we're engaged, aren't we? What's mine is yours."

She felt herself begin to cry. "I don't deserve you."

"It makes me happy to support you. Think of it as an arts fellowship. Besides, when you finish your book and get famous, you'll be the one supporting me."

She'd started writing recently—fiction, in fact—about (what else?) a girl who gets involved with her high school English teacher. But where William's novel had been narrow, solipsistic, even antisocial, and filtered through a single, authoritative consciousness that was terminally uninterested in the existence of others, Maya's ambition was to write something different. Something multifaceted, expansive, and philosophical, something shot through with social criticism— something Russian. The more she wrote, the more she saw that her involvement with William was just one episode in the history of her own life and the lives of her family and friends, from which she mined her most promising material. She wasn't writing, as William was, to argue on behalf of herself, to assert her side of a story as the truth. She was writing for almost the opposite reason, for the same reason she read, the reason she'd fallen in love with books in the first place: to inhabit lives other than her own.

She'd seen William only once since her weekend in the Hamptons, though she hadn't planned to see him at all. It was easier—cowardly, maybe, but easier—to avoid his countless calls and texts until he got the message. But there he was, one December afternoon, shivering in front of her building, looking so cold that in her embellished memory, there were icicles hanging from his sleeves. She kept her head down and crossed the street, ducking into a coffee shop through whose window she could monitor his movements. He looked small from where she sat, and slightly crazed, pacing back and forth without a proper winter coat, puffs of moisture proliferating from his mouth before fading into nothing. It was forty minutes before he kicked the trash bins in front of her building and faded into nothing himself. She didn't want to see him, and might never have again, had she not logged on to Facebook a few months later and seen his face in a photo in the middle of her feed.

The photo, posted by *Humans of New York*, showed a William she could scarcely recognize. His brittle hair hardly concealed the creases in his forehead, and Maya could make out the broken blood vessels in his hollow cheeks. The pores were dark and dilated on his dripping nose. Around his neck hung the ubiquitous green apron of the world's most successful coffee chain.

"The country is crawling with geniuses," the text below the photo read in the conversational style of all the account's captions. From the first line, Maya could tell that this was going to be one of William's speeches, the kind that had captivated her at seventeen, though the authority conveyed by that torrent of text was undermined by the image of the peaky-looking man in the picture. She read it in his voice. "You won't find them in fancy classrooms, chasing grades, and you won't find them in the so-called writing workshops either. You sure as hell won't find them on the shelves at Barnes & Noble, their pride of place paid for by the big publishing houses. You'll find them in a diner, the freaks, the madmen, scribbling the next great American novel on the back of a napkin, half-drunk after a twelve-hour shift. Those geniuses. The ones who do menial work. The ones who wash your car and bus your tables. The ones who brew your coffee. Sure, I might look like a barista, but goddammit I'm an artist."

Below the post was a cascade of comments. The first twenty or thirty were supportive, offering sincere words of encouragement. "Too true!" someone wrote. "Don't give up!" said another. Maya felt compelled to write a comment herself, noting that not only was William no genius but he had studied, and taught, in a number of those fancy classrooms and courted the favor of those big publishing houses. But as she scrolled, she saw a second wave of comments, calling William out for using such insensitive words as "freaks" and "madmen" when the correct term was "neurodivergent." A third wave of comments comprised the backlash to the backlash. There were those who felt the term "neurodivergent" was nothing more than "PC bullshit," and there were those who identified as neurodivergent and resented the implication that the word was a synonym for "freak." Others objected to the term "menial," and still others wondered about those busboys and baristas who weren't artists—what about them? Maya scrolled and scrolled. At the bottom of the thread, someone had compared William to Hitler, and, satisfied, she decided not to leave her own comment after all.

It wasn't even that she disagreed with William, or not entirely. She was the product of a fancy school, she had worked in a big publishing house, and neither institution seemed especially good at incubating genius. But William's romanticizing of the working poor, among whose ranks he apparently counted himself, made her cringe. He was only ever half-right, she realized, but never more than that, and the line between half-right and wrong was so fine as to be invisible.

More than family, more than money, more than anything else, it was her brother who inspired Maya to scrap the wedding ceremony. As far as she and her parents knew, he was in Israel working for an NGO, but early one morning at the end of August, she received a brief email from a strange address with the subject line CONFIDEN-TIAL!!, and body text composed in a voice that she knew to be her brother's.

The email was long and rambled. The sentences were hard to follow. Maya squinted over the screen, registering only certain words. DIF-FICULT DECISION . . . APOCALYPTIC ATROCITIES . . . WAGE SLAVERY . . . SUPERSTRUCTURE . . . What the message lacked in clarity, it made up for with momentum. The words came fast and sparsely punctuated. Maya couldn't follow her brother's logic, couldn't understand what he was driving at until she settled on a single bolded phrase near the bottom. AFTER MANY MONTHS OF SEARCHING I BELIEVE I HAVE FOUND MY PURPOSE: TO HELP THE KURDISH PEOPLE BUILD A HOMELAND.

It was as though he had reached out through the light of her phone and slapped her in the face. She lost the sound of Louis snoring in bed beside her. There was only silence. Silence, and her anxious pulse beneath it.

She rubbed her eyes and read it again, slower this time. He couldn't tell her where he was, exactly, not only for security purposes but because he didn't really know. All he knew was that he was in northern Syria at a training camp for the People's Protection Units, or YPG, a militia devoted to defeating ISIS and establishing an autonomous Kurdish state. He begged her not to tell their parents, who would try to intervene, but he wanted someone in the family to know where he was in case something happened to him. He trusted she could keep a secret.

Her first impulse was to fear for his life. Not one week earlier, she'd read that ISIS had beheaded an American journalist, their second, and filmed the whole thing. Her brother had no business being in the Middle East—he wasn't fluent in Arabic or even Hebrew—and Maya didn't know what to make of all that Kurdish business nor the Marxist vocabulary that appeared periodically throughout the email.

The bedroom was filling with funereal gray light. A chill slipped between the window sash and sill. Louis kept an herb garden on the fire escape, three small planters of basil, parsley, and thyme. Fall would be here soon enough, picking off the leaves. Louis always forgot to bring the plants inside, and it seemed to Maya, given the contents of the email, that though it was a simple matter of opening and closing a window, they would never get around to it now. The plants would freeze and die there.

Louis stirred, turned over in bed. Maya read the email again and then once more. Despite her fears, Gideon's mission seemed more honorable with each successive reading. He had always tried his best to be like Scott. Now he'd gone and done something for himself for once—something that was, paradoxically, selfless—and she admired him for it. It was a feeling she, being the older of the two, had never really known before. She wouldn't tell her parents anything.

"MY ONE REGRET IN COMING HERE IS THAT ILL MISS YOUR WEDDING," he'd written near the end of the email, "SINCE I SUSPECT I WONT BE GOING HOME ANYTIME SOON. I KNOW YOURE STRESSED ABOUT THE WEDDING AS IT IS AND THE LAST THING I WANT IS TO MAKE IT ANY HARDER. BUT IF I CAN GIVE MY BIG SISTER A SMALL PIECE OF ADVICE ITS THAT YOU SHOULD DO WHAT YOU WANT. NOT WHAT MOM AND DAD WANT FOR YOU. WHAT <u>YOU</u> WANT FOR YOU."

She didn't forgive him, not entirely, for embarking on this mission of self-discovery the same year she was supposed to get married. But she couldn't imagine a wedding without him, couldn't fathom entertaining random family friends when her actual brother was five thousand miles away. The more she thought about it, the more she decided he was right. Deb wanted a wedding, Patty wanted a wedding, but she didn't. She wanted Louis—and that was all.

Not that she admitted this to anyone. When, in September, she called her mother with the news that she and Louis had just said their vows at city hall, and Deb, dismayed, asked why she had done it, Maya answered, "Why does anyone get married? Health insurance."

●

Deb had been staying with the Nassers for two weeks when Scott called with the news about his mother. She'd had her doubts about Joan ever since her son moved in, but Deb was disturbed by how lightly, how *cheerfully*, Joan took the news that Gideon was staying on in Israel. She didn't seem to understand how dangerous it was and how unlike him to make such an impulsive decision. Nightly Deb dreamed of suicide bombs, buses blown to bits, bodies pitted with shrapnel. When she woke, gasping, in the middle of the night—when the desert sun of her dreams shrunk to the size of the streetlamp outside the window—she'd find Joan on her back, breathing evenly, a mask over her eyes, ears plugged with foam.

She couldn't be with someone who didn't love her children. She knew that, had known it for some time already, but it wasn't until the opening ceremony for Joan's new academy in Mattapan that Deb understood it was time to leave. Donors, members of the press, and politicians filled the auditorium chairs at the ceremony. The new mayor, Marty Walsh, introduced Joan, who delivered a version of the speech Deb had heard when they met at the Seaport World Trade Center, a speech she'd heard a hundred times since. Then Joan introduced the inaugural class, who marched into the auditorium, and down the aisles, bearing flags and holstered sabers. In their uniforms, they hardly looked like children at all.

Joan finished her speech as the flag corps assembled in neat rows behind her. "There's one more person I have to thank," she said, smiling at the crowd. "I couldn't have done this without my ally—without my *partner*—Deborah Greenspan. Deb? Where are you, honey?" She searched the crowd. "There she is. Stand up and take a bow."

Deb tried to stand, but her body stayed put. She commanded her legs to flex, her core to tighten, the blood vessels in her lower body to constrict, but she simply couldn't *move*. It was a feeling she remembered from her days as a dancer, this slackening in protest, the body's refusal to take orders from the mind. Deb heard the whispers shifting through the room, felt the confusion seeping in. Joan, jaw set, was staring at her. And still, she didn't move.

Their fight that night was like any other, except that it didn't end in sex. It ended, instead, with Deb packing a suitcase while Joan took an angry jog up and down the Commonwealth Avenue Mall.

The feeling that followed Deb out of Joan's apartment, the feeling of freedom, the air in her lungs, dissolved before her feet touched the pavement. She didn't know where to go. From Joan's stoop, she called one neighbor after another. They wanted to help, but they were out of town, or had family visiting, or had converted their guest rooms into home offices. It seemed a strange coincidence, the scarcity of spare beds, but by the fourth call, Deb had begun to suspect, if not a conscious conspiracy, a certain strain of NIMBYism among her civic-minded friends—as though Deb were a wind turbine or housing project, a worthy cause that would drive down the price of real estate.

In the end, it was Fatima Nasser who took her in. Fatima had redecorated the house in Dudley Square, and Deb was surprised to find just how different it looked from when she'd first moved in. The windows were adorned with heavy, tasseled drapes, and the sofa, where Deb slept, was encased in a plastic slipcover. It wasn't what Deb would have done, design-wise, but she was grateful to have somewhere to stay. She made every effort to help around the house. She woke before dawn each morning and put a pot of coffee on for Khalil, who had found work at a Greek bakery on Beacon Street. She watched Amina after school while Fatima attended English classes and driving lessons. But no amount of service could untangle the knot of guilt in her chest.

When Scott called, he was calm, if stern, speaking with the bedside manner of a man practiced in delivering bad news. He'd just heard from the staff at Green Pastures. His mother had fallen two days earlier, and for some inexplicable reason—Deb could hear him working to tame his temper—they were only telling him about it now. According to the on-call physician, Marjorie had bruised her hip and strained a few muscles. Her bones, miraculously, remained intact, and there was no apparent damage to her internal organs. More troubling was her change in behavior. She was, Scott said, apparently exhibiting all the classic symptoms of dementia: anxiety, irritability, loneliness, confusion, and limited social skills. "Then again," Scott said, "she's always been anxious, irritable, lonely, and confused. As for social skills? Forget it."

"Do you think she'll be all right?" Deb asked. She was surprised to hear from him, given the way their last call had ended. She knew about the anger that lurked below his calm exterior, but even she had never heard him talk like that before. She had no choice but to believe him when, before hanging up, he said, the words sharp as a surgeon's scalpel, that he didn't want to see her fucking face ever again.

"Maybe, maybe not. I won't know until I see her. I fly out this weekend. Which, I'm sure, is exactly what she wants. Her son to come see her, I mean."

"You don't think she's faking it, do you?"

"With my mom, you never can be sure."

Deb insisted on going with him, if only to act as a buffer between mother and son. He surprised her by saying she could come, and so, a few days later, they met at Logan Airport and boarded a flight, her first all year, to Washington, DC. Scott slept most of the way there, but when, on their descent, the plane began to tremble, he put his hand over hers.

The nation's capital never failed to arouse a patriotic feeling in Deb.

Even during the Bush years, when she'd taken a bus down from Boston with other members of her synagogue to protest on the National Mall, chanting, "No blood for oil! Get off Iraqi soil!" she was moved by the majesty of those white marble structures, their physical presence, the mighty durability of the American Dream. Now, at Scott's side, in the late summer heat, her indestructible mother-in-law in decline, she saw how fragile it all was. She envisioned the city sinking into the swamp on top of which it was built, the monuments submerged in sludge.

At Scott's request, Marjorie had been transferred from the hospital at Green Pastures to Sibley Memorial in the Palisades. Deb followed Scott into her room, where they found her surrounded by hospital staff, the picture of happiness. "Deborah!" she cried, exhibiting none of the symptoms that Scott had described on the phone. "What a pleasant surprise! I'd like you to meet my lovely nurse, Michel. I call him my hunk of Brie. Because he's French! And a hunk! Come in, come in. Sit, sit, sit."

Michel smiled and excused himself. Scott pulled up a chair, and Deb did the same while Marjorie praised the facilities. "I can't tell you how well I've been treated here," she said. "They serve a chocolate pudding that's marvelous, marvelous. Michel says I'm his favorite patient. I try to make it easy on everyone, you know."

"How are you feeling, Mom?" Scott asked.

"The world's gone mad," she said. "Just the other day, I was on the computer, checking my email, modern woman that I am, when I find a message from my dear friend Dottie. You remember Dottie, from my old building? In any case, I open the email, wondering why Dottie didn't call if she wanted to catch up. Then I see the email isn't meant for me alone. It's addressed very generally, to friends and fam-

ily, and it says that her husband, Ted, you remember Ted, has started
to succumb to Alzheimer's. Well, this is news to me, of course, as Ted
has always been one of the great minds, in my opinion, a full professor of political science at Georgetown, tenured at twenty-six, and at
a time when universities were not so welcoming to Jews as they are
now. I could have sworn Dottie would go first. But even more shocking than the news about Ted was Dottie's request that we all *help pay
for his treatment*. She even included a link to a page where you can click
a big green button that says Donate Now. I could hardly believe it."

"I'm sorry to hear about Ted. But how are *you*?"

"Asking for money like that. Can you imagine? Never before have
I seen something so shameless. And Dottie's family has money, believe me. These are not poor people! It's a mad world that turns tax-
payers into paupers."

"I know you fell. How's the hip?"

"I want you two to stay at my place tonight."

"Your hip, Mom."

"Green Pastures can be quite accommodating."

Scott sighed. "Last I checked, Mom, there was only the one bed."

"Don't be such a prude. You're husband and wife! Oh, I can't tell
you how happy it makes me to see you two together."

Scott shot Deb a glance before turning to his mother and asking
her questions designed, Deb gathered, to determine whether she had
dementia. But Marjorie kept talking, energetic as ever, as though her
guests weren't assembled around a hospital bed but a table set for
dinner. In fact, she seemed to be in such good spirits that Deb wondered if she was faking her illness after all. She took a long look at
her mother-in-law, but the smile on the old woman's face betrayed
nothing.

Epilogue

•

SEPTEMBER–OCTOBER 2014

G ideon learned a lot at the Academy. In his classes on political philosophy, for instance, he learned that capitalism was just one phase in the natural progression of economic systems that would culminate in communism. He learned that patriarchy was the ideological product of the nation-state. He learned the word "neoliberal," though he struggled to define it. He also picked up practical skills. He learned the basic principles of first aid: how to stabilize a bone fracture with a splint, how to properly clean and dress a wound. He learned how to fire a Kalashnikov; he learned how to clean one, too. He learned to distinguish between the Hi-Lux trucks belonging to the YPG and those favored by ISIS, which he learned to call "Daesh." He learned elementary Kermanji, a Kurdish dialect. He learned, albeit slowly, to respond to his new name. But it wasn't until he graduated, one month after his arrival, that he learned how boring war could be.

For six weeks, he'd been stationed at a defensive outpost near the Turkish border, not far from the Euphrates, a river whose name he recalled from fourth-grade social studies, when, with his father's help, he'd built a papier-mâché map of Mesopotamia. The outpost was a cinder block structure, haphazardly furnished, with sandbags buttressing the balcony on the second floor. Gideon found himself wondering where the striped sofa and the swivel chair had come from. These objects had belonged to other people once, but if the view from the outpost was any indication, those people were long gone. The land beyond was barren, a uniform beige, pocked in places where cinder block foundations stood supporting nothing.

Gideon was one of a half dozen graduates of the Academy living at the outpost. There was a former Marine addicted to adrenaline, a registered nurse whose parents believed he was backpacking through Europe, a Peace Corps alumnus with terminal cancer, a San Francisco gutter punk with bipolar disorder ("I'm not the sick one. It's the modern world that's sick"), and a Vietnam veteran's son with poor eyesight. Gideon was given an inflatable mattress that had belonged to an excommunicated member of their ranks, a born-again Christian who was caught snacking on the foot of a dead civilian.

Two weeks after his arrival at the outpost, Gideon received an email from his sister. She wrote to say that she wished him well and that she wanted to see him the minute he came home, which she hoped was soon. She also attached the novel she was writing, which she said was just a work in progress, though it seemed pretty polished to him. He recognized Scott and Deb in the parent characters, and he recognized himself in the character of the protagonist's brother. The portrayal wasn't always flattering, but the detail with which his character was rendered felt like an act of love nonetheless. He hadn't realized she'd been paying such close attention to him all these years.

He recognized, too, in the central love story, the familiar rhythms of the romance novels he'd devoured as a boy. All the elements were there—the naive yet headstrong female lead, the rakish male object of her affection—but with one key difference: in Maya's novel, there was no emotional justice. The woman didn't wind up with the man, or at least not that man. It didn't feel like a novel, but it did feel like life.

Apart from reading, there wasn't much to do most days besides work out and browse the internet. The gutter punk had pirated a number of nineties action movies, which the group took turns watching on his laptop, a busted old ThinkPad with the caps lock button permanently depressed. Some of the guys chatted online with therapy bots. The Marine liked to sit in the swivel chair on the balcony and sip a Monster energy drink, staring through the scope of his rifle at the hills beyond. The most action any of them saw was when the Marine played a game called "talking guns," exchanging casual fire with far-off combatants just to pass the time.

Part of the problem, Ernie surmised, was that the YPG was loath to send its Western volunteers to the front lines. Guys like Gideon were useful for recruitment; a live American within their ranks was far more valuable than a dead one.

Gideon would not have guessed this was the case. At the Academy, he'd received the same treatment as the rest of the recruits. He'd studied beside them, slept on dirty cots beside them, run in packs with them at dawn. He'd even sat before a digital camera and told his parents he loved them; the video file would be sent to them in the event that he lost his life in battle. Now, however, he understood why the YPG had been so quick to take him on. He would probably never see combat. His training, his new name, none of it mattered. Five thousand miles from home, he was still a Greenspan.

Ernie had grown tired of waiting. After a week at the outpost, he'd defected, catching a ride in the nearby town of J——, gone in search of more exciting subjects to photograph. It seemed heartless to Gideon, the ease with which Ernie had walked away. His fascination with the man had been, in its way, as passionate as a love affair, and he couldn't shake the feeling he'd been dumped.

One afternoon, his heartbreak exacerbated by boredom, Gideon joined the Marine on a "recon mission," which entailed nothing more heroic than walking into J—— and chatting up the locals. On the road into town, they passed a slanting telephone pole behind a bus riddled with rusting bullet holes. The sky was so vast and empty that Gideon could make out the curve of the planet in it.

The Marine talked for the duration of the walk, but Gideon wasn't listening. Since Ernie left, he'd grown wary of war stories—the embellished heroics, the empty hours edited out. He was thinking, instead, of the email he'd received from his mother that morning. After a lengthy preamble in which she expressed her hope that he was safe—she still believed he was in Israel, which was probably *more* dangerous than the outpost—she told him that she'd moved back into the house on Crowninshield Road. The news comforted him. Whatever anger he'd felt toward his father had dissolved considerably in recent weeks. Scott had made a mistake, it was true, but set against the blown-out backdrop of northern Syria, the mistake seemed small and remote. There was room in such a wide world for forgiveness.

But the news depressed him, too. Now that he had a home to return to, he felt homesick for the first time since leaving.

J——, once a city of ten thousand, had begun to shrink over the past few months as Daesh advanced across the country. The hot, paved street ahead of Gideon was empty save for a boy, about twelve years old, who was kicking a soccer ball as he came toward them. The boy looked like Gideon had at that age, with thick, black hair and long lashes. He wore denim shorts, sandals, and a blue T-shirt with the words KANSAS CITY emblazoned across the chest. His expression, even at a distance, looked strained, and there was something lopsided about his gait. Gideon saw a small bulge on the boy's right shoulder, some round object concealed beneath the T-shirt. The Marine saw it, too, and tensed. He bent his knees in a defensive stance and held his hand up to signal that they stop.

It was clear that the Marine perceived a threat, but Gideon kept walking until he stood face to face with the boy. The boy's skin was a shade darker than his, but otherwise, the resemblance was uncanny. Kneeling, Gideon laid a hand on the bulge of the boy's shoulder. The Marine was barking now, his voice a distant echo. Pools of oily water held the color of the sky.

It was such a small thing. Gideon took the boy's hand in his and raised it, slowly, until it hung over their heads. That was when he heard the sound that he was hoping for, the click of a dislocated bone returning to its place.

ACKNOWLEDGMENTS

This book would not exist in its present form—nor would I, in mine— without the patience and understanding of Erin Sellers, to whom *Hope* is lovingly dedicated. I cannot imagine life without her.

Sanjena Sathian and Janelle Effiwatt helped raise this novel from its infancy. If they are its aunties, Lee Cole is its uncle. All three provided critical feedback, and friendship, at every stage.

I am forever indebted to my agent, Peter Straus, and my editor, Allison Lorentzen, for (among many other things) their advocacy, passion, persistence, and faith. They are the reason you are reading this book.

I am also grateful to Camille LeBlanc, Elena Ridker, Todd Portnowitz, Nicholas Thomson, Oliver Munday, Ariel Katz, and Maria Goldverg for all their help along the way. Paul and Susan Ridker's support was invaluable.

Charlie D'Ambrosio, Ayana Mathis, and Tom Drury all helped shape an embryonic version of this book, as did Sam Chang, whose warmth, wisdom, and generosity are unparalleled on the planet Earth. Connie Brothers, Jan Zenisek, Deb West, and Sasha Khmelnik: there is no Iowa without you. Thanks as well to Jamie Powers for the clean, well-lighted place.

For their willingness to share their expertise, I would also like to thank Ruth Birnberg, Anne Jaffe, Bob Michaels, Brett Mead, Leah Sutton, and

Kallie Clark. Ann Calfas and the Schulze Fellowship helped fund the writing of this book.

The cover photograph was taken by the brilliant Melissa Ann Pinney. Major thanks to Mystery Inc. for helping seal the deal: Jordan Rodman, Sophie Summergrad, Noreen Malone, Eva Zenilman, Avi Zenilman, and the Sufrin family.

The romance novelist Jennifer Crusie coined the phrase "emotional justice" in an essay entitled "I Know What It Is When I Read It: Defining the Romance Genre," originally published in the March 2000 issue of *Romance Writer's Report*.

Lastly, I would like to thank my grandmother, Carol Ridker, the original artist in the family and the woman who taught me how to tell stories. Growing up, I thought you were a character. Now I see you were a writer all along.